An
Unfinished
Tapestry

An
Unfinished
Tapestry

·

Susan Leslie

·

St. Martin's Press

NEW YORK

DESIGN BY BARBARA M. BACHMAN

Library of Congress Cataloging-in-Publication Data

Leslie, Susan (Susan E.)
    An unfinished tapestry / Susan Leslie.
        p.   cm.
    ISBN 0-312-02995-0
    I. Title.
PS3562.E818U5   1989
813'.54—dc19   89-30155

FIRST EDITION

10 9 8 7 6 5 4 3 2 1

TO BARNEY, MY PARENTS, AND PLUCKY.
FOR ALL THE RIGHT REASONS.

An Unfinished Tapestry

quest had been my brother Elijah. And though I had been but seven at the time, I had swiftly assumed many of the duties of caring for him. There had been a nanny, of course, in those early years, but Father had never taken to a strange woman's presence in the house, and she was long gone by the time I was twelve.

But where responsibility had perhaps robbed me of the normal musings of a young girl, it had, I knew, given me a certain strength, a wisdom beyond my years. Even if I had had the inclination, I had not had the time to trifle with inconsequential matters. And as our social life was limited, I had progressed with studies far beyond those of my female peers. Rebecca oft advised that I should learn to hide my mental prowess, as it would one day clearly intimidate prospective suitors. I, however, had long before decided that any man to whom I could not speak my mind would simply not be a suitable marriage partner.

Not that thoughts of marriage preoccupied me in any fashion. In truth, during this last year I had given serious thought to asking Father if he would allow me to work as his apprentice. I sensed I had inherited his eye for porcelains and fine furniture, all objets d'art, and I thought that under his tutelage I might one day become an importer in my own right. He could scarcely argue against my interest in pursuing a career, for Mother had set a family precedent years before, becoming one of the most accomplished actresses of the English stage.

Of course, that was before the news had come which had plummeted me into a sense of despair unlike any I had ever known. It was not like me to be so disconsolate. There had been bleak moments before, and somehow I had always been able to muster the stamina and courage to press on. But this time I seemed unable to summon any inner resources. Grief had assaulted me, and as hard as I had tried to fight it, I had succumbed to it.

My gloved fingers played nervously with the manila enve-

1

A L I G H T rain had begun to fall as the carriage turned north on to Queen Anne's Street. Though accustomed to the inclement showers which were almost a daily occurrence in London in June, I had not thought to bring an umbrella.

That was not like me. If nothing else, I was organized, rarely if ever caught at a loss. Indeed, there were times when I had wished I could live life with more abandon, but circumstance had not permitted me to develop that part of my character. Responsibility, particularly at an early age, had been a sobering force. As the small bird, who, if its wings are clipped, cannot take flight, I found my horizons limited. I had not resented it. It had been of necessity. Mother's final bequest had been my brother Elijah. And though I had been but seven at the time, I had swiftly assumed many of the duties of caring for him. There had been a nanny, of course, in those early years, but Father had never taken to a strange woman's presence in the house, and she was long gone by the time I was twelve.

But where responsibility had perhaps robbed me of the normal musings of a young girl, it had, I knew, given me a certain strength, a wisdom beyond my years. Even if I had had the inclination, I had not had the time to trifle with inconsequential matters. And as our social life was limited, I had progressed with studies far beyond those of my female peers. Rebecca oft advised that I should learn to hide my mental prowess, as it would one day clearly intimidate prospective suitors. I, however, had long before decided that any man to whom I could not speak my mind would simply not be a suitable marriage partner.

Not that thoughts of marriage preoccupied me in any fashion. In truth, during this last year I had given serious thought to asking Father if he would allow me to work as his apprentice. I sensed I had inherited his eye for porcelains and fine furniture, all objets d'art, and I thought that under his tutelage I might one day become an importer in my own right. He could scarcely argue against my interest in pursuing a career, for Mother had set a family precedent years before, becoming one of the most accomplished actresses of the English stage.

Of course, that was before the news had come which had plummeted me into a sense of despair unlike any I had ever known. It was not like me to be so disconsolate. There had been bleak moments before, and somehow I had always been able to muster the stamina and courage to press on. But this time I seemed unable to summon any inner resources. Grief had assaulted me, and as hard as I had tried to fight it, I had succumbed to it.

My gloved fingers played nervously with the manila enve-

1

A L I G H T rain had begun to fall
as the carriage turned north on to
Queen Anne's Street. Though accustomed to the inclement
showers which were almost a daily occurrence in London in
June, I had not thought to bring an umbrella.

That was not like me. If nothing else, I was organized,
rarely if ever caught at a loss. Indeed, there were times when
I had wished I could live life with more abandon, but circumstance had not permitted me to develop that part of my character. Responsibility, particularly at an early age, had been a
sobering force. As the small bird, who, if its wings are
clipped, cannot take flight, I found my horizons limited. I had
not resented it. It had been of necessity. Mother's final be-

lope which bore the seal of my father's solicitor. It had been three days since I received his letter imploring me to see him at my earliest convenience, only eight days since I received news of my father's and young brother's death at sea.

It still did not seem real to me. I had read and reread the communiqué, totally disbelieving its contents. Somehow, someone must have been mistaken. Another ship perhaps. Father was strong. Even if it had been his vessel, he would have survived.

I do not know when the moment of acceptance finally came. I had promised myself that I would not give up, would not abandon hope. At first I had thrown myself into my daily routine, convinced we would find there had been some mistake. Indeed, if Abraham had not shown me that my frenzy of activity was only my own way of escaping reality, I might still be wandering aimlessly about, inventing unnecessary household chores.

Dear Abraham. He had been a godsend to me during those days. And it had not been easy on him. After all, he had been with my father since he was a little boy, indeed a fixture in our house as long as I could remember. I knew that in some ways he found it just as difficult as I to fathom the enormity of our loss. And yet he was the one who finally forced me to see that denial would not bring Father or Elijah back.

The carriage lurched slightly as the driver brought the horses to a halt. I leant forward, peering out as he climbed down and opened the door.

"Number eighty-nine is there te the left, miss, ye can't miss it," he assured me as he helped me down from the carriage. I withdrew several coins from my purse, adding a few pence extra for his helpfulness and, gathering my skirts above my boots, scurried towards the six-story brick building he motioned me to.

I fumbled for a moment with the heavy forged latch of the iron gate before proceeding along the cobbled walkway to the carved wooden double doors beyond. I had only a moment's

3

wait before the door was opened by a tall middle-aged man, whose eyes swept the full length of me with curiosity.

"I am Lillith Chatfield," I said, quickly pressing the manila envelope into his hand. "I believe you sent me this note."

He withdrew the paper from the envelope, reading its contents as I waited uncomfortably in the increasing damp.

"Sir Henry is occupied at present," he replied finally, "but I shall inform him that you have called. It is customary to make an appointment, but as you are here, if you would not mind waiting—"

"Oh, I shall wait," I interrupted, embarrassed that I had not thought to arrange an hour for the meeting, moreover that I had mistaken this man for the solicitor.

He nodded and ushered me through a large hallway to a small library at the rear of the staircase.

"I fear—Miss Chatfield, is it—that I cannot offer you any refreshment at this hour, as Cook is off Thursdays. We close early today, you know."

I, of course, simply muttered a polite thank you. When I was seated, he left me alone. Feeling that it would be presumptuous of me to peruse the papers and books cast with abandon about the room, I settled back into the wing chair and closed my eyes, prayerful my wait would be brief.

I had no idea how long I had been there, for the next thing I knew there was a slight pressure on my arm, and I heard my name being called repeatedly.

"Miss Chatfield. Miss Chatfield, Sir Henry will see you now."

I opened my eyes, startled for a moment by the unfamiliar surroundings. "Oh, I do apologize," I murmured, my hands flying up to adjust my bonnet. "I fear I must have drifted off."

The man, who I now gathered was either Sir Henry's assistant or his manservant, nodded and instructed me to follow him, which I did, back through the main hallway and up the staircase to a pair of double doors towards the front of the house.

4

.

With but a brief knock, without another word he ushered me into a cavernous room, which was spare of furnishings save an enormous tooled leather partners' desk faced by several chairs. The man behind the desk, which clearly overshadowed him, peered out at me over spectacles that sat high on the bridge of his nose.

"Well, well. You mustn't be afraid my dear Miss Chatfield," he called out to me. "Though I am loath to admit it, you shall find me quite harmless."

I moved forward tentatively. "I am Lillith Chatfield," I said, reaching the front of the desk.

He leant his corpulent midriff across the desk, and when he clasped my hand between two pudgy palms, even through my glove I felt perspiration.

"Of course you are, my dear," he said effusively, "but then I would know you anywhere. The image of your mother, you are. Ah, what a beauty she was! The theater lost a grand lady when she passed on. I shall never forget the first time I saw her on stage. Desdemona, she played—or was it Juliet? In any event, I believe I fell in love with her right then and there."

Seeing my look of surprise he added, "I only meant that there was hardly a gentleman who was not enamored of your mother's beauty and talent. But then, I am not telling you anything that you do not already know."

I pulled at the soft leather tips of my gloves and folded them into my lap. "On the contrary, Sir Henry, I knew very little of my mother, save her reputation as a great actress. She died in childbirth. I was but seven at the time. She was much celebrated on the Continent during my early years and 'twas really Abraham in whose charge I was placed."

He withdrew a large handkerchief from his vest pocket and dabbed the beads of perspiration which had formed about his receding hairline.

"Abominable, this heat," he muttered. "Now let me see. Your mother's death, yes, I recall now. That was when your young brother, Elijah, was born."

I nodded, fighting to hold back the tears. It was devastating enough to think of Father, but the memory of dear Elijah made it almost unbearable. How could God have snuffed out the life of one so young? He was such an innocent, those deep blue eyes, set under a shock of pale hair, always filled with such merriment and wonder.

I had begged Father not to take him. Not out of some ominous fear but from a motherly instinct, I suppose. I knew that, at nine, he should be occupied with his lessons and not traveling the high seas to quarters unknown. But Father had been insistent. "'Twill make a man of him," he had exclaimed. And so when my pleas had fallen on deaf ears, I had gone with Abraham to see them set sail.

Sir Henry poured a glass of water from the crystal decanter on the desk and handed it to me. "Here, drink this," he instructed. "You look a bit pale, my dear, and we wouldn't want you to go fainting, now would we." I accepted the glass and drank slowly of it as he mumbled on. "I realize this must be painful for you, my dear, but I cannot proceed as I am instructed to without discussing your loss."

I took a deep breath and, placing the glass back on the desk, said, "I feel better now. Perhaps we had best go on with whatever you wished to see me about. I am certain you have other, more pressing matters to tend to."

A deep frown furrowed his brow. "I wish I might say that were so, Miss Chatfield. Though not an intimate of your father's, I certainly have had dealings with him for many years now. Which makes my task more difficult than most. Dreadful, these matters, but then what can one do?"

I straightened myself against the cushioned leather of the chair. "I must say, Sir Henry, you give me pause. I had thought this but a routine call."

He collected the papers before him, squaring their edges against the surface of the desk. "It should have been such. Lord knows, I tried to direct him. But your father, Miss

Chatfield, was a stubborn man. Of course, he did not think clearly. Not after your mother passed on. I have never seen a man so bereft as he."

As much as I wanted to defend my father, I could not. Though oversimple, I knew what Sir Henry said was true. Father had never accepted my mother's death. At first he seemed unchanged. Perhaps because, though he had lost the woman he loved, he had been left with the son he had dearly wanted. But in the months and years that followed, that consolation had not been enough. I was very young, but not too young to realize that he had become obsessed by something that was larger than himself.

Perhaps Sir Henry was right, perhaps he had indeed lost his sense of reality. Certainly he had lost a sense of purpose. He went out most days, though I wondered how much time he actually devoted to his work. And as the years passed, he spent more and more evenings alone in the big overstuffed chair in the library staring before him, a snifter of brandy never far from his reach. That was why this voyage had puzzled me so. He had come home one day more ebullient than I had seen him in years, insisting that I fetch Elijah and meet him in the drawing room. It had been so good to see him so spirited, so animated, that I had at first not had the heart to tell him that his plan was daft. Elijah, of course, was beside himself with excitement, as delighted as any boy his age would be at the thought of sailing the high seas to unknown lands. I thought the scheme would be abandoned long before it ever took form, but I had been mistaken. What unknown force guided him in this quest I should never know, but his fervor of that first day never abated.

I looked across the desk as Sir Henry muttered to himself while tapping a pen against the sheaf of documents before him.

"As I was saying, my dear, I wish that this indeed might be a routine call. You see, some time ago your father requested

7
.

that I prepare a will, papers that would disperse all his worldly goods in the event of his death. Never did I think I should need to attend so soon to this unhappy task!"

I pressed my hands together, praying he would be done with it quickly. "Is there something unusual about his instructions?" I asked.

Sir Henry adjusted the thin wire bands of his spectacles behind his ears. "Unusual? No, I could not say that, Miss Chatfield. Unfortunate, but not unusual. You see, at the outset 'twas all rather pro forma, as we say. On his passing, the estate and all its holdings were to pass to you and Elijah. Of course, now, as you are the sole survivor, you would stand to inherit the lot."

It seemed to me a simple bequest, and 'twas therefore puzzling why Sir Henry looked so troubled.

"I say unfortunate, for though you indeed are the heir, my dear, I fear that all you stand to inherit is the accrual of bad debts."

I sat forward in my seat. "But that cannot be," I argued. "I do not presume to think that my father harbored great wealth, but we have always lived most comfortably. There has never been any hint that we were impoverished, much less in debt."

He mopped again at the moisture on his brow. "I am certain this comes as a grave shock to you, my dear, and believe me it causes me great discomfort to be the bearer of these rather ominous tidings, but I fear that what I say is true."

I leant back to find some support from the chair, feeling as though the wind had been knocked out of me. "I simply do not understand," I murmured.

"In many ways you are not alone, my dear," he replied. "It is simply tragic that it should have come to this. In any event, I shall try in simplest terms to reconstruct what happened.

"We know that your father did not come to terms with your mother's death. As far as I can see, from that point on he simply lost all perspective when it came to financial matters."

"Sir Henry," I interrupted, "my father was many things, but he *was* a successful importer. Surely one of the largest in all of England."

He cleared his throat. "The key word there, Miss Chatfield, is 'was.' In his heyday Jonathan was considered the finest. He had a keen eye and unending charm, and it made him a great favorite, both here and on the Continent. But as far as we can discern, from the moment of your mother's death he lost total interest in the concern. Indeed, our records show that the last major transaction he made was but three months after her passing."

"Three months?" I asked in disbelief.

He nodded. "Which, frankly, all things being equal, would not have been so damaging. He had amassed a more than comfortable sum. It would, if invested wisely, have left you a wealthy woman. As it is, I fear you are left destitute."

"What happened?" I gasped, clasping the arms of the chair.

He shrugged. "That I fear we will never fully know. With no additional revenue coming in he lived off his capital. And, though I am loath to burden you with such knowledge, I fear in the last years he had taken to the gaming tables."

"Are you saying my father was a gambler?" I charged.

Sir Henry cleared his throat. "At first I could not fathom it either. Jonathan was not profligate. He had always been a cautious but sound investor. But 'tis all here in these papers, the squandering of huge sums not in one but in almost every gaming house in the city. To finance that doomed voyage to America, he used his final resources, creating liens on Bost-worick Hall."

So it was even worse than I imagined. Not even the house had been spared his irresponsibility.

"Before you think too unkindly of him, Miss Chatfield, let me suggest to you that this trip was not, as I suspect the courts will assume, undertaken to flee his indebtedness. There is evidence to show he truly believed that great profit might be made in trade with America, and he was willing to put all at risk to prove it."

"Which became his greatest gamble of all," I choked out.

It was several moments before I could compose myself. The last thing I had thought about this past week was money. Indeed, I had never thought about it. I had always taken it for granted. It was not enough that the two people I loved most in this world were taken from me, but now in my darkest hour to find that I had nothing—no home, no resources—was almost unbearable.

"As I have explained," Sir Henry proceeded, "there are sizable debts, many of which cannot be paid. The courts will demand that restitution be made as far as possible. That will come from the sale of Bostworick Hall and all its contents."

So everything was to go: the paintings, the silver, the porcelains my father had imported from China.

"I realize, my dear, that this may seem like a meaningless gesture to you at this hour, but as I was fond of your father, I should like to help, even if it can only be in some small way."

I shook my head. "That is kind of you, Sir Henry, but I cannot accept charity."

"Oh, 'tis scarcely that," he argued. "Actually, you would be doing me a great favor. 'Twould be a mutually satisfactory agreement, I believe. You see, once all has been disposed of you shall need some small sum to tide you over until you can find employment. What I am proposing is only something which would afford you a little time. You have heard me say what admiration I had for your dear departed mother; though some years have passed since I have seen it, I do know there is a painting of her that I have long coveted."

I knew instantly the one to which he referred. It was a full-length portrait. She was dressed all in white, which, though it had not been in vogue at the time, was a fashion by which she had been known in the theater. The painting had hung in the library at Bostworick Hall as long as I could remember.

"You know the painting of which I speak?"

I acknowledged that I did.

"Well, I should be honored to purchase it from you," he continued. "And I am prepared to offer you, let us say, one hundred pounds. More than I suspect it is worth, but then—"

"Oh, I could not sell you that painting, Sir Henry," I interrupted. "Not that I do not appreciate your generosity, but, you understand, it has a sentimental value for me."

He adjusted the wire bands of his spectacles once again. "My dear Miss Chatfield, though I am sympathetic to your plight, I must apprise you of the fact that in your present position, you cannot afford sentiment. To be honest, I must tell you that what I propose is highly irregular, since by all rights you have no claim to anything within the house. But if a transfer were made, quickly and in private, we might be able not only to save the painting but to start you on your way as well. Otherwise, your mother's portrait will simply be seized by the creditors and wind up who knows where."

The full impact of what he was saying suddenly dawned on me. He was trying to tell me that I had no choice. I was to sell the painting to him for a meager sum or see it removed with the rest of my father's possessions for no gain.

Slowly I drew on the supple leather gloves. "You shall have your picture, Sir Henry," I said resolutely. "I know I should thank you for your generosity, but all I can do at the moment is to beg you to guard the portrait well. My only solace will be in knowing that it will go to one who appreciates its importance."

"Of that I assure you," he said, a slow smile spreading across his face. "Now, I need trouble you no longer, save to ask you to sign these papers. I shall arrange to have the painting picked up and the sum of one hundred pounds deposited in your account forthwith."

As he handed me the papers and pen I had a moment's

pause, thinking that by all rights I should read what I was signing. But I was drained of all energy, and to pore over the copious documents seemed too exhausting a task. I did not think I could bear to view evidence of Father's philanderings, or whatever it was that had brought us to this state. What good would it prove anyway? All was lost. The sooner I accepted it the better.

I rose to leave, extending my gloved hand to Sir Henry. "You have said I must vacate, but how long do I have?" I asked.

He released my hand and drew himself to a height far less than mine. "Not long, I fear. Five or six days at the most."

I wavered slightly. "Five or six days?" I moaned. "But where am I to go? I could not possibly—"

"Miss Chatfield, I assure you that that is the best I can do. Believe me, had your father not been a friend, and if I did not have influence, the authorities might indeed repossess before morning. As it is, you seem a competent young woman, certainly not without attributes, and I am left with the conviction that you shall make your way."

"From what you have told me, Sir Henry, I shall have to. Though to find myself suddenly in these circumstances, without prospects, I admit to you is less than comforting."

"Things will not seem so bleak to you tomorrow. There are those who should be delighted to employ you as a governess. And with your looks . . . well, your mother was certainly heralded on stage. You might well find that you possess her talent."

I shook my head. "I fear that is not my calling, Sir Henry. I am far too shy to think of going before vast audiences. Though I inherited some of her physical characteristics, I fear whatever talent my mother possessed was not passed on to me."

2

I HAVE no idea how I finally made it
out of his offices and onto the street,
where by chance a driver had paused to give his horses a rest.
With some reticence he agreed to return me to Bostworick
Hall.

I could not stop from trembling the whole of the trip back.
As much as I chastised myself for allowing the meeting with
Sir Henry to upset me, I could not steady my nerves. I had
never felt so alone as I did at that very moment.

Where was I to go? Where was I to turn? There were no
relations other than a distant cousin of my mother's who lived
in Cornwall, but it had been so many years since our last
communication with her that I had no idea if she was even

alive. When Mother had been with us, my parents had had an enormous coterie of friends, but that had dissipated over the years. My father had described them as merely acquaintances—"hangers on," as he had termed it—who felt important in the presence of one as celebrated as she.

No, there was no one, save Abraham and Rebecca. Abraham, I thought suddenly. What would become of him? Without funds I could not ask him to stay. He would be dispossessed, as would I. I unclasped my small bag and withdrew a handkerchief. Where would it stop? I wondered. Even Abraham, who was part of my family, would be taken from me. How could I tell him, much less imagine the day—now so near—when I might see him for the last time?

I had not spoken to Rebecca for three, perhaps four days now. She had come to me the moment she had heard. She and Abraham were the only people who understood my grief. We had been friends since childhood. Though she was from a titled family, our mothers, who had also been friends, had shared a bond that went beyond class. Sadly, as we had grown up we had seen each other less and less. But as her family's major estates were in Devon, it was not unusual that their time in London was kept at a minimum. I felt a sudden sinking feeling as I realized that Rebecca had told me that she and her family would be returning to the country at week's end. If my memory served me correctly, that would be this very day. And since harvest time would soon be upon the countryside, it was unlikely she would return to London before winter.

Winter. Where would I be when the frost was on the pumpkin? Sir Henry had seemed certain that my prospects were good. But, though I was strong and certainly well educated, I was ill-prepared for a life of service. And even if I were to attempt it, where would I begin? It had never crossed my mind that I would one day have to seek employment. My wish to dabble in importing had been born of desire, not of need. Though Father had apparently squandered our means, he had never even hinted that our lives would not always be as they had been. I had never imagined myself, like Rebecca, having a season, but I had assumed having reached a marriageable age, I would have suitors. We were not totally isolated from society, and though I never wanted to play off the memory of my mother's reputation, I knew that still, these many years later, it had influence.

I stepped down from the carriage and paid the driver, pausing for a full moment before unlatching the familiar iron gate leading to Bostworick Hall. How I loved this house! But then I had known no other. I had been born in the master bedroom on the second floor, with its magnificent view of the rose gardens to the south. The limestone front, which was sorely in need of cleaning, still spoke of elegance in line and symmetry. Moss grew in abundance between the bricks which lined the walkway to the massive oak door.

The house was painfully quiet. I called out for Abraham, but when there was no response I removed my bonnet and the velvet jacket of my walking suit and went to the library. The first thing I saw upon entering the room was the portrait of my mother. I moved towards it, falling to my knees on the wine-colored carpet.

I do not know how long I knelt there sobbing, only that when I heard Abraham's voice, felt his hand at the small of my back lifting me up, I thought that I should never shed another tear as long as I lived.

"Miss Lillith, this won't be doing you any good," he whispered, guiding me to the silk settee beyond. "Not that I can blame you, for my own heart is close to breaking as well, but all the tears in this world cannot bring them back."

I clung to his small thin frame as he embraced me. "I know, Abraham," I choked out, "but 'tis far worse than I thought."

He seated himself next to me, clutching both my hands in his as I explained the events of the past hours. When I was done he said nothing, but the shadow which crossed his eyes told me more than any words.

"Well now, we mustn't worry, must we," he commenced finally. "I have a little money set aside—not much, mind you, but enough to get us started again. And 'twon't be long, I expect, until I find a place. Not that it would ever be the same, but I have been in service with the best of them too many years not to be of value to someone. And once I get settled, then you can join me."

I squeezed his hand, feeling a thick lump in my throat. Dear Abraham. I should have known that he would make some gesture to secure my safety as well as his own.

I shook my head. "I know you would do anything for me," I assured him, "but I cannot ask that of you. Whatever funds you have must go towards your own care in the years to come. Even if you were able to find employment, I should only be a burden to you." I did not want to add that at his age it would be unlikely that he would be quick to find another position.

He scratched his grizzled chin. "But then where would you go, Miss Lillith?"

I smiled. "I have been asking myself the same question since I left Sir Henry's office. And I admit to you at this moment I do not have an answer. But once I have had a chance to think on it, I am certain some light will be shed. After all, I am young and healthy, and though it may sound immodest, I have a good mind. Surely, I can be of some service to someone."

" 'Tis far from immodest you are being," he counseled. "I have known since you were a wee bairn there is little you could not do, but it breaks my heart to see you in circumstances where you are forced into something beneath your station."

"Nothing is *beneath* me, Abraham. It may take some time to accustom myself, but I can learn."

He lowered his eyes. "Would that it might be so simple. 'Tis cruel, this world of ours, to those not of privilege. For myself I do not worry. But for you—so young, so tender—I cannot bear to think what might befall you."

It was the second time that day that I had been over-whelmed by a sense of fear—or was it dread? But I tried to keep my voice light as I replied, "It will all work out, Abraham, you mark my words."

3

How I saw the sun rise and set in the days that followed, I shall never know. It was Abraham who attended to dismissing the cook and the maid. Fortunately, Father kept a small reserve of cash in the house for emergencies, and I was able, though not to stake them well, to see them on their way with a few pounds in their pockets.

Much as Sir Henry had advised, the creditors swarmed over the house almost immediately, moving in small flocks like vultures identifying their prey. He had seen to it that Mother's portrait was removed the morning after our meeting and true to his word, a slip verifying a deposit to my name was delivered to me shortly thereafter.

On the third day of this violation, to preserve my sanity, I left the house, the *Daily Telegraph* in hand, and strolled to the park. I had a moment's amusement when, upon seating myself on a public bench and spreading the pages before me, I realized that in all the years of studying them I had never given notice to the section devoted to employment. At first my hopes were raised, for there was no dearth of listings. But on closer examination, the positive attitude I had brought to the task was quickly quelled.

Though I was in no position to be selective, I gave only cursory attention to those openings for a lady's maid. If I had to work, I wanted to employ my mind as well as my body, and currying favors with a pampered woman was not how I envisioned spending my days.

In the end I circled only two notices. The first was from a couple in Surrey, who, it appeared, were seeking a governess for an unspecified number of children. The other, though far more obscure, wholly captured my interest.

"Desired immediately," it read. "Comely woman under twenty-five for permanent situation in North Yorkshire. Must be articulate, unencumbered, and willing to commit for an undetermined period of time. References unnecessary. Reply in confidence to Darby Manor, North Yorkshire."

Certainly, it was a bit oblique. Likely 'twas a family who dared not mention that the position was to oversee a full lot of overbred, rambunctious children. But, I told myself, nothing ventured, nothing gained. And since I had circled only one other offering, I could not afford to dismiss this one out of hand.

I spent the whole of the rest of the day and evening penning letters to each correspondent. When I had finished and was rereading them by the guttering light of the candle, I thought that the best thing I could do would be to rip each epistle to shreds. That I had been raised with some privilege, that my studies had taken me beyond the realm of most my age, seemed suddenly so inconsequential.

I waited a day before posting the letters. As foolish as I felt about sending them, I could not afford to let pride rule my head. Though I knew that scanning the paper for employment opportunities ought to be a daily discipline, there was suddenly an issue far more pressing at hand.

I had but two days to remain at Bostworick Hall, and then I would, in effect, be turned out on the street if I did not find a place to live. My first thought was a hotel, but upon venturing to the two known to me it quickly became apparent that living at either for any length of time would be far beyond my means.

The concierge of the one hotel, a kindly man who took sympathy on my plight, had given me the card of a woman in the south end of the city who took in occasional boarders. It seemed a dreary prospect, but time was fleeting, and as I took the carriage to the rather ramshackle structure at the address shown, I decided if there was accommodation there I would take it, if only temporarily.

I was not prepared for the woman who greeted me at the door, and had I not instructed the carriage driver to wait, I believe I would have made some excuse and left posthaste.

"What kin aye do fer ye?" she demanded as her eyes traveled over me from tip to toe.

I withdrew the card from my purse. "I was given this by the concierge at the Excelsior," I replied. "He told me that on occasion you have rooms to let."

A heavily ringed hand almost snatched the card from me. "Aye run a proper 'ouse 'ere, ye know," she advised.

"I am only looking for something temporary," I explained. "Just until I can find suitable employment."

She shook her head. "Aye don't take on charity cases, duckie. Them that's 'ere pay a week in advance fer their room an' two 'ot meals a day."

"I am not asking for charity," I assured her.

She shifted her bulky frame in the doorway, giving me my first view of the dark hall beyond. "Aye've only one te let at the moment. Not the biggest, mind ye, but it's on the back, nice an' quiet like."

"Might I see it?" I asked.

She pulled her floral wrapper taut against her ample bosom. "Suit yerself, but it's three pounds a week—in advance, mind ye."

As I followed her into the long hallway and up the stairs, I struggled to keep from choking on the acrid cooking odors which permeated the house. If this gave evidence to the culinary skills of the cook, I expected I would not have much appetite in the weeks to come.

The room was on the third floor, and though small and sparsely furnished, it was surprisingly clean and tidy.

"Yer in luck that this is vacant. The last bloke was 'ere paid prompt, 'e did, but 'e was a carouser, an' aye 'ave no truck with that sort. 'Tis bad enough that aye've come to 'ave te take in boarders without frettin' over what they be doin' in their rooms."

I opened my bag and carefully withdrew three pound notes. "I believe this was the charge you quoted. I should like to take the room commencing Thursday."

She shook her head. "If ye want the room it'll 'ave te start today. Aye can't be 'oldin' it fer ye. Rooms in a proper 'ouse are scarce in this town, an' whether ye take it or not aye'll 'ave it let by dusk."

Though I found her demands outrageous I was in no position to argue. It could take me days to find another room, and beyond funds, time was the one thing I did not have.

"Agreed," I said, pressing the notes into her hand.

As she led the way back down the stairs I prayed that I had done the right thing. We had reached the landing when she paused and turned to me. "Aye don't mean to be pryin', but ye don't seem the type te be lookin' fer a room. Yer not in any trouble, are ye?"

I shook my head. "I have recently lost my father and young

brother. An accident at sea. And I have found myself with, let us say, financial reversals."

I struggled to hold back the tears as she reached out and patted my cheek. "There, there now, luv, Aunt Millie 'ere will take care o' ye. Sad, fer a young pretty thing like ye are. But ye'll manage. Why, aye expect some fine gent will whisk ye away from me afore we kin even get ye settled in."

Despite her tough, blowsy exterior, I decided Aunt Millie had a good heart underneath. "I doubt that will be so," I replied. "As I have no present suitors and little opportunity of meeting any, I think my first inclination to find gainful employment is the wisest course."

She looked up at me thoughtfully. "Ye know, aye've got another boarder 'ere. She's a little older than ye, but she 'as a nice spot, she does, in one o' them fancy shops. Maybe aye could speak te her an' see if there might be a place fer ye as well."

I thanked her but explained that I felt I would be more suited to a position as a governess, which, by her expression, I gathered she found a particularly distasteful prospect.

"Well, unless ye 'ave any other questions, then aye'll be lookin' fer ye two days hence. Dinner is served prompt at six, so ye'll want te be settled before then."

I assured her that I would be well ensconced by midafternoon and prepared to take my leave. I was halfway down the walk when I turned to see Aunt Millie scurrying after me.

"Miss, miss. Aye fergot te ask yer name."

"It's Lillith," I called back. "Lillith Chatfield."

4

I HAD not suspected that I would meet with such opposition to my newly laid plans from Abraham. He was resolute in saying that I was making a grave mistake, both in the room I had let and in my determination to find a position as a governess. I had been so proud of my resolve, so amazed that even in my grief I was functioning with some sense of reason, that his disapproval came as a great surprise.

Dear Abraham, he only meant well. Although I had told him of the severity of my financial situation, I do not think he was fully able to comprehend the enormity of the loss. He had made arrangements to travel to his widowed sister in Dartmoor and begged me to forgo my plans and join him, at least for a month or two, until the shock of these past weeks had passed.

It was tempting, I admit, but it was not an answer; it only postponed the inevitable. I had to make a way for myself in this world. Oddly, if Mother had lived I might not have been as prepared as I found myself at that moment. She had been very protective of me. But my own childhood had died when she did. Father had adored Elijah, but he was in no way capable of caring for an infant. I had acted as mother and nursemaid and tutor for so long now that it seemed only natural that I should direct my energies in such ways in the years to come.

Though I missed Rebecca dreadfully, I was almost relieved that she was not in London. She had begged me that first day to come and stay with her and her parents in the country. Indeed, her mother had sent a note imploring me to live with them for an undetermined period, saying she knew it was what my father would have wanted. But though I believed their pleas genuine and that I would be welcomed without question, in my heart I knew it would not be a solution. The Chatfields had never depended upon others, and I was not suddenly going to abandon that tradition.

The tide of creditors did not abate, but oddly, after my mother's painting had been removed, I was able to regard them at arm's length. Likely it was a protective device, for it was not easy to see these men wend through the house, examining with calculating eyes objects which were the memorabilia of my life. I learned quickly that nothing was sacred. Perhaps the worst moment came when I happened, on passing my parents' bedroom, to overhear one rather swarthy-looking sort exclaim over a set of combs he had found in my mother's dressing table. I had not even known of their existence, but to hear them discussed as "baubles" which would "bring a pretty penny" made me sick at heart.

Mother had had, I knew, an extensive collection of jewelry, given to her not only by Father but by a selection of admirers much taken with her performances. Abraham had tried to convince me to remove the better pieces, insisting they were mine by rights, but, perhaps foolishly, I could not. If Father had created this indebtedness, it was my responsibility to remove all blemish from the Chatfield name as best I could.

How I coped during those last days I will never know. I packed my trunks and valises, thankful I had always taken care with my wardrobe, since I suspected it would be some time before I could add to it. When the hour came for Abraham's departure, I could not bear to leave my room. I suppose I had held out the hope that some miracle would prevent this moment from ever happening.

I heard a knock at the door; I knew that it was Abraham and bade him enter.

"I know 'twas silly of me, hiding here like this," I apologized. "I do hope you understand."

His eyes, which were as red-rimmed as my own, gave evidence that he, too, was consumed by grief. "I only wish I could convince you to come with me, Miss Lillith. I feel by leaving you here I am not doing what your poor father would have wanted. Who will tend to your needs, or look after you if you should fall sick?"

I drew myself up from the small chintz-covered chair by the fireplace and went to him. "You must not feel that way, Abraham. I have always been in good health, though admittedly I have not been myself these past days. I shall make my way. You will see. Why, I imagine that before you are fully ensconced in Dartmoor I shall have word of some prospects."

He stretched out his arms and I fell into them, comforted by the strength of his embrace. When he finally let me go he withdrew an envelope from his pocket and pressed it into my hand.

"What is this?"

" 'Tis simply my sister's address," he assured me. "You promised me you would write, and I will hold you to that."

I broke away from him and went over to the dresser where

I withdrew an envelope. "We must have been of the same mind," I said, handing it to him. "This contains my address as well. I expect it should be no more than temporary, but 'tis a start." I did not add that I had included twenty one-pound notes. It was not much, but, though he had assured me he had put a sum of money aside over the years, I knew it must be a pittance. Until this tragedy Abraham could never have thought he would leave our family, far less under such diminished circumstances.

I had arranged for a carriage to be brought round at three, which gave me two hours to fill after Abraham had departed. I had not permitted myself to indulge in dwelling on the memories that lingered throughout the house, and though I knew it was unwise, I felt the need for one last picture to hold fast in my mind.

It had been such a happy house at one time. I could still see Mother, standing by the marble mantel which framed the drawing room fireplace, regaling guests with tales of her performances.

There were so many beautiful pieces. The table services of Staffordshire and Derby were irreplaceable. Sir Henry had been right when he had said my father had had a discerning eye. I wondered who would acquire them. I hoped it would be people whose interest would be more than mercenary.

The carriage driver was less than sanguine about the amount of baggage amassed in the front parlor. But with the staff dismissed, there was none to help him save myself. It actually took less time than I expected, for which I was grateful; the skies were darkening and I sensed there would soon be a downpour.

I turned in the carriage to look one last time on Bostworick Hall. Rivers of tears cascaded down my cheeks as it moved farther from my sight, and I wondered if I would ever again know a place I could call home.

Aunt Millie, whose last name I realized I had never learned, was waiting for me when I arrived. Like the carriage driver, she looked askance at my baggage, less perhaps at the amount than at the task of getting it up the narrow wooden staircase to the third floor. I could not help but be amused as the last trunk was hauled on high, for several doors had opened, revealing those curious to have a first glimpse of the new boarder.

Though the room had obviously not been aired, I noticed immediately that someone had taken care to place a small nosegay of flowers on the maple nightstand by the bed. "Was this your doing?" I asked Aunt Millie as I pressed the bouquet to my nose.

She nodded, the frizzy topknot on her head flopping back and forth as she did. "Aye thought 'twould add a bit o' cheer. Ye leavin' yer 'ouse an' all, it must be a bad day fer ye. But don't ye be tellin' me other tenants, or they'll be expectin' the like o' it."

I assured her I would not, wishing that she would leave me alone so that I might unpack and lie down for a while. As if sensing this, she bustled out the door, reminding me that dinner was served promptly at six.

I did not think I could swallow one morsel this night, but I knew she would take it as a grave insult if I did not appear at the appointed hour. It was tempting to think of leaving the unpacking for another day, but procrastination would not serve me well in the morning. The sooner I fitted myself into this new pattern of my life the better.

A basin had been left in my room, and as soon as the last gown had been hung in the narrow closet, I splashed the tepid water on my face and, for the first time in days, regarded myself fully in the freestanding mirror set atop the dresser.

As I unpinned the heavy dark coil of hair, letting the long tresses fall past my shoulders, I was struck by how tired I looked. Food had been the last thing on my mind these past weeks, and my high cheekbones had become more pronounced due to an obvious weight loss. My usually clear violet eyes were red-rimmed, and even the sweep of my dark lashes could not cover the circles under them.

I brushed my hair vigorously before pinning it up again with a large tortoiseshell comb. My traveling costume looked less than fresh, and I chose in its stead a simple blue muslin.

As it turned out, there were five boarders other than myself. Aunt Millie, it seemed, was cook as well as landlady for the group which assembled in the simple but friendly dining room. As I entered, the other guests eyed me with unabashed interest. I was introduced to two older gentlemen, one of whom was obviously hard of hearing, for no matter how many times I corrected him, he insisted on calling me Miss Cheswick. There was a man I guessed to be in his early thirties who had a distinctly professorial demeanor, a matronly woman who obviously overindulged in Aunt Millie's cooking, and a girl named Elizabeth Wren, perhaps three years my senior.

I gathered she was the young woman who worked in the shop, and as my plate of mutton was placed before me I endeavored to ask her about her position. If I had hoped we might become friendly, I was sadly mistaken, for she was less than responsive to my queries.

Indeed there was little conversation, save from Aunt Millie, who prattled on about one innocuous subject after another. I had barely finished my meat when the young serving girl removed the plates and returned with a dessert of strawberry cream, which I ate only because I was under the scrutiny of Aunt Millie.

The two older gentlemen moved to the front parlor after the meal, but I followed the example of the rest, who retired to their rooms.

The room was stuffy, for though I had opened the window at the back, the evening air was close. I undressed, slipped into a lightweight nightdress, and settled onto the narrow bed. I had not thought to test it before taking the room, and as I stretched out upon it, I wondered if I should ever become accustomed to its lumpy surface.

Though my limbs ached from exhaustion, my nerves were so taut that I knew sleep would not come easily. I took several deep breaths, feeling tears forming in my eyes. I bit my lip, telling myself that I would not sink again to the levels of depression I had experienced these past few weeks. Nothing would bring my father and brother back. And I was in no position to indulge my heartache. The months ahead would prove difficult at best, and I would need both my wits and my health if I were to see them through.

31

.

5

I LOOKED up as the clock in the
parlor struck one, realizing it would be
only an hour before the post was delivered. If anything had
become routine over the past four weeks it was my habit of
waiting for these deliveries. In all, I had found only six notices
in the newspaper to which I felt I could reply for possible
employment, and to date, there had been only one response.
It was from the family in Surrey, who had apprised me that
they had already filled the position.

It was getting increasingly difficult not to lose heart, for as
the weeks passed, my funds were fast dwindling.

I heard the parlor door open and turned, smiling as Aunt
Millie bustled into the room.

"Yer at it agin, aye see," she said shaking her head. "Aye can't think why ye won't be takin' my advice an' take yerself down te the shops off Grosvenor Square. With yer looks an' smart clothes aye expect they'd 'ire ye right out. 'Twould be a far lot better than takin' care o' a lot o' snivelin' young uns."

"You may be right, Millie, and if I do not hear something soon I expect I shall be forced to take your advice, but in my heart I feel more suited to governing."

She threw up her hands. "Ye've a stubborn streak, Lillith Chatfield, but aye'll be admittin' that part o' the way aye'm pushin' ye is me own selfishness. Yer a good tenant, clean and quiet. A real lady. An' ye pay real prompt. Aye'll go a far stretch before aye kin git the likes o' ye under me roof agin."

"You have been very kind, Millie," I replied. "I feel fortunate to have found this place, and I admit to you it is with some dread that I think of being uprooted once again."

We both looked towards the door, as there was some commotion in the front hall. "Aye be thinkin' 'e's early today," Millie mused. "Maybe 'tis a good sign."

I suppressed an inclination to bolt towards the door, for I had soon come to know that Millie enjoyed fetching the post, as it was a chance to indulge her curiosity. I waited, trying to calm my nerves, for her return. She reentered almost immediately, shuffling through the stacks of envelopes. My hopes had almost been dashed when she suddenly withdrew a long thin envelope, turning it over in her hand.

" 'Miss Lillith Chatfield,' it says," she murmured. "From North Yorkshire it is, an' penned by a fancy 'and, I would say."

"North Yorkshire," I repeated thoughtfully. "That was one of the first I replied to. 'Twas a rather vague notice as I recall."

I accepted the letter and moved to the desk, where I used the slim brass opener to cut the tongue of the envelope. Pulling out the tissue, I settled on the settee and commenced reading:

34

.

Dear Miss Chatfield,

It was not without interest that I received your letter of the month past. I regret my delay in responding, but I had only returned to Darby Manor two weeks ago, and it took me several days to sort through the surprisingly numerous responses to my inquiry.

Yours, I must say, impressed me the most. Your penmanship and grasp of the English language give evidence that you indeed are well educated for your tender years. And that you seem to understand the complexities of managing a household is laudable.

Though I know this is a time of bereavement for you, I admit that the fact that you now find yourself without relations is particularly appealing.

My need is immediate. I am certain you will find the remuneration and accommodations here at Darby Manor to be more than suitable. If you should be inclined to accept the position here, please contact my solicitor, whose name and address I have given below. He will arrange for a carriage and driver to bring you north.

I hope that I might expect your arrival in the immediate future.

Until then I remain,
Lord Edmund Darby

As I placed the tissues on my lap, Millie looked at me expectantly. "Well, d'ye 'ave an offer?"

"In a manner of speaking, I suppose I do," I acknowledged.

"From the looks o' ye, yer not too thrilled," she persisted.

"I think 'confused' is more apt," I replied slowly. "I have been offered a position, but I have no idea what that position is. To say Lord Darby is vague would be an understatement."

Millie's eyes widened. "A lord is it? Well, that should be whettin' yer appetite. Likely it's a big fancy 'ouse they live in. Does 'e say 'ow many little uns?"

I shook my head, handing her the letter. "See if you can make sense of it," I offered.

Her brow furrowed as her eyes scanned the tissues. " 'Tis a tad odd," she admitted. "But then, such types always are a little off in the clouds."

"Perhaps," I mused. "But, beyond his not defining the position, his seeming delight in my having no relatives strikes me as very strange. Why would that be of any matter to him?"

"Likely 'e doesn't want ye te show up on 'is doorstep with a wee bairn in yer arms or one in the pot," she replied.

I flushed at her reference. It still struck me as peculiar, but I supposed Millie had a point. 'Twould be simpler all round if I was unencumbered.

"Puts a chill in me bones, thinkin' about the North Country," Millie said, returning the letter to my possession. "Cold an' bleak the winters kin be up there."

I smiled. "What is far more bleak is the thought of not being able to afford to live once the winter is upon us."

"Then ye've made up yer mind?"

I shrugged. "Frankly, my dwindling purse has made it up for me. I shall go and see Lord Darby's solicitor tomorrow morning. Perhaps he can be a bit more informative."

I awakened before dawn the following day, and by nine I had had three different gowns on and off before settling on a two-piece black faille banded at the collar, cuffs, and hem with brown velvet. The first weeks I had worn little but black, appropriate to my state of mourning, but Millie had convinced me that the lack of color was only reminding me daily of my loss. Guiltily I had heeded her advice, but today all else seemed inappropriate. I coiled my hair high on my head and pulled on a broad-brimmed black bonnet, tying the full sash beneath my chin. Placing the letter in my purse I made my way down the staircase and out into the bright sunshine of the day. Thursday was Millie's shopping day, and so she had bade me luck the night before.

I had to walk some paces before I found a carriage to convey me to the High Street address given in the letter. I admitted to being nervous as the driver pulled up before a double-gabled brick edifice, whose windows I realized with some dismay were shuttered closed. Requesting the craggy-toothed driver to wait, I gathered my skirts and made my way up to the solid mahogany door. At first my heart sank, for my repeated attempts with the knocker met with no response. Dejected, I was just about to turn away when the massive door opened, revealing a petite woman in maid's garb.

I explained quickly who I was and the nature of my visit, but she informed me that the offices of Grout and Sons were closed on Thursdays. I should have remembered from my experiences with Sir Henry Willferth. Seeming to take pity on me, she abruptly asked me to wait a moment, explaining that her employer was in the library and she would inquire if he might make an exception.

Returning within minutes, she opened the door wide, ushering me through to an ornate oak-paneled library within. His back was to me and I was startled when he turned around. He was tall and there was a lanky, relaxed set to his frame. But it was his face to which I reacted most strongly. There was an open, almost boyish quality to the immediacy of his smile. I had anticipated someone of a more venerable age, and my face must have shown my surprise.

Clearly he was accustomed to such a reaction, for he said quickly, "I expect I do not look the part, but though I have not the experience of my late father, under whom I trained, I think you will find me not wanting in competence."

I felt a blush creep into my face. "It was kind of you to see me," I muttered. "I had no way of knowing that you are customarily closed today. But the matter at hand is pressing and—"

He held up his hand. "You need explain no further, Miss Chatfield. I received a communiqué from Lord Darby telling me that you might well be calling. In fact, it was his fervent hope that you would."

"Well, then you know that I am here to accept Lord Darby's offer," I proceeded.

His eyebrows raised quizzically, but if my response surprised him he made no comment.

"I see," he replied. "Well, then, I suspect all that is left is to make the arrangements for your departure."

It was now my turn for surprise. "You mean it is as simple as that?" I asked, amazed.

"Well, I surmise that you find the terms of the position agreeable, or you would not be here, Miss Chatfield," he retorted, taking a seat opposite the one he had indicated for me.

I cleared my throat. "Quite frankly, Sir Charles, the terms of the position, as you refer to it, are not fully known to me. Indeed I was hopeful you might be able to shed further light on Lord Darby's expectations."

He shook his head. "I fear I cannot. Beyond the fact that he has communicated naught of the matter to me, I am not even acquainted with his lordship. It was my father with whom he had formed an association, and regrettably, since my father's passing was recent, it is doubtful that he is even aware of it. I did, when I received his charge, look back into my father's papers to see if I might learn something of the history of their dealings, but curiously I found little of note."

"I see," I said quietly.

"That in no way is intended to dissuade you, 'twas only by way of explaining that I have no further information for you, save that, beyond being a man of title, Lord Darby is also one of considerable assets. I am certain whatever arrangement he would make with you would be more than generous. Indeed, should you accept his offer, I have been commissioned to employ a private coach and driver to take you to Darby Manor. Scarcely a miserly gesture."

I had many questions, but it was obvious that even if I were to press him, Sir Charles had no answers. Clearly the decision was mine, and though my mind wavered slightly, I knew I had come here committed to accept.

"When would I depart?" I inquired, becoming embarrassed by his openly admiring regard.

Composing himself, he replied, "Lord Darby was very specific that it should be as soon as possible. Tomorrow, if you should wish."

"Tomorrow?" I gasped. "Oh, I do not think I could possibly ready myself that quickly."

We compromised on three days hence. I was to expect a carriage and driver at my lodgings at eight in the morning. As the trip was to take several days, we needed to take accommodations along the way, which would be arranged by my employer. When Sir Charles offered me tea, I refused, explaining that I had a driver waiting and was facing a good deal of packing.

"Then it is settled," he concluded, extending his hand. "I do hope the situation meets with your liking, Miss Chatfield. I must say, it seems quite an undertaking for one so young and, if I might add, so comely."

I drew myself up to my full height. "I am certain 'twill be satisfactory, Sir Charles."

He walked me to the door. "Perhaps one day we shall meet again."

I must have looked surprised.

"As Lord Darby is a client, and as we are not personally acquainted, it would behoove me to travel north to the manor one day. In truth, if I could free myself I might suggest accompanying you on this journey, but matters are simply too pressing here at the moment. Perhaps come winter."

"Well, I shall be certain to tell Lord Darby how helpful you have been," I assured him.

I took my leave and rode back to Aunt Millie's pondering my lot. I had tried to appear confident before Sir Charles, but if he had sensed the truth, he would know that I was embarking on this journey with great trepidation. I could, I supposed, have declined the offer, but that was putting a good deal at risk. If none of my other inquiries led to anything I would be forced to start all over, which I could ill afford. For better or worse I had made my decision, and I would have to abide by it.

The next few days flew by. After repacking my trunks and penning a letter to Abraham, I had little time left for anything but meals and sleep. Millie fussed at me like a mother hen, insisting that I take myself to one of the shops and purchase a heavy wool melton coat, which would serve me well in the northern clime. Though I suspected it was a sensible suggestion, I was chary of spending any of my remaining funds. It was indicated my compensation would be good, but until I had money in my pocket 'twas best to be frugal.

As arranged, the carriage and driver pulled up at Aunt Millie's on the stroke of eight. It had not occurred to me until that moment that the day of my departure was a Sunday. Though not raised a churchgoer, I had always observed it as a day of quiet.

I took cheer in the fact that the sky was blue and boded no inclemency, at least not for the first portion of the trip. My driver seemed a jolly sort, for which I was relieved. Though we need not be intimates, we would be spending the better part of three days and nights together.

Millie had pressed a small basket of scones onto my lap before the carriage departed, making me promise to write when all was settled. She had a good heart, and I knew in an odd way I would miss her prattling. But, I was reminded as I bit into one of the biscuits, her cooking was something I would gladly leave behind.

Though I knew I should have been grateful for the privacy of the coach, I almost wished that we were to collect fellow passengers, for conversation would take my mind off myself. But as we reached the outskirts of the city I found myself occupied with the sights of the countryside.

It dawned on me suddenly that this was my first venture beyond the confines of London. Mother and Father had been well traveled, yet oddly I knew naught of the English coun-

tryside. Mother had been adamant that it was no life for a
child to be traipsing about with her, and though I oft longed
for it, I supposed she was right. When she died, Rebecca had
invited me for repeated summers to go on holiday with her
and her parents in Devon, but I could not bring myself to
leave Elijah, not that Father would have permitted it anyway.
At the moment I wished that I had not been so sheltered and
I prayed that Lord Darby was not expecting me to be more
of a sophisticate than I was.

As the carriage rolled to a stop, I opened my eyes, realizing
I had drifted off to sleep somewhere in the past hour. The
driver was suddenly peering in the window at me.

" 'Tis goin' on noon, miss. Aye thought we'd stop 'ere fer
a spell an' take some food whilst aye rest an' water the 'orses."

I peered out, catching sight of the inn. "That sounds a
splendid idea," I agreed. My appetite was not great, but I
welcomed the chance to stretch my limbs a bit and gathered
my purse to me as he helped me alight from the carriage.

The Sign of the Hawk turned out to be a pleasant enough
place, if wanting in quality of food and service. Angus
McMurphy, my driver, hovering at a respectable distance,
commenced to excuse himself once he had seen me seated at
a large rough oak table in the corner. I beseeched him to
remain, explaining that I would welcome the company, as I'd
become more than a little bored with myself these past hours.

Agreeably he joined me, and though I found myself slightly
unnerved at the amount of brown stout he consumed, I found
him a convivial companion. A Scot by birth, he was particularly pleased, it appeared, to have this assignment. He was
longing to see his mother, who resided just over the border
in Scotland, and planned to continue on after he had deposited me.

Listening to him, I began to become excited at the prospect
of my life at Darby Manor. He knew the North Country well,
and though I had imagined it as a cold, bleak land, his descrip-
tions more than warmed my heart. I had never known other

than the city, but I found the prospect of vast rolling dales and moors dotted with nature's bounty of flowers and trees and animals instantly appealing. It recalled to me that my own great plea during my childhood was that we might have a dog, but for whatever reason neither parent had ever seen fit to indulge my whim.

When the bill was presented for our meal of kidney pie, I searched in my bag for the payment and was surprised when Angus, as he insisted on being called, assured me that all had been taken care of. I remembered Sir Charles had told me that all accommodations would be met, but I had scarce thought that would include my meals.

I was feeling greatly uplifted as I climbed back into the coach and we started off again. Perhaps, I thought, despite all my quandary of the past few days, I had indeed made a wise decision.

That afternoon and into early evening I was amazed at how much of England I had not even imagined. Here in 1852 towns were springing up all about us. The railroads had, of course, done much to open the gateways throughout England, particularly in the north, but whereas I had imagined vast wastelands, towns and cities had sprung up throughout the countryside. Indeed, although coach travel was by no means extinct, it was now, I suspected, a lesser alternative to those who had become accustomed to this industrialization which had caused so much furor in the decade past.

It was almost dark when Angus brought us to rest at the next inn, a small dwelling nestled in a thatched-roofed village. I was shown to my room by a young serving girl. Though near my age, she regarded me with a certain deference, believing, I suspected, that I was from a notable family traveling alone by private coach. The room, though sparse, was somehow much friendlier than my abode at Aunt Millie's. Though the furnishings were of a practical nature, someone had provided an abundance of crisp linens.

The crowd which had gathered in the oak-pillared and

-beamed dining room could not be deemed rowdy, but it was indeed more boisterous than what I was accustomed to. Angus, not in the least a reticent type, had made himself a fast favorite with both the management and clientele. That night I realized how long it had been since laughter had been part of my world. At first, the sound of my own mirth startled me. It seemed somehow irreverent considering my recent loss. But as tears had been a release of sorts, this was too. Angus, to whom I had briefly recounted my devastation of the past months, seemed pleased that, if only temporarily, I was able to divest myself of the burden I carried. We were a motley crew, if examined closely, but somehow camaraderie superseded background and circumstance.

I slept better that night than I had since the news of Father's and Elijah's demise. I know not whether from sheer exhaustion or from the sense of being unburdened of the dark cloud I had moved under those past weeks. Awakening to the warbling of birds beyond my window, I appeared to regain hope.

6

S A D L Y, the remainder of the journey did not hold the promise of that
first day. The further north we progressed, the heavier the
cloud cover, and on the second day we were beset by a deluge.
Sitting alone in the coach, I commenced again to dwell on my
recent loss. Whatever courage I had mustered seemed to dissipate with every furlong we traveled. Even Angus, who had
been such an ebullient companion, was affected by the whims
of nature. Not that I blamed him, for while I was dry within
the carriage, he had to weather the storm. But he was unwa-
vering in his mission to continue onward, determined to deliver me within the arranged time.

By afternoon, though I thought I would have grown accustomed to the jogging and sway of the carriage, I began to realize that the warmth which spread throughout my body was more than just discomfort. There was a moment of vast embarrassment when, unable to make my head rule my stomach, I had to request Angus to pull by the wayside, where my stomach revolted.

I must have appeared feverish, for Angus, who until now had been adamant about making headway each day, suggested that we try to find a doctor in the next village. Assuring him it was but a temporary malaise, I urged him to continue on to Darby Manor, which we could reach by nightfall. He was not of a mind to argue and thus, within the hour, we had taken to the road once again.

As the lashing rains subsided to a pale drizzle, I became absorbed by the changing landscape before us. The intimate thatched and beamed dwellings of the Midlands had given way to industrial towns lacking architectural distinction. But now, as we seemed to climb higher out of the low-lying pattern of the cities, there was a sparse, raw texture to the countryside. I yearned to see more of this land which was to become my new home.

Save for the traditional yews, junipers, and boxwoods which were used to adorn the more stately houses in London, I was uneducated about horticulture. But here was a feast for the eyes, ranging from tall spires of evergreen to berried shrublike clusters dotting endless green hillsides. Sheep, whose color ranged from black to shades of cream, roamed these dales, where the tracks were so narrow that in places I thought we would be unable to pass. Though vegetation and animal life seemed abundant, I was struck by the dearth of houses. There were a few small stone dwellings sheltering in the undulating hillsides; these, I suspected, were the homes of tenant farmers and the like. If manor houses existed in these remote places, they were hidden from view. Indeed, it had been hours since we had encountered another carriage along the rocky road.

I pulled the blue serge jacket of my traveling costume close about my neck. Whereas I had indeed felt feverish hours before, now I shivered in the cool late afternoon air. It was the middle of summer, and if this was indicative of the weather in these parts, I should have taken Millie's advice and purchased a warmer coat.

My heart sank as a low growl of thunder rolled past the carriage, followed quickly by another and another. If we were due for a terrible storm, I did not know if we could continue. As if reading my mind, Angus halted the coach and, inquiring about my condition, advised that the horses were not unaccustomed to this weather; as we were but an hour, perhaps two, from our destination, we would forge ahead.

As darkness blinded my view I settled back against the tufted leather of the seat and closed my eyes. Now that we were so close, all my resolve of the past days seemed to abandon me. What was I doing in this wild undeveloped countryside, traveling to a place, to circumstances unknown to me? Had I been so beset with grief that I had lost all clarity of thinking? If I was going to be plagued by doubt, why now, when it was too late? My nature had always been impulsive. If only I had waited, I might have found some better solution. What if they did not like me, or found me unsuitable? Would this entire venture have been for naught?

I loosened the neck of my gown as flashes of heat spread through me. The rain pelted incessantly against the roof of the carriage. I felt our motion slow and realized we were turning off the road on which we'd been traveling. We had gone but several yards when suddenly the carriage lurched and I was thrown to the floor. I cried out as my head struck against something cold and sharp. The next thing I knew, Angus was lifting me up and easing me back into the seat.

"Damn fool," he muttered as he pressed some soft fabric against my forehead. " 'E could 'ave killed us."

"What happened?" I inquired, struggling to pull myself up to a seated position.

"Out o' nowhere 'e came. Ridin' like a madman an' did not stop even after the 'orses shied."

I could not fathom what would possess someone to be riding out not only at this hour but in this weather. "Is the carriage damaged?" I moaned, pressing the cloth more tightly to my head.

"Appears not," Angus assured me. "But the team's jittery now. If ye think ye'll be all right, aye be wantin' te press on. The manor is but a spell up the road."

I agreed, anxious at this point to reach our destination.

As we proceeded once again, I tried to straighten my bonnet, realizing as I did that I had been injured more than I first suspected. Although it was too dark to see, the cloth was now damp and sticky, I feared with my own blood.

It seemed only minutes later that Angus was reaching into the carriage to help me alight from it. I apologized as I almost toppled against him and did not protest when he instructed me to stand against the carriage door while he extended a broad umbrella above me.

"Aye'll be carin' fer the baggage, miss," he assured me, taking my elbow and leading me forward. " 'Twon't be helpin' if yer soaked through. Yer in no condition."

What with the pelting rain and the cover of the umbrella I could see naught of where I was being led, save that we seemed to have climbed countless broad stone steps before reaching what appeared to be a landing. As Angus lowered the umbrella I realized we were standing under a portico.

I shivered as the wind gusted against me. I do not remember Angus knocking at the door and was thus surprised when the door was flung open and a man whose outline I could perceive only in shadow demanded the purpose of our presence. I was vaguely aware that Angus presented the man with an envelope, but instead of welcoming us in against the storm he closed the door, instructing us to await his return.

"The nerve o' it," Angus muttered as he gave renewed

support to my arm. "I 'ave a mind to put ye back in the carriage an' take ye well away from this godforsaken place."

Had I not felt so ill, plagued by a throbbing within my head and a weakness the like of which I had never known, I might have urged an immediate departure. But the thought of traveling any further caused me to stand firm.

We waited only moments until the door was reopened and the man, who I could now see by his garb was in service at the manor, ushered us inside. I could barely lift my serge skirts, so heavy had they become with rain.

My first impression was of a cavernous center hall the scale of which I had never seen before. My boots, soaked through, squeaked as I moved across the sleek floors of black and white marble laid in an intricate circular pattern. A three-tiered chandelier, its serpentine branches festooned with teardrop crystals, hung from the vaulted ceiling just to the left of the sweeping staircase.

The manservant, a rather nondescript, wiry fellow, advised Angus to bring the team round to the stables where the lads would tend to them.

"Miss Chatfield, if you will follow me, Lord Darby will see you now in the library."

Although I knew it was inappropriate for Angus to accompany me, I wished that he had been included. He had been kind to me these past days, and his spirited brogue was a friendly note. I knew not what to expect on the other side of the ornately carved doors to which I was being led.

The library was very dark, so dark that indeed at first I did not see the figure bent before the fireplace stoking the embers. As I stood peering about he turned and rose to a towering height.

"Come forward, my dear, come forward," he urged. "You must be chilled to the bone from this night. I assure you 'tis not always so gloomy here in the dales."

I did as he bade me, feeling slightly awkward as his gaze

held mine. He motioned me to a settee by the fire, which was covered in a yellow silk damask. I hesitated, explaining that my skirts were wet, but he waved me off, exclaiming that he had always found the fabric too fussy for the room.

I sank onto the seat, wishing I could control the shaking which overtook me again.

"Now, now, Miss Chatfield, there is no need to be nervous," he advised, moving forward and taking a seat opposite me.

I looked up into dark, deep-set eyes framed by prominent unruly brows and topped by a shock of silver hair.

"You look surprised," he murmured.

" 'Tis only . . . well, I expected—that is, I anticipated," I flustered, "that you would be a younger man, Lord Darby."

"I see. Well, I admit you have me at a disadvantage, for though that is a charming bonnet, it does hide your face."

I untied the large bow under my chin and removed the broad-brimmed hat.

It was now his turn to look startled.

Immediately my hand flew to my forehead, where a crusty lump had already formed. "I must look a sight," I apologized. "There was a minor accident, and I was thrown down in the carriage."

His eyes narrowed. "I see that, and we must have it tended to immediately. You are very pale, Miss Chatfield, and I can see now that your tremors are due to shock, or even fever. But with all that, I cannot help comment that your resemblance is . . . well, it is uncanny. However, we can discuss that another time. For the moment I shall fetch Mrs. Horsley, our housekeeper, and she will see you to your room. With some rest and warm broth you should be in fine fettle by morning."

I started to protest, but he would hear none of it. By the time he returned with Mrs. Horsley, I was nearly burning with fever and unable to swallow.

Although I was barely in control of my senses, I could not help but notice that the housekeeper was less than pleased at being rousted at this hour. She was a heavy woman, so square of jaw and shoulders that she had an almost manly appearance. The black shapeless gown she wore did nothing to enhance her dour regard.

"See Miss Chatfield to Lady Anitra's room," Lord Darby instructed.

I could not dismiss her look of surprise. She turned on her heel, advising me to follow her.

I struggled to my feet, fighting the dizziness which swept over me. I vaguely remember Lord Darby assuring me that we could speak in the morning. How I managed to climb the stairs in pursuit of Mrs. Horsley I do not know, for my knees felt as though they would buckle under my weight.

The room to which I was led was at the far end of the second-floor passage. I remember being perplexed at having to wait when we reached it while Mrs. Horsley withdrew a ring of keys from her pocket and placed one in the large brass lock. She did not enter with me but stood aside and handed me the candle she carried, advising me that I would need it.

"I will have some broth or tea brought to you, whichever you prefer," she said in a flat monotone. "Due to the lateness of the hour, your baggage shall not be brought up until morning."

"There is no need," I assured her, leaning against the frame of the door. "I am feeling poorly I fear and—"

"Up to you." She shrugged. "I'll be taking my leave then. There's a bell by the bed, but don't bother ringing it. No one will hear you at this hour."

I stepped into the room and crossed the length of it to a massive canopied tester bed at the end. Placing the candle holder on the gateleg table beside the bed, I began to fumble with the buttons of my jacket. When I had finally managed to divest myself of my traveling costume and boots, I pulled the heavy crewel coverlet back and climbed between the sheets, thinking as I did that there was a musty smell about the room which seemed to cling to the linens. By the candlelight I could see that the room had a series of windows along one wall, but I had not the strength to rouse myself. Placing my hand tentatively to my forehead, I realized with alarm that the swelling had increased. It had been foolish not to request a basin; a cool cloth might have helped.

I do not know at what hour I finally drifted off to sleep. I was vaguely aware that two people were in my room, but as much as I struggled to focus, all seemed but a blur. I had some sense of dread, but I could not fathom why. I kept asking them to bring Elijah to me and I could not imagine why they would not heed my request. And Father—where was Father? Moreover, why did these people, whoever they were, refuse to talk to me? Why did they move and talk in hushed tones? Could they not see that I was there?

Suddenly I was aware that someone was calling my name. It was a man's voice, but I couldn't place it.

"Miss Chatfield. Lillith. Open your eyes," he repeated over and over again.

I tried to tell him that they were open, but I could not hear the sound of my own voice.

"Try, Lillith," the voice urged. "You can do it. Open your eyes. We cannot get you well again unless you try."

Well again? I thought. Have I been sick? My eyelids felt so heavy.

"That is right," the voice encouraged me. "Now, open them wide."

I struggled to bring the face hovering close to mine into focus.

"Good, that is excellent." I started to ask where I was, but he pressed a finger to my lips. "Hush now. You need to conserve your strength. You are at Darby Manor, and I am Dr. Rendcomb. You have been a very sick young woman. But in a few days I suspect we'll have you up and about."

"How long?" I murmured.

"How long have you been ill? 'Tis a full three days now.

You have been delirious for the most of it. Lord Darby has been very concerned."

Three days I had languished.

"You have had a dangerously high fever," he told me, "and you sustained a nasty crack on the head, but there is no cause for worry. Now I must take my leave, but I will be back to see you two days hence. In the interim I want you to try and eat. I shall leave a tonic with Mrs. Horsley. I fear it has a bitter taste, but it is important that you take it."

When I awakened the next time, the room was dark. I looked out over the bedstead as a young girl tiptoed forward and placed a tray on the night table. Seeing I was awake, she brought the candle over, and smiling down on me, she said, "My name is Mary, miss. Aye've some chicken stock an' tea an' crumpets fer ye. An' yer medicine too."

I struggled to pull myself up in the bed but fell back against the pillows, unable to muster any strength.

"Ye lie still, miss," she advised, tucking a napkin under my chin. "Aye'll spoon this te ye. First the tonic though." She giggled as I made a face when the vile-tasting liquid passed my throat. " 'Ere, take a bite o' crumpet, an' it'll take the bitter away."

I marveled at how one so petite managed to support both my head and shoulders while feeding me the hot, thick soup. I had not thought myself hungry, but I was amazed at how much Mary was able to cajole into me. Afterward she removed the tray and brought a basin of water, sponging my face and neck with amazing gentleness.

"Where did I get this gown?" I inquired, suddenly noticing I was wearing a nightdress which was unfamiliar to me.

" 'Twas Lady Anitra's," she murmured. "Aye put it on ye last night. Soaked through five of 'em, ye did, till the fever broke."

"Who is Anitra?" I queried as she unwound the coil of my hair and brushed out its length against the pillow.

"Ye've beautiful hair," she said admiringly, seeming to avoid my question. "Mine is such a frizz. Aye envy ye."

She drew my hair into a long plait, and though I warmed to her company I suddenly felt exhausted.

When I next awakened it was to find sun streaming through the windows along the south side of the room. I raised myself slightly in bed and for the first time looked about, taking note of the room's appointments. It was not a very large room, but it was one of the prettiest I had ever seen. The intricate crewelwork of the coverlet and canopy had been carried to the swagged hangings at the windows. A chaise and two large overstuffed chairs picked up the Dresden blue of the crewelwork. The woodwork and dentil moldings had been painted in a shade of pale celadon. The chimneypiece was of white marble with side pilasters. There was a serenity about the room, and yet its elegance confounded me. This was scarcely a room assigned to a governess. Likely it was but a temporary arrangement, I decided, an accommodation made since I had fallen ill. I hoped whoever Anitra was that I had not displaced her, for I knew how important my own room had been to me at Bostworick Hall.

My eyes clouded with tears as it came to mind. It had been six weeks since I had left it. Somehow I knew that no matter how much time passed, I would always think of it with some emotion. In my heart, Bostworick Hall would always be home.

7

THAT day and the next passed with much unchanged. Mary, of whom I had quickly grown fond, looked in on me regularly, ever amused by my distaste for my medicine but as ever determined that I should take it.

Mrs. Horsley visited me exactly twice—once to announce that the doctor had returned, and the next time to say that Lord Darby had inquired after me and was pleased to hear of my progress. Each time she visited, her messages were delivered from the doorway to my bedroom. It was difficult to discern whether she harbored some unreasoned hostility towards me or whether her character was simply as saturnine as her appearance. For whatever reason, she made no move to approach me or even venture into the room.

With Dr. Rendcomb's assistance I arose and sat briefly in a chair by the windows on the second day of my recovery. He appeared a kindly man, and though I had had since childhood a perhaps irrational fear of doctors, I found his presence reassuring. Beyond his obvious pleasure with my progress, I could feel myself growing stronger by the hour. My appetite, once reduced, had grown enormous, and my interest in the sights and actions about me convinced me I would, as he promised, recover fully.

The first sights I saw from the chair beside the windows indeed gave me renewed hope. As I gazed out over the gardens and the undulating verdant lawns beyond, I thought I had never seen anything quite so peaceful. The sun having climbed to its zenith had gained sufficient strength to bring warmth to the rain-soaked atmosphere, burning the lingering morning mist from the flowers and greenery. It was while seated there on the second day that the stillness of the scene was suddenly interrupted by a movement near a circle of stone statuary depicting the four seasons. Straining forward in my chair, I could see no further, and so, tentatively, I drew myself to my full height and peered out at the landscape beyond. 'Twas just in time to see a woman gather her skirts and dart from where she had stood back beyond a row of junipers. I paused, waiting for her to reappear, curious as to who of the household bounded about in the garden, but when the vista before me remained motionless I settled back into my chair.

On the morning of that third day, when Mary arrived with my tray, I sat resolutely up in bed and announced that today I intended to be up and about.

Mary looked askance at me. "Oh, miss, aye think 'tis too soon. Lord Darby were real specific that ye shouldn't rouse till ye were strong enough."

I shook my head. "I admit I barely feel like a gallop through the dales, but I am here to work, and I have lain about here too long as it is. You might do me the favor, Mary, of inquiring of Lord Darby when he should like to see me. 'Twill take me but an hour or so to bathe and dress."

She left, returning moments later with ewers of hot water and informing me that Lord Darby would meet me in the drawing room at ten. I longed to ask her the questions that had been floating in my mind these past days, but I knew that to do so would be indelicate. Thus far, the only people I knew existed in the house were Mary, Mrs. Horsley, the manservant, a cook, obviously, and Lord Darby. I had decided if young children were about they were indeed well mannered, for the house had been so still that at times it had seemed almost disconcertingly so.

After I bathed I moved to the massive armoire where, as Mary informed me, my clothing had been placed. I withdrew a morning dress of pale yellow muslin with a white lace shawl collar and lace banding at the elbow. Donning my petticoats and leather slippers, I seated myself before the inlaid satinwood dressing table and began brushing my hair. The swelling on my forehead had reduced considerably, and I suspected the dark blotch which remained would disappear in time. My skin, which tended to alabaster, needed a bit of color, and though I rarely rouged my cheeks, I did so now. I drew my hair high on my head, catching its weight with a maize satin ribbon which matched my gown. I was scarcely satisfied with my appearance, for these past days had taken their toll, but Lord Darby would, I assumed, be more interested in my mind and character than in my looks.

It was with some trepidation that I left the confines of my bedchamber. I had been so out of sorts when we arrived at Darby Manor that I had little if any recollection of the house itself.

The passages were long and broad with polished wood floors strewn with oriental rugs of the style my father had oft imported from Turkey and Persia. The ceiling was richly crafted with ornamental motifs of anthemion and griffins banded together with scrolls and arabesques. There were numerous doors off to each side, which I presumed led to a series of bedrooms. All were shut tight, giving a forbidding impression. The most unusual thing, however, were the mirrors: they were everywhere, so that the entirety of the hall seemed to look back on itself. I wondered who in the household needed to satisfy his vanity with such decoration. That no expense had been spared was perhaps clearest from the stairwell, which formed an oval supported by massive Doric columns of stone. The elliptical staircase, also crafted of stone, had a lyred iron balustrade with a mahogany handrail.

I clutched the polished wood as I commenced my descent. My eyes, which had been directed downwards, were drawn to the curve of the stairwell. There, hung in staggered succession, was a series of portraits, each more elaborately framed than the next. I crossed towards the first, fixing on the engraved gold plate set into the fine carving of the oval. EDWARD DARBY, I read, "1786–1830." I breathed a sigh of relief. The artist's depiction was of a man at once pompous and stern, and I doubted we would warm to one another were he still alive. The expression of the woman whose portrait was immediately below was so disdainful that I concluded that Sarah, who had predeceased Edward by some thirty years, must have suffered the misfortune of being his wife. I had only met Edmund Darby briefly, but though time had blanched the once-black hair and furrowed the once-clear brow, his likeness was instantly recognizable. The two paintings which followed were of women, most remarkable for the differences between them. More than their physical characteristics, it was the attitude of the subjects which distinguished them. The one whose plate bore simply the name JESSICA was clearly bemused, as though all she suppressed was laughter. The portrait following of Caroline Darby, though flattering to its subject, was by contrast empty of expression.

The pattern of the portraits was broken here, for the next, unlike its predecessors, was a full-length canvas. The subject, a man on a horse, was in profile, the set of his jaw as determined as the flared nostrils of his mount. I crouched down to read the name emblazoned at the base: DAMIEN. Only one other portrait hung below it. The eyes of the young girl whose coppery hair fell with unstudied abandon about the strong arches of her face met my own with disarming directness. I concluded that whoever Amanda was, she had a fearless sense of self.

I was about to cross to the handrail when a shadow on the wall several feet below the last portrait drew my attention. Stepping down I realized it was not a suggestion of light, but rather the remembrance of a painting which had once occupied this space. Was there a Darby who had fallen from grace? I wondered. Immediately I scoffed at my own imaginings. Likely it was simply being cleaned.

The chimes of a clock resounding through the sweep of the stairwell reminded me I could not afford to linger, and I moved purposefully towards the marble landing. Though I was not unaccustomed to being surrounded by beautiful objects, the scope of what lay before me was overwhelming. Indeed, the center hall was undoubtedly used as a place of entertainment as much as an entry hall would be. The splendor of this expanded Palladian house was so great that it gave me pause. With some temerity I moved towards the large paneled doors at the far end of the reception hall. When there was no response to my knock, I opened the doors and peered inside.

Though the room was vacant I knew immediately that I had reached the main drawing room. I am unusually tall, but the scale of the room seemed to dwarf me. Such opulence was almost beyond imagining. The room faced south, with rows of sash windows whose red velvet curtains were corded and tasseled with gold braid. The massive marble chimneypiece was adorned with exquisite Chelsea and Wedgwood plates and miniature gilded torchieres. Here again, mirrors were hung throughout the room.

Wood paneling, intricately carved and gilded, extending from ceiling to floor, incorporated candle brackets in the design. Console tables, rich with marble and gilt, surrounded the perimeters of the room. As in the upper hall, rugs of varied hues were strewn about the floors, though here they were French rather than oriental.

But for all its richness there was a strange remoteness to the room. There was no abandon here, no carelessly tossed coverlet, no book awaiting its reader. There was beauty here, but there was no warmth.

I moved forward towards the windows and looked out to the terraces and gardens beyond. My heart lifted, for by contrast there was a serenity about them which was calming.

I turned suddenly as I heard movement by the door.

"Am I to take it you are a nature lover, Miss Chatfield?" the voice inquired.

I nodded as Lord Darby came into the room. "Admittedly, though in London one has little opportunity. Indeed, never have I seen the like of this."

"I am gratified it pleases you," he murmured, studying me intently.

As he offered me a seat on a settee by the chimneypiece, I was aware that I had not realized before how tall he was—six foot three at least.

"Might I say that you look much improved, my dear, though you will pardon my staring. It is just that your resemblance to Salina Kent is so remarkable. She was a very great actress, lost to us now I fear."

I smiled. "The resemblance is not mere coincidence, Lord Darby," I replied. "Salina Kent was my mother."

"Your mother?" he said, amazed.

"Chatfield was her married name."

His heavy brows knitted together. "Your letter made no mention. Of course, you told me that your mother had passed away some years past and that you recently lost your father and young brother, but I had no idea."

"It was not that I avoided telling you, Lord Darby," I replied. "I just did not see that it had any relevance."

He became so quiet that I began to grow alarmed.

"Actually, your background may serve us well, my dear," he mused. "That is, if you have inherited any of your late mother's talent." I thought it indeed an odd thing to say but had no chance to inquire of it as he proceeded. "Now that you appear improved, if not indeed fully recovered, I expect you are anxious to know why I sent for you."

I nodded. "I assume, Lord Darby, that there are charges who might need my care or tutoring, or both."

He eyed me curiously as he bit his lower lip. "There is but one charge, Miss Chatfield—Lillith, if I may call you that. But of a far different nature than you might suspect. Frankly, I know of no way to be subtle about my reasons for bringing you here. In short, I have a son. A son who may one day inherit all of what is known as Darby Manor. A substantial amount, I can assure you. And it is as a bride to my son, Damien, that I wish to employ you."

At first I thought I had misheard. He could not possibly have said that he wanted to *hire* me as a wife to his son!

"It is only natural that you should be surprised, but I assure you, Lillith, that though up in years, I am scarcely suffering from dementia. To the contrary. Indeed, I think this—shall we say, proposal—is one of the most sensible I have ever made."

My voice was barely audible as I fought to recover some composure. "I do not mean to interrupt, Lord Darby, but I fear that I must. Had I known that this was the companion you sought, I should never have responded, much less traveled to Yorkshire. You must see that what you suggest is

6 1
.

impossible. I admit I owe you a great deal for having cared for me so well these past days, but what you propose . . . well, it is nothing less than preposterous."

His gaze was steady. "Less so than you think, Lillith. I only ask that before you judge, you hear me out."

It seemed to me that there was nothing left to be said, but I felt I did owe him the courtesy of listening.

His regard relaxed. "As is evident, I am not a young man. Indeed, Damien was born to my wife and me somewhat late in life. Darby Manor was built by my great-grandfather. There is much history, much tradition here, and it is my very dearest wish that it shall survive not only my death but for many, many years. As Damien is my only son, he is also my proposed heir. Which serves for the immediate future, but not for the generations to come. However, were Damien to have a child, most preferably a son, this trust we have inherited would indeed be handed down, one to the other."

I felt myself grow outraged at the mere suggestion. "What you are telling me, in effect, Lord Darby, is that you are looking for a brood mare for your son," I charged.

I was appalled to find him laughing. "Good, I like spirit, Miss Chatfield, though I find your reference somewhat exaggerated. No. What I want, and want of you, Lillith, is that you become a wife in all meanings of the word to my son Damien. That I want grandchildren I admit freely. But my proposal is not as selfish as you are likely to assume. My son, for reasons I do not wish at this time to pursue, would be aided, I believe, by the kind of companionship a young woman such as yourself might provide. And though I scarcely mean to insult you by reminding you of your present position, I do ask that you think upon it well.

"You were more than candid in your letter in describing your financial circumstances. And though I am certain that you are, as you indicated, not only well schooled but accomplished in certain matters, I suspect at the moment you are nearly destitute. You have obviously been raised with some privilege, and now that I know of your mother, I think it likely you were well exposed to things far beyond a working-class situation. Though I certainly do not denigrate one who needs to work for his survival, I expect you would find that life tedious beyond measure. What I offer you is perhaps bizarre, but if you think upon it, it is a quite attractive alternative. As my son's wife you would become a lady of title with naught to want. You would live here at Darby Manor, which I assume you have already found pleasing, and you would benefit from all the accoutrements which accompany that position. Fine clothes, jewels, a lady's maid, the society of the county's notables. And, instead of being a governess, you would one day be employing one. There is, of course, one more matter. Upon your marriage to my son, that very day in fact, you would become the beneficiary of twenty thousand pounds, which would be deposited to an account in your name with my solicitor, Sir Charles Grout, whom you have already met."

"T-twenty thousand pounds?" I stammered in disbelief.

He nodded. "Not that you would be needing it, but it would be there for your use for whatever purpose you saw fit. An economic independence, shall we say.

"On the birth of your first child," he continued, "an additional ten thousand pounds would be deposited. If that child were to be a son, that sum would be doubled."

The man was mad. He had to be. How could he sit there before me with a calm complacency and say the things he did.

"You should take care for your thoughts, Miss Chatfield, for your face is indeed expressive. I have assured you that I am of sound mind. But let me finish: if, after that son is born—admittedly it would have to be in my lifetime—you find the arrangement untenable, I should not only release you from it but see that you are removed to a place of your choosing, where you should live freely for the rest of your life. The only accommodation would of course be that the child or children would remain here at Darby Manor."

I gathered the muslin of my skirts and stood up. "I have heard quite enough, Lord Darby," I exclaimed. "I may be needful financially, as you point out, but I also have some morality, which perhaps you did not expect. That a father would even conceive of such a plot is maniacal, but that a son would accept is pathetic. Is he such a spineless sort that he would permit you to orchestrate his life? Or does he have any say in the matter? What did you say to him when you received my letter? 'Here, Damien, this looks a good prospect.' Or did he have the benefit of choosing from the applications? And if I had been a hagged-toothed spinster, would I have been turned out the night I arrived?"

Again I was indignant at his laughter. "*That*, my dear Miss Chatfield, I knew you were not. Though I had no idea that you were a beauty, my solicitor, who had observed you for several weeks before I responded to you, assured me that you were indeed comely."

"Are you saying that I was surveyed before, that Sir Charles or his assignees *watched* me?"

He nodded. "One cannot be too careful, my dear. Particularly when one is seeking a wife for one's son."

This time it was not what he said but his tone which startled me. If I had not known better, I would have thought that there was disdain, if not hatred, in his voice. I smoothed the folds of my gown. "If you will excuse me, Lord Darby, I shall retire to my room and commence packing. Perhaps your housekeeper will apprise me when I might commission a coach to return me to London."

He raised his fist and I thought for a moment that he would strike me. "Sit down, Miss Chatfield," he instructed.

Out of fear or shock, I knew not which, I sank back into the settee.

"I cannot hold you here under duress, but I ask, no I insist that you do not make up your mind so quickly. In any event, there is not a coach for days, at least none which returns directly to London. So, whether you favor it or not, you are captive to our hospitality for at least a few days. Not to mention that to travel so soon after your illness would be foolhardy. Having said that, I will tell you that though my son knows of my decision, I would not say he is enamored of it."

"Can you blame him?" I blurted out. "I mean, what did you say, Lord Darby—'Oh, by the way, Damien, I have employed a wife for you. She will arrive the week next'?"

A wry smile spread about his face. "I would not say that it was quite as terse as you might think, Lillith, though I freely admit to you he is less than receptive to the idea."

"And that surprises you?" I asked, amazed.

"Frankly, it is of no matter," he replied.

I was incredulous. How he could sit there, showing no emotion, and almost as a tradesman bargain his son's future was beyond me. Though I felt a certain sympathy for Damien, I decided he must be a mindless sort, spineless, as I had challenged. Through Lord Darby's own admission, he did not take well to the proposal, but any man worth his salt would decry it as not only unsavory but the scheme of one who was unbalanced.

Lord Darby suddenly withdrew his pocket watch. "You will forgive me, my dear, but I have a luncheon commitment. A tray shall be brought to your room, but I shall expect you to dine with us this evening. We observe a certain formality during our evening meals. Service is promptly at six. And now might I say you look fatigued. I would suggest you retire to your room and take some rest. If you require anything, you need only inform Mrs. Horsley, with whom I believe you are now acquainted."

My indignance was irrepressible. That I had been summarily dismissed was clear but almost unfathomable. Indeed, I was so nonplussed that I could not comment when he rose and crossed to the doorway of the drawing room.

I thought he was going to leave without another word, but as his hand clasped the heavy brass handle, he turned to face me.

6 5

"Before you make any decisions, Miss Chatfield, I suggest you mull over what I have said. Tonight should prove interesting, if you allow it to be such. I leave you with the thought that we all must make compromises in life. I would not regard this one too harshly were I you." And with that he was gone.

I was overwhelmed with such despair that I thought at first I would dissolve into tears. But my anger suppressed all other emotions. I do not know how long I sat there. Instead of it proving a calming influence, I simply found myself becoming more incensed. I had entered this greatly vulnerable, but I suddenly had the feeling that I had been rendered altogether powerless. When I finally rose up from the settee, I did so mechanically, paying no heed to my surroundings.

I made my way back to my room weighed down by the circumstance I found myself in. I had had second thoughts about my impulsiveness, and I wished with all my heart that I had listened more closely to my instincts. I nearly collapsed on the bed, wearied by the events of the past few hours.

Had Mary not brought me a luncheon tray, I would likely have slept the afternoon away. Indeed, after I had consumed far more than I would have thought possible, I curled up on the bed with a book of pencil engravings which I found in the room. When I awoke it was late afternoon, and through the windows I could see that a strong cloud cover was rolling in from the west.

How dare he instruct me about dinner, I thought. I determined that until I departed Darby Manor, I would remain sequestered in my room.

As much as I tried to dismiss our conversation, it was not easily shaken off. "Think on it," he had instructed me. I had raled against Lord Darby, yet what troubled me most was that I found I could not dismiss his proposal entirely.

Here, in the confines of my room, I had been forced to examine the alternatives. I had enough money to see me back to London and, if Millie would take me in again, to live there for three, perhaps four weeks. But where would I go from there? Situations, I had quickly learned, were not easy to come by. Were I able to afford a hiatus of three, perhaps four months, I fully believed I could find employment. But I did not have the funds.

Yet, despite my predicament, I concluded that I could not entertain Lord Darby's proposal.

I was sound asleep when Mary jostled my elbow, advising me that dinner would be served within the hour. When I told her I had no intention of joining Lord Darby, she ignored me.

"Aye wouldn't be tellin' ye what te do, miss," she offered, "but aye wouldn't be crossin' Lord Darby if aye were ye. Besides, ye 'ave to eat, an' the cook will be preparin' somethin' special. If ye don't mind me sayin', aye think the mauve gown would be appropriate."

Without another word she moved to the armoire and withdrew the silk gown with green tassle bandings, which had always been one of my favorites.

"Ye'll look like a vision in this," she enthused. "Besides, Miss Amanda will be 'ere. A grand lady she is, an' unless aye'm mistaken, ye'll like 'er, ye will."

"Who is Amanda?" I asked, my curiosity piqued.

She looked surprised at my question. "Well, 'tis Lord Darby's daughter, o' course."

"But who is Anitra then?"

She appeared suddenly alarmed.

"Who is Anitra, Mary?" I repeated.

She shook her head. " 'Tis not my place to be sayin'. Lady Anitra was Lord Darby's daughter. Youngest she was. But . . ."

Before I could say anything, Mary curtsied and in haste left the room.

So Anitra was Lord Darby's youngest daughter, yet Mary had referred to her in the past tense. Where was she? What had become of her?

I lifted the mauve gown above my head, letting its silky taffeta fall around me to the floor. I decided to be civil until

I could take my leave from the manor, but nothing would alter my opinion of Lord Darby's proposal.

As I piled my hair high on my head, plaiting the sides in wickerwork to hold its weight, I knew with certainty that the source of my ambivalence about the evening was the prospect of meeting Lord Darby's son. Damien, he had made it clear, was not favorably disposed to his father's plan. In that at least we were of like minds. But that I should figure as a pawn in this duplicity was an embarrassment. Had I agreed, I would appear to be a fortune hunter. Had Damien been told that I had arrived at Darby Hall unaware of what awaited me?

I took such trouble with my toilette that evening; I think I did not want to seem so much in need. I had not come begging, and I told myself I needn't apologize for either my character or my countenance.

Mary had been very specific about the hour of dining, and smoothing the folds of my gown, I commenced the long descent to the floor below. At midpoint on the stairs I sensed the presence of another; I turned round, but there was no one about. My eyes flew to the portraits on the wall. I knew it was an artifice of light, but for a second it seemed as though I was under the scrutiny of both the living and the ancestral Darbys.

I reached the reception hall, and drawing a deep breath, I guessed where I would find the dining room, and crossed quickly to it. Hearing no voices beyond, I opened the paneled doors with some trepidation. The imposing aspect of the house did not stop with the halls and drawing room. Every detail had been carved and designed by a master. The plaster ceiling, with its painted lunettes, was matched by a carpet of the same design in robin's-egg coloring. A marble chimneypiece hosted a painting I suspected to be by Reynolds, and the insides of the mahogany doors were decorated with elaborate yet graceful ormolu mounts. The side niches contained epergnes and porcelains so like those Father had imported that it brought a lump to my throat. A mahogany table, the size of which I would never have imagined possible, occupied the center of the room, almost dwarfing the flower-filled urns at the perimeter.

Alone in the room, I hesitated momentarily before seating myself. Though I had thought to go in search of Lord Darby, the appointed hour was six, and the mantel clock rung that time as I settled into a Hepplewhite chair with Prince of Wales feathers carved at the shield back. Beyond the fact that no expense had been spared on any aspect of the house, the taste exhibited was also faultless. It caused me to realize how much I had indeed gleaned from Father's tutelage over the years. His knowledge of periods, of styles, and of the turnings and colorings which befitted pieces of superlative standard had been the one thing he had shared with me without restraint. I knew not now how it would ever be put to practical use, but it had instilled in me a knowledge and appreciation which made all this come alive for me.

When a good fifteen minutes had passed, with only the sound of my own breathing and the ticking of the clock, I began to feel awkward. I was just about to rise to go in search of Lord Darby when the doors to the dining room opened. A cold draft wafted through the room, causing the flames of the candles to drift down against the wax tapers.

"Well, here you are," Lord Darby exclaimed as he entered, followed by a woman perhaps five years my senior. She had the reddest hair I had ever seen. It was like a crown of fire. Her eyes were dark, her gaze so direct it was almost unsettling. She was the image of her portrait.

Moving forward from behind Lord Darby, she strode towards me. "You see, Father, I suspected as much," she said effusively. "Mary is a love, but I should place ten that she quite forgot to inform you that Father always takes a nasty brandy and a bit of snuff before dinner."

"Amanda," Lord Darby rebuked.

She laughed, extending her hand. "Do not mind Father. He is a bit of a dodderer, but then one forgives those one loves.

I am Amanda, Amanda Craigmoore, née Darby. And you are Miss Chatfield."

I was taken aback but also somehow warmed by her forthrightness. Her grip of my hand was firm, and I found myself smiling in return. "Please call me Lillith."

She took the seat opposite mine, chattering on as she did. "Oh, I *am* indeed pleased you have come, and I do hope you will like it here. A bit daunting at first, perhaps, but really quite beautiful. Though of course that is my opinion. In any event, I do hope we shall become friends. 'Tis ever so dreary in the winter, but we are not entirely bereft of entertainment, though Father has become so stodgy these past years."

Lord Darby had reached his place at the head of the table. "You must forgive my daughter, Lillith; she tends, as we say, to 'go on.' Harmlessly, you will find, but she is not without opinion."

"I am grateful for her welcome," I murmured.

His coarse eyebrows lifted. "Ah, then may I take it you have reconsidered your earlier decision?"

"I fear not, Lord Darby," I said resolutely. " 'Twill simply be a matter of when a coach is made available."

Amanda looked surprised. "You mean then that you intend to leave Darby Manor?"

"I do," I replied, wondering if she had any knowledge of the ruse under which I was summoned.

The look which passed between Lord Darby and his daughter gave me hint that she did.

I had not heard the dining room doors open again and was thus a bit surprised when I heard a woman's voice saying, "A wise decision, Miss Chatfield."

My eyes raised to meet those of a woman whose beauty could only astound. She was tall, like myself, with flaxen hair, which was curled and coiled in perfect symmetry, caught by a round of gem-studded combs at the crown. Her gown was of sage green and white, so embroidered it reminded one of jasperware. Save for my mother's stage costuming, I had never seen one whose appearance was so artfully studied.

Whereas Amanda's ebullience now seemed to dim, Lord Darby's stony mask warmed to a slow smile. He rose immediately and brought the woman to the end of the table, opposite him. He seemed solicitous as she lifted her satin skirts and took her place.

Leaning forward, his hand steadying against the mahogany of the table, he kissed her ever so lightly on the cheek. "As ever, you are worth waiting for, my dear."

Amanda, who had grown quiet during these last moments, whisked her napkin off the table. "It appears to me, Father, that it has become de rigueur for Marisse to make an entrance."

Lord Darby drew himself up to his considerable height. "I would suggest to you, Amanda, that your tongue has loosened beyond etiquette. You were an unseemly child, but I do not expect you to be an unseemly adult, and therefore I would remind you that silence is the better part of valor."

If I had expected Amanda to argue, she did not. But as the muscles grew taut about the line of her jaw and her eyes grew dark as black pearls, I knew she was seething from the rebuke.

"I must apologize for our manners, Miss Chatfield," Lord Darby murmured as he returned to his chair. "Might I present Lady de Wentoff."

I turned and nodded in acknowledgment; her regard, though her face was almost expressionless, was far from welcoming.

As if reading my mind, Lord Darby, tasting the wine which was just being served, continued, "Lady de Wentoff is staying as a guest with us for a while."

Seeing that the place laid beside Amanda was still vacant, I hesitated to commence eating the cold pike which had been placed before me. "Shall I fetch Damien, Father?" she asked.

He shook his head. "I fear you shall have to excuse my son

this evening, Miss Chatfield. He was feeling . . . well, a bit out of sorts."

"You really do let that boy off with far too much, my dear," Lady de Wentoff said critically.

"Not that it is your place to comment, Marisse, but I should remind you that at twenty-six, Damien is scarcely a boy," Amanda charged.

Undaunted, Marisse continued. "Might I remind you, my dear, that one day soon it *shall* be my domain."

"What she refers to, Lillith, is that Marisse has consented to marry me," Lord Darby explained. "And if you find it unusual that one of such beauty would deign to marry a man of my age, let me be the first to assure you I cannot believe my own good fortune."

" 'Tis not the man but the circumstances," Amanda mumbled.

I was surprised to hear Lady de Wentoff laugh. "You must not take Amanda's barbs too seriously, Miss Chatfield. Indeed, I do not. Though she took a husband and lives most times apart from the manor, she sees me as encroaching upon the territory of her mother, Caroline, Lord Darby's first wife. I suspect that were it I, I would be as quick to resent my presence here."

"How uncommonly generous of you," Amanda snapped.

"You and your husband live near to Darby Manor then?" I asked, trying to hide my dismay at their blunt comments about one another.

Amanda avoided my gaze. "My husband died two years ago," she said quietly. "Terrence, my young son, and I live about twenty miles from Darby Manor."

Before I could express my condolences, Lord Darby reached across the table and clasped his daughter's hand. "I fear, Lillith, as much as I have tried, I have not been able to coerce Amanda into returning to live here at Darby Manor. Perhaps you might talk some sense into her."

Amanda shook her head. "Middleton Hall was my husband's home. My brother feels it is important for Terrence to be raised there." I noted a trace of bitterness in her voice.

"I can appreciate that," I said slowly. "Houses are filled with memories, many of them happy ones. And it is his heritage, after all."

Amanda looked across at me. "I fear I view Middleton only as an inheritance, Lillith, but, given you recently were forced to leave your home, that must seem a somewhat cavalier attitude."

I nodded, fearful that if I were to speak, my voice would break.

Happily, the next course was served, and Lord Darby and Lady de Wentoff commenced talking about a ball they were planning some weeks hence. Indeed, they seemed an odd match, not so much because of the difference in age but in temperament. Clearly, it was she who was enamored of the idea of receiving the prominent families of Yorkshire, and I was amazed that a man who had seemed so willful was so accommodating to her whims.

Although I was almost relieved that Damien had not joined us for dinner, I had to admit to some curiosity. I wondered whether he was truly feeling poorly or whether the prospect of an encounter was as distasteful to him under the circumstances as it was to me. Realizing that my departure would be delayed, I knew it was likely we would meet. I could only hope that Lord Darby would have imparted my decision to leave Darby Manor to his son, so that we might at least be civil with one another.

The one thing I decided I would regret in leaving was not having an opportunity to get to know Amanda better. There was an indescribable quality, an intensity which compelled one. She could not be called beautiful, but there was a sultry assurance about her face and carriage. We were of similar ages and though different, we obviously both bore our own sorrows. Instinctually I had the feeling that we could become friends. She had the same spirit as Rebecca, and I suspected she shared her tenacity. That she cared not for Lady de Went-off was obvious. Although she made no other deprecating remarks, her expressions told me she found her stepmother-to-be tedious at best.

Though the dinner was superb I was enormously relieved when the last of it had been served. Lord Darby suggested that we retire to the library, but I excused myself, explaining as it was my first day up and about, I had grown more tired than I otherwise might have. Amanda, taking my lead, accompanied me to the staircase.

As we ascended she exclaimed, "That woman is enough to drive one to overindulge in spirits. Father is a fool. I cannot imagine why he allows her to make a mockery of him. And contrary to her little speech, I would *not* be jealous if Father remarried, I just do not want him to marry Marisse."

"She is very beautiful," I allowed.

She turned to me. "Do you really think so? Perhaps her character has colored my sight. Frankly, you, Lillith, far exceed her in appearance. Which, by the way, is but one reason she would make things very difficult for you here."

I felt a bit uncomfortable as we reached the second-floor landing. It was not my place to be discussing Lady de Went-off.

"Perhaps I shall see you in the morning, then," I said, putting my hand about the flickering candle I carried.

"Regrettably, I suspect not," she said. "I must leave very early if I am to make it back to Middleton Hall by nightfall. My son is there, and though certainly well cared for he does not take well to my absences. Usually he accompanies me, but as he loves to ride his pony while the weather is still warm, I had not the heart to drag him about."

I extended my hand. "You remind me of a great friend of mine, and it shall be my loss, I know, if we will not have an opportunity to know each other better."

She studied me for a moment, keeping hold of my hand. "I will admit to you that I was infuriated with Father over his scheming to bring you here. But now I find myself wishing you would reconsider. Your presence here could prove far more interesting than I had first thought."

I thought it an odd turn of phrase. Withdrawing my hand, I shook my head. "I fear my mind is made up, Amanda. As I told your father, had I known what he was to request of me I should never have left London."

She regarded me curiously. "I do believe you speak the truth, which is even more reason why I hope that you shall stay."

I was about to turn and start down the long passage but I paused. "Amanda, may I ask you something?"

"Of course."

"The room I am occupying is Anitra's. But no one seems to make mention of her."

Even in the shadowed light I could see her grow pale. "Anitra was my younger sister. She is dead."

Without another word she turned and moved off down the hall. The rustle of her taffeta gown hushed as she closed the door behind her.

Slowly I made my way towards my room. Halfway along I stopped suddenly. I had the distinct feeling that I was being watched. The flame from my candle repeated its shimmer in the mirrors, creating an almost fiery presence. Dismissing it as merely an illusion, I moved forward, my pace quickening as I drew nearer my room.

A fire had been laid in the hearth, and though it seemed peculiar to find one burning there at this time of year, the night had indeed brought a slight chill to the room. So Anitra had been Amanda and Damien's younger sister, I mused as I removed my gown and slipped into my nightdress. I do not know why, but I suddenly felt strange being here in her room. This was not a child's chamber; I surmised that Anitra had been fifteen, perhaps sixteen when she died. Was it coincidence that Lord Darby had placed me here? Could that be the reason that Mrs. Horsley refused to enter the room? Was the memory of it too painful or perhaps too fresh to cope with it?

As I tucked myself under the covers I wondered if it had been in this very bed that Anitra had slipped from life. Darby Manor was a beautiful house, but those who resided here had known tragedy.

8

I AWOKE with a start. Though the candle still burned on my nightstand the room was dark, save for a few embers flickering in the fireplace. I listened for a moment, thinking that I had heard a dog bark. 'Twas not remarkable, I decided, for though I had seen none about the house, Lord Darby likely kept several for hunting. I closed my eyes, willing myself back to sleep, but when the bark turned to a whimper I sat up and pulled on my robe and slippers. Taking the silver candlestick in hand, I went to the door and waited for a moment. The barking had come from below my windows, and deciding there must be a back staircase, I moved gingerly towards what appeared to be an aperture at the far end of the passage.

Though I felt foolish wandering about at this hour, I could not permit myself to just lie abed while the poor animal might be cold or hungry. When I had reached the landing I raised the candle high and looked about me. The ceiling was crafted of wood beams and rafters and the flooring was of flags. I determined that the kitchen must be off to my left. There was to my right a long hallway with many sashed windows. I moved along it as I heard a scratching at the far end. On reaching the heavy oak door there, I paused, confirming that the whimpering was indeed coming from beyond it. Pulling open the door, I peered out into the night and, lowering the candle, spied a spaniel, who backed off the moment he saw me.

I knelt down and, trying to keep my voice low, called out to him. "Come here, fellow. I will not hurt you." I held my ground, calling to him until slowly he crept forward. I stretched out my hand for him to sniff, hoping as I did that I was not being naive.

"There, that is better," I whispered as he licked my hand. I started to rise, exclaiming as a gust of air extinguished the flame of my candle. Now what, I thought, chastising myself for having ventured down here in the middle of the night.

I did not know whether the dog knew better than I, but he scampered from me down the length of the hall. As he scratched at a door, I waited, half expecting it to be opened. When there was no response, I tapped lightly at it. I was loath to enter unannounced, but with no light I was in no position to honor formality. As I opened the door, the brown and white spaniel bounded in. It was obviously a private sitting room. The pale green walls and white plasterwork set off the simple cornice and dado. A white marble chimneypiece inlaid with colored marbles representing ivy leaves sheltered a low-burning fire. An unusually large pianoforte in rosewood and satinwood monopolized the far end of the room. Books of every shape and subject not only filled the bureau bookcase but were strewn about the colored wool carpet. Tidiness, I decided, was not habitual to the person who inhabited this chamber.

The spaniel, who had curled up on a mahogany-framed sofa, cocked his ears and eyed me with curiosity as I leant towards the fire to relight my candle. I had just straightened up when I heard a sound by the door.

I whirled about as a man with the darkest eyes I had ever seen wheeled the chair in which he sat into the room.

"What in blazes," he shouted at me.

I was so startled that I was almost breathless. "I am so sorry," I spluttered nervously. "You see, I heard the spaniel barking, and I thought he might be hurt."

"Come here, Chips," he demanded.

The spaniel scampered off the sofa to the side of his chair.

"He seems fine to me," he said, ruffling the dog's long, curly ears, "but then I suspect your fetching Chips was but a ruse, was it not, Miss Chatfield?"

"First off, I cannot think what you mean by a ruse," I replied indignantly. "But more than that, how do you know who I am?"

"Stop the pretense," he stormed as he rolled the chair towards me. " 'Tis bad enough without your lies. Did my father put you up to this, or was this a clever little scheme you concocted all on your own?"

"Your father?" I said.

"Lord Darby," he said wryly. "If I did not know better I would think you really *are* surprised. But then, as your mother was an actress, I suspect you are adept at deceptions as well."

"Leave my mother out of this," I retorted angrily.

An insidious look crossed the angular planes of his brow. "Now, is that any way to speak to your intended, Miss Chatfield? Or should I call you Lillith?"

"You are Damien?" I said in amazement as he wheeled the chair across the room to a cut glass decanter, pouring an ample amount of the amber liquid it held into a snifter.

He whirled the chair about to face me. "Ah, I see they did not tell you. Well, I suppose I cannot fault him for that. 'Twould be awkward, now, would it not, to have placed a notice which read, 'Wanted, wife for crippled son.'"

"The notice you speak of," I charged, "did not even mention the word 'wife.' Indeed, if it had, I should never have shown my face at Darby Manor, of that I assure you."

"Oh come, come, Miss Chatfield," he retorted, downing the remaining contents of the snifter. "What did you think you were coming here for?"

I pulled my robe closer about me. "I did not know," I admitted, feeling distinctly foolish. "I had thought to be a governess."

His dark eyebrows, as prominent as his father's, raised. "Well, if that is true, then you must be beside yourself with your good fortune."

I knew it was absurd to stand there arguing with him, but I could not leave, having been insulted so wrongly.

"Good fortune?" I cried. "You do have a rather lofty idea of yourself, sir."

He shook his head. "To the contrary, Miss Chatfield. I am very much a realist about myself. When you sit in this contraption long enough, you lose romantic notions in more ways than one. By good fortune I only meant that you have seen Darby Manor. It does not take an educated eye to see that my father is a very wealthy man. And though I think he would wish it otherwise, I stand to inherit all this one day. That is, if I marry. As my wife, you would have benefit of that. You cannot tell me that that is not attractive to you. Why, as a governess, you would never even be able to afford the furnishings in this small room alone, not if you worked a lifetime."

I gathered the skirts of my robe. "I do not have to stay here and listen to this, sir, I—"

"Damien," he interrupted.

"Whatever," I retorted. "I thought I was doing a kindness by fetching your dog there, and instead you berate me for things you are very mistaken about. Your argument, if you have one, is not with me but with your father, who concocted this bizarre scheme. I am as much a victim here as you. But since I will soon be gone from here, you will not have to worry about that fact."

He paused for a moment. "That my argument is with my father is true. But that either by his command or your own initiative you came here intending to seduce me is likely. Since I believe that you did not expect to find a cripple, I cannot blame you for wishing to retreat. However, although I am confined to this, I am not totally incapacitated."

I flushed deeply and crossed the length of the room to the door.

"You seem more spirited than that, Miss Chatfield," he thrust at me. "I rather thought you would rise to the challenge."

I whirled about as my hand clasped the latch. "I feel sorry for you, Damien, but not because of your confinement to that chair. It is not your body that is twisted, but your mind."

I was shaking as I closed the door behind me. I drew a deep breath and moved cautiously back along the hallway to the landing of the back staircase. Curling my hand around the barley-sugar twist balusters I felt my way up to the second floor and back to the sanctity of my room.

So that was Damien Darby, I thought as I sank down onto the bed. Well, if I had ever given any consideration to his father's proposal, certainly the meeting with him had dispelled that. How dare he have defamed my character so. Could it have been that he was testing me? I wondered. If so, he had a particularly cruel way of doing it. I might under different circumstances have felt sorry for him, but he hardly seemed one to be pitied. How different he was from Amanda. In appearance alone they were opposites, she with her titian hair and pale skin, and he with those charcoal eyes and black wavy hair. I thought of Anitra and wondered which parent she had favored.

As angry as I was with Damien, I could not dismiss the fact that, though far more civil to me, Lord Darby was detestable in his own right. Arranging a wife for a crippled son so that he might beget heirs? It was monstrous, and I would not be a party to it.

When Mary brought my basin the next morning, I was amazed to discover it was so late.

"Mornin' te ye, miss," she greeted me as she drew back the heavy draperies, allowing a hazy sunlight to fill the room. "Lord Darby's been askin' 'bout ye, wants ye te take breakfast in the mornin' room with 'im, 'e does."

It was the last thing I wanted to do, but I felt I had no option. While accepting his hospitality, albeit under duress, it was not my place to be contentious.

I bathed quickly and donned a taffeta gown in a plaid of greens and blues. I wound my hair in a loose coil, noting as I did that the mark on my forehead had all but disappeared.

The morning room, it turned out, was at the rear of the dining room. Lord Darby rose as I entered.

"I hope I did not rouse you too early, my dear," he said, pulling back the veneered Chinese beech armchair.

I shook my head. "I had not realized it was so late. And I had so wanted to see Amanda off this morning."

He looked at me and smiled. "I am pleased that you two got along so well. We are oft of different minds, but then she takes after her mother. Caroline was a very unusual woman."

"Is her loss to you recent?" I said, pursuing the subject as I was served a plate of kippers and eggs.

His eyes darkened. "It was a little over three years ago. But let us not talk about the past. I know that you have said that you are determined to return to London, and I can scarcely keep you a prisoner here. But as a coach will not be passing until four days hence, I have decided we should make the remainder of your stay here at Darby as comfortable as possible. So, as I am to take a round of the grounds, I thought you might do me the favor of accompanying me. The fresh air will do us both good, and it even might have some remote influence on your decision."

I assured him that nothing would dissuade me from returning to London, but I accepted his offer. It was purely selfish; while confined here I thought I might at least benefit from experiencing the countryside.

We agreed to meet in the center hall at the stroke of ten. I admit I was relieved when it appeared that Lady de Wentoff would not accompany us. I would form no judgment solely based on Amanda's opinion, but I suspected the less interaction between us the better.

I was somewhat dismayed when Lord Darby, tucking my arm in his, led me over to the library. I must have stiffened, for he said, "There is nothing to be afraid of, Lillith. I happen to know that my son is in there, and though I acknowledge his rudeness of last evening, I do want you two to meet. As he is as resistant to my proposal as you, you will have that in common if nothing else. I do forewarn you that he is . . . Well, there is no need to go into that."

Before I could protest he had propelled me into the library. The first thing I noticed was the spaniel, Chips, who perked up, his inquisitive regard moving between Lord Darby and myself.

"Damien," Lord Darby called out, "I have brought someone for you to meet."

I stood transfixed as Damien whirled his chair about. He looked up at me, his eyes boring into mine.

"Well, I suspect this is the famous Miss Chatfield," he said, extending his hand. "You needn't look so frightened, I promise you I am quite harmless."

I moved forward, tentatively placing my hand in his. His grip was firm. "She's a beauty, is she not, Father? Though I somehow imagined you in looser garb. And your hair, it should be cascading about your shoulders." I could feel the flush creep into my face and neck. He was referring, of course, to my appearance the night before, and though he had protected our encounter, he was, I knew, mocking me.

Chips had moved from where he lay beneath the partners' desk and come to my side, pawing lightly at the hem of my gown. I noticed Damien's look of surprise as he released my hand.

"Well, that is something we do not often see," I heard Lord Darby comment. "Chips there is exclusively my son's dog. I cannot think when I have seen him sidle up to another."

I leant down and petted him as he wriggled his brown and white body against my leg.

"Well, I would say he has good taste," Damien murmured. "Or perhaps he is only trying to ingratiate himself with his intended mistress."

Lord Darby looked from one to the other of us, puzzled, I knew, by the repartee. "I have invited Lillith—Miss Chatfield—to accompany me on a tour of the estates. I thought you might care to join us."

It was with enormous relief that I saw Damien shake his head. "Two is company. I fear I would have little to offer. Besides, I suspect the two of you have a great deal to discuss."

He had turned the back of his chair to us before either Lord Darby or myself had a chance to comment.

Lord Darby, who had been amazingly placid during this exchange, mumbled, "Suit yourself."

He had seen to it that the carriage would be waiting for us in front of the house. It was the first time I had stepped outside since my arrival at Darby Manor, and my first opportunity to reflect upon the edifice.

Seeing my fascination, Lord Darby said, "It is magnificent, is it not? It was designed by Colen Campbell, a Palladian architect of note, though I admit I have heard it said that my great-grandfather put his two pence in."

The facade of the house was at once plain and monumental,

indeed almost severe. A rectangular central block crafted of polished stone was connected to side pavilions by low galleries and colonnades. The whole scheme was symmetrical, with careful attention to Roman classical proportion. The entrance front faced north and the long elevations by the garden facades were adorned with central classical porticos with pediments. The exterior was decorated only by rectangular sash windows and a balustraded parapet. The overall effect was impressive but somehow austere.

Lord Darby took my hand and helped me into the carriage. Try as I did to settle back comfortably against the seat I could not ignore his scrutiny.

"I must say you surprise me, Lillith," he said, tugging at the top of his boot.

I turned to face him. "And why is that?"

He shrugged. "Only that you seem to have great aplomb for one of such tender years. Most people are taken aback at the first sight of Damien. But you seemed quite unruffled by his condition."

"If you refer to his confinement to a wheelchair, then I can only reply that I would be less than honest if I did not perceive it as unfortunate. Though I suspect it troubles me less than it does you, Lord Darby, since when you informed me of this scheme of yours you specifically avoided mention of it."

He shrugged. "And if I had, Miss Chatfield, would you have been more inclined to accept my offer? Of course not. Though my eyesight is not what it once was, it is very clear that you are quite a beautiful young woman. Indeed, if Damien were not himself so opposed to my proposal, I should think even he might succumb to your very appearance."

"Well, we need not trouble ourselves with that, for in a few days my stay at Darby Manor shall be but a fleeting memory."

"Of that I would not be so certain, Lillith," he replied. "But for the moment, as I offered you an outing I shall not fall short of my promise." As the driver started the horses down the long drive, Lord Darby brought to my attention the parkland and gardens which filled the vista.

"You must take time to visit the gardens," he said. "The dales have a raw, spare beauty that appeals to me, but Caroline, my late wife, always found them forbidding. 'Flowers,' she used to say, 'what is a world without flowers?' The rose garden was her particular pride."

The drive, perhaps three furlongs in length, led us out to a main road which, I remembered from our approach, tended to jostle one a bit. There was a haunting quality to this land. Save for the wheels grating along the road and the distant bleating of sheep, all was silent.

The hills were bare, stark, treeless heights dotted with squat gray dwellings which housed tenants, Lord Darby explained. Barren ramparts of grass, rock, and shale punctuated the landscape.

"It is quite spectacular, is it not?" he said as I leaned forward to better capture the view.

I nodded. "Spectacular is an apt description. There is no prettiness about it, but it compels one. It seems to beckon."

"The River Cover, after which Coverdale has come to be called, commences there on high," he continued, "and coils its way throughout. There you can see one of the gills which feed it. We will be going on to Middleham, which though not a big village is one of great history. As I must go to the post, you may want to make a few purchases, though I shan't be long."

As we rounded an endless series of bends I looked up to see an enormous structure, its ravaged frame outlined against the clear blue sky. "What is that?" I queried.

"The ruins of Middleton Castle," he explained. " 'Tis a tragedy it has been allowed to decay so. It was once host to the Royals, but since the time of Henry Tudor it has not been inhabited."

I chose to remain in the coach as Lord Darby entered the small stone building at the center of town. It had been a perplexing morning. It was difficult to imagine that this man, so atuned to the land and history of the region, could be the same man who seemed so insensitive to his son. Lord Darby was far more complex than I had first assumed. Indeed, if I had not seen his other side, I sensed I might have been quite taken with him.

Our return to Darby Manor passed in silence. There were myriad questions crossing my mind, but Lord Darby made no further effort at conversation, withdrawing into the hush of the landscape. Indeed, as we reached the house and he helped me alight from the carriage, he excused himself, telling me that if I should like some tea I need only inform Mrs. Horsley.

Rather than finding myself fatigued, I discovered after the somewhat lengthy carriage ride that I longed to stretch my legs a bit. I had seen the Coverdale that Lord Darby loved, and strolling out towards the gardens, I hoped that I might get some sense of the nature of his late wife.

Lord Darby had not exaggerated when he had exclaimed about how she had transformed the landscape. Formal gardens spilled from terraces, whose circular steps were flanked by massive carved stone lions keeping guard over the sea of color below. The scent was heady, the roses, with their late summer bloom, fragrant in the air. The proliferation of hues ranged from the purest white to deep crimson, and the lawns spread with gentle undulations down to a lake nestled below the swell of the hillsides.

Thinking that I heard my name being called, I looked about to detect the source.

"Miss Chatfield. Miss Chatfield, wait on there," a voice called out.

As I was momentarily blinded by the sun I had to squint through the blur to see Lady de Wentoff moving towards me.

"Goodness, you *do* stride out," she gasped, obviously short of breath. "Did you not hear me calling you?"

I shook my head. "I fear I did not till the last."

"Edmund—Lord Darby told me that he thought you had come this way. I thought it might be pleasant if we could walk together. I do, on occasion, long for female companionship."

Somehow her words did not ring true, but I made no comment.

"You had a pleasant ride, I assume," she inquired.

"Very," I nodded as she opened her parasol.

"The sun you know, 'tis death on the skin. But then once back in London you shan't have to worry about it."

Though I had made my intentions known, I was nonetheless surprised at her comment.

"I cannot think what Edmund finds so thrilling about a lot of rock and drying heather," she continued, falling into step with me. "For myself, I find it dreary beyond measure."

"Then you are not from Yorkshire?"

"Indeed not," she exclaimed. "My family was from Devonshire. Far more civilized. But my late husband was from the area. Not far from here."

"Then you have known Lord Darby for some time."

"Of course," she acknowledged. "But let us not talk of me. I would far prefer to hear about you."

"There is not much to tell," I replied.

"Nonsense," she argued. "With a mother as famous as yours you must find our life here terribly mundane."

I denied this but found myself rambling on more than I would have intended.

We began a descent on the far side of the house when I spied what appeared to have been a small building set in the distance.

"What is that?" I queried, pointing down the hillside.

" 'Twas the summerhouse," she replied, slowly lifting the weight of her skirts and turning suddenly.

"It looks as though there was a fire there," I mused, noting the charred rafters.

"We should turn back," she replied resolutely. "There is nothing there of interest."

Perhaps not, I thought, but it was indeed puzzling that here within these impeccable grounds lay a dwelling whose charred remains left a distinct mar on the landscape. I was startled by a firm hand on my elbow. "Come, Lillith, there is nothing to be seen down there. It makes me shudder to think of it."

Indeed her composure seemed shaken. "Perhaps 'tis none of my concern, but I cannot help but wonder," I mused.

"Wondering does one little good, Lillith," Marisse advised, propelling me back towards the house. "But as this shall all soon become a memory for you, I suppose there would be no harm in explanation. Three years ago there was a fire. Caroline, Edmund's late wife, and Anitra, his youngest daughter, were killed. Damien was left . . . well, as you have now seen him."

I stood stock still along the path. "Oh, how ghastly," I exclaimed. "But how? What happened?"

Her pale green eyes studied me for a moment. "That, my dear, one does not discuss. It is tragedy enough that it occurred."

With that she turned and started back to the house. Realizing she had no intention of embellishing on this shocking revelation, I quickened my pace to catch up to her. As loquacious as she had been, her face was now masked in stony silence. Puffs of low-lying clouds now hid the sun, chilling the air. There was no doubt that as far as Lady de Wentoff was concerned, the subject was closed. But though I was not wont to pry, I could not suppress my desire to learn more about this fire which had claimed two lives, while perhaps wreaking its greatest destruction upon a third. Somehow I felt if I knew more about the fire I might better understand Lord Darby, and, yes, even Damien.

We had rounded the circle out of the gardens when Lady de Wentoff paused suddenly by the sundial. "Miss Chatfield—Lillith," she said, folding her parasol, "Lord Darby is not a man to take rejection easily. Were you to know him better, you would find that he is many things, but most of all resolute. Though you have made known your intention to return to London, I should advise you that I am quite certain he will try to dissuade you. Openly, and also in perhaps subtler ways. I forewarn you of this because I know he can be most persuasive. Darby Manor is not the place for you, and certainly marriage to one who is . . . Well, let us just say 'twould be a bad bargain. I understand that you met Damien this morning. He can be quite charming when he wants to. But there is a dark, brooding side to his nature, which I fear you would find disconcerting. What I am trying to tell you is that you must make certain to be on the next coach to London. You may feel little awaits you there, but, believe me, you have no reason to remain here."

As I followed her back to the house, I wondered whether she was advising me or warning me. Since I had made my intentions clear, why should she think I might be so easily dissuaded? And if Darby Manor and its inhabitants were of such an ominous nature, why did she, who expressed her dislike for the place, intend to remain here? There was something about her comments which made me bristle. Perhaps she was just being kind, but when I left Darby Manor, I wanted it to be of my own volition, not because I had been told to go.

9

I T was four thirty when I returned to
my room. I found that I was truly
weary, less from my outings than from the machinations of
my mind. I wished I could ignore the questions which
plagued me; I knew I should focus on what to do once I left
Darby Manor.

I lay down on the bed thinking that I had a good hour
before dinner. The portfolio of sketches which I had commenced looking at the day before was next to the bed. I picked
it up, opening the marbelized parchment cover. I had not
intended to study them the other day, but now as I perused
each I was struck by their beauty. Most were of landscapes.
The artist, whoever she or he was, had an uncanny ability to

capture the terrain that my eyes had feasted upon earlier in the day. The steep bare hills, the gullies carved by the Cover, the humpbacked bridges and slopes of bracken were all here. It did not take a trained eye to know that each of these sketches wrought purely in black line were jewels in themselves.

I started suddenly, for at the very last there were several which stood apart from all the rest. They were portraits of a girl. Though one knew that she was young, there was a distant, thoughtful quality to her gaze. My eyes looked down to what appeared to be a small signature at the bottom of the paper. I picked the candle up off the table and pulled it closer.

Anitra, it said. So this was Anitra, I murmured to myself. I wondered how long before her death this had been done.

As I closed the portfolio a small manila paper fell from the back of it. I was about to replace it when I discovered writing on the reverse side.

"To Anitra," I read. "Who sees a world apart from our own." It was signed "Your loving Damien."

I was flabbergasted. Could it be that it was Damien who had done these sketches? If so, he indeed possessed an enormous God-given ability to put a specter of life to paper or canvas. It confounded me that one who seemed so sullen and suspicious could create such beauty. What had Marisse said? That he had a dark, brooding side. Perhaps. But it was certainly veiled in these sketches.

I hurriedly replaced them in the portfolio, realizing suddenly that the hour was growing late. Selecting a gown of garnet taffeta with ruching about the scooped neckline and capped sleeves, I set about doing my hair. Pulling the dark masses high on my head, I clasped them with several combs, allowing the rest to fall in tendrils down my back.

I pulled my robe closer to me as there was a knock at the door. "Who is there?" I called out.

" 'Tis only me, miss," I heard Mary respond.

I bade her enter.

"Aye don't mean te be disturbin' ye, but aye thought ye'd want te know that there be guests tonight at the manor. Lord Darby said ye were te join 'em in the drawin' room."

"Oh, dear," I moaned, thinking it odd that no one had made mention of it earlier. "Now I am not certain this gown is suitable."

Mary crossed to the bed and gently lifted it up. " 'Tis lovely, miss. Ye'll shine above the rest," she reassured me.

"I hardly think that," I countered, "but 'tis too late to worry the matter. In any event, it is not as though I were the guest of honor."

Mary started to leave but then paused before the doorway. "Miss Lillith, please don't be thinkin' aye'm bein' rude, but, well, there's talk, an' aye'm not one fer gossipin' but—"

"But what, Mary?"

"Well, aye wasn't real sure why ye be 'ere at Darby Manor—not that aye'm sorry. Yer a real lady, ye are, an' bin ever so nice te me. But aye know ye told me ye were te be workin' 'ere, an' there's some that say . . . Well, Sommers says yer 'ere te marry Master Damien."

Sommers, I knew, was Lord Darby's manservant. It angered me, perhaps irrationally, that I would find myself the subject of the staff's scuttlebutt.

"I would not give much credence to what you hear," I replied. "Truth to tell, I shall be leaving Darby Manor on the next available coach."

Mary's eyes widened. "Leavin' are ye? Well, now, that's a pity, as 'ere aye was 'opin' we were to 'ave a weddin' at Darby Manor. An' Master Damien such a fine gentleman an' all—an' ever so 'andsome." Suddenly, sensing she had perhaps said too much, she curtsied and excused herself.

As I slipped the gown over my head, I pondered Mary's reaction. Unless I was mistaken she seemed to have genuine regard for Damien Darby. Her opinion was certainly in opposition to Lady de Wentoff's.

Satisfied with my appearance, I took my candle and wound

my way along the hall. The flame became fifty as it shimmered in the procession of mirrors. I paused midway down the staircase, drawn by the portrait of the figure atop the stallion. It was a pity that the raw power the artist had captured had been reduced to bitterness. But given what I now knew, I wondered if I had been too quick to judge Damien. It did not really matter, save that my own loss allowed me insight into his. Voices were emanating from the drawing room, and I took a deep breath as I descended and crossed to it.

As I opened the door Lord Darby strode deliberately to greet me. "Well, there you are, my dear. Come meet our guests."

I had taken but one step when I spied Damien, his chair placed close to the chimneypiece. He was staring at me as though he were looking right through me.

Lord Darby propelled me forward. "Now, let me see; you know Dr. Rendcomb, of course." The doctor took my hand, saying, "I am pleased to see you looking so well, Miss Chatfield. We doctors like to see examples of our medicinal powers. It breeds confidence."

"And Dr. Rendcomb's wife, Martha," Lord Darby proceeded, "and Lord Farklan and his sister Lady Maude Farklan."

As tall, sleek, and dandified as the viscount was, Maude, by contrast, was a small, softly rounded girl. There was a cherubic prettiness about her, save for an unfortunate down-turned pair of razor-thin lips which suggested a petulant nature.

I noticed that while Lord Farklan's eye roved my torso with some admiration, his sister's regard was cool at the least.

Marisse, who was standing at the far side of the fireplace, flashed a smile at me. "You look charming, my dear. You should wear your hair like that more often."

Her comment, I felt, was somehow patronizing, for my gown was the height of simplicity next to hers, not to mention that the necklace which lay against her flawless skin was a rainbow of priceless jewels.

"Well, now that we are all here, why do we not proceed to the dining room. Will you do me the honors, dear?" Lord Darby extended his arm to Marisse. Dr. Rendcomb and his wife followed.

"May I have the pleasure, Miss Chatfield?" Lord Farklan inquired of me.

I turned about, my eyes meeting Damien's. A willful smile played about his lips. "I am certain nothing would suit Miss Chatfield better," he murmured.

I hesitated a moment, but as Maude moved swiftly to the back of Damien's chair I allowed Lord Farklan to take my arm. We had reached the door when I heard Damien exclaim, "Really, Maude, this fussing is unnecessary. I am perfectly capable of wheeling myself to the dining room."

It was with some embarrassment that I found myself seated to the right of Lord Darby but also with some relief that I found Damien placed at the opposite end of the table.

The conversation tended to trivial matters. The viscount and his sister had returned but weeks past from a seaside sojourn at Brighton. Though I found their conversation banal, Marisse seemed wholly entertained by their recounting of social events.

For the life of me I could not fathom why this group had been gathered together. Dr. Rendcomb and his wife, I surmised, were only of recent acquaintance, and the Farklans were obviously far from being intimates of Lord Darby's. Lord Darby was painfully polite, keeping his responses brief. It was difficult to discern whether he was merely allowing Marisse to have center stage or whether he was preoccupied.

Only Damien was quieter than myself. Save for one instant, when I looked up to find him staring at me, he appeared lost in his goblet of claret, which I noticed was replenished with alarming frequency.

As the course of leg of mutton and caper sauce was served,

Lady Maude filled a moment's pause in the conversation by turning to me and inquiring, "Now, Miss Chatfield—"

"Lillith," I corrected.

"Lillith then," she replied, brushing a tendril from her face. "You must tell us what brings you to Darby Manor."

A deathly stillness seemed to fall upon the room. I could feel the flush spread about my face.

"Miss Chatfield has come to assist me, Maude," I suddenly heard Damien say. "I have found it quite impossible to catalogue my paintings, and she will bring some organization to it all."

Had I not just placed a morsel to my mouth my shock would have been audible. To my amazement neither Lord Darby nor Lady de Wentoff questioned his statement.

"How dreary," Maude murmured, seemingly satisfied with his response. "Not your paintings, of course, Damien. 'Tis just that to me it would seem a tedious job. I envy you not, my dear, save that it will permit you to spend your days with that attractive scoundrel."

I took a sip of wine. "One does what one can, Lady Maude."

With the presentation of the plum pudding the viscount seemed to make a concerted effort to engage me in conversation. Though he was the epitome of studied charm, all I desired was to excuse myself for the evening. Indeed, when everyone had retired to the library, I feigned weariness and, bidding all a good night, moved to leave the room. I had taken but four steps when Damien called my name.

"Now do not forget, Miss Chatfield. Be in my studio promptly at nine."

I whirled about to see a look of pure amusement on his face. I nodded and, clenching my teeth, nearly flew out of the room and up the stairs.

He was impossible. Admittedly the story he had concocted had saved me great embarrassment, but that final comment— meet him in the studio, indeed! His very look told me he had done it specifically to annoy me. Why I allowed him to exasperate me so was beyond me. Well, if he thought he could get the better of me he must think again. I might be stuck under this roof for the next few days, but I certainly would not allow him to goad me.

As I settled into bed I thought back to a comment of Lady Maude's. She had implied that she would envy me my days with Damien. Something told me she would like to occupy his nights as well. I blew out the candle, wondering why I was even thinking such thoughts. But if indeed Maude was interested in Damien, why would Lord Darby not promote a union between the two? They were obviously acquainted. What purpose indeed to have sent for me?

I closed my eyes, thinking again that if nothing else there were complexities here at Darby Manor that I did not understand. And the sooner I would be freed from it the better.

I awakened early the next morning. A young girl I did not recognize arrived to freshen my basin, explaining that it was Mary's day off. Sally, as she was called, seemed put off by my request for additional water, but my hair, I decided, was sadly in need of washing.

I missed Mary more than I might have expected, for Sally had an unfortunate habit of staring. But by nine I had brushed dry the last strands of my hair and wound it in loose coils. These early hours had been disquieting ones, for just as I felt that I was beginning to suppress the pain of my recent loss, my mind was crowded again with thoughts of Father and Elijah. A part of me wanted to believe it was all a bad dream, that I would awaken in my room at Bostworick Hall to the familiar sound of their voices below. Abraham had advised me it would take time. How long? I wondered. 'Twas not that I ever wanted to forget, only that I wondered if this feeling of desolation would ever leave me.

I had not written to Abraham, for which I felt guilty,

though the omission had also been deliberate. To tell him I would be leaving Darby Manor to return to London with no prospects, not even an address to impart, would only cause him greater concern.

The day was warmer than the last, and I donned my blue muslin and best cobbled boots, thinking that, after taking some breakfast, I would be inclined to walk the grounds again. Though I did not want to admit to it, I suspected that some inexplicable fascination would lead me to the charred summerhouse on the knoll above the lake.

My earlier sadness seemed to leave me as I wound down the staircase and crossed to the morning room. As I opened the door there was a bark, and Chips ran full tilt to greet me. I stroked his glossy coat and, rising, saw Damien as he called the dog. Somewhat reluctantly Chips scampered away from me back to his master.

"I did not know you were here," I muttered.

He did not look up, but replied, "I thought I told you to meet me in the studio at nine."

I was so dumbstruck that when I answered I could hear my voice falter. "Damien, we both know that that direction was issued for the benefit of your guests. Or perhaps for your own benefit. Even if I were to have paid it any notice, I do not even know where your studio is."

He turned his head to me. "Ah, but you seem to know that I paint."

"There was a portfolio of sketches in my—in Anitra's room," I retorted.

"You had no right," he said accusingly.

I moved forward. "I beg your pardon, but there was nothing to indicate that they were personal property. 'Twas not as though I was intruding on you. They were there in the room. And I looked at them. That is all."

He paused. "And what did you think of them?"

"I thought they were good. Very good. Indeed, superlative—not that I believe you care about my opinion."

He looked surprised. "The lady is quick to judge, I see. If I might say so, you look fetching but ridiculous standing in the middle of the room, Lillith. You are obviously hungry, so why not sit down. I promise you I shall be on my best behavior. 'Tis the least I could do for my intended."

I would have turned and left the room except that the night before I had promised myself that I would not allow him to intimidate me. He returned to his meal, seeming to ignore me as I moved forward, seating myself at the place opposite his. Without a word he picked up a small silver bell at his side and rang it. Within seconds a serving girl arrived.

"Miss Chatfield will have eggs, two slices of ham, and do bring more of these biscuits. They are delicious."

She left without a word. "Do you always order people about?" I asked.

"Only when I know what is best for them," he retorted.

"And what makes you the arbiter of what is best for someone?" I challenged.

He grimaced. "I have many faults, Lillith, but lack of perception is not one of them."

I bit my lip as the girl returned and placed the full plate before me. As I commenced eating he said, "Now, that is better. I expect a clean plate. I like my women with a bit of flesh on them."

My fork dropped to my plate with a loud clatter. "Well then you should apprise your father that the next notice he places should be more specific about your desires."

His expression told me my retort had struck a nerve, and I could not help feeling a small sense of victory.

"You know, Miss Chatfield, I think for both our parts 'twould be best if we did not harp on the actions of my father. That it is a sore point between us is obvious. Nonetheless, I would far prefer to call a truce."

I looked at him suspiciously. "I wish I could believe that," I admitted. "For in a few days I shall be gone from here, and whatever antagonism there is shall soon be forgotten."

We finished the meal in silence.

"What are you planning to do with your day?" he queried suddenly.

"I had not thought about it," I lied, realizing I could scarce tell him of my intentions of visiting the place which had felled him so cruelly.

"Then why do you not come with me to my studio," he replied. "As you have evidenced some interest in art, it might amuse you."

I was torn. I was not convinced that we could continue to be civil in each other's presence, and yet I was curious to see more of his work. "I should not want to intrude," I said slowly.

"You will learn, Miss Chatfield, that I am not a man easily intruded upon. The invitation stands."

"Then I accept," I concluded, avoiding his gaze.

He reached down and patted his spaniel. "Chips, it appears we shall have company this day."

I followed him, aware for the first time of the enormous strength his arms possessed to propel the chair forward with such ease. He moved down to the very back of the center hall and through a door leading to a passage, which though narrow seemed to go on forever. He had some problem with the lock on the door at the end of the hall, but I knew better than to offer him any assistance. Chips scampered through immediately, and holding the door back for me, Damien ushered me in.

I knew my gasp must have been audible. I had never beheld a structure of such majestic proportion. The ceiling soared perhaps some forty feet, and the entire end wall was glass, so that the room was flooded with the most extraordinary light. There were canvases everywhere; on the walls, tucked into rows of slotted supports, and stacked haphazardly about the floor.

"You must forgive the disarray," he apologized, moving a

palette of dried paints aside. "I fear it has all gotten beyond me."

I moved along the perimeter of the room, my eyes feasting on the proliferation of canvases. Whereas the sketches in the portfolio had been lacking any color, this room was filled with it. Again, his focus was with the land that surrounded Darby Manor—the reed-sprinkled fields, the rocky combs about the Creg, the escarpments purple with heather bloom; the wild loneliness of the dales was all here, at once frightening and evocative.

"I fear Father finds this a rather frivolous pastime," he said as I moved from one painting to another.

"How could anything so beautiful be frivolous?" I asked.

For a fleeting moment his gaze softened. "You like them, then," he ventured.

"They are," I replied, searching for the right word, "re-markable. But it is a pity that they are all locked up here. These ought to be shared, appreciated."

He wheeled his chair closer to me. "You flatter me, Miss Chatfield, but this is purely, shall we say, my indulgence."

"Then it is a selfish one," I admonished him.

"Perhaps I am a selfish man," he replied sardonically. "I fear that even if I wanted to show them, I would not know where to begin. Have you any idea what a task it would be to catalogue these pieces? Frankly, I prefer to paint."

There was some truth to what he said. The scope of his work was indeed enormous. "Could you not employ someone to help you?" I suggested.

He shook his head. "In this forsaken land about us there is no one with either the time or the knowledge."

I stepped up to a small platform to have a closer look at one of the smaller paintings, which was of a village hamlet.

"That is, unless you, Miss Chatfield, would consider taking the position?"

I nearly fell from the platform.

"Well, you needn't look so startled," he said. "Admittedly

it had not occurred to me before, but it is rather an ingenious idea, if I do say so myself."

I studied him, wondering if he was baiting me. "You *are* serious, are you not?"

He regarded me thoughtfully. "Oh, quite. You were quick to say yourself that I needed help. I have admitted there are no local prospects. It seems ideal to me."

I stepped down gingerly. "I believe you forget, Damien, that I am leaving Darby Manor on the next coach. That is but two days off. It would take months to sort out this work and catalogue it."

"Precisely. But there is nothing compelling you to return to London. And unless I am mistaken, you are not exactly in a position to refuse an honest income. That is what I am offering you. Obviously you'd have your quarters here at Darby Manor, and, let us say, twenty pounds a week."

"Twenty pounds!" I exclaimed.

"Thirty then, but no more," he retorted.

I gasped. "You know there have been moments when I thought your father was quite mad. You have obviously inherited some of his characteristics."

He whirled his chair about and propelled himself towards the door. "You may be right, Lillith," I heard him say. "But the offer still stands."

I realized I had been dismissed. He opened the door and waited in silence until I preceded him through, Chips bounding on ahead of me.

I walked ahead of him down the hallway and back through to the reception hall. Whatever good humor he had exhibited seemed to have suddenly disappeared. I could not say that he had grown morose, but certainly distant. He looked tired, and for the first time I felt some sympathy for him. No one had explained the exact nature of his injury to me, but I could see the pain in his eyes.

"I shall be taking lunch in my rooms," he said. "I expect I will see you at dinner."

Standing in the middle of the center hall, dwarfed by the chandelier above me, I felt terribly alone.

"Thank you for showing me your studio, Damien," I called out.

For a moment I thought he was going to reply, but without another word he wheeled away from me. Though I had intended to walk the grounds, I was tired suddenly and decided instead to go to my room. The sun was high, and I curled up on the window seat, relishing its warmth. The wind scattered the first leaves to be shriveled and darkened by the onset of fall across the still-verdant pastures of lawn. It was a peaceful vista, but I was not at peace. Whereas I should have taken some relief from Damien's offer of employment, instead I was unsettled by it. A part of me felt it was foolish to give it more than a cursory thought. But a more practical voice reminded me that it was a chance I could ill afford to let go. There were no other prospects on the horizon. And if I was diligent, I suspected I could sort and catalogue the works within two to three months. Even if I accepted half of what he had offered, I could live comfortably until I secured a position as a governess to some kindly family. I determined to accept his offer, albeit under my own terms.

When the hour for dinner approached I selected a midnight-blue silk taffeta gown from the armoire, laid it atop the bed, and moved to the dressing table, where I uncoiled my hair and commenced brushing it. It had become tangled and my brush, catching in a snarl, flew from my hand. I cried out as it smashed against the table, fearful that I might have broken the fine inlay. As I bent down to retrieve the brush, I saw that beneath the apron of the table a small drawer had become dislodged. I was about to push it closed when I spied a small leather-bound volume at the back. I withdrew it and laid it in my lap. The name ANITRA was emblazoned in gold leaf on the front and the whole book was bound by a leather strap with a small lock. As my fingers traced the outline of her name I wondered about the contents of this diary. How curious I was about this girl! Did the thoughts and experiences recorded here provide a clue to the nature of the girl whose thoughtful gaze Damien had captured in his sketches? Impatient with my morbid fascination, I quickly replaced the volume and pushed the drawer shut. As I did I spied a piece of paper on the patterned carpet below. Retrieving it, I placed it on the flat surface of the dresser. It was a page from the diary, dated 1847; that would have been the year before Anitra's death. Though I felt I was invading the dead girl's privacy I could not keep myself from pressing the paper out and reading it.

Father has been away, but Aunt Jess has arrived, so the servants have been polishing and scrubbing. Mother wanted me to help her in the garden, but one does tire of her obsession with her flowers. I have been to the summer-house again. How I love it there! Indeed I should be able to dwell there forever. Were it not for Chips, Damien would never have discovered me. He watches me so. And daily I am more disturbed by it. I seem not able to escape him. And I am frightened for what

Here the writing broke off. The page was neither torn nor concluded, so I surmised that the entry had been halted abruptly. I reread it slowly. What did this mean, I wondered, feeling a sudden chill in the room. What could possess a young girl to write such a thing? My eyes focused on the sentence "I seem not able to escape him." Was she afraid of her own brother?

I was sorry now the diary was sealed, for there was a possibility that the answer was locked away in its pages. This entry was too disturbing to dismiss, particularly because everyone seemed so determined not to even mention this young girl who had died so tragically. Anitra was an enigma. Was it because I occupied her room that I felt such fascination with her? I did not know. But if I remained here at Darby Manor I knew I would be compelled to learn the story of her life, and of her death.

It was early when I reached the center hall. Deciding it would be somewhat tedious to sit alone in the dining room awaiting the others, I crossed to the library. I found Damien seated there in his chair, his gaze fixed on the orange and amber flames leaping against the massive stone inset of the firewall.

I was within a few feet of him when I spoke. "Am I intruding?"

He whirled about. His face had an almost plaintive expression.

"Are you all right, Damien?" I inquired.

He sighed, seeming to slump in his chair. "It is you," he murmured.

"I am sorry if I startled you," I said.

"I fear I find apologies as useless as insults, Lillith, but actually I am glad you are here. I wanted to know if you have given any further thought to our earlier discussion?"

"You mean your offer to employ me as your, as your . . ."

"As my assistant," he concluded.

"You *were* serious, then," I ventured.

"I do not mince words, Miss Chatfield. My offer stands."

I drew a deep breath, wishing that I could stop my hands from shaking. "Well, then, I accept. On certain conditions, of course." He looked amused as I continued. "First, that I shall indeed be employed as your assistant—nothing else. Second, that I shall be paid the sum of fifteen pounds per week. And, third, that if my work cannot be completed within three months, you will release me from the agreement."

He rubbed his chin. "On the second point I would say you are a fool. I have offered you far more, but if this is the bargain you wish to strike, I will agree. On the third point I would tell you I am an impatient man. If the work cannot be accomplished within that time, then it would be I who had made the bad bargain."

"And on the first?" I ventured with trepidation.

"Frankly, it amuses me that it should even be a 'condition,' as you term it. You shall be my assistant, Miss Chatfield, pure and simple. That is, of course, unless *you* deign to change it."

I could feel a flush spread through me. "I can assure you I shall not."

He wheeled himself over to the decanters on the butler's tray. He poured two glasses of port and turning to me said, "I fear you must claim one for your own. 'Tis one of the inconveniences I live with."

I nodded and moved over to him, taking the glass in my hand.

He paused. "Before we toast our new association, I must tell you that I too have certain conditions."

I tightened my grasp on my glass. I knew I should have trusted my initial instincts.

"First, I wish to tell my father this very evening. Second, and far more important, I shall want you to respect my privacy. By that I mean that I shall inform you daily of those hours you are to work for me. You will forgive my saying so, but at times you would be, well, an intrusion. As long as you can abide by that, I foresee no problem."

I relaxed somewhat. Bringing my glass forward to meet his, I announced, "Then we have an agreement."

A smile played about his lips. "You shall have your work cut out for you, I fear, but I sense you shall not shrink from it."

"I am not unaccustomed to work," I assured him. "Indeed, many times I assisted my own father in cataloguing."

He downed his glass and replaced it on the tray. "You must tell me about that one day, but for now I suggest we proceed to the dining room. Edmund has a fetish about promptness."

Lord Darby and Marisse were already seated, their figures

appearing strangely dwarfed by the expanse of table between them. A look of surprise registered on both their faces as Damien wheeled himself to his place and I took my own. The room was quiet, save for the sound of the serving girl ladling a steamy fish stock into the Imari bowl before me.

"Since you both appear to have been rendered speechless by seeing Miss Chatfield and me together, let me suggest you become accustomed to it," Damien quipped.

"Then you have reconsidered, Lillith?" Lord Darby asked with satisfaction.

"Not really, Lord Darby," I replied.

Damien laughed. "Contrary to your belief, Father, you cannot control everyone's life. The simple truth is that I have persuaded Miss Chatfield to become my assistant."

I looked up as Marisse, wide-eyed, exclaimed, "Your assistant? You weren't really serious about that nonsense the other night?"

Damien nodded. "Absolutely. As 'twas foolhardy to think that she might become my wife I have done the better thing and taken her into my employ."

Lord Darby swallowed his wine. "If this is a joke—"

"I assure you, Father, it is not. Although your ridiculous plan has gone awry, I find this may work to my benefit. Our mutual benefit, I hope, Miss Chatfield. Since my accident, as we all know, I have been unable to keep up as I once did. The studio is in chaos and with Miss Chatfield's help it will at least have organization. Just think, Father, there is a chance that the Darby name will have a future after all. As much as you detest my paintings, in my own way, I may leave a greater legacy than you."

The venom in Damien's tone made me catch my breath. I looked quickly at Lord Darby. If I had not known how angry he must be, I might have thought he was afraid.

"You have agreed, then, to this arrangement, Lillith?" he inquired finally.

I nodded. "Your son has made me a most generous offer, one which frankly I am in no position to refuse. Unless, of course, you are opposed?"

"Opposed? No, I am not opposed," he said. "To speak candidly, I am surprised. I do not pretend to know you well, but I thought you were cleverer. Whatever Damien has promised you would be paltry compared to my own offer."

"As you say, Lord Darby," I replied, "you do not know me. I prefer an honest wage. And whereas your proposal insulted my intelligence, Damien's might make good use of it."

"Bravo," Damien championed admiringly. "I know you cannot understand her logic, Marisse, but I find it quite refreshing. A woman with both a mind and a soul. A unique experience for Darby."

Marisse, who had been particularly fidgety during this exchange, coughed. "How gallant of you, Damien. If I did not know better I would think you were quite taken with little Lillith here. But then we both know that—"

"Be very careful, Marisse," Damien interrupted, his eyes flashing. "A coiled serpent is unwisely challenged. Its poison could prove fatal."

As Marisse's mouth fell open it was clear that the arrow of Damien's threat had pierced her veneer.

My expression must have given clue to my reaction, for Damien's mood lightened suddenly. "Goodness, Lillith, you actually look frightened. You mustn't be, you know. It is just idle palaver. Is that not right, Father?"

Lord Darby nodded, avoiding Damien's gaze. As he reached for his glass, I noticed the tremor of his hand. Until that moment I had thought him amazingly robust for his age, but I now wondered whether his appearance was deceptive. Was his determination to see Damien married and the father of an heir stronger than I had first imagined? Did he, sensing his own demise was not far distant, simply wish to see the Darby line perpetuated while he still lived?

Though I wished I might take some relief if not pleasure

from my determination to accept Damien's offer, I was merely resigned. I told myself as the dinner proceeded with stilted conversation that it had in fact been my decision. No one had coerced me. But the thought of living here for the next few months was not comforting. My life at Bostworick Hall had not been without moments of consternation. But even in the worst of times we had managed to rally as a family. That was what seemed so different here at Darby: they were as strangers, living together and yet apart. If there had ever been a common ground, they seemed unable to find it now.

10

As I climbed into bed that night, stretching my limbs against the cool of the sheets, I still agonized over my decision. I had no idea of the hour when I was roused from a deep sleep. I had neglected to draw the draperies, and the sliver of the quarter moon shone bright through the panes of glass. Thinking that it might be the illumination which had disturbed me, I rose and moved to the windows. I began to draw the hangings when I paused, certain that I had seen a figure dart across the grounds below. I waited, curious as to who would be wandering the outskirts of the manor in the dead of night. When the scene remained still I decided I must have been mistaken. I had come to learn that the winds rolling the bracken in the barren straits beyond made images of their own. 'Twas possible their gusts had caused the disturbance.

Tentatively I went to the door, waiting for some sound, but as my room was far removed from the reception hall it was difficult to hear anything. Climbing back into the softness of my bed, I determined that I had no cause for concern and soon, burying my head in the pillow, I fell asleep again.

I knew the hour was early when my eyes opened and drank in the sweep of the room. Try as I would to will myself back to sleep, I could not, and dressing quickly, I decided if I wished to explore the ruins of the summerhouse this would be an ideal time to do so.

I did not know why these charred remains seemed to beckon to me. Certainly there was nothing there, only an echo of those who had died. But it seemed to stand as some decadent monument amid all this splendor. It fascinated me and, admittedly, it troubled me, for it was like some macabre reminder of the devastation it had wrought on all the Darbys.

As the fire had gone out during the night, the room was cold, and I withdrew a navy serge wool suit which, though not a favorite, was warm. I did not bother to dress my hair. I could do so upon my return.

I tiptoed along the hall, stopping suddenly with the distinct impression that I was not alone. I turned slowly around. There was no one in sight, only my own reflection looking back at me from the silvered glass. The shadow was an illusion, I decided. But there was definitely a haunting quality about the placement of these mirrors. When you walked past them you felt as though other people, crafted in your image, walked with you.

I stepped up my pace and, crossing the reception hall, tried quietly to turn the locks on the front door. I cringed at the loud noise when the bolts were thrown. The last latch released, I stepped into the mist of the morn.

There were several paths I could take, but I chose the one I knew. I chastised myself for not having brought an umbrella, for moisture hung in the air. I wound my way through the formal gardens along the paths below the terraces. What had once been a small lane down to the summerhouse had become overgrown by prickly wild plum and brambles, making the walking somewhat difficult. The bell heather in the fields beyond perfumed the air with a pungent scent. I halted where the lane forked into two paths. It was impossible to know which one to take, as dense hedgerows rising almost two feet higher than myself blocked further view. I chose the one to the left only because it appeared to be the one most oft taken.

It was a rather eerie feeling, walking through this tunnel-like maze. I had almost determined that I had gone in the wrong direction when suddenly I came upon a clearing. The land fell precipitously from it to what appeared, through the morning brume to be a small stone house. I was tempted to continue, but fearing I was intruding, I turned back. My inadvertent detour had cost me time, and I scurried quickly through the labyrinth back to the fork. It was but minutes later when I came upon the scarred remains of the summerhouse.

By its foundation one could see it had been sizable. The only things that seemed to have escaped totally unscathed were the massive Doric columns carved from stone, which had flanked the entrance. Charred blackened beams rose like decayed medieval relics. Indeed, the visual impact was so overwhelming that for a second I thought I could actually, even after these years, smell the flame-seared wood.

It must have been an inferno, but how, I wondered, had they all come to be trapped here? Surely there must have been some opportunity for escape. Had no one from the manor seen the flames or the smoke? Possibly not, I decided, at least not until it was too late. Or was that how Damien had come to be injured? Had he heard their cries and come running and perhaps been engulfed as Lady Caroline and Anitra had? But if so, how was it that his face and especially his hands had not been injured? He bore no scars. But no one who survived this blaze would have been spared the emotional pain of it.

I looked up, suddenly realizing that what had earlier been drizzle had turned to rain. Gathering my skirts, I turned back along the disused path, wishing now that I had not decided to defy the elements. As the pelting rain became more insistent, I determined to take a shortcut to the house. The overhang of the eaves would provide some shelter, and I would surely be able to find a rear entry to the house. I slid several times as I climbed the hill and was gasping for breath as I reached the north end of the edifice. Spying what appeared to be an entrance some fifty feet beyond, I dashed towards it. My hand closed about the heavy doorknob. Finding the door locked, I pounded on its nail-studded oak face.

"Hello," I called out, "is anyone there?"

When my repeated cries went unheeded, I set out towards the terraced gardens, resigned that at this hour I might have to go to the front entrance. I had progressed another thirty feet when drifting aromas told me that I was near the kitchens. The kitchen door was just beyond and I had just reached it when there was a loud crack of thunder. A maid, who could have been no more than sixteen, opened it, eyeing me with trepidation.

" 'Tis all right," I assured her. "I am Miss Chatfield, I am a guest here at the manor."

She eyed me suspiciously, blocking the entrance.

Fortunately, Mary had just started breakfast at a small table. She rose quickly and, drawing the other girl aside, said quickly, "Now, Flo, that be no way te treat our Miss Chatfield. Lord, ye're soaked through."

She led me quickly to the fire. "Now ye stand there whilst aye get ye a cup o' tea or ye'll be catchin' yer death."

I did as she bade, feeling more than a bit conspicuous. The kitchen, which I gathered was the rear kitchen to the main, was crowded with perhaps twelve young girls, each of whom eyed me with open curiosity.

"Miss Chatfield's the lady aye bin tellin' ye about," Mary announced as she poured some tea from the coal black kettle. She handed me the cup. "Aye know aye should be givin' ye this in the mornin' room, but 'tis better ye git it in ye fast."

"You needn't trouble, Mary," I said quickly. "I would not have bothered you if I could have gotten in through the door at the back of the left wing."

"Oh, ye wouldn't be gettin' in there, Miss Lillith," she advised. " 'Tis locked up good an' tight. An' a good thing, cause there's work enough, mind ye, in the main 'ouse."

Realizing I was keeping her from her breakfast I bade her to return to it.

She looked relieved. "If ye don't mind, aye will. Aye bin scrubbin' since five, an' 'tis the only time aye'll be 'avin to eat till tonight."

Her breakfast consisted merely of bread and drippings. Indeed, the atmosphere in this kitchen was dismal. For all the grandeur of Darby Manor, the conditions here were appalling. That none of the girls save Mary smiled was not surprising, considering the stygian gloom surrounding me.

Downing my tea, I excused myself, explaining that I had best change if I were to commence my work in the studio at the appointed hour. I left hurriedly.

I had just come down from my room and reached the center hall when Marisse emerged from the library. She looked at me, her reddened lips forming a perfect bow about her gleaming teeth. "Well, what a surprise. I was just going to take breakfast. Now you can join me."

I shook my head. "I fear not. Damien was most specific that I be in the studio by nine."

"Goodness, you are taking this seriously," she retorted, smoothing the lace elbow sleeve of her gown.

"I have to, Marisse," I insisted.

She sighed. "You are a fool, Lillith, not to have taken my advice. But just remember that I gave it, when all goes awry."

I felt myself stiffen. "Might I remind you that the condi-

tions under which I am remaining at Darby are quite different from those you cautioned me about."

She crossed to where I stood. "If you are wise you will keep
it that way. I am not certain that you are not more ambitious
than you appear. I just hope you are bright enough to keep
your aspirations confined to your work. You may not believe
me, but it is for your own good."

Without another word she swept past me, leaving only the
rustle of her skirts to remind me that, at least for her, my
presence at the manor was unwelcome.

The center hall clock chimed nine as I made my way back
through the series of passages to the studio. The door was
closed, and I rapped on it gently. I was startled when the locks
clicked. He had warned me about his demand for privacy, but
now I realized the lengths to which he went to assure it.

His eyes swept the length of me. "Where have you been?"
he demanded.

I flushed, realizing that my boots, which I had not taken the
time to remove, still bore traces of the dried mud.

"I simply took a stroll about the grounds," I replied.

"From now on keep to the confines of the manor, Lillith,"
he instructed.

"You neglected mentioning that I was to have no freedom
here," I charged.

He turned his chair, allowing me to enter. "I am only
advising you for your own good. You are not accustomed to
the mists which rise from the moors. It can be dangerous.

"I shall not think to tell you how to do your job, Miss
Chatfield," he continued, wheeling himself into the center of
the studio, "save to say that most of the sketches are stored in
those drawers there at the far wall. As some are preliminaries
to the paintings you see hanging about, you might wish to
commence there."

I scanned the room for some niche where I might seclude
myself with the blank ledgers he had provided. A stripped
pine table wedged under a small eave seemed suitable to use

as a desk; hoisting the cumbersome ledgers in my arms, I moved them there directly. Damien wheeled himself to the opposite end of the studio, where a canvas stood atop a large oak easel. I was struck by how agile he was for one so confined. But then, I supposed, one learned to make adjustments over the years.

The number of sketches I found in the first case of drawers caused me to question whether I had been too optimistic in estimating how quickly I could complete my task. The amount of work was astounding. That one could be so prolific, yet so masterful, was almost hard to comprehend. Even the rough sketches were worthy of note.

Crouching before the drawers, I withdrew a stack of renderings and carried them over to the desk. I had just seated myself when Damien peered from behind the draped canvas at the far end of the room and inquired, "How did you gain entry back into the manor? The doors are always locked."

I brushed a still damp lock from my forehead. "I fear I was caught in a downpour and gained admission at the kitchens. Such as they were."

"Do I notice some criticism in your tone?" he inquired.

"How can it be else?" I challenged. "But then, I suspect neither you nor your father have ever set foot in the kitchens. One might expect to find such conditions in some of the derelict sections of London, but it is appalling to see young girls working in those surroundings."

He put down his brush. "Not that it is any of your concern, but I assure you, Miss Chatfield, the servants at Darby Manor are well compensated for their labors. My late mother was the most humanitarian of women. A position at the manor is an enviable one."

"That might well have been," I acknowledged, "but I hardly think one meal a day of bread and drippings constitutes a charitable household."

I at once regretted having been so outspoken, for the last thing I wanted was to start an argument between us. I knew

Damien was angered, for he had a habit, when agitated, of locking his jaw, causing muscles to rise about the angular planes of his cheeks.

Without another word he picked up his brush and returned to work on his canvas. We were silent for the next two hours, each engrossed in his own labors. I had established some rhythm with the cataloguing and was pleased to see it moving at a more rapid pace. Having finished the original lot of sketches, I returned to the drawers and withdrew another. The next group my fingers clasped were bound by a braided silk cord. Untying it, I looked through them, thinking how different these were from the first. Whereas the earlier ones captured the starkness of the dales, these spoke of a different landscape. Though rendered in ink, one sensed that there was more color in these panoramas of rounded hills and meandering rivers. Here were hay meadows and copses, a glittering weir, white farmsteads and patches of mottled sheep on green fields. The whole of it became a foreground to windbreaks of pine and limitless moorland overhung by clouds.

"Might I interrupt?" I inquired.

"You already have," he answered, annoyed.

I carried the sketches towards where he sat, startled as he commanded, "Stay where you are. I do not like anyone to view my work in progress."

I did as he bade, waiting for him to reach me. Gently I placed the sketches in his lap. "I fear I have no idea where to commence with these," I acknowledged. "On most others there is some small inscription."

"I had almost forgotten these," he murmured, his long fingers caressing them as he laid each aside. "Here, this is up on Cross Fell in the High Pennines."

"What is that?" I motioned, stopping him at what appeared to be the ruins of a castle.

"Ah, the majestic Barnard," he mused, "long the home of the Nevilles, earls of Warwick, to whom the Darbys are related, though I take little pride in that. If I remember rightly, there should be another . . . ah, here. Yes," he continued, withdrawing another sketch. "Though not as renowned, Richmond Castle is far my favorite. 'Tis an eleventh-century Norman keep little known for battle, save a few Scottish raids, but legend claims that King Arthur and his knights sleep in a vast hall beneath the castle, waiting to be called by England."

"What a charming tale," I replied.

"Perhaps 'tis not, Miss Chatfield. Sometimes there is little difference between fact and fiction."

"It is a sacrilege that these have not been catalogued before," I said as he returned the sketches to me.

He looked amused. "You had best be careful, Lillith. I could grow accustomed to your flattery."

I lowered my eyes, realizing that I was blushing. "It is not flattery," I countered. "What I infer is that these should be offered for public viewing. I am certain Prince Albert, for one, would be interested. He is a great champion of the arts. Were he to select even a few of your paintings 'twould be a grand coup."

He looked surprised. "So you know of our Prince Consort's dedication to the arts?"

"You forget, Damien, that my father was an importer of some consequence."

He regarded me curiously. "I suspect there is a great deal I do not know about you, Lillith."

I waited, sensing that he wanted to ask something of me. But I was obviously mistaken, for he simply remarked that we were both late for luncheon.

"Would you mind making my excuses," I begged. "There are a few matters I must attend to. I would prefer to take a tray in my room."

He shrugged. " 'Tis of no consequence. I shall inform Mrs. Horsley."

I thanked him and left the studio, going directly to my room. As I changed my boots I reflected on my first morning of cataloguing. It had been full, but surprisingly pleasant. Damien had managed to curb his usually ascerbic remarks, making me optimistic that we might put our hostilities aside and work in relative peace these next months. I hoped so. I was still too fraught with the emotion of my recent sorrow to endure verbal combat. And sensing how diminished Damien's life must seem to him since the fire, I doubted he relished unpleasantness any more than I.

The rain had quieted to a drizzle as I drew myself into the window seat. Now that I had settled into a routine at Darby, it was time to write to both Abraham and Rebecca.

I made a concerted effort to keep both letters light and cheerful. Although I knew Rebecca would find the circumstances under which I had been brought to Darby mysteriously romantic, I knew Abraham would be appalled. In the end I told them about my position, describing the manor and countryside surrounding it. I avoided mention of any doubts I felt about its inhabitants. Their eccentricities puzzled me, and my preoccupation with Anitra would only strike my friends as morbid.

A maid, unfamiliar to me, brought my lunch tray, and though the turbot smelled most appetizing I only picked at it, preferring to finish my letters. It was near two when I sealed them and, gathering both in hand, decided to return to the studio. I had just reached the middle of the upper hall when from a recess in the south wall Mrs. Horsely appeared before me.

Startled, I misstepped, the letters falling onto the oriental rug. Before I could recover them, she leant down to retrieve them, studying the addresses with blatant curiosity. I put my hand out to accept them, but she held them securely away from me.

"May I have my letters?" I inquired.

"In a moment," she replied, her bulky frame barring my way. "I understand, Miss Chatfield, that you find the accommodations at Darby Manor less than satisfying."

I could not understand what she was referring to.

She took a stride towards me. "I should not be making comments on the affairs of Darby Manor were I you. Now that you are in the employ of Master Damien, I should remind you that you have no voice in this household. What the servants eat or do not eat is not your domain. We shall be far better served, you and I, if we keep to our own tasks. And, frankly, I cannot account for what might happen to you if you do not. There are many things you do not understand here at the manor. For your own good, I would suggest you not put your nose where it is not wanted."

Her surly manner threw me off guard; her imposing figure loomed, seeming to challenge me. It dawned on me that Damien must have repeated my comments on the conditions of the kitchen to her.

I drew a deep breath. "*I* would suggest, Mrs. Horsley, that you do not threaten me. I have no intention of causing you ill, but you cannot forbid my observations. It should please you that my stay at Darby Manor is but temporary. I have no influence in this house, nor do I desire any, but I think it would be far pleasanter if we remain amicable during my residence."

She glowered at me. "I don't take being crossed by the staff, and I won't take being crossed by you. As long as you keep to your own, Miss Chatfield, there shall be no problems."

"Good. And now, since the letters are already in your possession, I would ask that you see that they are posted when the regular mail goes out."

She tucked them into the pocket of her shapeless gown, nodding in assent. I turned and had started to cross the hallway when she called out, "Oh, Lady de Wentoff wanted you to know that there shall be guests at the manor again this evening. She expects you to dine with them."

I nodded and made my way back to the studio. This time, when Damien opened the door, Chips nearly bowled me over.

I knelt down and ruffled his long curly ears, sensing Damien's surprise at the dog's welcome.

As I made my way to my desk I commented, "I suppose I should tell you that Mrs. Horsley and I have had a bit of a set-to. I assume you must have relayed my comments of this morning."

"What did she say to you?" he demanded.

"Little really," I answered, "but she clearly resented my interference. And I suppose, were the shoe on the other foot, I would too."

He dabbed thoughtfully at his palette. "The less exchange you have with our esteemed housekeeper the better."

"I gather by your tone that you are not enamored of her," I replied.

"What I think of Mrs. Horsley is inconsequential. She has worked for us for many years. If there is value in longevity, then she has value to Darby."

"Does Marisse like her?" I asked, pulling the ledgers towards me.

He stopped, brush poised in midair. "What in heavens name does Marisse have to do with it?"

"Well, she is . . . I mean, she does intend to marry your father. And—"

"And you find it indelicate for her to be openly residing under this roof before she becomes Lady Darby?" he retorted. "You need not look so embarrassed. I am certain you are not the only one who finds it a curious arrangement."

Recovering my composure, I replied, " 'Tis only that she made mention that her late husband's estates were near here. I would think it would be difficult for her to absent herself from them for too long a time—until she marries, of course."

Damien started to laugh, but it was a mocking laugh, not one of pleasure. "You have a great deal to learn," he scoffed. "Marisse de Wentoff has resources, but they are not monetary. Jared de Wentoff, her late husband, died penniless. Frankly, it was as much of a surprise to me as it was to her."

"But the estates?"

"My dear Miss Chatfield, manors such as these do not care for themselves. There is no estate without the monies to support it. Oh, the land is there, the house still stands, but Marisse could not even afford a chambermaid."

"Then that explains why she is here," I concluded, feeling some sympathy for the woman. Not much time had passed since I had lost my own home.

"Does it?" he retorted. "Suffer no delusions about Marisse de Wentoff, Lillith. Let that be my father's domain."

If I had hoped Damien might volunteer further conversation I was mistaken. He addressed himself to his canvas again, leaving me to concentrate on my annotations.

I started to grow anxious when by the stroke of five Damien had made no move to dismiss me. Tonight's dinner was a command performance, and as I had already offended one member of the household that day, I wanted to be prompt.

"Must you fidget, Miss Chatfield?" Damien demanded suddenly.

"Was I? I am sorry. 'Tis just that I was told there are to be guests at dinner and—"

"And you would prefer to indulge in vapid conversation rather than continue cataloguing works which you *now* inform me I should offer to Prince Albert."

I clenched my fist, willing myself to be silent. There was no point in responding to his sarcasm.

He shrugged. "It's too dark to go on anyway."

As I moved towards the door, Chips trotted after me. When I bent down to cuddle him, Damien said, "You have obviously made a conquest."

"You sound surprised."

"You mistake me," he retorted. "I credit him with more perception than most people have."

"Is that to be taken as a compliment?" I inquired as I drew to my full height.

123

His eyes met mine. "It is an observation, Lillith. That is all."

I returned to my room, chastising myself for even imagining that he might do or say anything in praise of me. I didn't know why it bothered me, but it did. He was, after all, only my employer. He was paying me generously, and he owed me nothing more. I had been chary of the arrangement from the first; obviously it was foolish to think that we might become friends. Marisse had warned me to remember why I was here at Darby, and I was not certain she was wrong.

The hall clock chimed six as I fastened the last of the covered buttons along the face of my gown. With my hair piled high on my head, I decided I needed something to soften the barren neckline of the dress. Remembering a cameo Father had given me for my fifteenth birthday, I withdrew the delicate ivory carving from its satin case and hooked the velvet band behind my neck. 'Twas far from grand, but I knew I needn't apologize for my appearance.

I realized as I went down the stairs that I was late, for everyone was already making their way across the reception hall into the dining room.

"Ah, there you are," Marisse called up to me with a cool glance, her eyes sweeping my countenance. "Don't you look sweet."

Lord Farklan stepped forward, extending his arm to me. "I would say 'ravishing' is more befitting."

I placed my hand on his as I descended the last steps, aware that all eyes were upon me.

Lifting the skirts of her cream faille gown, Marisse stepped between us. "That is what I adore about James. He is always so gallant."

I flushed as she drew me forward to the other guests.

"You of course remember Lady Maude Farklan," she said effusively. "And may I present the earl of Shropshire, and of course Reverend Ghent, who will be presiding over our upcoming nuptials."

I took an instantaneous dislike to the earl, who regarded me with a slow, lascivious smile. The reverend, by contrast, appeared to be a jolly man, but his unfortunate stutter caused me to wonder about the length of his sermons. As I turned, Damien wheeled his chair next to me.

"I would escort you, Miss Chatfield, but then I suspect 'twould be easier for you to fall into step with Lord Farklan," he said wryly.

Before I could reply Lord Farklan had taken my arm saying, "Sporting of you, old chap."

I was seated to the left of Lord Farklan, with Lady de Wentoff to his right. Lady Maude, who had been placed beside Damien, seemed to titter at his every word. As I had never known him to be particularly loquacious and certainly not amusing, I could not fathom what delighted her so.

Lord Darby seemed particularly out of sorts that night. It was not his quiet manner but his countenance which disturbed me. He was pale and appeared anxious. I had the distinct opinion he was suffering this dinner only for Marisse's benefit.

The earl, a churlish sort, monopolized the conversation, droning on about the Royals and Lord Melbourne's health; there was talk of a seizure and it appeared likely his career was at an end.

"Poppycock," Marisse interrupted. "Lady Lyttleton has oft told me that his downfall will be the consommés, truffles, ices, and anchovies which he devours every day."

I looked up in time to see Damien roll his eyes. "And when, my dear Marisse, did you become an intimate of Lady Lyttleton's?"

"I would suggest to you, Damien, that there is a great deal you do not know about me," Marisse charged.

"Let us say I know enough, Marisse. More than enough."

Marisse, who always seemed a study of composure, looked frightened.

As the servants removed the remains of the grouse from the

table, the viscount leaned forward, saying, "Come now, you two. I am certain there are more interesting things to talk about. Miss Chatfield, for one. You know, Reverend, her mother was the great actress, Salina Kent. What an illustrious career she had! It must have been thrilling to have been her daughter."

I was discomfited at being the center of attention. " 'Thrilling' is not the word I would choose," I replied quietly.

Marisse leant towards me. "Come now, do not be modest."

"It has nothing to do with modesty, Marisse. My mother died when I was quite young. I doubt that a child's memories would prove amusing to your guests."

I squirmed uncomfortably in my chair as James Farklan persisted. "Well, for myself, I have many memories. Maudy, of course, would not, she was too young, and our mother—well, I fear she viewed theatricals with a rather jaundiced eye. But when Father would take me to London we would go to the theater to see your mother perform. What a beauty she was, and you are so like her."

I did not know why, but I sensed there was ridicule behind his flattery.

"I shall never forget her as Juliet," he went on. "The pure passion in her voice when she uttered:

> *I have no joy of this contract tonight.*
> *It is too rash, too unadvised, too sudden,*
> *Too like the lightning, which doth cease to be*
> *Ere one can say "It lightens."*

"You are a student of Shakespeare then, Lord Farklan," I murmured, surprised at this brief soliloquy.

"In a small way," he replied. "Now, I shall put you to the test. I shall give a clue. 'Tis from *Antony and Cleopatra*. I shall give Antony's line, and you respond."

I wished someone would say something to make him stop. "Really I am not very good at this," I protested.

"Nonsense," he said shortly. "Now, here's the line: 'There's beggary in the love that can be reckon'd.'"

The room was so still it almost seemed suffocating.

"'I'll set a bourn how far to be beloved,'" I murmured, feeling a flush to my cheeks.

"'Then must thou needs find out new heaven, new earth.'"

I looked up, startled, for it had been Damien who had spoken the last. A small smile played about his lips as his eyes bore into mine.

"Upstage me, will you, Damien! Now, I would have thought Brutus would be more to your liking," Lord Farklan charged.

"Don't take your test too far," Damien warned, glaring at James.

"Well, 'tis all too erudite for my tastes," Marisse interrupted. "I suggest we all retire to the library, as I am certain Edmund for one is longing for brandy."

"Actually I am afraid you are going to have to excuse me," Lord Darby said. "I have been a bit off my fettle today. Nothing that a good night's sleep won't cure."

"I am going to retire as well," I said.

"Edmund, I am not going to argue your leaving us, but I wish, Miss Chatfield, that you would reconsider," the earl said. "I was hoping we might get to know each other better."

"Since those were precisely my thoughts, I should warn you that you shall have a rival to your intentions," James chided.

"I believe I heard the lady say she was retiring," Damien said, as he wheeled his chair away from the table.

"I thought you were her employer, not her keeper," James retorted.

Damien laughed. "Lillith, I am coming to know, is quite capable of taking care of herself, gentlemen."

"And I have a full day ahead," I said. "So if you will excuse me."

As Marisse made no effort to encourage me to stay, I gathered she was just as well pleased to have the attention to herself.

"Be forewarned, Lillith," James called out as I started to climb the stairs. "The next time I shall not let you off so easily."

I puzzled over the evening's events as I returned to my room. I supposed most women would have been pleased by Lord Farklan's attention. He was not unattractive, and he had an accomplished surface charm. But he was not a man, I suspected, to have anything but a dalliance with a woman he considered beneath his station. It embarrassed me to think that Marisse might have encouraged his overtures towards me. But as she was so adamant that I should keep a distance from Damien, it was not beyond the realm of possibility.

As I undressed and slipped into bed I found myself hoping that James's attentions would prove ephemeral. The last thing I needed now was something to further complicate my life.

I closed my eyes, willing my mind to be still. I must have drifted off, for when I awakened, it was with a start. I pulled myself up in bed, and as I did there was a loud clatter emanating from the windows. I waited for a moment, and when the sound came again I drew back the covers and scurried slipperless towards it. Tugging at the heavy crewel draperies, I slipped my knee onto the window seat. As I did, something slammed against the outside of the house. I smiled to myself, realizing that it was simply a shutter which had become unhinged. I had started to withdraw when I was certain I saw a light flicker. Crouching forward, I watched as a figure darted across the end terrace. The light was extinguished suddenly. I waited, thinking I would see some further activity, but it was almost as though the person had been swallowed by the pitch black of the night.

Realizing my feet were almost numb from the cold I hurried back to bed. As I lay there shivering, I tried to fathom who was making these nocturnal forays about the manor.

There was no reason why the comings and goings of those who resided at Darby should interest me, much less trouble me. It had to be one of the servants. It was foolish to afix any ominous connotation to someone walking the grounds at night. Why, then, could I not dismiss it?

11

I AROSE early the next morning and had almost finished dressing when Mary arrived with my tray. "Yer up with the birds," she said as she pulled a basket of fresh linens from behind the door.

"I slept a bit fitfully," I admitted. "There is a loose shutter which was catching the wind most of the night."

"Aye'll tell Mrs. 'Orsley," she said, stripping the sheets.

I finished my coffee. "Mary, perhaps 'tis none of my business, but do you know if any of the servants are given to walking the grounds at night?"

"Oh, aye don't think so, miss," she replied quickly. "We're all so plum tuckered 'tis all we kin do te fall into bed. Course, aye can't be talking fer Sommers or the stable'ands or Perse."

"Who is Perse?" I inquired.

" 'E's the gardener," she informed me as she straightened the coverlet.

"That must be who lives in the stone house," I mused.

"Beggin' yer pardon?"

" 'Tis nothing. I was just talking to myself," I answered.

She grinned at me as she removed my tray. "Aye be doin' that all the time. Me mum says 'twill get me in a 'eap o' trouble one o' these days. Kin aye get ye anythin' else?"

I shook my head. "As a matter of fact, I think I shall take advantage of this early morning sun before going to the studio. I suspect 'twill be near the last of it for the season."

Mary left, and I followed quickly on her heels. As I reached the reception hall, Sommers came from the doorway heading to the studio with Chips in tow. The spaniel dashed towards me, his feathered haunches wriggling as he slipped on the smooth marble.

"Blasted animal," Sommers swore as he reached down and grabbed Chips by the scruff of the neck. "He thinks I've got nothing better to do than walk this dog."

"I am just going out myself, Sommers. I would be happy to take him."

"You are sure you can handle him?"

I nodded. "You'll be a good fellow, won't you, Chips?"

The spaniel looked up at me dolefully. I couldn't blame him for preferring my company; Sommers was not a man one warmed to. There was a distinct surliness about him. Actually all the servants save Mary were a peculiarly quiet, almost dour lot. But then Lord Darby was hardly a sympathetic sort. Since he felt he could order his own son about, there was no reason to think he would give those in his employ the time of day.

I took a deep breath as I stepped outside. The air was balmy, deceptively springlike. I had intended to stroll towards the terraced gardens, but Chips, who had scampered ahead of me, took the lead. The lawns at the front of the house were more gently undulating than those at the rear. Towering clusters of elms rose in random formation, their trunks and swaying limbs overshadowing the dense grasses. I halted, suddenly thinking I heard a rush of water. Chips had bounded towards the area from which the sound emanated. I quickened my pace, suddenly coming upon a body of water. At the far end huge arches and plinths sculpted in stone served as tunneled supports for a waterfall. I watched as the clear water cascaded into the pool, feeding back into the lake.

It was so beautiful, so peaceful here! What a contrast to the ruins of the summerhouse. I watched the water lap against the edge and wondered if Damien had used to come here before the accident. Had he sailed small boats here as a child, pretending he was on the high seas? Had he played with Anitra or Amanda in the ferneries along the borders?

I would probably never know. It would be several months before I left the North Country, but I suspected however long I stayed Damien would remain an enigma to me. My eyes lingered over the sweep of lawn up to the house. Had laughter ever echoed through those walls? I wondered. Had those who inhabited Darby always lived in worlds of their own? Had their tragedy changed them as I knew my own tragedy had in some way changed me?

Chips's barking drew me out of my reverie, and I lifted my skirts and hurried to catch up to him. I sensed he followed a routine as he took his morning constitutional, for he ran purposefully ahead, this time towards the stables. It was some five minutes before I reached the back courtyard leading to the bridle paths.

I turned about; Chips was nowhere in sight. I dashed towards the stretches of stalls. I had just rounded the brick path when I heard a man's voice.

"Thinks she can buy me off, she does, 'er an' 'er fancy airs. Well, let me tell ye this won't be the last she's 'eard o' me."

"What d'ye mean?" demanded another male.

"What do aye mean? Aye mean aye'll bleed 'er till she's dry. Ain't no one gettin' rid o' Heathy 'ere. Mark my words, she'll pay fer this."

" 'Twere me, aye'd take the money an' run. Place gives me the willies. Aye'd take the missus an' 'ightail it out o' 'ere."

I was just about to intrude when I spied Chips through the archway, bounding up one of the paths.

I ran towards him, hopeful he would not bark. Something told me it would be best that the men in the stables remain unaware of our presence. I do not know which of us was happier to see the other, but Chips seemed to accept my command that he follow me.

As I had no intention of going back through the stable area again, I started the climb back up to the house through the meadow on the northerly embankment. Mown paths rounded the edge, but I chose a swath which had been cut through the center. Chips clambered through the overgrown vetches and bedstraw which bowed into the narrow path.

I realized with some surprise, as the density gave way to open ground, that the formal gardens were ahead, the pillars of clipped yew rising in perfect symmetry in contrast to the wild grasses.

I moved through the vine pergola into the clearing, the scent of the last blooms filling my nostrils. The paths leading to the terraces were shaped in a quadrangle, and choosing one, I pressed forth, Chips brushing against my skirts. Beyond the beds etched like stencils on the parterre I saw a figure, his form crouched near the earth. I moved towards him, watching as he judiciously pruned the rangy cultivars.

I was upon him when I realized that he was oblivious of my presence. I leant forward and tenuously said hello. I was totally unprepared for his reaction, for he jumped back, his stocky frame nearly knocking me over.

"I did not mean to startle you," I said as I regained my footing.

My apology was met only with a wary stare. "I am Miss

Chatfield," I continued. "I am a guest at the manor."

I had begun to wonder whether he had heard me, when he removed his cap with a gnarled weathered hand and nodded to me.

Chips whimpered suddenly. "We had best get back," I said. "I think my companion here misses his master, and I would not want to keep you from the gardens. Even late in the season they are still a joy to behold."

He looked away, and I went past him, Chips at my heels. I had gone about ten steps when I realized that he was following me. I quickened my pace, but I felt his hand at my elbow. As I turned he thrust a single stem towards me. I took it from him, putting the rosy-orange blossom to my nose.

"It is exquisite," I said admiringly. I held it out for him to take back. He shook his head, and realizing he wanted me to keep it, I murmured my thanks.

Without a word he went back to his pruning, and Chips and I were left to return to the house. As we entered, a serving girl came running up to me.

"There's the little fellow," she exclaimed. "Aye bin lookin' all over fer 'im. Cook's got the mornin' scraps, an' she don't be takin' well te 'avin' 'im about after she starts the soups."

I looked across at the hall clock. "The time got away from me, I fear."

As the girl took Chips in tow, I hurried up the stairs to my room, where I removed my bonnet and quickly repinned the coil I had fashioned at the nape of my neck. I was back downstairs within ten minutes and was crossing by the library when I heard my name being called. I peered through the half open door.

"Was there something you wished?" I inquired.

Lord Darby nodded. "Come in for a moment, will you?"

I strode over to where he sat, wondering what was in store for me. "You are feeling better, I trust," I ventured.

"Your concern is refreshing, but unnecessary," he said. "Won't you sit down?"

"I should not stay long," I advised. "Damien will be expecting me."

He regarded me thoughtfully. "You really are serious about this cataloguing nonsense."

"I am surprised you would think otherwise," I responded.

"You seem to have forgotten I am intent on an heir, not a gallery of paintings."

"That is a pity, because your son has a special talent," I countered. "I am hardly an authority, but one need not be to appreciate the beauty and scope of his work."

He looked across at me. "You really think he has ability?"

"I do."

"Caroline thought so too," he murmured. "When he was but a little boy, she would take him out into the gardens and prop him there with a sketch pad and pen. Of course, I could make neither head nor tail of the child's squiggles, but Caroline would say, 'Edmund, he has an eye. You mark my words, he shall be a great painter one day.'"

"Did Anitra by chance share Damien's talent?"

His face suddenly twisted, causing me to shudder. "One thing you had best learn, Miss Chatfield, if you are going to remain here at Darby Manor, is that I forbid any discussion of my younger daughter. Damien is a daily reminder to me of—"

He broke off. I waited for some explanation, but none followed.

"Enough of that," he said suddenly. "What I wished to speak to you about was Sir Charles Grout."

"Your solicitor?" I asked.

He nodded. "You made mention that he had been efficient in his dealings with you."

"I can only tell you, Lord Darby, that Sir Charles seemed capable, though admittedly vague as to why you sent for me.

But then, had he been otherwise, as you well know, I should never have come."

"Aha," he exclaimed. "But you see I paid him to be vague. You will learn, Lillith, that everything can be had, for a price."

"Not *everything*, Lord Darby," I retorted, stiffening in my seat.

His eyes roved my face. "There we disagree. Even our principled Miss Chatfield has had to succumb to the power of the pound. 'Tis true you refused my offer. Given the generosity of it, I admit I was surprised. But you are still here. And I do not deceive myself that it was because of affection for those who reside here. I do not know to what extent my son is compensating you. It was obviously sufficient to convince you to remain."

I wanted to argue, for he had made me sound avaricious. I had not been bought, as he implied. But it was quite true that my decision had been made because of my finances.

His expression made it clear he knew he had won this round.

"We were talking about Sir Charles. I do not know the chap. 'Twas his father I dealt with. He died recently, which has put me into rather a quandary about whether to remain with the firm."

"He made mention of his father's passing," I acknowledged.

"There are numerous things which need tending to," he continued. "As I had a long association with the father, I suppose I should at least give the son a try, but Marisse is against it. She thinks someone in York would be better. Closer to hand, you know."

I found it odd that Lady de Wentoff would be recommending solicitors. "I am not certain what this has to do with me Lord Darby," I said.

"Let us just say that I was interested in your opinion. After all, you are the only one who has met him."

"I met him once," I retorted. "That would hardly justify a recommendation."

He raised his bushy eyebrows, his dark eyes peering from beneath them. "Well, we shall soon see. I have sent for him, and as my sister was planning a trip north, I expect they will arrive together."

"If there is nothing else, Lord Darby, I really must get to the studio," I said.

"No, there is nothing else, Lillith," he said in dismissal.

I left the library. I was baffled by my little tête-à-tête with Lord Darby. I did not really believe that he cared for my opinion. If his intent had been to insult me for having remained at Darby, I supposed he had been successful. The news that Sir Charles was due to arrive I found unsettling, and his complicity in Lord Darby's scheme still infuriated me. I did not relish his presence here.

I knocked at the door of the studio several times before Damien opened it.

"You are late," he charged.

"I was with your father," I replied as I swept past him to the desk.

"What are you scheming about now?"

"If there is any scheming at Darby, it is not I who is doing it, Damien."

"And what do you mean by that?" he demanded.

I took my seat and opened the ledger. "Nothing. Let us just forget it."

"Well, aren't we irascible today."

I whirled about as Chips, who had been curled by the window seat, gamboled over to me.

"You know, this started as a very pleasant day. Chips and I had a nice walk outside. I came here ready to resume my work, and all you can do is make snide comments. You have the most vile nature, Damien Darby. Did it ever occur to you to just say, 'Good morning, Lillith. How are you today?' Or

'Good morning, Lillith. I want to tell you how pleased I am with the work you are doing'?"

At the conclusion of this outburst I found I was shaking.

Damien wheeled his chair towards me. "This lowly soul offers his apologies," he announced, a small smile curving the corners of his mouth. "Let us make believe that you have just knocked at the door. I open it and say, 'Good morning, Lillith. You look particularly lovely today.' "

"You needn't mock me," I said, flustered.

"Oh, don't be stubborn, Lillith. I am doing my best to say I am sorry for my behavior. And I will even go myself one better. I would like us to be friends. We started out under strange circumstances, but my anger has been misplaced. I have been taking out on you what is really an issue between my father and myself."

Chips, who had seated himself next to me, nudged my hand.

Damien winked at me. "There, you see? Even Chips thinks you should forgive me."

"It is not a matter of forgiving, Damien," I said finally. "It would be nice if we became friends, but all I really want is that we not be abusive to one another. There is an enormous amount of work to be done here, and I would like to think it can be accomplished with the least possible friction."

"Fair enough," he agreed, extending his hand.

As I reached down and put my hand in his I was struck by how his enveloped mine so completely. When he did not release it immediately, I found myself blushing.

"If you are going to praise my work, I had best get back to it," I murmured as I slipped my fingers from his grasp.

"Our Miss Chatfield is a taskmaster, Chips," Damien said. My expression must have been one of consternation, for he quickly added, "And how fortunate we are that she is."

I watched him as he wheeled towards the easel at the far end of the room. I decided that, if nothing else, it had been an interesting morning. First the strange exchange between the stablehands, then the silent encounter in the garden, the unfathomable conversation with Lord Darby, and now Damien. I found myself hoping his plea was genuine. He had admitted a prejudice against me. I couldn't really fault him for that. We were both victims, he more so than I. I would leave Darby at least having gained by it, but every day Damien would be reminded of his father's duplicity and manipulation.

The remainder of the sketches I had worked on the previous day were still stacked against the leg of the desk, and as Damien seemed to settle into a rhythm I struggled with my notations.

When about an hour later I found myself staring off into space, I absently pushed the ledger aside. As I did, it tipped precariously and fell to the floor with a thud.

Damien peered round from his canvas. "For one normally so quiet, you seem quite the fidget today."

"I am not fidgeting," I protested. "I dropped something, that is all."

He put his palette knife down. "My concentration is broken anyway. What would you say to a change of scene?"

I replaced the ledgers on the desk. "I am fine, truly," I assured him. "I shan't interrupt you again."

"You mean that you will venture out with my father, but the thought of my company doesn't amuse you."

"I did not say that," I snapped.

He wheeled towards me. "Good. Then fetch a cloak and meet me in the reception hall in an hour."

"Where are we going?" I inquired.

He smiled. "Most women like surprises. And since you seem very much a woman, I shall keep our destination a mystery for now."

I could feel the color creep into my neck and cheeks. I averted my eyes from his gaze as I straightened the ledgers and went to the door. "I will see you within the hour then," I murmured.

It was almost with a feeling of elation that I returned to my room. Since my carriage ride with Lord Darby, I had longed to see more of the countryside and though I had taken easily to the cataloguing, it was a demanding discipline. I had almost concluded that I had made a terrible mistake by remaining at Darby. There was an undercurrent of hostility and anger here. I couldn't really put my finger on it, but it was, I was convinced, not in my imagination.

And yet, just as I had begun to resign myself to Damien's disdain of me, he had astounded me by his frank admission this morning. I prayed it was not a whim of the moment, for it would be far pleasanter to think that the tension between us might be eased.

I redid my hair not once but three times before I tucked its weight into the full frame of my bonnet. The walking costume I had changed to was violet, an almost perfect match for my eyes. As I stood before the mirror smoothing the succession of gathers along the back of the skirt, I told myself it was ridiculous to be fussing so with my appearance. Damien would likely not notice, and even if he did, it meant nothing.

I had just descended to the front hall when Marisse appeared through the drawing room doors.

She regarded me quizzically. "It appears you are going out for a stroll. If you could wait for a moment, I will join you."

I shook my head. "Actually I am going for a ride. With Damien."

Her eyes narrowed. "Have I heard you correctly?"

"I am going with Damien in the carriage," I repeated. "I think he is hoping to find inspiration for some new paintings."

"Is that what he told you?" she persisted.

"No," I admitted, "that is my own assumption."

"Don't assume anything about Damien, Lillith," she cautioned. "You choose not to heed my advice, but I shall give it again: keep your distance. You will find it is healthier all around."

"Are you telling me I cannot even take a ride with Damien?" I challenged.

She stepped forward, her hands clasping my shoulders. "I would not put myself in situations which breed familiarity. You are not a child, but I sense you are inexperienced in these matters. I know that you consider yourself to be in Damien's employ, but I am not certain he views you with as much detachment. You are, after all, a young woman many men would find pleasing to the eye, and though he is—well, as he is, his manliness, let us say, is not diminished. And I would not overlook the fact that Edmund is determined that he shall have an heir. Though the two seem, on the surface, at odds, I would not dismiss a collaboration. Damien may be stubborn, but he is not a fool. He has much to lose and even more to gain if—"

"Marisse," I interrupted, stiffening under her grasp, "I really think this is unnecessary. I am here only as Damien Darby's assistant, nothing more. And if you knew the antipathy which has existed between us, you would see that your suggestion is ludicrous."

She released me. "Now there, you see, I have only angered you. But please believe me, Lillith, it was not my intention. If I seem overly protective, it is only that I understand this house and those herein far better than you. You know I feel you would have been wiser to have departed from here, but as you are determined to stay, I simply do not want you to be hurt by it." She sighed. "And now, as I have obviously said enough, go off on your ride and have a pleasant day."

Even if I had wanted to pursue the conversation I could not have done so, for the driver came to tell me that Damien was waiting for me in the carriage. I was surprised when he assisted me into the brougham to find that Damien was not alone. Chips whimpered a greeting, wriggling over and wedging himself between us.

"I hope you do not mind," Damien said, "but he looked so woebegone I acquiesced."

"Of course not." I laughed as the spaniel nuzzled me.

"You should do that more often," Damien said, studying me.

"Do what?" I asked, perplexed.

"Laugh," he replied, "it intensifies the violet of your eyes."

The carriage lurched suddenly and I clasped Chips so that he would not topple forward. When we had cleared the drive, the carriage turned in a direction opposite to the one I had taken with Lord Darby.

Damien was very quiet. He seemed so completely absorbed in the countryside spread before us. It was as though he was trying to capture every aspect in his mind's eye. We had gone some distance when we appeared to be climbing to an altitude which seemed almost dizzying. At the sides of the little-traveled road were deep gullies gouged in the limestone sheltering treelike outcroppings, whose roots crouched in the water carved hollows.

"We are traversing Buttertubs," he said suddenly. "There at the top you shall see Swaledale."

I sat forward, my arm braced against the rest. Across the horizon, as far as the eye could see, stretched the rampart of fells, their flanks dappled with subdued browns and mottled greens.

"The Swale," he continued, "is forged by the dashing together of two streams, Great Sleddales Beck and Birkdale Beck. In spate, the river is ferocious. It trundles boulders along like marbles."

I found the scene at once magnificent and frightening. I must have shuddered, for Damien said suddenly, "You are cold."

I shook my head, but he insisted I draw the wool lap robe about me.

We rode on to a sloping site near the entry of a tributary to the Swale. "What is that there below?" I inquired.

Damien grimaced, and I thought for a moment that he was in pain. "The blasted mines," he muttered. " 'Tis the scourge of Yorkshire."

"But I thought that lead mining was a highly prized industry about the North," I retorted.

" 'Tis profitable, but only for a few. I regret my grandfather was much at the center of it."

"But it brought employment to many people," I argued.

"Employment and death," he replied sarcastically. "If they survive the collapse of the walls about the shaft, not an infrequent occurrence, they will likely be felled by the foul air. 'Tis only this very year, because of the Restrictive Act, that we are no longer sending women and children to their untimely demise."

Whenever I seemed close to having some understanding of Damien Darby, he said or did something which gave me pause. I had decided he was totally self-centered, and yet here he was, expressing what seemed a genuine compassion for a group of people who meant little to him personally.

The carriage moved on, until suddenly Damien leant forward, requesting the driver to pause at the foot of an enormous escarpment, about which lay ruinous stone walls.

"It is called Whitcliffe Scar," he said, as if reading my mind. "Some say it was built after the Roman Legions left England, designed to withstand attack from wandering marauders. Others suggest 'twas an Anglo Saxon hunting lodge. Those are meadow pipits and curlews nesting in the crevices."

The site had an aura of melancholy.

"We used to come here often," he said almost in a whisper. "Anitra loved this place."

I started at the mention of her name. Why did it seem that she was never very far from me? It was as though from somewhere beyond the grave her presence forced itself upon me. The very sound of her name fascinated me; indeed she had become an obsession.

I looked about me, studying the cliff as though it could give me some clue, some insight into her. What I saw was a massive edifice of nature, which evoked a haunting sense of desolation, even despair. Damien had said she loved it here. I found it difficult to fathom how it had stirred a responsiveness in one so young. There was nothing here that was light or carefree. The harsh angles were stark and cold. They seemed to assault one's senses.

Whitcliffe Scar. Could it have been this place that Anitra was contemplating when Damien captured her in thoughtful repose?

Suddenly, Damien said, "We must be going back. The weather will change soon."

"How do you know that?" I inquired turning to face him.

He pointed beyond. "There, you see those small streaked clouds? In North Riding they are called henscrats and are likened to the marks of fowls' feet in the dust. Their appearance foreshadows strong winds and rain."

I settled back as we were jostled about once again by the sway of the carriage. I had taken my hand off the armrest, and as the wheels rode over a suddenly rocky terrain, I was thrown sideways, my cheek brushing against Damien's waistcoat. His hand flew out to grasp my shoulder, and I flushed as I felt the pressure of his fingers against my skin.

"I am so sorry," I murmured. " 'Twas foolish of me not to hold on."

He eased me back against the seat with his arm. "More's the pity," he replied. "Here I thought you were throwing yourself at me."

I bristled at this. "You know 'twas nothing of the sort."

"Oh, come now, Miss Chatfield. You can admit to a small indiscretion, though it seems that Chips here rather thwarted your advances."

Without thinking, I slapped him. "How dare you," I exclaimed in anger.

I became even more incensed as his lips curled upwards. "You know, earlier I suggested you should laugh more often. But indeed I think anger becomes you even more."

Rarely if ever was I as nonplussed as I was at that moment. I wanted to demand that he immediately let me descend from the coach, but as the barren hillsides were now being pelted by a steady rain, I knew that I would only be spiting myself. I pulled the crest of my bonnet forward as I felt my eyes well suddenly with tears. Vowing I would not permit him to see my humiliation, I turned towards the window, gazing blindly ahead.

If I had questioned Marisse's intentions before, I now knew she had only been acting in my own interest. How dare he even suggest what he had. Damien Darby certainly had talent. But, I decided, he had no scruples whatsoever. Well, he would not deceive me again. I would no longer allow him to take pleasure in goading me, nor would I stand for his abuse. He would have a catalogue of his works, and I would have a sum of money which would give me a stake in the future.

Our return to the manor seemed endless. The sky was almost black now, and through the rain Darby loomed before us like some mythic fortress. When the carriage had finally come to a halt in the drive, I did not even wait for the driver to help me alight but, gathering my skirts, bolted from it. A voice called out to me, but I did not pause, racing up the steps, through the front door, and across the marble floor towards the staircase. So preoccupied was I with putting distance between Damien and myself that I did not see the figure emerging from the drawing room until it was too late.

The impact of our collision sent me reeling, and had I not grabbed at the balustrade I would have taken a nasty fall.

"Good Lord, are you quite all right," a male voice inquired as I straightened myself.

"Just a bit shaken," I admitted. "I fear 'twas my fault. I did not see you." I squared my bonnet and looked up into the face of the man before me.

His eyes widened. "Why, it is you, Miss Chatfield."

"Sir Charles," I said, amazed. "I thought you were not expected till tomorrow."

He nodded, grinning down at me. "Ah, but you have never traveled with Jessica Darby. She is a fountain of energy. I do not know who is more tired, myself or the horses. But that is not the point. Are you quite certain you are all right?"

I assured him that I was.

"The way you were running," he continued, "it almost seemed as though you were frightened of something."

I shook my head. " 'Tis nothing really. If you will excuse me, I really must return to my room."

He looked genuinely disappointed. "Of course. But I hope I may look forward to seeing you later."

"At dinner," I informed him.

I turned and scurried up the stairs to my room. Removing my bonnet and the jacket of my suit, I repinned a plait of my hair which was coming down, and I noticed that some time earlier a tray had been left. On it was a berry cobbler, and when I had finished eating it I sat down, wondering what I should do with the remainder of the day. The last thing I wanted was to go to the studio. But to avoid doing so was to admit that I had allowed Damien to unsettle me. No, I had to go, and I had to act as though nothing was wrong.

That my instincts had been correct was confirmed by the look of surprise on his face. "I assumed you wanted to work," I said, brushing past him.

He closed the door and wheeled towards me. " 'Tis likely that we will find ourselves interrupted," he replied. "My aunt and my father's solicitor have arrived a day early."

I stood by the desk, hauling the ledger towards me. "Actually, I saw Sir Charles when we returned."

"Well, that did not take long," he mused, yanking the drape from the canvas he had been working on.

I pressed my nails into my palms, willing myself to stay silent.

"He seems a pleasant enough man," he continued. "Though I wonder if he shall prove a match for Marisse. 'Twill be amusing, I wager, to see how that evolves."

"You sound as though you would almost welcome conflict," I remarked.

"Ah, there you are wrong, Miss Chatfield. What I seek is a resolution of conflict. But that is a higher goal to aspire to."

I thought it an odd comment.

"I admit I am surprised, Miss Chatfield," he continued after a moment. "You, as I have come to know, are rarely without an opinion."

"If you are asking me for one, I will tell you that I expect Marisse and Sir Charles will find much in common. Marisse is a lovely woman and certainly an accomplished hostess. I see no reason why the two should not be amicable."

"Lord, what nonsense you speak," his voice boomed back at me. "What, pray tell, has caused you to be a sudden champion of Marisse? You are stubborn, Lillith, but I did not take you for a fool."

I slammed the ledger closed. "That is enough, Damien," I said, my voice cracking. "If I am a fool it is because I actually believed you were genuine this morning. But no matter what I do, what I say, you have some sardonic reply. That you and Marisse are not on the best of terms is clear. Frankly, given the way you treat people, I am not surprised she appears wary of you. The longer I remain here, the more I believe that Marisse has been a friend to me. And, in this household, that is a rarity."

I had risen during my outburst, striding over to where he sat. I found myself suddenly at the wall of glass at the far end of the studio. As I caught sight of the canvas before me, I could only gasp. For there, rendered in the gentlest of strokes, with color which seemed to breathe life itself, was my own image.

The very sight of it struck me speechless. More than the shock of discovering that this canvas, which Damien guarded so jealously, was a likeness of myself was my appreciation of the beauty of the work. It stirred my soul.

It was Damien who finally broke the silence. "Do you like it?" he inquired, wheeling about to face me. "It is not finished, of course."

I did not know what to say. "I had no idea," I murmured finally.

He turned back to the canvas. "That is how it should be. A portrait should be like a landscape. The rock, the gully, the flowers in a field do not know that their presence, their existence is being caught in time, and thus they do not preen, hopeful that only the best parts of them shall be preserved. Art should be a replication of what the naked eye sees. It is, after all, a reflection of life."

I felt a veil of moisture cloud my eyes.

"From your reaction I suspect I should withhold this one from the Prince Consort," Damien said.

I shook my head, fearful whatever words I might find would be insufficient to express emotions I was experiencing.

"I wish I could tell you that you are an easy subject, but I cannot. You are not a simple woman, Lillith Chatfield. I am not certain I have captured that—what shall I call it? That rebelliousness, that fire that burns within you, but then I am not certain it has yet been brought to flame."

"Perchance you have seen more than is there," I suggested.

"I only paint what I see," he answered.

I moved to touch the painting before me.

"No," he cried out, his command startling me. " 'Tis only that it is still wet," he said more gently, "and there is still work to be done. You can see it there, in the mouth."

I shook my head. "What you cannot know is that it bears a striking resemblance, save for the gown, to one which was painted of my mother. I do not know the artist, but I had always treasured it, particularly after her death."

"And where is this painting now?" he inquired.

Sadly I told him of Sir Henry Willferth's purchase of it.

"Well, then I shall, when I have done with it, make you a present of this one," he replied.

"Oh, but I could not accept it," I argued, amazed by the generosity of his offer.

"And why not? Certainly, as the artist, it is mine to give."

I shook my head. "I am flattered but—"

"But," he interrupted, "when you leave Darby Manor you would prefer not to take with you any memories of the unpleasantness of your stay."

"I . . ."

He wheeled past me and threw the drape over the canvas. "You need say no more, Miss Chatfield. Indeed, the less said the better. Now, if you will excuse me, I should go and see my aunt. As I will lock the studio before I leave, do what you will with the rest of the day. Perhaps a visit with my father's solicitor would amuse you. Or, since you are suddenly so taken with Marisse, perhaps you should seek her out."

I did not argue. 'Twould have proved pointless, I knew.

In the sanctuary of my room I lay down on my bed, realizing that there was a good hour until dinner. I had actually enjoyed the ride. That is, until Damien had spoiled it. I did not know why he seemed to take perverse pleasure in unnerving me, nor why I allowed myself to be so sensitive to his remarks. I should have learned by now that those glimmers of gentleness would always be snuffed out by the darker side of his nature. It was hard to know whether his sarcasm was a deliberate attempt to mask his feelings or if his character was as strident as it oft appeared.

The sight of the painting had unnerved me. I could not fathom why he had chosen me as a subject. Indeed, the body of his work, excluding, of course, those few sketches of Anitra, was landscapes. People seemed to play little importance in Damien's life, personally or artistically.

I withdrew the portfolio of sketches and laid them out on the bed before me. Had Anitra, as I, been caught unawares, or had she sat for her brother? I suspected I would never know. I wondered what she had been thinking when Damien had captured her on the verge of womanhood. It was the eyes which compelled one. Initially I had found them thoughtful, almost wistful, but now as I studied them more closely, I wondered if I had misread them. In this light there was an almost haunting quality to her expression. Indeed, if the corners of her finely drawn mouth did not turn up slightly in the suggestion of a smile, I might conclude that there was a portentous aura about her countenance. Certainly she could not have had a vision of her impending demise. But, unless I was reading more into these sketches than was there, I could swear I saw fear in Anitra Darby's face.

I shuddered as I carefully gathered the heavy watermarked pages and replaced them within the portfolio. If only I had not found that page from her diary, I would not now be reading meaning into these drawings.

Then why, I wondered, could I not rid myself of this preoccupation with her? As macabre as it seemed, it was as if Anitra was reaching up from the grave, demanding not to be forgotten.

12

As I heard the clock chime the half hour I realized I had dallied too long and hurriedly rose to change my clothes. I withdrew three gowns from the armoire before finally settling on a magenta silk brocade with pearl-button closings along the bodice and skirt. I scolded myself for being nervous about the upcoming evening. However Sir Charles's complicity in Lord Darby's scheme to get me to marry Damien still rankled. I had nothing, after all, to apologize about. I was earning my keep, and I was proud of the job I was doing. I was far from the vulnerable, insipid female the solicitor must have thought me when I had agreed to accept the admittedly vague conditions of employment at Darby Manor. I had no reason to believe that he would mock me, but I had more than I could handle with Damien's taunts, and I was not about to suffer ridicule from other quarters.

I spun the last tendril about my fingers and laid it along the nape of my neck, took a deep breath, and started on my way downstairs. Just as I reached the reception hall landing, I heard a woman's voice call my name.

I turned to see Maude Farklan, who was handing her wrap to Sommers, raise her hand in a little wave.

"Miss Chatfield, how pleasant to see you again," she said, her eyes sweeping over me with obvious uninterest.

"I did not know you were expected," I told her, wishing now I had selected a less conservative gown.

"Well, it was quite impromptu," she admitted, "but then, as we are nearly family, one need not stand on ceremony. Though I confess I did not know until this moment that other guests were expected."

"Was your brother not able to accompany you?"

She smoothed the folds of her gown. "I did not realize you had taken such an interest in James. He *is* devilishly handsome, but I would not have expected you to delude yourself about any prospects with him."

"Whatever would cause you to suggest such a thing?" I said, astounded.

"You needn't be embarrassed, Lillith. You would not be the first to succumb to his charms. And I assure you, you will not be the last."

I was not going to be permitted the privilege of a denial, for at that moment James burst through the front door. " 'Tis a good thing I had one of the men look at that wheel," he exclaimed. "One of the spokes was nearly broken off."

Maude came forward. "Well, it gave Lillith and me a chance to chat."

Sommers took James's outer vestments and escorted us to the library.

"Ah, there you are," Marisse gushed as she came forward,

embracing Maude and her brother while I hung back, feeling
like an intruder. "You both know Edmund's sister, Jessica,
and this handsome new addition to our party is Sir Charles
Grout, our solicitor."

Her use of the plural possessive did not escape me. By
Damien's expression I knew it had registered with him as
well.

I turned as the figure in the large embroidered Jacobean
chair lifted the cane at her side and pointed to where I stood.
"Who is that?" Jessica Darby demanded. "Come in here so I
might see you."

I did as she bade me, realizing as I did that all eyes were
upon me. When I had come within three feet of her, she
lowered her cane and adjusted the spectacles which sat on the
high bridge of her nose. "Come closer, my dear," she said
encouragingly. "They tell me I should see perfectly well
through these damnable things, but they're all alike. They
just want to take my money."

I moved forward as I heard Damien say, "Why, you old
reprobate, Jess. Here you have told me all these years that you
were impoverished. Holding out on us, have you been?"

She leant forward as I reached her. "Do not listen to my
nephew, Miss, Miss . . ."

"Chatfield," I provided. "Lillith Chatfield."

"Ah, so you are the angel of mercy who is helping Damien
with his cataloguing," she replied. "Much too pretty to be
locked away with the disarray in that studio of his. Wouldn't
be my cup of tea, but then I never could sit still long enough
to discipline my mind."

I smiled at her forthrightness. If, as Lord Darby had said,
she was years his senior, she was a woman to whom time had
been kind. Even though she was seated, one could see that she
was of remarkable stature, with broad shoulders and a long
neck. Though large, she would never have been called ample.
Indeed, the melton jacket stretched taut across the bodice
suggested that she had almost no bosom. Her hair, in both

color and fashion, reminded me of a snowdrift undulating in waves about the crown of her head. Somehow I knew Jessica Darby would never have consented to bother about a crimping iron.

"Your pace has slowed considerably since I encountered you earlier," I heard a voice say.

Marisse came to stand by me. "How foolish of me. I was about to introduce you two, but then of course you and Sir Charles are acquainted. But I must admit I *am* curious as to what set you at such a run, Lillith."

I could feel myself flush. Before I could reply, Damien wheeled his chair forward, saying, "That was my doing, Marisse."

I turned to face him, my knees growing weak. Was he going to humiliate me again by recounting the events of the morning?

Damien's eyes were stony as they bore into mine. "You see, I had persuaded Miss Chatfield to humor me by accompanying me on a drive. We returned later than I expected. As I was anxious to get back to work, I fear I set her scurrying so that we might return to the studio. Now I admit that I am embarrassed by what a taskmaster I must have seemed."

It was only with effort that I was able to restrain myself from gaping at him. He had every opportunity to publicly mortify me, and yet he had chosen to guard my honor. At the very least, he was unpredictable.

Jessica Darby shook her head. "Incorrigible, that nephew of mine, Miss Chatfield. Do not let him think he can have you hop about like a jackrabbit. He is strong-willed I admit, but you need not put up with that nonsense."

I shook my head. "There is much to do," I replied slowly. "As your nephew and I have an agreement about the duration of this project, I cannot fault him for wanting to see progress made."

Maude Farklan suddenly interjected, "Well, I agree with

Aunt Jessica. It was simply naughty of Damien to push poor Miss Chatfield so. Heaven knows, I cannot think of a woman of my acquaintance who would endure the drudgery that he expects her to. In truth, I know of no one who would even consider such a task."

"Well I, for one, admire a woman who can put her mind to things other than embroideries and such," Jessica Darby said, her eyes meeting mine. "Frankly, if our father had been more forward-thinking, I might have spent less time busying myself with other people's causes and focused on my own. In any event, I do not know about the rest of you, but I am famished after that journey. Perhaps if we move to the dining room, that staff of yours will take a hint, Edmund."

As Lord Darby went to assist his sister, Marisse, who, I sensed, was less than sanguine about Jessica Darby's taking control, slipped her arm through Sir Charles Grout's, saying, "Since you traveled with my soon-to-be sister-in-law, I suspect you will understand why I have learned not to argue with her."

As Lord Darby assisted his sister to the door, she called back, "Well, do not just sit there, Damien. Escort Miss Chatfield to the dining room. I am anxious to get to know this young woman better."

Maude Farklan was clearly incensed as Damien wheeled towards me, saying, "I fear you have no choice, Lillith. To countermand my aunt would be to take my life in my hands. And though there are some here who feel that it is of little value, I have no intention of parting with it just yet." Though his delivery was flippant, I suspected there was a kernel of truth in what he said.

"Damien, you are such a tease." Laughing, Maude moved forward and began propelling Damien towards the doors, leaving James and me well behind. I knew Damien was loath to have anyone assist him, but he was surprisingly silent as he disappeared from view.

"It seems we are paired again, Lillith," James said as he strode forward and offered me his arm. "How fortunate for me."

That he was attempting to be gallant mattered not to me, for though his sister had suggested I carried some romantic notions about her brother, it was the furthest thing from my mind. It was with some distress that I found myself seated opposite Sir Charles. In spite of myself I felt some sympathy for him. Lord Darby was not particularly gracious in welcoming the younger man.

I suspected that Jessica Darby was less than enthusiastic about her brother's impending marriage to Marisse. She studiously avoided talking to her during most of the dinner. It was having an impact on Marisse, who, though affable, was noticeably piqued.

As a desert of cranberry fool was placed before me, I looked up to find Sir Charles studying me. I flushed as Jessica Darby repeated her question to him.

"I am sorry. My mind seems to be wandering," he apologized.

She leant over and patted his hand. "No need for apology. My sight may not be what it was, but I am not blind to your preoccupation. Were I a few generations younger I might be distressed, but age robs us of many things, vanity included. Though I should warn you that you are not alone in your admiration. My nephew's obvious interest has not escaped me either."

My blush deepened as I heard Marisse say, "Really, Jessica, you are embarrassing the poor girl."

"And when have you become so considerate of Miss Chatfield?" Damien challenged suddenly.

I started as the table shook. All eyes turned to Lord Darby, whose fist remained clenched upon the highly polished surface. "Damien, I will not have you—"

"Edmund, calm yourself," Marisse said quickly. "I am certain Damien meant nothing. The truth is, I have become very fond of Lillith. Perhaps it is my maternal instinct. But that shall soon be put to the test."

It was now Lord Darby's turn to be embarrassed. "Really, my dear," he blustered, "I scarcely think it appropriate—"

Marisse laughed. "Balderdash, my dear. We are all adults, and it's common knowledge that I will soon be Lady Darby. Therefore it's hardly improper of me to hope that within the year a newborn can be expected at Darby Manor."

If shock had been her intent, then Marisse should have been pleased, for there was not one of us who did not appear visibly stunned by her pronouncement, save Damien. I did not know why I found her comment so surprising. Marisse was, after all, still of child-bearing age. And since her former marriage had not produced any offspring, it was, I supposed, natural that she would anticipate motherhood in this new union. But why, if Lord Darby and Marisse intended a child, was it so important that Damien produce heirs?

I was greatly relieved that no one tried to dissuade me from retiring after dinner. It had been a full day and I longed for the quiet of my room. As I undressed and crawled into bed, I thought that the longer I remained at Darby the less I understood it. Each day revealed some new puzzle. Not the least of these was Damien's painting of me. In retrospect, I knew I should have accepted his gift. The last thing I wanted was to insult him. I had just been so startled, even embarrassed, that he would have chosen me as a subject. 'Twas a pity, for no matter how hard we tried, we seemed to spurn one another. I wondered, if we had met under different circumstances, whether things might have been more peaceable.

13

I AWAKENED early the following morning. The room was dark and
the dying embers in the fireplace did little to illuminate the
surroundings. I reached for my robe and, pulling it about me,
threw back the covers and scurried over to the north windows. It took several tugs to open the draperies, and when I
turned to peer out, I was startled by the sight before me.
Sometime during the night a blanket of snow had covered the
landscape, giving a light of its own to the early hour.

Certainly I had experienced many snowfalls in London,
but never had I experienced the like of this. The delicate
white crystals amassed on the limbs and branches of the massive oaks and spires of evergreen gave an almost mythic ap-

pearance to the countryside. My first reaction was to suppose the storm to be some freak of nature, an early warning of winter in these northern climes. But I realized, I had lost a sense of time. In several weeks it would be November. Where had the time gone, I wondered. It seemed only yesterday that I received the news of Father and Elijah.

It was probably foolish to go out in this weather, but the panorama of white seemed to beckon me. I dressed quickly, taking care to pile my hair high under the hood of my cloak. The clock chimed the half hour as I slipped down the stairs.

Although the snow had stopped, there were sufficient gusts of wind to cause the fine powder to dust about me. I took particular care on the first steps, aware that the drifts might cover a layer of ice. As I did so I noticed that someone had preceded me, for there were distinct footprints leading down the steps and turning towards the garden. Intrigued to discover who else in the household had been restless at this hour, I chose to follow on the same path. The rose canes climbed out of the crystal carpet, their buds and full hips swaying, the last mark of color on the low horizon.

I had reached the stone lions which framed the southern terraces when I spied the figure ahead of me. He turned suddenly. Recognizing Sir Charles, I started to go back to the house.

Unfortunately, he had seen me as well, for he called out to me. I would have preferred to ignore him, but that, I decided, would solve nothing. Like it or not, he was going to be ensconced in this household for the next few weeks, and whatever my opinion of the man I could not permit myself to show my own feelings.

He crossed to where I stood. "And here I thought I was the only early riser," he said as he knocked the snow from his boots.

"Usually, I am not," I replied, keeping my eyes lowered. "Actually, 'twas foolish of me to venture out in this. I really must be turning back."

"I hope you are not running off because of me," he replied.

"Of course not," I retorted. "I cannot think what would make you even suggest such a thing."

As I moved to go past him he put his hand to my elbow. "Lillith, wait. Please. I shan't keep you long, but our meeting here is perhaps providential. You see, I had quite determined to seek you out today. I think we need to talk. In private, that is."

I made no move. "I cannot think what we have to say to one another, Sir Charles."

"I can understand it if you feel that way." His smile caught me off guard.

"Can you? I rather doubt it," I said coldly.

He grimaced. "I must say I did not expect you to be charmed at the sight of me, but I had hoped that by now—"

"That by now what?" I challenged. "That I would have forgotten or somehow overlooked that you conspired with Lord Darby to bring me here under false pretenses?"

"Now, hold on one moment, Lillith," he demanded. "I need not apologize for my dealings with Lord Darby. I was employed by him to fulfill a request. An unusual one, I admit to you, but, if you recall, at the time of our meeting my own father had recently passed on. Lord Darby had, as best I could conclude, been a prominent client, though I had amazingly little information about him."

"What is the point of all this?"

"That day," he continued, "when you arrived at our offices, I was taken aback, frankly. Until that moment you had simply been some young woman who had responded to a notice placed by a client."

"That is not true," I bristled. "Lord Darby himself admitted that you had had me investigated. What did you do? Lurk about Bostworick Hall for some glimpse of me, to see if I would be suitable for this prominent client of yours?"

He slicked back his straight hair, the dampness causing it to cling about his narrow skull. "I swear to you, Lillith, I had

163
.

not seen you until the day we met. And when we did, well, it seemed too late to go back on my agreement. Truly, the day before I knew you were to depart I almost called on you to explain."

"What stopped you?" I challenged.

He shrugged. "I knew that you had no choice but to find employment. And though the veil of secrecy in this case is unusual, arranged marriages are scarcely barbaric. Why, oft times they even prove quite satisfactory. Of course, had I known the circumstances, I could never in full conscience have gone through with it. You must believe I had no idea of Damien's condition. I cannot believe that Lord Darby made no mention of it."

"Damien's condition, Sir Charles, is irrelevant," I argued.

He looked surprised.

"As it has turned out, it is really of little consequence," I continued. "Lord Darby did not get what he bargained for. Admittedly, I was humiliated. But Damien has paid me amply for cataloguing his paintings. More, certainly, than I would have received as a governess. So perhaps instead of damning you for deceiving me, I should thank you."

I started past him, but he fell into step with me. "I wish I could believe that. Like it or not, I shall be at the manor for the next few weeks, and it would be of some consolation to me if I felt that we might get to know each other. I suspect neither of us relishes the necessity which keeps us here. It strikes me that in this hostile environment one needs a kindred soul. Perhaps each of us can be that, one for the other."

Silently I continued on towards the house.

"Oh, come now, do give me a chance," he cajoled. "If you knew me better, you would discover that I am a decent sort after all."

I paused to wipe away the snow which had accumulated along the hem of my cloak. "Sir Charles, I really wish no antagonism between us. As you point out, you were only carrying out instructions. But I remind you that I too have a task, and it more than occupies my time. If you are trying to establish a truce of sorts, then let me assure you that you have it. That does not mean that I forgive you for your part in Lord Darby's scheme, simply that it would be foolish of us not to be affable with one another. As you have quickly realized, there is sufficient enmity at Darby Manor already."

He sighed. "I would hope for more, but I suppose it is a start."

I accepted his arm as we climbed the steps, feeling some sense of relief when we reached the door. His overture had been unexpected, but it was not unwelcome. I had enough to ponder without suffering the anxiety of his presence at Darby.

"It would be good of you, Lillith, if you would tell me one thing," Sir Charles entreated, his hand on the door.

"If I can," I demurred.

"I understand I am to deal with Lord Darby's daughter as well. Amanda, I believe."

I nodded.

"You know her, then?" he pursued.

I conceded that I did.

"And what is your opinion of her?"

"Amanda? She is forthright, really quite delightful," I replied. "Were I to remain at Darby, I suspect she and I would become fast friends."

He looked relieved. "I confess I have had reservations about meeting her. I have not exactly experienced a generous reception from Lord Darby—or from Damien, for that matter."

"Well, the women are different," I concluded.

He brushed the shawl of his coat. "The women?" he ruminated. "I was led to understand there was only one daughter."

"There is. Now," I murmured.

Before he could pursue the conversation further I reached forward, grasping the door handle. "You really must excuse me. Damien will be expecting me."

He followed me in, and as he closed the doors behind us I

turned to see Jessica Darby, who was poised on the landing. Her eyes squinting through the wire-framed spectacles moved between us, but if she was curious she had the good grace to remain silent.

I murmured a greeting and then whisked by her up the stairs to my room, where I found Mary changing the linens on my bed.

"Aye see ye were up with the birds," she said gaily.

I removed my cloak and, shaking it out, replaced it in the armoire.

"Ye'll be wantin' te change yer boots," she advised. "Clear soaked through they look."

As I untied the laces, Mary chattered on. "Aye can't be thinkin' why ye'd want te be roamin' about in that damp. Now fer me, aye be 'appy te be tendin' the fire in this weather. Guess yer jest like Miss Anitra. Me mum told me she'd go wanderin' at the oddest hours. The wet didn't stop 'er neither."

I started at the mention of Anitra's name. It was only the second time I had heard Mary utter it since my arrival at Darby Manor.

"Your mother worked here at Darby?" I ventured.

"Oh, fer years."

"Then she would have known Anitra," I suggested. "And talked to you about her? What was she like, Mary?"

"Aye wouldn't know, Miss Lillith. Gone she was, afore I was hired on to Darby."

"But your mother must have said something more about her," I persisted.

She shook her head. " 'Twasn't that aye didn't ask. But she's always said there's no good in 'arpin' on the past. Left sudden, she did, after eleven years' service."

"Why?" I exclaimed.

She drew the coverlet taut over the bed. "Aye don't know. But aye can't be complainin'. Took swell care o' 'er, they did. An' now aye've got me place 'ere. Which, since ye were te the kitchens, aye'll be tellin' ye is a might different. Believe me, aye know the extra blankets an' food ain't my lady Uppity de Wentoff's doin'. Course, we still 'ave Mrs. 'Orsley."

I drew the laces of my boots tight. "I notice a disparaging tone in your voice," I mused.

Mary gathered the used linens from the floor. "Aye don't mean te be rude, Miss Lillith, but aye've a load o' chores. Will ye be wantin' anythin' else?"

"No, you may go," I replied, moving to the dressing table. "I am going to be late myself if I don't hurry."

I gave a quick brush to my hair and followed close on Mary's heels.

As I went across the reception hall, I paused to pick up a few letters which had fallen from one of the consoles. I was about to replace them when I noticed that one envelope bore my own name. The penmanship was unmistakenly Abraham's.

Excitedly I tore at the sealed tissue, quickly scanning the single sheet of paper within.

My dear Lillith,

I have tried to tell myself that you are likely well and too occupied to fuss about me, but I cannot dismiss the feeling that something is amiss.

It is simply not like you not to write. Admittedly, I have not been as faithful a correspondent since my illness, but though still abed I am feeling stronger day by day. My indisposition likely boded well for you, as I had near decided to make my way up north to let these old eyes see for themselves how my little Lillith is faring.

My sister suggested that such a trip might be for naught, as you might well have moved on. But as my letters have not been returned, I must assume you are still in residence at Darby Manor.

If it would not trouble you too greatly I would be much relieved to receive some word from you. I have always thought of you, Lillith dear, as one of my own, and I long to know of your safety and well-being.

> With loving concern,
> Abraham

Hearing footsteps behind me, I hurriedly tucked the tissue into the pocket of my skirt, turning as Marisse reached me.

"I understand our prim Miss Chatfield had a full morning," she murmured. "Not that I blame you. He *is* a most attractive man."

"What are you trying to say, Marisse?"

"Don't be coy with me, Lillith. I know you and Sir Charles had a rendezvous this morning. And you needn't look like that. I shan't say a word. Edmund is rather a prude about these things, but—"

"Marisse," I interrupted, "I fear you are mistaken. The 'rendezvous,' as you term it, was a chance encounter. Nothing more."

She studied me curiously. "If you insist. But you must admit he would be a good catch. Why, his dealings with Edmund alone should yield no paltry sum. And though not titled, you obviously have had breeding. With a bit of encouragement and perhaps some subtle strategy on my part, I should think we might just accomplish a match."

"I cannot fathom why you would even suggest such a thing," I exclaimed.

Her lips turned upwards in a small smile. "One day you might thank me for it. You will be leaving Darby soon, and believe me it is always better to have something, or shall I say some*one,* to move on to."

"Frankly, Marisse, at present 'tis the furthest thing from my mind. I have just received some very disturbing news and—"

"News?" she interrupted.

I withdrew the letter from my pocket. "This came for me.

I found it quite by accident. My friend indicates that he has written often. Yet this is the first letter I have received."

"Perhaps he was mistaken about the address," she offered.

"I rather think not," I countered.

"What are you suggesting?" Marisse queried, annoyance unmistakable in her voice. "Surely you do not think that someone deliberately kept the correspondence from you?"

I stiffened. "What else am I to think?"

"I do not mean to insult you, Lillith, but I cannot imagine what anyone would want with your letters. This is not London, and the post here is less than regular. They were probably just misdirected."

I had no choice but to accept her explanation. Even if I believed that someone had taken them, I had no proof.

"You are right, of course, Marisse," I said quietly.

We parted, and I made my way to the studio. I was in such a hurry that I opened the door before remembering that Damien insisted that I always knock before entering.

"I am sorry," I muttered as Chips bounded forth to greet me.

When there was no response I moved forward tentatively. "Damien?" I called out. "Are you there?"

"Of course I am here," he replied tersely. "I shan't bother to ask where *you* have been."

Deciding it would be wisest not to dignify this with a response, I went to my desk and commenced working without reply.

Try as I did to concentrate, it was exceedingly difficult, for Damien, though he had said nothing, seemed to be venting his anger and frustration on the floor, his palette, on anything which might produce noise. Finally, when the clatter became intolerable, I moved to the platform at the far end of the studio and began to create my own commotion by ceremoniously stacking the canvases against each other.

It took only moments before Damien's voice boomed,

"What in damnation are you doing, Lillith?"

I turned as he wheeled his chair towards me. Our eyes met and simultaneously we began to laugh.

"I suspect I more than deserved that," he concluded finally. "Will you join me in a cup of tea? I promise I will keep the cacophony to a minimum."

I nodded. "I could do with one of Cook's crumpets."

"Be careful climbing down from there," he cautioned as he wheeled over to where the silver service had been placed. Pouring the liquid was awkward for him, but I refrained from offering him any assistance. I had come to know that pride burned deep within Damien Darby, and I had come to respect his independence.

I accepted the cup and sipped of it, relaxing back into the loosely cushioned chair.

"You seem thoughtful," he murmured as he, too, partook of the warm brew.

"Do I? I was just realizing that this is really the first time we have actually sat together like this."

"Thus far I find it quite painless. And you?"

My eyes moved to the windows beyond. "I used to sit like this with my father," I reflected.

"You were close?"

I set the cup on the saucer. "Very—or so I thought. But I have found that it is possible to think that you know someone, and then to discover that you really do not know him at all. Does that sound strange to you?"

I looked up to see Damien swirling the tea in his cup. "No," he replied slowly. "That does not seem strange to me."

"Seeing the snow this morning reminded me how many months have passed since I learned of the death of my father and brother. They say time is the ultimate healer, but I suspect I shall never forget. Not that I would want to."

"That is where we disagree," he mused. "I find some things are best forgotten." I knew he meant his accident. He smiled as I reached for a crumpet. "I was wondering how long it would take you to succumb."

I took a large bite. "I shall miss these when I leave."

His eyes narrowed. "And is that all you shall miss?"

I could feel myself flush under the intimacy of his gaze. The cake seemed to stick in my throat as I struggled to swallow. "No," I admitted. "Frankly, I have enjoyed my work here. Who wouldn't, surrounded by all this?"

His mouth formed a wry smile. "So you are impressed by Darby Manor."

"The house is very beautiful, but it was your paintings to which I was referring," I explained.

"You flatter me, Miss Chatfield."

I shook my head. "I only speak the truth, Damien."

"Then you are a minority of one. Truth is rare with the Darbys."

I set my cup on the table and rose, smoothing my skirts. "If I am to complete the cataloguing in time, then I had best get back to work."

"It is not as if we are forcing you to leave Darby Manor. Your goal was self-imposed," Damien replied as he wheeled his chair back to his easel.

"You almost sound as though you are sorry I shall be leaving," I said quietly.

"What I meant was that there is no reason for you to rush off. It is not as if I were getting ready for a show. If the cataloguing were to take you weeks, even months longer, it would be of no consequence. That is, unless you have made some other commitment."

I acknowledged I had not.

"Perhaps it is none of my business, but I admit to being curious about where you will go when you leave here," he went on.

"To London, I expect," I replied. "But first I shall go to the south. I have just had word that the man who cared for our family has been ill. I should want to see that he is fully recovered before I sought other employment."

"There is, of course, another option you might consider."

I was puzzled. "And what is that?"

"You could accept my father's offer."

For a moment I thought I had not heard correctly.

"It was quite generous, as I recollect."

When I recovered my composure, I said, "I do not know what possessed you to bring that up, Damien, but I resent your suggestion."

"I gather from your response that the idea is even more distasteful to you now," he replied bitterly. "But then, of course, the offer was made to you before you knew that your intended was a cripple. Perhaps no sum would have been generous enough."

"I am not going to listen to this. You know perfectly well why I did not accept your father's proposal. I thought he was mad. And sometimes I think the son is like the father. You suggested that you wanted us to become friends, and yet when I draw closer to you, you attack, shattering all hope of that. I do not know why you do it, Damien. Perhaps you, yourself, do not know. I told you once that I feel sorry for you. But it is not that chair that confines you. You are trapped by your own bitterness."

"Where are you going?" he called out to me as I went to the door.

"I do not know," I said, closing it loudly behind me.

I marched out along the passage and soon found myself at the library door, without having given any thought to where I actually was going. As I entered the room I realized it was not vacant.

"I am sorry, Lady Jessica," I apologized. "I did not mean to intrude."

"Miss Chatfield, what a pleasure. I was sitting here longing for some company. My brother is off somewhere with Sir Charles. Nice chap, don't you think?"

"He seems pleasant enough," I replied.

She patted the cushion of the love seat. "Come sit with me a bit. I am relieved to find that Damien gives you some time for yourself."

"I fear today I just took the time," I admitted.

She looked at me over her glasses. "Do I sense a rift between you two?"

"I suspect I made too much of it," I replied. "I knew I should just ignore him but . . ."

"But Damien is hard to ignore," she said, completing my thought.

I nodded.

"He is not an easy man," she continued. "Of course, since the fire . . ."

I waited for her to finish.

"Yes?" I prompted gently.

"It was a great tragedy." She sighed. "His mother was a lovely woman. You would have liked her. Everyone did."

"Lord Darby indicated that Amanda is like her," I reflected.

Her finely drawn brows arched at my comment. "Curious that I should never have drawn that association. Amanda is a far more purposeful woman than Caroline was. But I suspect she is as fragile as her mother in her own way. Edmund, I fear, was never a real father to the child. Caroline had a very difficult time carrying her, and my brother always blamed Amanda for her mother's indisposition. Thankfully she had Damien. Even as a youth he championed his sister.

"Perhaps you find me indiscreet, but I have wondered about Amanda's husband," I admitted. "Was his death sudden?"

"Very," she confided. "It was a riding accident. He was killed instantly. I was in London and am somewhat muddled about the details."

I drew a deep breath. "It must have been devastating for her."

"I expect so," Jessica replied. "It was strange. I think only Damien sat a horse better than he. But the Lord moves in strange ways. Every day I survive this life I realize how fleeting it is."

"And Anitra?"

She looked away from me, down at her hands clasped tightly in her lap.

"Why do you ask?"

"Because I do not understand," I replied. "There are no pictures of her, no one speaks of her. I have been warned never to mention her. Sometimes I feel as if there is a conspiracy to pretend she never existed. And yet I feel her everywhere at Darby Manor."

There was a distinct sadness in her voice when she said finally, "You must understand, Lillith, my brother adored Anitra. He would do anything . . . In any event, when she died he forbid anyone to mention her name again in this house. He dismissed servants. He removed paintings, he refused to see old friends. I do not understand it, but I have never understood Edmund. That does not change the fact that I have given my oath that I shall never raise the subject again."

We talked for a good hour. She inquired of my family and I found myself talking easily about my youth. She had a direct, almost brusque manner, but one sensed a warm sensitivity underneath. I was surprised how openly I spoke with this woman who until yesterday had been a stranger to me.

"It must have been a great blow," she concluded as I finished telling her of Father and Elijah. "It is not good for a woman to be alone."

I wondered if she spoke from her own experience.

As if reading my mind she continued, "Oh, do not mistake me. I am quite certain that we women are as capable as men in many things. But with society as it is, we simply do not have the rights men do. And that makes us far more vulnerable. I admire your working for Damien, but I fear for you, my dear. That is not a life with much potential."

I shrugged. "Perhaps not, but it is my only recourse."

"That is not what I have been led to believe."

I flushed, sensing that she had been told of the ruse under which I had been brought to Darby Manor.

"Sir Charles told me," she confessed. "You mustn't be angry with him. Actually I believe he is quite taken with you and feels guilty for having helped perpetrate this scheme of Edmund's. I admit that I was at first shocked myself."

"You will pardon my saying so," I retorted, "but I find it unforgivable that a father would do such a thing. Damien may not have the use of his legs, but he *is* a man, and an enormously talented one. Oh, I find him exasperating at times, but perhaps if Lord Darby showed him some care, some respect, he would be different. His paintings display such insight, such sensitivity. Beneath that hostile guise, I sense there is a man of great depth. He can even be quite charming, though I admit those times are infrequent."

Lady Jessica studied me. I had no right to speak as I did. And, given how angry I had been made by Damien earlier, I could not understand why I spoke so adamantly on his behalf.

"I am sorry," I said quickly. "It is not my place, I cannot think what caused me to say what I did."

She leant forward and clasped my hand, smiling at me. "I suspect, Lillith, that you truly do not understand why you speak as you do. And yet, though I am a spinster, I know what it is to be in love with a young man." She broke off as the door to the library was flung open and Damien wheeled in.

"So there you are," he exclaimed.

"My nephew seems to have forgotten his manners," Lady Jessica advised. "I have just been getting to know Lillith. Perhaps you will join us. We might order some tea."

I shook my head. "I really must be going. I shall return to the studio, if that suits you, Damien."

He shrugged. "Do what you will. I left the door unlocked."

As I returned to the studio I reflected on my conversation with Jessica Darby. Her feelings about Damien puzzled me. Surely she was not implying that she thought I was in love with him? Had she mistaken my defense of him against his father as something other than it was?

Restless, I went to the windows. Chips, who lay before them, beat his tail as I approached. As I was alone, I decided to seize the opportunity to look again at the canvas Damien had done of me.

I removed the drape and seated myself before the easel. He had worked on it since I had seen it last. It took me some time before I could pinpoint what was changed. As I did I found myself embarrassed by what I saw. It was an excellent likeness, but there was a sensuality there which I did not recognize within myself. It reminded me of the painting of my mother. She had always had a certain something, a smoldering quality which was evident in the eyes and mouth.

What was it Damien had said? That there was a fire that burned within me. Did he perceive a quality in me which I did not even recognize myself?

As I drew the drape back over the canvas, I inadvertently knocked something off the table behind the easel. I knelt down to retrieve the small tin box, noticing as I did that a paper had been thrown from it.

I recognized the writing immediately. It was Anitra's.

I could feel my heart pounding as I moved into the light. If Damien discovered I had read this, I could not think what he might do. But I had to read it. I had to try and know this young woman. If I did not, I sensed that long after I left Darby Manor I would still be haunted by her.

"Damien," it read. "I want you to know that I know what you are planning. You see, you cannot fool me any longer. No matter how hard you try, somehow I will prevail. I cannot think why you want to hurt me so. I beg you to take me to

Whitcliffe Scar. Perhaps there you will see reason. Anitra."

As I had done with the page from her diary, I reread this note again and again. What could it mean? Even if I had dismissed the diary entry, I simply could not put this aside. Why would Damien want to hurt Anitra? What had he been planning?

I folded the note and was about to replace it in the box when something made me hesitate. If I were going to put this growing obsession about Anitra to rest, this paper might prove helpful. What I would do with it I had no idea. I certainly could not thrust it before Damien, demanding to know what it meant.

Amanda was due to return to Darby. Surely she would have some idea. If I could get her to talk to me about it, perhaps I could finally dismiss this preoccupation of mine. I folded the note and placed it in my pocket.

Ironically, the first drawings I withdrew when I returned to my cataloguing were unmistakably of Whitcliffe Scar.

I worked steadily the next hour, and when I was done, I searched out another stack of sketches. Noting that they seemed to be preliminaries to a group of particularly large paintings at one end of the studio I carried them over to better study them. Seeing that one of the canvases was set at a precarious angle, I set the sketches aside and, taking a firm grip of the slat frame, struggled to prop it steadily against the wall. As I did I realized that it had been placed over a door. I would have thought nothing of it, save that it appeared the door had deliberately been blocked off. Balancing the weight of the canvas with my left arm, I reached around the frame, trying to grasp the door handle with my right hand. As I did I nearly jumped out of my skin at the sound of a booming voice behind me.

"What in damnation—" I heard Damien explode. "Get away from there."

The shock nearly caused me to lose my footing, and it was several moments before I could right the painting safely against the wall. When I had done so I whirled about. "You nearly frightened me to death."

I think I have never seen anyone so angry. His entire visage seemed masked in fury. "I do not take well to anyone spying on me, Miss Chatfield," he charged. "I leave you alone here only to return and find you cannot be trusted."

"Trusted?" I managed to choke out. "How dare you accuse me of anything. If you were rational, you would see that I was only trying to relate those sketches there to the paintings. I believe that was part of my assignment."

"Then what, pray tell, were you doing at that door?" he demanded.

"I was trying to open it," I conceded.

"Ah, so you admit you were spying?" he pursued.

I felt at my wit's end. "I was not intruding, and I have no idea why you would think I would be spying. Even if I were so deceitful, you would be the least likely subject of my interest."

His eyes caught sight of the sketches to my left. "I thought I made it clear, Miss Chatfield, that I demanded privacy as part of our arrangement. What am I supposed to think when I return to find you snooping about?"

I clasped the fold of my skirt and took a step forward. "What you *should* think is that I am doing my job. What you *do* think is another matter. I believe our arrangement, as you call it, is at an end. I shall inform your father of my decision and be gone on the first coach returning to London."

I was shaking with anger but grew even more infuriated when his derision turned to amusement. I tried to go past him, but as I did, he spun his chair about, blocking my way.

"Oh now, come, Miss Chatfield, 'tis not so dire. Though you bargained badly, I am still compensating you well. To spite yourself would only be foolish."

"Let me pass," I insisted.

His hand reached out and took hold of my wrist. "Do you really mean to tell me that you would leave me here to my

178

own devices? I did not think you were so cruel."

"Do not talk to me of cruelty, Damien," I spat back. "That is *your* specialty."

My accusation had an immediate effect. His fingers uncurled from my wrist and fell to his lap. Our eyes met, and for a fleeting moment I beheld an expression of sadness the like of which I had never known.

"Do as you will," he said dully.

I paused for a moment, thinking that he was going to say something else. When nothing was forthcoming, I left the studio to seek sanctuary in my room. As I flung myself onto my bed, rivers of tears wet my cheeks. That I should permit him to affect me so was indeed foolish.

I lay there seething for perhaps fifteen minutes when I decided that I would make myself ill if I were to go on this way. Today was Wednesday. The coach would leave, if I remembered rightly, on Thursday, tomorrow. Even if it did not, I would somehow find my way to Richmond, for the service there had to be more frequent.

I pulled out my valises and had just begun laying my gowns carefully across the bed when there came a knock at the door. When it was followed swiftly by another, I went to open it and found Amanda before me.

"What are you doing here?" I said, amazed.

"It is—or was—my home, in case you have forgotten."

I clasped her hand, drawing her into the room. "You know I did not mean it that way. I just thought you were not expected until week's end."

There was a certain smugness to her smile. "I always prefer to do the unexpected, Lillith. I might have thought you would have guessed that by now."

I released her hand and ran to remove some paraphernalia from the chairs. "Come and sit down."

"You are packing," she said, noting the baggage placed round the foot of the bed.

I nodded. "I think it best that I leave here, Amanda."

She paused. "I know about the disagreement you had with my brother."

"He told you?" I gasped.

"Not the nature of it, simply that you had had a row. He worried that you might prepare—well, that you might decide to leave us."

"Worried," I exclaimed. "I quite expected he would be shouting it from the rooftops."

She sat down on the window seat. The glare of the white outdoors set off the coppery flame of her hair. When she turned to me her eyes had a faraway, thoughtful look.

"Damien often speaks before he thinks, Lillith," Amanda said slowly. "He knows it was wrong of him to shout at you. Indeed, he even sent me here to plead his case."

"Is he not man enough to do his own pleading?" I accused.

She winced. "That is a bit unfair. It is not a simple matter for him to come upstairs."

"Then he could have sent for me," I responded.

"And would you have gone if he had?"

I knew I would not.

"I believe he is truly sorry," Amanda continued. "It is obvious that he is most pleased with your work. Frankly, I have not seen Damien in such good spirits since . . . well, I cannot remember. I had a feeling from that first day, Lillith, that you would be good for him. Selfishly, I ask that you reconsider. Not for Damien, for me."

"Even were I to do what you ask, Amanda, how could I be certain this will not happen again and again?" I demanded as I sank into a chair opposite her.

She shrugged her shoulders. "You cannot, except that, if this red hair of mine is a mark of temper, then you can imagine what happens when it is unleashed. Damien in particular would not want to incur my wrath."

She turned and looked out the window and with her index finger traced the single letter *D* into the condensation on the frosty glass.

"Amanda," I ventured, "may I ask you something?"

Her eyes stayed trained on the snowy landscape. "That depends, Lillith."

"I know it is unfair in a way to ask you about Damien," I went on, "but if I could try to understand him better, perhaps I could prevent a recurrence of today's events. It is only that he is so mercurial. One moment he is reaching out to me, and the next, taunting me. There is so much anger in him."

She turned to face me. "Damien does not like to be confined. He is a fiercely independent man."

"It is just for that reason that I cannot understand why your father concocted this ridiculous scheme to bring me here," I continued.

"That is very simple," she murmured, her voice barely audible. "Father cannot forgive Damien."

"Forgive him? Forgive him for what?"

She pressed her hands to her temples, pulling the skin taut against her brow as though she was trying to eradicate some pain. "For the accident. For my mother's death and—and Anitra's."

"But why?" I exclaimed.

Her face contorted. "The fire . . . it was Damien," she choked out. "It was Damien's fault."

"Damien," I gasped. "But how?"

Her eyes took on a haunting look of anguish. "He used to paint down at the summerhouse. One day, he apparently left his oils very near a candle. The authorities said it had been careless. Mother and Anitra were there. By the time he got back, it was an inferno. He tried to help, but it was too late. A beam fell on him, but he managed to escape by dragging himself out."

"But it was an accident, Amanda," I insisted.

She looked at me with a dreamy expression. "An accident? Of course it was an accident. But Father never got over it. He adored Anitra. She had always been his favorite."

"Surely he must see how devastating this must be for Damien."

She shook her head. "One would have thought so. But instead of being grateful that Damien survived he . . . well, it is as though Damien took two lives, and Father now feels he can claim Damien's."

If that were true, I thought, then it was Lord Darby who had become the real victim of the fire.

"Why are you looking at me that way?" she demanded suddenly.

"I am sorry. I was just thinking how tragic all this has been for you. Coupled with the loss of your husband, at times it must have seemed insurmountable."

"No, not really," she said softly. "I have Damien."

"And Terrence," I offered.

"Speaking of whom, I had best get back to him," she said, rising.

"You have brought him to Darby?" I inquired.

She nodded.

"I am so anxious to meet him."

"Perhaps later. Father wants me to meet his solicitor," she explained. "What is he like?"

"Understandably, my opinion is slightly colored by the difficulty he has caused me," I conceded, "but he is attractive, and I expect you will find him pleasant enough."

She cocked her head. "This might prove more interesting than I had first thought."

I followed her to the door.

"I *can* tell Damien you will stay," she entreated me.

"I will stay," I agreed, "but he has you to thank for that."

She laughed. "I rather fancy the idea of having Damien indebted to me."

She had started down the hall when I darted after her. "I seem to be full of questions today, but you are the only one who seems willing to give me any answers. I was out with Chips yesterday and I encountered a man I assume was the gardener. The strange part was that he seemed almost wary of me; in fact, he did not utter a word to me."

"That must have been Perse," she replied. "You needn't take offense. He is a mute."

"I see. There is a stone house down on the westerly path. Does he live there?"

"No, he does not," she retorted shortly. "Now if you will excuse me, I really must get back to Terrence."

I returned to my room. I had the distinct impression that I had annoyed Amanda. It was the last thing I wanted to do. We both, I conceded, would be better served if I kept my curiosity to myself, and that meant deciphering the note I had found in the studio, without her help.

There were still several hours of daylight left when I finished straightening the room, and I decided to take advantage of them. As I reached the staircase I saw that Mrs. Horsley was on her way up. I waited until she reached the second-floor landing. I foiled her attempt at ignoring me by stepping directly into her path.

"Is there something you wanted?" she said in a surly way, thrusting her hands into the pockets of the shapeless black gown which hung on her like a shroud.

"I received a letter today," I said, watching her expression carefully. "The writer indicated he had not had word from me. And yet I specifically gave you several letters to mail to him. Before you think I am accusing you, let me assure you I am just trying to understand why my letters never reached their destination."

"You take great stock in yourself for a miss nobody," she scoffed. "I've a load more to worry about than your little letters. As far as I know they went out with the rest."

With that she withdrew one hand and pushed me aside. The force of the thrust sent me reeling, and had I not caught myself on the finialed balustrade, I would have plummeted down the stairs. When I recovered myself, I turned back to see her bulky frame hovering over me.

"You should be more careful, Miss Chatfield," she jeered. "Darby Manor can be a dangerous place for those who don't know their station."

I was too shaken and frightened to attempt a retort. Clinging to the railing, I descended to the hall below. I had crossed the width of it when I realized that I was still suffering the aftereffects of my confrontation with the housekeeper, and I sank into the gilded chair steps away from the library.

As I did I heard a man's voice say, "I take you for many things, Marisse, but not stupid. If you allow this to go on any longer, he will never marry you."

"Ah, there you are wrong," the woman replied.

"You may not have noticed, but Edmund is not getting any younger. And I do not think he looks well. Not to mention the little complication with Miss Chatfield."

"I have taken care of that," Marisse responded.

"Have you?" The man, whose voice I now recognized as James Farklan's, said with disdain, "Then why during those dreadful dinners does Damien not seem able to take his eyes off of her?"

"I admit I have noticed it myself," Marisse replied. "Frankly, I was violently opposed to Edmund's bringing Sir Charles here, but now I think it quite a stroke of luck. And of course with Amanda having . . ."

I leant towards the door which was slightly ajar, but their murmurings were no longer audible. Concerned that one or both might emerge from the library at any moment, I rose, and gathering my skirts high above my boots I tiptoed through the rear door towards the studio.

I knocked and waited several minutes before the bolt was thrown. Damien looked up at me warily.

"Am I to take it that you have reconsidered?" he ventured.

"Only because of Amanda," I said.

"What did she say to you?" he asked, wheeling his chair back so that I might enter.

"That is really unimportant, Damien."

"You really don't have to resume cataloguing today," he offered as I crossed to my desk.

"The sooner I get back to it, the sooner I will be done with it." I drew the ledgers open.

"You mean the sooner you'll be done with Darby," he answered with irritation.

I whirled about. "Damien, I have no desire to be done with Darby, as you put it. Sometimes I think there are those here who would like to drive me from it, but that is another matter."

He studied me thoughtfully. "And do you include me among those who would drive you away?"

I sighed. "Sometimes."

"I expect I have myself to blame for that," he murmured. "What you do not know is that it is the kindest thing I could do."

"Why?" I said, astonished. "So that you can go back to plodding about this studio, wallowing in your grief, allowing your father to continue to torture you?"

"Stop it, Lillith," Damien exploded. "You don't know what you are talking about."

"Don't I? Look around you. That's right, look. What do you see?"

His dark brooding eyes looked back at me. "I see paintings and a very beautiful, very desirable young woman."

Feeling myself blush, I put my hand to my neck.

"You needn't look so shocked, Lillith. I am certain I am not the first admirer you've had, and I am only sorry that I shall clearly not be the last."

"You are missing the point," I said, flustered.

The planes of his face softened as he smiled. "No, it is you, I fear, who are missing the point. I don't want to drive you from here, Lillith. I want you to stay."

"I have already said I would," I replied meekly.

His eyebrows knit together, forming a solid black band

across his forehead. "As my assistant. But would you stay if I asked you to be more than that?"

I was too stunned to do more than stare at him.

"I must say, it is the first time I have seen you at a loss for words, Miss Chatfield."

I drew a deep breath. "That is because we both know it does not merit a response. You know I came back here hoping that I might find you the least bit contrite over your earlier behavior. What a fool you must take me for."

"Now where are you going?" he demanded as I closed the ledgers and stood up.

"If you are asking me whether I am quitting, the answer is no. I said I would stay and I will, until the task is completed. But I am starting to see that there is no dealing with you when you are like this. Henceforth Damien, I suggest that you and I have as little to do with each other as possible. I will leave you to your work, and you will leave me to mine. I will be gone soon enough; I think we can refrain from insulting each other while I remain."

Chips sat up on his haunches as I crossed purposefully to the door. It stuck, and, frustrated, I jiggled the knob.

"You see there really is no escape, Lillith," I heard Damien say.

The door released suddenly and I swept through it. I ran blindly back through the reception hall and up the stairs to my room. As I slammed the door behind me, Mary dropped a load of kindling to the hearth.

"Now look what aye've gone an' done," she murmured.

"It was my fault," I said as I rushed to help her gather the wood. "I certainly have no cause to vent my frustrations on you."

"Now, ye needn't fret," she replied. "This place kin get te one. Me mum's always sayin, 'Now Mary, ye mind yer tongue, else they'll put ye out straightaway,' but sometimes this place gets te a body. If jobs weren't so scarce up north aye'd leave 'ere in a minute."

I stood up, dusting my skirt. "I thought Damien had taken steps to improve conditions, in the kitchens, at least."

" 'Tain't the kitchen that gives me chilblains in the 'eight o' summer," she replied. "An' 'tain't my imaginin's. Things are not right 'ere."

"What makes you say that?" I asked anxiously.

Her dark eyes grew wide as she looked past me towards the door. I started to ask her what was wrong, but she pressed her index finger to her lips. We both stood transfixed, staring at the massive mahogany door.

When not a sound came from beyond it, I crossed the room, clasped the curved brass handle, and flung it open. I stepped out into the dark hallway, peering to either side of it. Satisfied that no one was about, I returned to the room, assuring Mary that no one was there.

"Ye can't be too careful," she murmured.

"You don't really think someone was eavesdropping?" I asked her.

She picked up the ewer from the washstand. " 'Tain't my place te be advisin' ye, Miss Lillith, but aye'd be careful what ye say or who ye say it te. Them don't like nobody nosin' about 'ere. Take me friend, Flo, fer instance. One day she's 'ere, right as rain, an' the next, gone. Just disappeared. Mrs. 'Orsley says she took another spot, but ain't no way she'd leave without a word te me. No, she knew somethin'. Somethin' so terrible that they got rid o' 'er."

"What are you saying? You aren't implying that some harm came to your friend?"

She clutched the sculpted pewter to her breast. "Aye dunno. But aye'm not takin' any chances. An' if yer smart, ye won't neither."

I started towards her, but she darted past me. "Mary, please do not go," I entreated, "not until we have a chance to talk."

She paused as she reached the door. "Please don't be askin' me anythin' more, Miss Lillith. Like me mum says, aye probably got fancies in me 'ead. But just in case aye'm right, ye watch yerself."

With the opening and closing of the door, a cold draft wafted into the room, and I started at a loud crack from the fireplace. Darting over to it, I picked up the live ember and threw it back into the flames. As I replaced the embroidered fire screen, I winced in pain. Chastising myself for my stupidity, I ran and plunged my hand into the newly refilled basin, praying that the water would soothe the searing pain. When I finally withdrew it, I realized that the puffy blanched skin was quickly forming blisters.

I sank down onto the edge of the bed, clutching the wrist of my injured hand and trying to will the pain away, but as the swelling increased I realized that I needed help. I left the room and headed towards the back staircase, deciding the kitchen would be the best place to find a remedy. As I started down the stairs, a door slammed below and the sound of a woman running across the floor drifted up to where I stood.

Had I not stepped aside, I would have collided with the figure racing up the stairs.

"Amanda," I gasped, "are you all right?"

Even in the dark I knew I had startled her. "What are you doing here?" she demanded breathlessly.

"My hand, I fear I burnt it," I replied. "I thought perhaps they may keep a salve in the kitchens."

She reached out and clasped my shoulder. "You poor thing. Come with me, Lillith. I have an ointment I am certain will help."

I followed her back up to the second-floor passage and struggled to keep pace with her as she moved purposefully along it to her room.

"Come over here by the light," she instructed me as she fetched a small jar and a roll of gauze from a satin case atop the dressing table.

"It was stupid of me," I said, chagrined, as I stretched out my hand so that she might apply the ointment. When she made no move I looked up at her in time to see her recoil, shutting her eyes at the sight of the fiery patch of skin before her.

"Let me do it," I offered.

She handed me the jar. "I am sorry," she murmured, "I simply cannot bear the thought of burning flesh."

As she left the room I realized that she had not been spared the emotional scars of the tragedy in the summerhouse. Slowly I wrapped bandages over the cooling cream. When she returned she was not alone.

"You must be Terrence," I said as the young boy peered from behind her full skirt.

"Say hello to Lillith," Amanda encouraged him, pushing him forward.

He stood his ground, eyeing me warily.

"Well, he certainly is a Darby in appearance," I replied.

"Do you think so?"

"Absolutely," I insisted, studying the boy. "Those dark, deep-set eyes, the square jaw—he is the image of your father."

Seeing that the child appeared fascinated by the bandages, I extended my hand to him. "This is not as bad as it looks," I said. "I burnt my hand and your mother was kind enough to help me. You see, it is only a bandage."

Gingerly he stepped forward, placing two small hands about the gauze. Suddenly he clapped his hands together with such force that I screamed out in pain.

Amanda darted forward, grasping his stiff lace collar. "Now look what you have done," she exploded.

"He meant no harm," I assured her as he struggled to pull away from her.

"He never does," she murmured as she dragged him from the room. "And not a morsel of dinner," I heard her say as she reentered the room.

"Isn't that a bit harsh?" I asked. "He's just a little boy."

"I expect you are right," she admitted, twisting a lock of

hair nervously about her fingers. "You know, sometimes, Lillith, I wish Terrence had never been born. I love him, of course, but it is not easy raising a child alone."

"I am certain it is not," I replied sympathetically. "I know it is none of my concern, Amanda, but have you ever thought of moving back to Darby? It might be good for the boy to have male companionship, and it would certainly ease your burden."

"I have considered it," she acknowledged, "but there are those who do not take well to the idea."

"You mean Marisse," I concluded.

Her eyes darted across the room as the French enamel wall clock chimed the hour. "Good Lord, I had no idea of the time," she exclaimed. "We had best get down to dinner."

"I should like to freshen a bit," I said.

"Can you manage?" she inquired as I crossed to the door.

"Thanks to you, I will be fine. I will see you downstairs, then."

I returned to my room, and as I struggled out of my walking suit and into a peacock-blue silk gown, I realized how the bandages made the simplest of tasks difficult to perform. I was anxious as I made my way to the dining room; Lord Darby was a punctilious man and I did not want to incur his wrath.

The mood was solemn as I crossed the cavernous room and silently took my place next to Sir Charles. As he smiled I was struck by the boyishness of his grin.

"Amanda tells us you have had a little accident," Lord Darby offered.

"It was very foolish of me," I said.

"Miss Chatfield will do almost anything to get out of working with me," Damien added dryly.

"Somehow I do not see her going to such extremes," Sir Charles retorted.

Damien laughed. "I see you have made another conquest, Lillith."

"Has everyone in this household forgotten his manners?" Jessica Darby exclaimed.

"My thoughts precisely," Marisse broke in, "which is why I have been trying to convince Edmund that we should be more festive about this house. It has been years since anyone has given a ball at Darby."

"Let us not start that again," Lord Darby objected.

Marisse pursed her lips.

"Marisse may have a point," Jessica agreed. "I have never set great store in being a Darby, but it does obligate us to some extent."

"Exactly," Marisse said. "You know, James mentioned that there is talk. Our postponement of this marriage is beginning to be awkward."

"I really do not think this is the time or place, my dear," Lord Darby fumed.

Marisse appeared distraught. "But, Edmund, I have already written to Lady Lyttleton and Dr. Brathwaite and . . ."

I jumped as Damien's fist pounded the table. "You invited Brathwaite?" he demanded, his face a mask of fury. "Why, you scheming little—"

"Damien, I won't have this," Lord Darby warned.

"The two of you stop," Marisse pleaded.

Damien pushed his chair back from the table. "Stay out of it, Marisse. You have done quite enough."

Lord Darby stood up and strode around the table, blocking his son's way. I sat dumbstruck as I saw him raise his arm as if to strike Damien.

"Father, please," Amanda beseeched him as all eyes focused on the tableau unfolding before us.

He lowered his arm, but his look remained one of glazed fury.

"Afraid, Father?" Damien, who had sat unflinching in his chair, charged. "Afraid of what you might be capable of?"

There was a deadly hush in the room.

"Get out of here," Lord Darby whispered hoarsely.

"Would that I could," Damien retorted as he spun his chair about and wheeled himself from the room.

"What was that all about?" Sir Charles whispered to me as Lord Darby returned to the table, obviously struggling to regain his composure.

"I do not know," I replied, turning to see how Marisse was.

Far from being upset, she almost seemed to be relishing the confrontation. "Everyone eat, please," she urged.

I did not know about the rest, but I had suddenly lost my appetite. I had no idea what it was about Dr. Brathwaite that had made Damien react as he had, but nothing merited the extent of his father's wrath. I had previously experienced Lord Darby's verbal abuse of his son, but it was terrifying to think that his torment burned so deep that he was capable of causing Damien physical harm as well.

I could not wait for dinner to be over and I suspected that Amanda shared my sentiments, for instead of following the others to the drawing room for coffee, she announced she, too, wished to retire early. We climbed the stairs together in silence.

"I am just going to look in on Terrence," she said as we reached the landing. "Would you care to join me?"

"Of course I would," I replied, "unless you think I might disturb him."

She put her arm through mine. "Nonsense."

We went to a room at the end of the hall. "Fortunately, the nursery was kept intact," she whispered as she pressed the handle of the door adjoining her room. "Mother was sentimental about those things." I followed her as she tiptoed forward to the bed where Terrence lay sleeping.

"He looks so angelic," I whispered as she pulled the coverlet up about his shoulders.

She smoothed the hair back from his brow and then beckoned me to follow her back to the master bedroom.

"Just let me light these candles," she said. I had been so preoccupied earlier that I had not taken particular note of the room. It had a distinctly masculine decor, but there was an easy comfort about it.

Amanda signaled me to join her by the fire.

"Was this your parents' room?" I queried as I seated myself in the large leather wing chair.

She placed the candle on the table between us. "Why do you ask?"

I shrugged. " 'Tis only that it adjoins the nursery."

"It was theirs originally," she replied stifling a yawn. "But after Anitra was born it became Damien's. He used it until . . . Since the accident, his quarters have been below."

"Perhaps I should let you sleep, Amanda," I offered. "You seem tired."

"I am, a bit," she admitted. "I have had my hands full with Terrence these past months."

She followed me to the door, handing me the candlestick. "You had better take this."

I thanked her and had turned to leave when she said, "I am amazed that you have not asked me about what happened at dinner tonight."

"I hesitated to do so," I admitted.

"It is the wisest course," she advised. "If you will take my advice I should not mention it to Damien."

"You seem to understand him well, Amanda," I replied. "Therefore, I will assume it is good advice."

"I do not pretend to understand him, Lillith, any more than I understand myself, at times. But I love him, and I know what is best for him."

"I hope he knows how fortunate he is to have you," I told her. "And now I shall bid you good night."

The manor was hushed as I edged back along the length of the hallway, but, as before, I found no peace in its silence. For all the splendor that was Darby, the house was somehow lifeless. It was like an ancient oak, its majesty corroded by some unseen decay within its core.

As I opened the door to my room, I paused. It was faint, but there was a distinct scent permeating the air. I breathed deeply, struggling to identify the heady fragrance. I held my candle high, my eyes sweeping the room. It was empty. Something told me to retrace my steps. Leaving the door ajar, I moved back along the hallway, trying to avoid the mirrors. It was an illusion, of course, but the replications of my reflection made me feel as if I were being followed.

I had just reached the landing when my eye caught some movement below. I leant against the balustrade and peered down through the intricate stairwell in time to see a figure dart across the marble floor to the entry door. There was a quick click as though a latch had been turned. I shivered, feeling a sudden chill, and quickly put my good hand up to guard the flickering candle.

Who was this person who roamed the manor in the dead of night? I wondered. I waited a few moments, but when all was silent I gathered my skirts and moved swiftly back to my room.

The draft from the hall had removed all traces of the earlier scent. The fire was lit, but Mary had neglected to draw the draperies. Putting the candle down, I moved swiftly to the windows. A three-quarter moon played its beams on the snow-laden ground, which radiated a light of its own.

I clasped the heavy silk tassels and began to draw the hangings when I saw a figure dart across the landscape. It happened so quickly that I could not discern whether it was a man or a woman. My face was pressed so close to the window-pane that my breath on the glass fogged my view. Hurriedly I wiped away the condensation, but whoever it was had disappeared behind the high privet hedge leading from the lower terraces.

Pulling the draperies closed, I began undoing the buttons on my gown. My bandaged hand was throbbing by the time I climbed into my nightdress. I had dismissed Damien's barb insinuating that I had injured myself purposely, but now I wondered whether it would not actually impede my work. The sooner I finished the cataloguing, the sooner I would be free to leave Darby. But where I felt I should have been excited about the prospect, it also harbored an undeniable sadness.

I tried to tell myself that this was only natural. No matter how strained or tempestuous these last weeks had been, Darby had become a haven of sorts for me. I had hardly been taken to the bosom of the household, but I found a certain security in the known.

But what was the known? Did I really understand any more about the manor or the people who lived here than I had that first day? I had gathered snippets of information, but nothing which offered any conclusions. I tried to tell myself it was simply an odd household, that after my relatively uncomplicated upbringing it was natural that it would seem alien to me. But to do that I would have to dismiss more than just the personality of those who resided here. No matter where I let my imagination take me, I always came back to the one person who even in death would not let me put my anxiety to rest.

I had suggested to Jessica Darby that there was a conspiracy of silence about Anitra, and in her own way she had confirmed it. Had I not found the diary entry or the note in the studio I might have reasoned that the denial was simply Lord Darby's eccentric way of dealing with his grief. But these writings, I was convinced, were not the result of mere temperamental annoyance with an older brother. What if anything they had to do with the mysterious night forays or the perplexing conversation between Marisse and James Farklan or the threatening talk of the stablehands I could not fathom. Yet I felt compelled to find the answers. It was as though someone had placed an unfinished tapestry and needle in my hand and was urging me to weave the tableau to completion. As much as I wanted to see the picture, I wondered if there was good reason to leave it unfinished.

14

I AWOKE the next morning to an insistent knocking.

"Lillith, are you awake?"

Recognizing Amanda's voice, I gathered my robe and pulled it about me as I went to answer the door.

"I hope I did not disturb you," Amanda said, "but Terrence and I thought you might like to join us for a stroll outside."

"How could I refuse an invitation like that," I replied, smiling at the little boy. His dark eyes peered up at me from behind his mother's cloak. "Could you give me about ten minutes, or shall I catch up with you?"

"Take your time," Amanda replied. "I need to get some hot

porridge into Terrence before we brave the elements. How is your hand, by the way?"

I flexed my fingers within the gauze bandage. "It is stiff, but the nagging pain has disappeared."

"It should be right again within a few days," she assured me.

We agreed to meet in the reception hall. I gave a moment's thought to going to the studio and informing Damien where I would be, but as it was still early, I decided he would not miss me.

"This really was a splendid suggestion," I said as Amanda and I each took one of Terrence's hands and descended the steps to the drive. "The air is so fresh and clear it almost demands that one be out of doors."

Amanda laughed. "Wait till you have a child, Lillith. You will long for those days when you could languish inside."

"And what makes you think I will have a child?" I replied, grasping Terrence's hand more firmly as he kicked at the soft powder on the ground.

"Do not tell me you never considered it?" she said, amazed.

Before I could reply, a male voice called out to us. "Whoa there."

We turned simultaneously in time to see Sir Charles slip on the icy surface of the steps and tumble down, landing a few feet from where we stood.

"Oh, Lord, are you hurt?" Amanda cried out as she sprang forward to help him.

He struggled to his feet, dusting the snowy crystals from his coat. "Just my pride," he said. "That serves me right, I suppose, for being so eager to catch up with you ladies."

"I did not think we were to meet until later this morning," Amanda said.

He adjusted the brim of his hat. "We were not, but I thought if I asked in my most endearing fashion, you might permit me to walk with you."

"Ah, but there you are mistaken, Sir Charles," Amanda retorted.

Sir Charles looked genuinely disappointed.

"What I mean is that the person you should be asking is Terrence here."

Without a word he crouched down before Terrence, who had not let go of my hand. "Would you mind if another man came along?"

I nodded in encouragement as Terrence allowed Sir Charles to take his other hand.

As soon as he seemed to have gained a certain confidence, I let the little boy go and fell back with Amanda. We had gone some paces when the drifts deepened suddenly, and Sir Charles swung young Terrence up on his shoulders.

"Seeing them like that only serves to remind me how little male company Terrence experiences."

"Have you ever thought of remarrying, Amanda?" I asked as we followed the rangy figure of Sir Charles toting Terrence towards the gardens.

She shook her head. "Not really. My marriage was . . . well, let us just say I do not abide by convention. Unfortunately, there are those who think it would be the best course. I expect it of Damien, I suppose, but not Marisse."

"Marisse? Why would she have cared?"

Her eyes narrowed, their dark pupils like the jet cuffs of her gown. "Marisse is never without purpose, Lillith. It is ironic that she thought a solution might be an alliance between James and me."

"James? You cannot mean James Farklan?"

She slowed. "Does that shock you?"

I thought about it a moment. "I would say rather it puzzles me. To tell you the truth, Marisse embarrassed me when I first came to Darby Manor by almost foisting me on him. 'Twas absurd, of course. I am not so inexperienced as to suppose he would have an interest in me. And I certainly have none in him."

" 'Tis even more absurd, but I shall tell you that James actually proposed to me," she admitted. "It could not have been more than two or three months after Robert's death."

"I see," I murmured. "Perhaps that is what Damien meant."

She whirled round to me. "Damien? What did he say to you?"

"I cannot recall what it was exactly," I admitted. "It was merely an inference. I gather he has no liking for James Farklan. Which surprises me, because of Maude."

"Now you have me at a disadvantage," she replied. "How does Maude figure in this?"

I cleared my throat. "Because of her relationship with Damien. Even if he did not particularly care for James, I would think he would be more generous, if only for appearance sake. It would not make for a comfortable association if they were to marry."

Amanda clasped my arm. "Marry? Good Lord, you do not truly think . . ."

"Well, Maude has made it very clear," I said. "But then I know 'tis awkward. Your father has not helped."

"You will pardon my saying so, Lillith, but I assumed that you were more insightful than this," she chastised me. "Maude Farklan is nothing but a pretty little snit. You have worked with Damien now for some time; you cannot truly believe that he would be interested in such a woman."

"Who your brother is interested in is none of my concern," I retorted.

"Well, for one who has no concern you seem to have a great number of misconceptions, and to have a misconception you must have given thought to it."

"No," I argued. "But, Amanda, you know the ruse under which your father brought me here. I was merely a pawn in a complex but expedient plan. I cannot say that there is any empathy between Lady Maude and myself. But were I in her position, and as taken with Damien as she appears, I expect I would have many confusions."

"My dear Lillith, there is only one thing which Maude Farklan cares for, and that is herself. No—she also cares for money," she replied. "She might have been an amusement for Damien at one time, but I assure you there is naught between them now."

I was about to pursue it when suddenly Terrence twisted about in Sir Charles's arms and called out, "Mummy, Mummy."

"You go on," I urged her.

I watched as Amanda ran forward, laughing. Terrence was swung into her arms, and the two frolicked ahead. I did not know why, but I sensed her expression of gay abandon was more of a performance than real merriment.

As I reached Sir Charles he said, "I am relieved to see the child shows some responsiveness to his mother at least. I could elicit nothing from him, but you are right about one thing."

"And what is that?" I pursued.

"The Darby women. They *are* different. Or at least, they appear to be."

The chill of the stones had crusted the snow along the path at this juncture. "I am pleased you agree," I mused.

He paused to pull on gloves over the slender musculature of his hands. "Oh, I suspect, Lillith, that we would agree on many things, were I to know you better."

"There is little chance of that," I conceded.

"That needn't be so," he replied.

Something in his tone brought my eyes up to his. His regard was of such unstudied tenderness that I started at the pure intimacy of it. Through the cold of the morning I felt a scarlet flush spread upwards from my neck.

"What I mean to say is that I hope you will permit me to call on you once we have returned to London. I know we did not start on the best footing, but perhaps you will allow me to make it up to you."

I put my hand to the crown of my bonnet as the wind gusted. "I do not recall saying that I was returning to London."

He looked surprised. "You have other plans, then?"

I admitted I did not.

"Perhaps I can be of some assistance to you," he said slowly. "In securing employment, that is."

"I think you have done quite enough on that score," I retorted.

He grimaced. "You do not forgive easily, do you. I expect I am owed that. Which is why I would like to make up for having helped to get you into all of this. Of course, to be honest, my motives are not without some selfishness."

Amanda and Terrence turned to rejoin us.

"We had best turn back," she said. "Terrence is sneezing, and the last thing we need is to have him take cold."

"I should be getting back to the studio anyway," I agreed.

Amanda waved me off. "Do not be silly. You two stay. I shall join you later this morning, Sir Charles."

Ordinarily I would have returned, but we had come a fair stretch, and we were not far from the paths leading down to the ruins of the summerhouse.

"The snow deepens here. Are you certain you wish to venture on?" Sir Charles inquired.

I nodded, seeing that Amanda and Terrence were now well out of sight. "You needn't stay," I offered. "I know my way."

The specks of green in the hazel of his eyes glinted mischievously. "I am always game for a bit of adventuring. But I wish you would permit me to take your arm."

I allowed that it was wise, and the two of us maneuvered our way down the hillside to the path below.

"You certainly seem purposeful. Can you give me a hint where we are going?"

"You will see soon enough," I assured him.

"It looks as though you are not the only one who finds this route compelling," he murmured.

I peered up at him. "What do you mean?"

He pointed ahead along the path. "You see there, the snow is compacted. Someone else has been along here earlier."

I went to where he indicated and, crouching down, brushed the light flakes away to reveal distinct boot impressions. "There was more than one person here," I murmured, straightening up.

His brows knitted together. "Why do I feel a party to sleuthing of some sort?"

"Sleuthing? Oh, heavens no! I was just curious," I replied, making a distinct effort to keep my tone light.

His laugh was hearty. "Well, you could have fooled me."

I signaled him to follow me. "It is only a bit further." I proceeded, keeping the footprints in sight until I reached the fork in the path.

Sir Charles caught up with me, saying, "I hope that puzzled look you have does not mean that you have led me astray. You did say that you knew where you were going."

"I do," I assured him.

"Well, obviously you are a woman who chooses the path less traveled," he replied as he followed me.

I quickened my pace, and within minutes I was face to face with the charred ruins.

"It looks different," I murmured as I heard his step behind me.

"I do not know what it looked like before, but this . . . well, it is not exactly what I expected."

"The snow covering the timbers that way makes it look almost ethereal," I mused.

Sir Charles stepped forward. "Might I ask what this is—or shall I say, was?"

"The summerhouse," I offered as I moved forward precariously. "This is where the accident happened that took Lady Darby's and Anitra's lives."

"And where Damien was injured," he added.

I nodded.

"I must say, it presents a rather macabre picture. There must be other vistas about which would be gentler to the eye."

I could not deny that there was something sad about the desolation here. And yet my fascination with this place had in no way diminished.

"You know, Lillith, I would not advise you to walk about this place," Sir Charles said. "This skeletal structure could be dangerous. Besides, the wind is increasing, and I think it would be wise to turn back."

"I know," I conceded, "but just let me remain a moment longer." When I finally turned back to him and we had returned to the path, he asked, "Did you find what you were looking for?"

I shook my head. "The most difficult thing is that I am not even certain what it is, if anything."

We continued on in silence. "Will you tell me something, Lillith?" Sir Charles asked as we approached the fork in the path.

"If I can."

He stopped and turned to face me. "What is your relationship with Damien Darby?" He paused. "I will understand if you do not care to answer."

I shook my head. "It is not that," I assured him. "I just cannot think what would cause you to ask. He is my employer. You know that."

"Yes, but that does not tell me how you feel about him."

"He is extremely talented," I replied quickly.

His eyes explored my face. "And?"

I shrugged. "And I do not know what you want me to say."

He smiled. "You are not making this easy for me, you know. What I have no right to ask is the very thing which I most want to know. And that is whether you have any real feelings for Damien Darby."

My eyes widened. "What in heavens name would make you think that?"

He looked at me sheepishly. "Last night at dinner, for one thing. You seemed genuinely concerned about what happened."

"I would be inhuman if I were not. The incident was upsetting to everyone."

He agreed. "I suspect if it had not been followed by a conversation with Jessica Darby, I should have dismissed it."

"I fear you have me at a disadvantage," I said.

" 'Tis more something she inferred than anything specific."

"That being?"

"That you have indeed formed deeper feelings for Damien."

"That is preposterous," I protested. "If she had been privy to our arguments she would never even suggest such a thing."

"Hold on, Lillith," Sir Charles interrupted. "I only make comment of it because I find Jessica Darby to be a rather perceptive woman. She is certainly a character. But if she was misguided, then I admit it comes as some relief to me. I would not want to see you matched with someone so volatile."

"There is another side to Damien," I countered. "Do not be too quick to judge. What appears on the surface at Darby Manor is not necessarily what exists."

"If you are trying to titillate my imagination, then you are being quite successful. Am I to understand that things I find unsettling hereabouts have their roots in darkness?"

I thought that a peculiar turn of phrase. "You will undoubtedly depart from here finding it all quite mundane. My reaction, I suspect, has more to do with the peculiarity of my existence here. Or perhaps I am overly imaginative. In any event, we really should not be discussing the Darbys in this manner."

We had reached the terracing and continued to make our way towards the house.

"If I promise not to continue to be so inquisitive, will you tell me what I might encounter if I were to take the other fork along the path?"

" 'Tis a house," I replied.

"Who lives there?" he asked.

"I do not know," I admitted. "I surmise it is vacant."

There was a sudden gust, and his hat flew off and rolled along the crusted surface of the lawn. He let go of me and ran off to retrieve it.

"Why do you ask?" I pressed as he returned to where I waited.

"Let me see. Oh, yes. 'Twas only that last night—it must have been very late—I was certain that I heard someone or perhaps something outside. Then when we saw the footprints below, well, I was just curious. Am I to take it that you heard it as well?"

"No," I lied as we reached the front steps of the manor.

He shook the snow from his cloak. "Likely 'tis just being in the country that has me a bit ill-at-ease. I admit to you I cannot wait to return to London. This seems rather a waste-land in comparison. I cannot think how you have managed it these past months."

"Actually, I have been quite comfortable here," I told him as he held the door for me and I stepped inside. "This is not the best of seasons to experience the North Country, but I have found it quite—"

"You have found it quite what, Miss Chatfield?" It was Damien.

"I did not know I had an audience," I bristled as he wheeled towards Sir Charles and me.

"Well, from the expression on Sir Charles's face, you have been more than a bit entertaining this morning."

"I think that is a bit out of hand," Sir Charles accused. "In fact, I think you owe Miss Chatfield an apology."

I reached out and put my hand on Sir Charles's arm. "Please, there is no need," I urged, praying that there would not be a scene.

Damien laughed. "You see, old chap, our Miss Chatfield is perfectly capable of taking care of herself. You will find her to be quite independent of spirit. I should keep that in mind, if you intend to pursue her."

"Damien," I gasped. "That is outrageous."

"Is it?" he challenged. "I rather think my approach is simply more direct than Marisse's. And Charles, you needn't look so scandalized. There is no doubt that Miss Chatfield makes a rather fetching sight with that bonnet askew as it is."

My hands flew to my head as I struggled to straighten the full felt brim.

"Not that I wish to stand in the way of affairs of the heart, but my father is rather anxious to see his solicitor," Damien continued. "I suspect this is due more to the encouragement of my future stepmother, but then what Lord Darby wants, he usually gets."

I gathered my skirts and swept between the two men. "I am going to my room. I shall be down to the studio as soon as I have changed my boots."

I could feel their eyes upon me as I climbed the stairs, and when I reached the second-floor landing I headed purposefully to my room, shutting the door loudly behind me.

I threw off my cloak and tugged angrily at the ribbons of my bonnet, which had grown stubborn from the damp. How dare he try to humiliate me so! The worst of it was that it appeared that in some sadistic way he had actually taken pleasure in our embarrassment. If indeed Damien had rejected Maude Farklan, as Amanda had told me, she should consider herself fortunate. Damien had no regard for the feelings of others, particularly, it seemed, of women. He was insulting and abusive. How could I ever have felt sympathy or compassion for him? He was insidious. Anyone who delighted in the pain of others as he seemed to do was warped.

I shuddered suddenly. What had it been that Anitra had written? She had asked why he hurt her so. Had she, too, been the object of the cruel streak he seemed to possess? But his own sister! Why would he have displayed such antagonism towards her?

I changed my boots and hurriedly made my way down to the studio, taking a deep breath before I knocked at the door. Chips must have heard me, for he commenced scratching on the other side until Damien turned the latch.

"You really did not think I expected you to work today," he mused.

"And why not?" I asked challengingly.

"Well, I thought you would far prefer to dither your time away with Sir Charles. Then of course, there is your hand."

I gathered my skirts and pushed past him. "You know, if I did not know better I would actually think you are jealous."

I heard him turn the chair and wheel towards his easel. I climbed to my work area and withdrew a set of sketches, realizing as I did that my right hand was less facile than I had thought earlier. The familiar sound of the drop cloth snapping off the canvas told me that he would not deign to reply. Carefully I placed the quill between the wedge of bandage and laboriously resumed my task. The silence was almost deafening, but this day I rather welcomed it. I was not having an easy time of it, and I did not need the usual strife between Damien and myself to produce further discouragement.

It was a good hour later when I heard him mumble something.

"Are you talking to me?" I inquired tentatively.

He put his palette aside. "I said perhaps you are right."

"Did I miss something?" I called out in reply.

"Perhaps I am jealous," he ruminated.

I clenched the rough pine of the table with my good hand. "Must you make a mockery of each day, Damien?" I said in despair.

I felt a sense of dread as he wheeled purposefully towards me. "Why must you always challenge me, Lillith? Why would you not think that I might resent the way Charles looks at you? Not that I blame him. Any man in his right mind would find you desirable. You cannot think that I have spent these last days and weeks with you alone in this studio with total dispassion. If you do not believe me, look there at the portrait I have done of you. Is that painted by one who mocks you, Lillith?"

I did not know whether it was bewilderment or shock which rendered me speechless, but I could only sit gazing down on him.

"Am I to take your silence as my answer?" he demanded finally.

My mouth was so dry that when I replied it was a mere whisper. "I do not know what you are asking of me, Damien."

His brows knit together emphasizing the deep set of his eyes. "You really do not see it, do you?"

"I do not know what you want me to see or what I am to say. I cannot read your mind. Why are you trying to confuse me?"

He wheeled his chair closer to me. "Why are you crying, Lillith?"

"I don't know," I whispered as salty tears ran past my lips. I fumbled in the pocket of my gown for a handkerchief.

"Here, take this," he said, offering his own.

As I reached out to accept it his hand clasped mine.

"What are you doing?"

"I am trying to talk to you. Would that I could rise up to you. As it is I have to use the powers I have."

"Please let me go, Damien," I begged.

"Only if you promise not to go running off, as you usually do."

"I need promise you nothing," I blurted out.

"That is true. But you should learn to discern between what one needs and what one wants."

"What I want is to be left free to go back to my work," I said dully.

His eyes searched my face. "I don't believe that, Lillith. I think that you want me as much as I want you."

I felt my knees grow weak. "Don't do this, Damien," I gasped. "You don't know what you are saying."

"Oh, but I do. You choose to see the tension between us as antagonism, but I think it is only our mutual attempt to deny the attraction between us. Don't mistake me. I was prepared to detest you, but that first evening when you returned Chips to my quarters . . . Well, let us just say I did not sleep that night. On the surface you are the comely and prim Miss Chatfield, but as I watched you here in the studio day after day I discovered a smoldering quality about you. You can see it there in the portrait. There is a fire that burns in you, Lillith, as it does in me."

"How dare you speak to me that way," I said accusingly. "Do you think because you pay me to catalogue these paintings it affords you some right? What you believe you see in me is your fantasy, Damien, it is nothing to do with me. By your very words you show me that you know me not at all. I am not some trollop you can seduce at whim."

"God, you are mulish. Is that how you think I view you?"

"What else am I to think? Now I see that I was a fool to question Marisse's motives."

"What are you talking about?"

"I do not intend to carry this conversation any further," I averred. "If you will be so kind as to unhand me, I—"

"What did Marisse say to you?" he interrupted, his grip tightening about my wrist.

"If you really must know, she warned me about you. But I chose to dismiss it, when I should have realized that, other than Amanda, she may be the one friend I have here."

He released me so abruptly that I fell back a step. "I take you for many things, Lillith, but not a fool. You can argue with me all you will, but I am not wrong about you—about us. I can't force you to see it. I can only hope you will see it for yourself before it is too late. I swear I will make no move towards you again. But I will wait and hope that you will come to me."

"That day will never come, Damien," I seethed. "Now, if you are quite finished, I will return to the one thing I do care about—finishing the job I started."

"You'll have to forgo your work today, Lillith. There is something I have to do—alone. And on your way out you can ask Sommers to fetch one of the stablehands to take Chips for a good run. Just because I am tied to this chair is no reason for him to wither away with me."

I was trembling as I left the studio. All I could think of was getting to the sanctuary of my room. I reached it just as Mary was leaving.

"Oh, aye'm glad yer 'ere," she said gaily. "Aye just left a tray fer ye. Lady de Wentoff was real specific that everyone was te take trays fer luncheon. She's up te somethin', but 'tis not my place te be guessin' what."

"I am not very hungry," I demurred.

"Ye feelin' all right, Miss Lillith?" she queried. "Now that aye look at ye, yer lookin' a bit pale."

"I am fine really," I assured her.

She started to leave, but I called her back. "Mary, you might do me a favor and give Sommers a message for me."

"Oh, aye would, miss, but 'e's off te town. Is there somethin' aye kin do fer ye?"

I shook my head. "No, I will see to it."

I was fond of Mary, but it was with an overwhelming sense

of relief that I closed the door behind her. The tray was on the table in front of the fireplace. I knew I would not be able to take even a morsel of food, but I told myself that the tea might settle my nerves. I removed the tea cozy and poured the brew into the fine porcelain cup. As I clasped the gold handle the shaking of my hand caused the liquid to spill over onto the tray. Tears streamed down my cheeks as I clumsily struggled to blot up the tea with the napkin.

"How dare he," I stammered to myself. In some ways I felt I had only myself to blame. If I had not allowed Amanda to dissuade me, I would have been almost back in London by now. But never in the farthest stretch of my imagination could I have anticipated today's conflagration. Worse than his declaration was his having the gall to suggest that I shared his wanton desires. Did he think that I was so naive or would be so flattered by his attentions that I would succumb to some afternoon tryst?

But why today, suddenly and without warning, had he spoken to me this way? Amanda had indicated that he no longer fancied Maude Farklan if he had ever done so. Had he simply tired of her and decided to sate his desires with whoever was at hand? What infuriated me most was that he had not even tried to mask his intentions. He had made it clear that his desires were physical; there had not even been a hint that he cared for me in any way. I expected I should actually be grateful for that; at least he did not try to seduce me with endearments which were grounded in lies.

What if he had chosen to lure me to his bed with professions of more than pure lust? Might I then have succumbed to his advances? What good did speculation serve? Of course it would not have made any difference, I told myself. Then why did I mentally belabor it? The last thing I cared about was Damien Darby's feelings for me. Jessica Darby had been wholly mistaken when she suggested that I had formed some attachment to her nephew. The suggestion that I loved him bordered on blasphemy. I did not even like the man. Certainly this knot in the pit of my stomach and the state of constant tumult he kept me in were not expressions of that most sacred of emotions.

Why did he have to do this? Why now? The cataloguing was almost completed. Why could we not have parted amicably with the quiet knowledge that we had managed to make the most of what had been a bad bargain for us both? Now what was I to do? I could not suffer the indignity of continuing to work with him, and yet if I fled Darby, I would only give him the satisfaction of knowing I had done what he expected of me. He thought me a simpering woman who would cower from anything. Pride told me I should leave, but it was pride, I knew, which would keep me here to see an end to the work I had started.

I realized that well over an hour had passed since I had left the studio. Whatever rage I felt towards Damien, I had promised to see that Chips was exercised. The little fellow certainly did not need to be penalized for his master's behavior. Since I had been dismissed for the afternoon and Sommers was not about, I decided I might as well take the spaniel for a run. If nothing else, the fresh air might prove salutary.

I dressed warmly. It was a cold sky. The landscape from the window showed no movement, save for a few grouse foraging in the peat hags under the crusted snow.

As I approached the studio my heart was pounding so furiously that it resounded in my ears. I paused some ten paces before the door, willing myself to be calm. I could not allow Damien to see me this distraught. I had to remain poised, deliberate. I was about to step forward when I heard a crash from inside the studio. I stood still, and then suddenly I realized that if Damien had fallen he might be hurt. There would be no one to hear him at this end of the house. I flew forward and began pounding on the door. It was with enormous relief that I heard the lock turn.

"Amanda," I gasped as she flung open the door, stared at me stonily, and swept by me without a word.

I was so startled that I did not at first see Damien, who had been directly behind her.

"What are you doing here, Lillith?" he demanded. "I thought I told you not to return here today."

"How dare you shout at me," I retorted. "I was doing you a favor. No, I was doing Chips a favor. Sommers is away, so I have come to walk him."

"How long have you been standing there?"

"Oh, I suppose now you are going to accuse me of spying on you again. From the look on Amanda's face, your own sister finds you as detestable as I do. And I have good reason to believe she is not the first."

"You do not know what you are saying, Lillith. If you came for Chips, then take him and leave me alone."

"Gladly," I answered, leaning down to the dog, who had maneuvered himself between us.

When I reached the center hall I looked about for Amanda, but she was nowhere in sight. Whatever Damien had said to her had obviously upset her greatly. Obviously no one was spared his mercurial temperament. Perhaps it was no wonder that Anitra had been frightened of him.

The wind whistled through the avenue of trees leading down to the stables. Chips darted on ahead, coming back every few moments and circling me, as if for reassurance that I would not abandon him. I reached the outer courtyard in time to see him bound inside. Despite my calls he did not return, so I followed him in, where I found that one of the grooms had him in hand.

"Hello," I said as the heavily bearded man pulled his woolen cap off and peered up at me.

"I am Miss Chatfield. Chips and I were just taking a walk."

He looked relieved. "Sure am glad ye didn't want me to be saddlin' up one o' the 'orses. Aye kin barely keep the stalls cleaned 'ere by myself."

"Surely you are not here alone," I ventured.

He picked up a set of loose shoes off a straw bale. "Today aye am. It's Wills's day off an' Heathy's up an' disappeared."

"What do you mean, disappeared?" I inquired.

He shrugged. "At first aye thought 'e'd just taken too much stout, like, but then 'is missus came round lookin' fer 'im."

"Has he gone missing before?"

"Naw. Oh, mind ye, 'e's a rowdy when 'e wants te be, but 'e's a good worker. Ye mark my words, 'e's fallen quarry te some misdeed."

"What makes you say that?"

He pulled out a large file and commenced shaping one of the iron shoes. "Ye can't 'ave bin round these parts too long. There's a lot o' strange things that goes on 'ere."

"Strange in what way?" I asked, puzzled.

He looked across at me. "Ye know, ye ask a lot o' questions. An' if ye take my advice, it ain't 'ealthy 'bout these parts. Besides, 'ow do aye know wasn't the lord 'imself sent ye down te find out what aye know?"

"I assure you nothing could be further from the truth."

"Whatever. But aye can't sit 'ere jabberin'. Ye better take the dog there an' 'ead on back. There's a storm brewin', an' aye've te bed the 'orses down or they'll be kickin' free o' their stalls."

I called Chips, who came to me reluctantly. As I started the climb up to the house I realized that though the air had warmed, a zephyr had rolled down from the north, causing the few remaining leaves to give up their perches and cascade in undulating sweeps to the hardened surface below.

I stepped up my pace and it was with some relief when I finally climbed the steps to the manor. I stood hesitantly in the reception hall wondering if I should return Chips to the studio. Damien had made it inordinately clear that he did not want to be disturbed, and since I had naught with which to occupy myself I decided to take the spaniel to my room. He appeared wary of following me but finally trotted after me up the staircase.

As I reached the landing I had the sudden sensation that I was not alone. I removed the hood of my cloak and saw ahead of me the figure of Mrs. Horsley.

"What's that dog doing up here?" she demanded as Chips approached her, sniffing up at the tray she was carrying.

"I am caring for him for the day," I explained.

"Well, keep him in tow," she commanded. "I don't need some beast roaming about where he doesn't belong."

"If that tray is for Amanda, I should be happy to take it to her," I offered.

"It's not," she replied, lumbering past me.

I put my hand down to Chips and he fell into step with me. I would not have seen it save that my eyes were trained downward on the dog. I bent down and picked up a cut rose very like the one Perse had given me days past. As I did, the petals, which had been preserved only by frost, fell onto the Tabriz below. I gathered them up, and as I straightened I caught sight of Mrs. Horsley watching me from the opposite end of the hall.

I started, for in clutching the thorny stem too tightly, I had pricked my index finger. Blood trickled from the puncture, and I placed my tongue to it to staunch its flow. When I looked up again Mrs. Horsley had disappeared. Where, I wondered, had she taken the tray? But I resisted following, for the incident on the staircase had made me more than a little frightened of her strength.

I passed the remainder of the afternoon writing a letter to Abraham. I chose my words carefully, using Marisse's explanation of the unreliable post to dismiss the problem of my letters having gone astray. He knew me well, and if he sensed I had any misgivings it would only increase his concern for me.

Shortly after five there came a knock at my door. Chips,

who had been curled at my feet, looked up expectantly as I bade my visitor enter.

"Am I disturbing you?" Amanda asked, peering round the door.

"Never," I assured her, thinking that her demeanor had certainly changed.

"I wanted to apologize for being so rude earlier."

"You need not apologize, Amanda," I said as she took a seat opposite me. "Frankly, I was worried about you."

"Nonsense," she said stoutly. "It was just a disagreement between Damien and myself. . . . You did not by chance overhear, did you?"

I shook my head.

"It is just as well," she said, as if relieved. "Damien was in a foul mood."

I could feel my cheeks grow red.

"Am I to assume that you two had another rift?" she pursued.

"I would rather not discuss it," I murmured.

"I saw his portrait of you today," she ventured. "It is quite extraordinary. But then, so is the model."

"You are too kind. But I did not sit for it. It was a great surprise to me."

"Damien is full of surprises. A faint smile played upon her lips. That is what makes him so attractive. He has an uncanny sense about people. Particularly women."

"I fear on that point I would disagree," I mused. "But then I do not pretend to know your brother."

"But you spend a great deal of time together," she persisted.

"He to his work and I to mine," I replied slowly.

She toyed with the heart-shaped amethyst about her neck. "And nothing more?"

I had the sense that she was being deliberately inquisitive, and though a part of me wanted to confide in her, I could not bring myself to do so. Damien, after all, was her brother, and

I could not ask her to take sides. Besides, I did not think I could suffer the embarrassment of relating our confrontation.

"Now I've gone and been a busybody," she exclaimed. "You must forgive me; I have so little opportunity to enjoy the conversation of women."

"It is not something I am very artful at," I admitted. "Father became a recluse of sorts after my mother passed away. My leisure was spent principally with my young brother Elijah."

"Now that you know him better, what do you think of Sir Charles Grout?"

Her question startled me only because he was the person furthest from my mind.

"Sir Charles?" I repeated. "I do not know. Perhaps if I set aside his duplicity in bringing me to Darby, I would find him quite pleasant."

"You are not taken with him then?" she pressed me.

"If you are asking whether I have any romantic notions, I assure you nothing could be further from my mind."

She drew forward in her chair. "You must think it foolish of me, but I had to know. He is certainly a champion of yours, and if I thought—"

"Are you saying you are interested in Charles?" I asked, amazed.

"He is attractive in a rather boyish fashion, don't you think? I rather thought a liaison might prove amusing."

She read my expression clearly, for she quickly added, "Oh, Lillith, you needn't look so shocked. The attention is not uncalled for. Father seems to have taken to him. Even Jessica is beguiled."

"I was only thinking that you scarcely know him. You might find in time that you had little in common."

Her eyes narrowed. "Is there some reason you are trying to dissuade me?"

"Of course not," I assured her.

"Then you will help me," she replied. "Of course, it must be our little conspiracy. 'Twould not do at all if anyone knew I had set my cap for him."

"Amanda, you can trust I will say nothing of this, but I cannot fathom how I can help you."

She rose and went to stand by the fireplace. "Well, as he seems to have a high regard for you, it might help matters if you were to make some considerate mention of me. I do not know—say something like how lonely it must be for Amanda in these northern climes, or 'tis a pity that Amanda is ensconced in that house alone, or I understand Amanda's husband's death left her a very wealthy woman or—"

"Amanda," I protested, "I could not possibly say any of those things. Indeed you almost sound as though you hope to appeal to his avarice, if he has any."

She smiled slowly. "Greed, my dear Lillith, is a seductive force. And since he has not exactly succumbed to my other charms, why should I not use my station as a lure of sorts?"

"Because you need not," I said emphatically. "You have beauty and kindness; he will not be blind to that."

She looked across at me. "Damien was right."

I stiffened at his name. "What does he have to do with this?"

"He finds you very sweet. A romantic, I think he called you."

"What Damien thinks is of little concern to me," I snapped. "And I resent being talked about. He would be far better served by addressing his own character. Or lack of it."

"A lack of character is not what Damien suffers from, Lillith," Amanda retorted. "You can accuse him of many things, but not that."

"I wonder if that would be Anitra's response," I murmured under my breath.

"Pardon me?"

I shook my head. " 'Tis nothing. I simply cannot bear to be the object of your brother's ridicule."

"That hardly sounds like one who is uninvolved," she reasoned.

"It is strictly a matter of decency, Amanda."

She smoothed the folds of her skirt. "Say what you will. I had better dress for dinner if I am going to be my most fetching for Charles."

"I had not realized it was so late."

Amanda crossed to the door. "You won't forget to play my champion, will you?"

"I will do what I can, Amanda," I assured her, "but I think you credit me with far too much influence. If you are to win Sir Charles, you will do it all on your own."

I sat and mulled over our conversation after she left. I told myself it was foolish of me to be put off by her blatant intentions towards Sir Charles. There was no reason that she should not desire to build a new life. It was a reasonable expectation for a woman of her age, particularly one with a young son. But I was dismayed by her aggressiveness. She made no attempt to veil her pursuit. Were it not Amanda, I would view her as brazen, but she was far from a shameless sort. In any event, it was not my place to stand in judgment. The last thing I knew about were affairs of the heart.

When Chips nudged my knee I started, realizing I not only had to dress but get him back to his master. My hand felt considerably improved, and I decided to remove the bandages. I remembered seeing a small sewing box in the closet and went to search it out. Carefully I lifted the chinoiserie papier-mâché box down and took it over to the dressing table. The satin tray at the top contained only a variety of threads. Lifting it I found a small pair of scissors below. As I withdrew them I realized that there was an envelope beneath. Placing the scissors aside, I picked it up, turning it to see if there was any writing on it. There was none, but whoever had penned its contents had taken the time to seal it. I shocked myself, prying at the cold wax without a second's hesitation. Had I lost all scruples since I had come to Darby?

I knew before I even unfolded the single sheet that I would find it written in Anitra's hand. But if I had hoped it would offer some insight into her mind and the mysteries at Darby, I was sadly disappointed. It read simply, "D, I have the proof I need. I am certain they will acquiesce rather than suffer the shame. It really needn't have come to this. A."

I read it several times before replacing it in the envelope. Why did I persist in this inquisition, I wondered. Each fragment that I happened upon, each provocative innuendo, drove me not closer but further from the truth. According to this note, Anitra, rather than fearing Damien, was in allegiance with him. She referred to proof, but proof of what? Who were "they"?

I picked up the scissors and awkwardly cut away at the gauze. My fingers were still stiff, but the fiery splotches had quieted, and I doubted there would be any scarring. Hurriedly I replaced the box in the closet and changed to a gold brocade gown. A knot formed in my throat as I smoothed the brocade-trimmed side aprons over the skirt. This and two other gowns had been the last gifts I had received from Father. I could still see him seated in his favorite chair, watching me lift the gowns, one after the other, from the enormous box which had been delivered. He was so pleased that he had dealt with the dressmaker all on his own. When I had asked him what the occasion was, he had smiled that slow faraway smile of his and said simply, "I am just proud of you, Lillith. And I wanted you to know that."

"How proud would you be of me now?" I murmured in challenge to the mirror's reflection.

I was glad the glass was silent, for I did not want to be taunted by what I knew would be the answer.

Calling Chips to me, I left the room and went to the back stairs. The light was gone and I was certain Damien would have abandoned the studio by now.

The candle burned bright as we began our descent. My slipper had just touched the lower floor when Chips broke into a run. I looked after him as he nearly collided with the figure of a man poised by the outer door. As I called to the dog, the man spun round. He hesitated but a moment, and then, almost like an apparition, he was gone. I moved forward tentatively. Though Chips had seemed untroubled, as if familiar with him, I felt somewhat unnerved by the sight of this man who fled furtively into the night without a word. He seemed a stranger to the manor—at least, he was a stranger to me.

222

I steeled myself before I knocked at the door to Damien's quarters. The door opened immediately. As Chips scampered past his chair, Damien looked up at me, his face distorted in such a pernicious mask that I stepped backwards.

"What are you doing here?" he demanded.

The flame from my candle flickered as I fought to steady my hand. I heard my name repeated again and again as I turned and fled back along the passage to the back stairs. Clasping the roughly hewn wood of the banister, I hauled myself back to the second floor. Sinking back against the wall, I struggled to regain my composure. What was it that caused me to react to Damien as I did? I knew his behavior; why did I expect anything else from him? And why did I always allow him the satisfaction of acting as he predicted I would? It was a pattern: he thwarted me and I ran. And then I always felt as I did at this moment—frustrated and vulnerable. Why could I not have said simply, "I was returning your dog, Damien. Nothing more."

With these thoughts buzzing in my head, I found myself at the top of the main staircase. I was so absorbed in the occurrence of the past moments that I did not hear anyone behind me. When a hand clasped my elbow, I gasped aloud.

"I did not mean to startle you, Lillith," Sir Charles said, pulling me to him. "You nearly tripped and fell down those stairs."

"I am all right," I assured him, embarrassed to find my face nestled against the curve of his shoulder.

"Then why are you trembling?" he persisted.

I drew away from him. "As you said, you startled me, that is all. We ought be getting down to dinner."

"I expect you are right, though I cannot feign much enthusiasm for these little family gatherings. I do not know how you have suffered it for so long."

I began my descent and he fell into step beside me. "Like you, I am being compensated for my tenure here. If I find the company less than amiable, it is not really relevant."

"I fear I am not so stoic," he murmured. "With the exception of Jessica Darby, you can keep the lot of them, as far as I am concerned."

"Surely you cannot mean that," I replied. "You have already indicated that you like Amanda."

I did not hear his reply, for there was a loud knock at the front door, and Sommers, who had been under the eave of the stairwell, strode forward to answer it.

I shuddered in the draft that whipped through the entry hall as we reached the bottom of the stairs. As Maude Farklan divested herself of her fur-trimmed cloak, she exclaimed, "I do not know why we had to come out on a night like this. I cannot tell you how tedious this is becoming."

James, who had seen us, strode forward. "How charming you look this evening, Lillith," he said effusively. "Seeing you takes the chill off one's bones."

I took his compliment as merely an attempt to silence his sister, who appeared embarrassed that she had been overheard.

At that moment Marisse flung open the drawing room doors. "I thought I heard voices," she exclaimed. "Come in and warm yourselves by the fire."

I followed her back through the double doors, feeling Damien's eyes following me as I went to sit by Jessica Darby.

"Where is Edmund?" James inquired.

"He is a bit under the weather," Marisse replied quietly.

"The poor dear, I fear all these discussions of financial matters are taking a toll on him."

"Nonsense," Jessica Darby said briskly. "There is no one who prefers talk of money more than my brother."

"Save perhaps Marisse," said Damien coldly.

Lady Maude, who had paused before a mirror and was primping the damp ringlets about her face, turned to say, "Well, I am far more interested to hear about the ball you are planning, Marisse."

Damien laughed, "My father will never acquiesce to such frivolity."

Marisse rearranged her lacy shawl, revealing the smooth curve of her shoulders. "Ah, but there you are mistaken, Damien. We discussed it over luncheon today, and I feel certain Edmund will give his blessing."

"What else is he to do, Marisse?" Amanda charged. "You have taken it upon yourself to extend invitations unbeknownst to him."

Marisse was clearly becoming agitated. "And what if I have? You know, when your father and I are married things are going to change around here. This house has been shuttered up for too long. You all have made it your own private mausoleum. Well, let me tell you, you have created more talk by retreating like this. And to what good, you—"

"I should like a sherry," said James, who had been standing some twenty paces away. He came quickly towards her, taking her arm. "What about you?"

"That is a fine idea," Jessica chimed in. "You know, Damien, I do not remember this house being so cold. There is a positive draft coming from the west wing. I spoke to Mrs. Horsley about it, but all she did was tell me I had allowed the fire in my room to burn too low. If you are so intent on making changes round here, Marisse, you ought to start by getting rid of that woman. She's a queer lot."

An odd expression came over Marisse's face. Her mouth

bowed in a supercilious grin. "Oh, I could not agree more, Jessica."

Damien, who had obviously begun imbibing long before we had gathered, downed a glass of port and returned the crystal to the onyx-topped table with a clatter.

"Mrs. Horsley stays," he said dully. "If you do not care for her, Marisse, you may take your leave of us."

I winced at the insult, fully expecting Marisse to give some retort, but James, whose arm was at her side, seemed to keep her in check.

Fortunately, Sommers announced that dinner was served and Damien set his chair in motion and led the awkward gathering from the room.

Were it not for Amanda, I should never have been able to endure the remainder of the evening. She was at her most charming, managing somehow to keep the conversation light, even amusing. I sensed she was making the effort for Charles's benefit and was heartened when there seemed to develop a warm repartee between them. I purposely avoided Damien's regard, though I was discomfited by the constancy of it. He was drinking heavily, and I sensed there were words or actions brewing within him which, if he were crossed, would be vented directly on me.

I learned a great deal about Charles that evening. Amanda had an ingenuous nature and elicited more information about him in two hours than I might have done in weeks. His mother, like mine, had died when he was very young. And whereas I had become the maternal figure for Elijah, he had an elder sister, Jane, who had nurtured him while his father immersed himself in the practice of law. The two were clearly very close, though the sister had married and now resided in Devon with her husband and two small children. I gathered that they were a family of some prominence and wondered if they might be acquainted with Rebecca's family.

It troubled me somewhat that his connections had come to

light, for the facts had piqued Maude's interest. We were almost finished with the warm berry tarts when Maude decided to try and monopolize him, and I could see Amanda was seething at the threatened rivalry.

When we left the dining room, Jessica Darby, who had been all but silent during dinner, drew me aside.

"I hate to intrude upon you, Lillith, but might you spare a moment and help me to my room? I do not know if it is these damnable chilblains, but I am feeling a bit unsteady."

"Of course I will," I assured her.

Charles, who was making for the drawing room, called out, "Are you coming, Lillith?"

I shook my head. "Please extend my apologies. I will see you on the morrow, I am certain."

As I put my arm through Jessica's, she murmured, "You need not have done that on my account."

"I did not," I told her.

"Well, Charles there looked clearly disappointed. And I gather he will not be the only one."

"On the contrary," I argued as I supported her up the stairs, "at least one of them will be delighted."

When we reached the landing, she guided me towards her room. Fortunately, the candles in the wall sconces still were effulgent, and we managed easily.

"You know, it *is* colder in this wing of the house," I murmured as I turned the handle of her door.

She tapped her cane on the floor. "There, you see? It is just as I said. Several times a day a draft comes through here that is unnatural, I tell you."

"Perhaps you should change your room," I offered.

She glowered at me. "Never. This is my room, and I shall not be put out. That is one of the few advantages of age, my dear. I can be as fractious as I choose, and no one dares contradict me."

"Save Mrs. Horsley."

She smiled up at me. "Touché. Perhaps that is why I find her so unpleasant. She does not bend to my whims."

"I do not think you are alone in your dislike of her."

"Am I to conclude that she has been less than obliging to you, Lillith?" she queried, pushing her glasses up on her nose.

"It is nothing, truly," I demurred. "I expect it was my fault in part. But I should let you rest now."

Jessica Darby limped towards the fireplace, where she sank into an early Jacobean chair covered in a faded animal tapestry. "Come sit with me for a while, would you? We have not have much opportunity to visit, and from the first I had the sense we might be kindred spirits, you and I."

"I fear I am not very good company these days," I apologized as I seated myself on the downy love seat opposite her.

She leant forward, the flame from the fire creating a silvery halo about her head. "I sense that something has changed for you at Darby since I first arrived here. On the one hand, you appear almost remote. And on the other, Lillith, I feel you are struggling with this detachment."

"It matters not, really," I sighed. "Soon I shall be gone from here, and Darby shall in time become simply a memory."

Her eyes roved my face. "Is that truly what you want, Lillith?"

"Why do people keep asking me what I want?" I bristled. "Do I seem so fey as not to know my own mind?"

Her eyes softened. "I am assuming that Damien is among the people you refer to. And I suspect that he is not inquiring of the determination of your mind, Lillith, but of your heart. My sight is diminished, my dear, but I see better than most. My nephew is not an easy man." She chuckled. "Lord knows, that is an understatement. But he is obviously taken with you. I have known him all his life, but never have I seen him like this. I watched him at dinner tonight. He could not take his eyes off you. Not that he was alone; though my niece was making an obvious play for Sir Charles, he would have far preferred to attend to you."

I knew not how to respond. She clearly meant to flatter me, but how could I tell this woman that she was mistaken? As with Amanda, I could not visit Damien's earlier indiscretion on her. That would be asking her to take sides. She had warmed to me, and certainly I had to her, but she knew her nephew less well than she thought.

"You need not respond, my dear," she continued. "You likely take me for an eccentric old spinster who harbors romantic notions personally unfulfilled. But life has not escaped me as fully as some might expect. It is selfish of me, but I should like to see Damien lead a full life. And that includes marriage and children. My brother wants the same thing, though I admit our motives are different."

"I am certain there are many women who would be happy to marry your nephew," I offered. "Lady Maude Farklan, for one."

She laughed lightly. "She is as avaricious as her brother, but not clever enough to capture my nephew. He has only disdain for her."

"He has disdain for women in general I fear," I charged.

"Not for you, Lillith," she countered. "You have managed to gain his respect, and unless I am off the mark you have also gained his love. He may not be able to articulate it, but I saw it straight off in his very regard of you. And deny these feelings as you might, you are as drawn to him as he is to you. Just the other night, when Damien and Edmund had their quarrel, I watched you. The concern in your expression was undeniable."

"I was horrified," I objected.

"I believe you were," she agreed. "As was I. But your countenance did not reflect the regard of employee for employer: your heart went out to him. And before you go looking so dour, let me tell you there could be worse things. True, I am his aunt, and I am prejudiced. And I would be the last to tell you that it would be an easy road to be married to Damien Darby. But any road worth traveling has its ruts."

"It would be the last road I would take," I argued, recoiling at the very suggestion.

"Do not be so quick to decide, Lillith," she implored. "If I am being selfish, then God forgive me. But though I find Edmund's scheme to bring you here quite despicable, I have found myself praying that you will accept his offer."

"You mean you actually expect me to marry Damien?" I murmured incredulously.

She nodded. "If you care for him as deeply as I suspect, then what could be the harm? I see by your expression that you think I have had more to imbibe this evening than tea, but I assure you of my sobriety. In that I may be unique amongst the Darbys. If it pains you to admit that you care for my nephew, then I beg you to try and see it from another perspective. You are a young woman alone. Capable, undeniably so, but with few prospects. Not that that might not quickly be remedied. I see how Sir Charles regards you. And with proper introductions, he would be only one of many. However, one has to be practical about these matters. Without benefit of social resources, with a need to support oneself, there would be little time, and subsequently little opportunity."

I felt myself stiffen. "So you are recommending that I marry Damien in order to escape the rather depressing future you foresee for me otherwise," I challenged.

"No," she argued emphatically. "I only suggested that because I suspect you are either too confused or too proud to admit to me—but more important to yourself—that you truly do care for Damien. Believe me, I am not saying these things to frighten you. If you give it consideration you will see that I would have no motive in that. Perhaps I simply do not want to see you make the same mistake that I did years ago. As I said, God help me if I am being selfish. But for reasons far too complex to detail, I want to see Damien married. He *needs* a woman in his life. I think he needs you, Lillith."

My mind was racing as I countered, "Why me?"

She shrugged. "Call it instinct. But I sense you might be the one person, the one woman who could enable him to rise out of this tangled web he has spun about himself."

"Are you saying you think Damien might walk again?" I asked, amazed.

Her hand rubbed the burnished silver handle of her cane. "That, I cannot say. What I referred to was escape more from an emotional, a mental confinement than a physical one. There may be a link. And there may not be. That would be your challenge."

I had experienced emotional turmoil in my life, but I had never felt so muddled, so little in control of my own being. My instinct was to dismiss her entreaties as the ramblings of an addled woman. And yet I could not. The more she talked, the more I questioned. Could it be possible that Jessica Darby, whom I barely knew, had perceived something which I had not seen within myself? Had my confusion these past months had less to do with Anitra and Father and Elijah than with Damien?

"Hmm," Jessica Darby murmured. "You are perhaps a bit suspicious."

"Suspicious?"

"That Edmund has put me up to this."

I shook my head. "I had not even considered it."

"You will," she concluded. " 'Twould be only natural. But let me assure you my brother has nothing to do with this. Oh, he would no doubt be ecstatic if he thought I was pleading his case, but I promise you that our motives are disparate."

I took a deep breath. "I do not know what to say to you. The idea that I marry Damien is inconceivable to me. Even, at the wildest stretch of the truth, if you were correct that my feelings for him are greater than I have admitted, what makes you think that he would even begin to entertain this proposal?"

"Damien will do what his father commands," she replied resolutely.

I felt myself stiffen. "You know, I am terribly confused. You seem to express great feeling for Damien, and yet you would be as quick as his father to condemn him to some emotional penury."

"Ah, that is where you mistake me," she countered. "My only want is to see him escape it."

"And you think I could help him do that?"

"I would hope so."

"But why should I?" I demanded.

"Only you can answer that, Lillith," she replied quietly.

I wrung my hands together. "Even if you are right and I do have deeper feelings for Damien, to what end? Are you suggesting that I return to the studio now and say to him, 'Oh, by the by, Damien, your Aunt Jessica thinks we are well suited and should marry. When would you like to post the bans?' "

Her eyes narrowed. "Cynicism does not become you, Lillith. But I cannot fault you. I would be disappointed if you did not display some question, some anger at this advice of mine. But if, on reflection, you conclude that I am less than mad, admit that there is only one recourse. And that is to accept my brother's offer to you."

"What?" I gasped.

"Before you express shock, let me explain. To admit feelings for Damien is going to be a large enough challenge. I do not expect, if you were to do that, that you would then go to him and declare yourself. My brother's offer, though it insults your pride, is not without merit. No matter what the outcome, you would be secure for life. That may not mean much to you now, but five or ten years from now it could make a great difference."

I was incredulous that this woman, who on the one hand suggested that I had developed an emotional attachment for her nephew, would in the same breath suggest that I should profit from him. She had read me improperly. Her very suggestion that I avail myself of Lord Darby's offer was so repugnant to me I actually shuddered at the thought.

"I fear, Lady Jessica, you have wholly misjudged me," I said emphatically. "I am neither an opportunist nor a fortune hunter. I am not without resources. Though I admit to you my prospects at present are dim, I have managed thus far. Even if I were to admit to having feelings for Damien, I could never be a party to this sadistic scheme of his father's. It would give me even greater reason to decry it."

"Perhaps," she admitted, "but it might be the only way."

I could not believe that she was persisting in this absurdity. "Let me phrase it differently. What do you think Damien's reaction would be? You cannot think that he would welcome the idea? He found it as despicable as I from the first. Why would he feel any different today?"

She sighed. "Because I am certain that Damien is in love with you, Lillith."

"Damien does not know the meaning of love," I scoffed. "He taunts me, he tests me—but loves me? No, I think not. I am not certain that Damien cares for anyone beyond himself, and I do not even know how much he likes himself."

"I cannot blame you for thinking that," she conceded. "But if you had known him before . . ."

"You mean before the accident?" I finished.

She nodded.

"Damien never speaks of it," I offered. "In fact, no one does. I have said before it is almost as if you all pretend it never happened."

She suddenly looked very tired. "It was a very sad time, Lillith. 'Twould come to no good to dwell on what is done."

"I can understand that, Lady Jessica. I shall never fully recover from my own loss. But I can still talk about Father and my young brother. Indeed, it is often some consolation to remember them. But the very mention of Lady Darby and particularly of Anitra is taboo. Even the servants have been intimidated to the point of silence."

"There are things that are best laid to rest. Opening old wounds could serve no one well."

"Save perhaps Damien. It is he who carries the burden, the misplaced guilt. 'Tis no wonder he is so full of rage."

She looked up suddenly as the clock chimed eleven.

"It is late," I acknowledged. "I am certain you are tired."

"Truthfully I am not. But the doctor has me on a regimen of rest and medicines which he insists is keeping me alive. I tend to think 'twill be what kills me, but I continue to humor him."

I stood up. "Might I borrow this?" I asked, fingering the brass candle holder on the table. "Just until the morning, of course."

"Please," she consented. "That Mrs. Horsley darkens the hallways so early is ridiculous. It is not as though we cannot afford candles. I have been hearing noises night after night, but I would not dare venture out to investigate in that blackened space."

I paused halfway to the door. "What kind of noises?"

"Now I have gone and frightened you," she fretted. " 'Tis nothing, truly. Nothing ominous, in any event. I should not let that woman rankle me so."

I sighed, realizing that she could offer no information which would give a clue to the strange nightly occurrences I had experienced since coming to Darby.

"I hope you will sleep well," I said.

She peered across at me. "I would rest far better if you would assure me that you will at least think on what I have suggested."

I nodded. "That is easy, since I cannot imagine that I should be able to blot it at will from my mind. At the same time I want you to know that I cannot consider it. My place is not here at Darby—and it is certainly not with Damien."

The door clicked behind me, but I stayed there a moment leaning against it. I felt so drained. When I finally started down the hall it seemed an effort just to put one foot in front of the other. Reaching my room, I undressed by rote. Even the soft down of the bed did not seem welcoming. I tossed, pulling at the constricting covers. It was preposterous, I told myself. If I had told her of Damien's earlier actions, if I had recounted the endless squabbles, if she knew that I had found proof that his own sister feared him, she would never have suggested that we had any feelings for each other. She could not have been serious that I should consider Lord Darby's offer. Yet I knew she had been. And something told me that Jessica Darby was not only a woman without malice but a woman of perception. By age alone she was my superior. Was I, as she had suggested, blinded by stubborn pride? I had qualms about what the future would hold, and yet I had remained silent on that subject. Although I had fallen sadly behind in the cataloguing these past days, with diligence I knew the task would soon be completed. Was my argument that I was not without prospects mere bravado to cover my real fears?

It was ridiculous, I silently chastised myself. Even if the future now appeared dim, the unknown could not be so ominous as to require that I compromise myself. Marriage to Damien was not an answer. I would have the nobility and protection of the Darby name, but nothing else. I could not imagine a life based on a loveless union. And to accept Lord Darby's offer would be an act of pure greed. Damien would never agree to it. And his father could not force him to marry me. Or could he?

But to what end? If Damien displayed antipathy for me now, what would that become if he were bound to me in marriage? Whatever feeling he might have had for me would quickly turn to loathing.

Tears dampened the corners of my eyes as I stared at the

shadows cast on the ceiling by the dying fire. There seemed such futility about it all. I had thought those last days at Bostworick Hall, with the pain and indignities I suffered then, to be the worst of my experience. Had I known that they were simply a precursor to these dark days, I wondered if I could have mustered the strength to go on.

15

I AWAKENED to the sound of knocking at my door.

"Who is there?" I called out.

" 'Tis me, Miss Lillith," Mary's voice called back to me.

Wearily I swung my legs from the bed and, fumbling with my robe, scurried across the chilly floor.

"What time is it?" I asked as she swept passed me and set the tray down.

"Nigh unto eight," she replied gaily. "Ye musta bin exhausted. Yer usually up with the birds."

"The odd thing is that I do not feel as though I slept a wink," I said.

"The tea an' biscuits will perk ye up," she advised. "Aye

won't be doin' yer room till later. With Flo gone aye've got double the load."

I sat down before the tray and removed the cozy from the glazed pot. "Who is Flo?"

Mary pulled the white circle cap down over her unruly curls. "Ye remember 'er. That day ye came te the kitchens she let ye in. Real young kind o' brazen type, but pretty, leastways the men always gave 'er a big play. Remember I told ye she just seemed te disappear a while back."

I sipped at the tea. "Vaguely. Do you know where she went?"

Mary shrugged. "Just up an' left, aye guess. Aye thought she'd gone 'ome fer a visit, but then Mrs. 'Orsley just says Flo won't be back an' they're not replacin' 'er. If aye didn't need this spot aye'd a mind te quit meself. But aye shouldn't be troublin' ye with this."

"You never trouble me, Mary," I assured her. "Frankly, there are days when I do not know how I would make it through without your morning cheerfulness."

Lines furrowed her brow. "Ye 'aven't been 'appy 'ere at Darby, 'ave ye, Miss Lillith?"

"I have nothing to complain about, Mary," I replied thoughtfully. "Compared to you I live like a lady of leisure here."

"For a while aye thought . . ."

"Yes?"

"Well, aye thought maybe that ye an' Master Darby . . . aye mean spendin' so much time an' all—"

"Damien is my employer, Mary, nothing else," I replied resolutely.

" 'Tis a pity 'es in that chair," she ventured. " 'E always looks so sad, kinda far away, if ye know what aye mean. But 'e's always been good te me. Takes the time te ask me 'bout me mum an' all."

It surprised me that Damien was solicitous of anyone other than himself.

"Now that Sir Charles, there's someone if aye was grand aye'd set me cap fer," she rambled on. "A real gent, 'e is. Always got a smile an' a 'ow-do. Real different from the Darbys."

I sensed she was baiting me, but I was not about to bite. Amanda's interest in Sir Charles had been a confidence. As fond as I was of Mary, I could not chance that she might inadvertently say something that would translate to gossip.

I stood up. "You may take this tray, Mary. I really am not very hungry."

She appeared disappointed but within moments she had removed it and left me alone.

I dressed quickly, noticing as I plaited my hair that my hand was far more limber. At least I could be thankful for that. I needed to make great strides these next days if I were soon to commence the next uncertain journey in my life.

When I had finished dressing I looked into the mirror. "Get a hold of yourself, Lillith Chatfield," I instructed my reflection.

As I went down to the studio I pondered my conversation with Mary. Something she had said had struck a distant chord. It had something to do with the girl, Flo, but I could not fathom what it was. I was so deep in thought that when the door to the library was suddenly flung open I jumped back.

"Lord Darby," I gasped, "you startled me."

For a second I thought he was ignoring me, but as I looked up at the figure looming in the doorway I became alarmed. His face was ashen, and he clutched the doorframe for support.

"Are you all right?" I cried, darting forward.

His voice barely audible, he said, "In the left drawer of the desk. The bottle. Bring it to me."

My heart was pounding as I brushed past him. I breathed a sigh of relief as my fingers closed about the dark green vial.

I raced back to him and he snatched it from me. The cork fell from his hands as he gulped desperately at the contents.

Moments passed. The fiery agony which had distorted his face suddenly abated, and as if dappled by a painter's brush, color flooded back to his skin.

"Might I help you?" I offered tentatively as he turned to go back into the room.

He looked down on me, and for one instant I read gentleness in eyes which until now had seemed as cutting as a northern zephyr. "Just stay with me a while," he murmured, sinking into the cushions of the love seat.

I did as he bade, taking a seat opposite him.

"You needn't look so serious, Lillith," he said. "I am not going to expire. At least, not at this moment."

I drew a deep breath. "I am sorry. But you can well understand my concern."

He rubbed his chin pensively. "I do believe you actually are concerned."

"Why would I not be?"

A smile played about his mouth. "I do not deceive myself that I am a favorite of yours, my dear."

"We are not opponents, Lord Darby."

"Neither are we comrades," he reminded me.

"No," I replied slowly, "but I expect by this point we ought to put our differences aside. 'Twill not be long before I am gone from Darby. Neither of us got what we bargained for, but then we both made bad bargains."

He regarded me quizzically. "Am I to take it that you regret your decision to do this cataloguing for my son?"

"I needed employment, and Damien provided it."

"If you had taken my offer you need never have worked again."

"We both know it was untenable," I argued.

His brows knitted together. "Curious. I rather thought the two of you had taken to each other."

"Then you are mistaken, Lord Darby," I was quick to answer.

"And where will you go from here?"

I loathed admitting that I did not know.

"Well, if you should have a change of heart, Lillith, you need only let me know. My offer stands. It is not an unattractive one. Say the word and I shall have Sir Charles draw up the papers."

I rose. "You can keep your money, Lord Darby. Though I know I overstep my bounds, forgive me if I suggest that you not seek to make another arrangement. Damien is not a pawn to be toyed with. He is many things, but he is foremost a brilliant artist. That is the part of your son which should be encouraged."

He was clearly rankled. "I want an heir, Miss Chatfield. Nothing more. You can give me that. Since you seem so vehement about my son's talent, perhaps I ought to make an addendum to my original offer. I will see that Damien's paintings receive the attention you think they deserve, if you will marry him. I cannot guarantee his success, but if your instincts are correct his work should soon be sought after."

"Lord Darby," I began.

He put his hand up to silence me. "You ought to learn to be less quick to respond. The wisest decisions demand thought."

I strode past him. "Unless there is something else you need I must get to the studio."

"There is only one thing, Lillith," he replied. "I should be most grateful if you made no mention of this little spell of mine. There is no need to go alarming the household. And as you can see, I am quite recovered."

I agreed, though I did not think it wise. I cared little for the man, but he was obviously unwell. I was not certain that any of the household realized the seriousness of whatever malady plagued him.

I left the library and went directly to the studio. The lock turned quickly in response to my knock.

Chips bounded to the doorway and nuzzled my hand.

"What are you doing here?" Damien demanded.

"I think I rather prefer Chips's greeting," I quipped.

"After your theatrics of yesterday I did not expect you to return here."

"I shall try to overlook that comment," I retorted. "If you do not mind, I should like to get to work. We have lost quite enough time as it is."

"The model of efficiency," he jeered, wheeling back so that I might pass.

I clenched my teeth as I swept past him to my work table.

"I see that your hand is recovered," he remarked as he went past me towards his easel.

"Quite nicely, thanks to Amanda," I replied, hauling the bulky ledgers towards me.

I did not know what I expected of him this day, but I was enormously relieved when the silence of the morning spread before me. It took me a good half hour to get back into the rhythm of the work, but when I finally laid the portfolio of sketches aside, I realized that I had made great progress.

I withdrew the next lot, and as I leafed through the series of pen and ink images I recognized that these were of the Darby stables. I had begun recording them when something clicked. "That is it," I murmured.

"That is what?" Damien inquired.

I stared across at him. "Oh, 'tis nothing. Just something that Mary said."

"Are you going to let me in on the secret?" he persisted.

I shrugged. "It is scarcely a secret. One of the stablehands has disappeared. And Mary told me that one of the serving girls left about the same time. I was simply postulating that there might be some connection."

He appeared amused. "Such a fanciful notion for one who allows no passion in her life."

I lowered my eyes as a wave of heat raced through my body. "I warned you it was of no consequence."

He laughed. "Not to you perhaps, but I expect it is of monumental consequence to the stablehand."

I dipped the pen in the inkwell and drew the sketches closer.

"I am going to stop for a while," he continued. "Would you care to take lunch with me?"

"Actually I was going to ask Cook if I might have a tray in here," I replied.

"It is up to you. I expect I ought tell you that I shall be gone from Darby for a day or two."

"Does that mean that I shall not have access to the studio?"

He looked round. "I expect you can do no harm. I shall leave the key on the sill above the door. But I do not want anyone else in here. Do you understand?"

I did not truly comprehend why he insisted that his work be guarded so jealously from the sight of others, but I agreed. It was small consolation that I might continue with the cataloguing, and I did not want to risk his changing his mind.

"What will you do with Chips?" I inquired.

"I shall take him down to the stables, I expect."

The spaniel, who seemed to understand his master's words, regarded me woefully.

"I should be happy to keep him," I offered. "He is accustomed to me now."

"You are certain it would not be an imposition?"

I assured him it would not.

"Then I shall see that Cook sends a tray round for you," he said as he wheeled towards the door. "I shan't ask if you will miss me. It would be tempting to think that you might, but I expect it would be asking too much of my proper Miss Chatfield."

243

My eyes were trained on the back of his chair as it receded from me; I thought he was well through the door when his voice carried back to me. "Not even a wish for a safe journey, Lillith?"

I drew a deep breath. "Be safe, Damien," I managed to say.

16

T H E R E was a different mood about Darby with Damien absent. I had hardly considered him to be the catalyst of the family, and yet the household seemed almost adrift without him. I knew not how long he would be gone, but I decided to use the time to best advantage. I took all but my evening meals in my room, keeping mostly to the studio and making occasional forays out with Chips.

Sensing that Amanda felt snubbed by my refusal to take luncheon with her two days in succession, I finally acquiesced to a late-afternoon tea. I was surprised to find Terrence in her company. I did not know how the child spent his days, but obviously he was not allowed the run of the house. And with

Amanda putting her affairs in order with Charles, I suspected he was alone far more than was healthy for a child of his age. I had been tempted to ask if I might care for him during the day, but Damien had been so specific about not wanting anyone in the studio that I was loath to chance it.

As I watched her pour a cup of the steamy brew, I thought there was an uncommon tension about Amanda this day. She seemed particularly thoughtful, and having handed me the tea, her fingers withdrew and plucked anxiously at the textured threads of her gown.

"Your gown is most becoming," I said admiringly.

"I am glad someone noticed," she replied dryly. "Sometimes I think if I were to attend these meetings with Charles in nothing more than my petticoats he would take no notice."

I laughed. "I trust you say that in jest."

"No, I do not," she said with some heat. "He is so damnably businesslike. I am beginning to wonder if anything can shake him."

"I am certain he is eager to please your father, Amanda," I offered.

"Well, he is being most uncooperative," she complained. Terrence squirmed off the seat beside her. "I had hoped I might make more progress before . . ."

I waited for her to complete the sentence, but she changed the subject.

"Enough of me. Tell me about you, Lillith."

"I fear I have little to relate these days," I admitted. "Save that I realize my work here is almost at an end."

"And then what do you intend?"

"I shall go to London," I replied. "Once I have secured accommodations there I shall go south briefly, to visit a friend who has been ailing. And then I expect I shall have to search for a position."

"I wish you would consider your other option, Lillith. You strike me as so sensible about most things, and yet I find your dismissal of my father's offer foolhardy."

"Why is it that you all think I should even entertain such a proposal?" I said with asperity. "Do you not understand that even if I agreed, even if Damien agreed, it would not be a solution for anyone."

"There I disagree," she argued earnestly. "My father wants to see Damien married. Why not give him what he wants. In a manner of speaking, of course."

"And what does that mean?" I inquired.

She leant forward in her chair. "Look, Lillith, my father has only so much influence. He can see you wed to Damien, but he has no control over whom you do or do not take into your bed. If you were to accept his offer you would have money, position; you would want for nothing. You would be mistress of Darby, and you could do it without ever being a mistress to Damien."

"I cannot believe you of all people would suggest such a thing," I exclaimed.

Her eyes widened. "And why not? Frankly I see it as the ideal arrangement for us all."

"I cannot think what importance it could have for you."

She took a sip of tea and replaced the cup on the silver tray. "It is very simple really. My father would have what he wants, or he would think he did. You would remain here, and I should not lose one who has become a good friend. And Damien would have his rightful inheritance and yet also his freedom."

"His freedom?" I gasped. "You think that to be married to a woman he does not love is freedom?"

"It might be hard for you to understand, but yes, Lillith, for Damien that would be a liberty which I rather think would suit him well. I know you have trouble believing it, but he likes you. I rather think he even respects you. Would it be so wrong to enter into an arrangement of mutual benefit? You should be free to come and go as you please and Damien could continue his work, but with my father's blessing. You would never need fear any unwanted intimacy and in time you might—if you were discreet, of course—even manage to take a lover."

I stared at her incredulously. "You know if I were not certain that I was sitting here with you, Amanda, I should swear I was having hallucinations. I am astounded you would champion such deceit. I thought you and Damien were close. I thought you loved him."

"It is because I love him that I beg you to consider it," she implored. "I know it seems selfish on my part, Lillith, but it is not wholly so, for you would have gained as well. Oh, I know you are independent of mind and think you can go off and secure employment and be content as a governess or whatever you intend to become, but I wish I could make you see the fallacy of it. You have breeding, Lillith, and to find yourself destitute as a drudge in some household would be such a waste."

"Beyond it being preposterous," I retaliated, "there is one enormous flaw in your plan, Amanda; your father wants Damien married, but solely to beget an heir. When there is no child, what do you think should happen to me then?"

She fingered the silken tassels along the front pleat of her gown. "Have you never heard of a barren woman? 'Twould be a pity, of course, but he could not condemn you for that. Besides, unless you have not noticed, my father is not a well man. I know he tries to keep the extent of his illness from us, but I am not blind to it. One day he shall pass on. And then there would be nothing to keep you here, unless of course you chose to stay."

I was appalled at the callousness with which she discussed her father's impending demise. I had felt so close to Amanda, and yet at this moment I wondered if I might have misjudged her. I started to explain how impossible her suggestion was when there was a loud yelping from the far side of the room.

I turned to see Terrence wielding a poker at Chips, who was cowering in obvious pain. I sprang up and went to him, placing myself between the boy and the dog. As I extended my hand to remove the implement from his grasp, he flung it, the blackened tip just grazing the side of my skirt.

Amanda, who until now had been a silent witness to this, bolted forward and, grasping the child by the linen collar of his shirt, shook him so furiously that I feared she might do him harm. Reaching forward I clasped her wrist, loosening her grip.

"Amanda, he is only a child," I exclaimed. "I am certain he did not comprehend what he was doing."

As she whirled about, I started. Her eyes were wild with rage. "Stay out of this, Lillith."

I looked down at the boy, amazed by the placid expression on his face. He had not cried out once, indeed he appeared almost unperturbed by the entire incident.

"Go up to your room at once," Amanda ordered as I stood transfixed before her. When the child did not move she grabbed his arm and, thrusting him forward, said, "I am sorry you had to be witness to this, Lillith."

"It is not so serious as all that. Perhaps—"

"Forgive me, but this is between Terrence and myself," she apologized. "You and I will talk later."

I stood stock still as she pulled the child from the room. It was only when I heard Chips whimper that I remembered I was not alone. I knelt down on the needlepoint carpet, entreating the frightened spaniel to come to me. Assured that the danger was past, he wiggled towards me, nuzzling into my encircling arms as I whispered reassurance. I ran my hands over his body to ascertain that no harm had come to him.

"What do you say we take a walk, my friend? I expect we could both do with a bit of fresh air."

His tail beat appreciatively.

"Then you wait here while I fetch a wrap."

I went quickly to my room, changed my walking shoes to sturdier boots, and fetched my cloak.

Chips awaited me patiently where I had left him in the morning room, and within minutes we were descending the mellow stone steps to the drive. The weather had warmed since the storm of several days past and here and there the earth showed through the melting snow. As Chips bounded down through the avenue of trees I followed in pursuit. It was late afternoon, with the winter sun casting soft illumination over the landscape.

I drew a deep breath, releasing ghostlike vapors as I expelled it. The events of the afternoon weighed heavily on me. Amanda's suggestion seemed so calculated. She seemed utterly unabashed in recommending that I dupe her own father. Yet the incident with Terrence preoccupied me even more. I had been quick to come to his defense, arguing that he was only a child, but that was because I saw no virtue in corporal punishment.

Moreover, there was something about the boy that alarmed me. He was so taciturn; it struck me I had never seen even a suggestion of a smile cross his face. Of course, there was a certain tedium for him at Darby. Certainly, I had never seen anyone shower attention on him. And probably Amanda was right in believing that he needed a male figure whom he might emulate. But that did not explain the viciousness with which he had attacked the spaniel. I wished that I might be able to discuss this matter with Damien. He was, after all, the boy's uncle, and though not given to selfless acts, he might see the wisdom of taking the boy under his wing.

I looked ahead, and realizing that Chips had vanished from view I quickened my pace. I soon learned his whereabouts, for he had commenced a fury of barking. Following the sound, I made my way down to where the series of pools spilled to form a small lake. A thin veil of ice formed a natural dam, and where there had once been a rushing cascade the stream only trickled into the body of water below.

I called out to the spaniel as he darted to the ornamental arches, but he paid me no heed.

"You silly dog," I scolded as I reached him, " 'tis likely some rabbit that has built its warren near the warmth of the stone."

When he scampered suddenly to the water's edge I decided I could allow him his freedom no longer. I reached him and grabbed at the scruff of his neck, but he wrestled from me and resumed his barking.

Realizing that he was intent not on the reedy embankment but on the lake itself, I peered out to where his frenzy seemed to be directed. At first I thought it was a growth of fronds reaching from the depths, but as I trained my eyes upon it I recoiled in horror. The lumpy mass was no vegetation. Unless my eyes deceived me, it was a body. I was trembling and I could taste the bile of my own fear, but I knew that I had to be certain. I bade Chips to be silent and turned back to the inert form but an inch from the water's edge. I needed no one to tell me that life had long ebbed from this man whose face stared blankly into the watery element. His clothing was dark, and one leg was somehow buoyed up. I knew those boots. They were the kind the men wore down at the stables. That poor man, I agonized. I had imagined him running off with young Flo, when in fact he had met his untimely demise.

I turned away from the lake, commanding Chips to follow me. Dusk was turning into dark and there was nothing I could do but bring this news to the house as quickly as possible.

My billowing cloak hampered my movement, and I almost cried out in relief as I reached the drive and saw the house looming before me. It was only then I realized an icy rain had begun falling.

I ran across to the entrance, taking the steps pell-mell. There were a few more to climb when my boot slid out from under me. I thrust my hands out to break my fall, but my body careened down along the icy steps until I came to rest

251

some eight feet below. Pain shot through my leg, and I struggled to right myself. Chips had recommenced his barking, for
which I was grateful, as it was immediately evident that my
spill had wounded more than my pride.

When the doors opened I was actually happy to see Sommers, who, taking a quick stock of the situation, told me to
stay put until he could fetch help. Only seconds later he
reappeared with Sir Charles beside him.

"Good grief, Lillith," Charles exclaimed as he reached me.
"Are you hurt?"

"I am not certain," I admitted as he knelt beside me. "I am
afraid it is my ankle."

He instructed Sommers to support my other side while he
drew me up.

"Can you put weight on it?"

I shook my head.

"Then we will simply lift you up. Just one step at a time."

I felt almost faint by the time we reached the reception hall.

Without a word Charles curled his arms about me and
swept me off the floor. As he placed my head on his shoulder
I felt his lips lightly brush my forehead.

"Where are you taking me?" I whispered.

"The library," he replied.

Sommers moved ahead of him, opening the doors.

"Well, isn't this touching," came Damien's voice from
across the room.

"This is not a joke, Damien," Charles charged as he lowered
me gently onto the silk couch. "She's had a nasty spill, likely
seeing to your dog there."

"Listen to me, both of you," I insisted. "I shall be quite all
right, but something terrible has happened. I was down by
the lake, and there is a body there, floating not far from the
edge."

Damien had wheeled his chair over to where I lay. "Over
there on the side tray, Charles. Get her a brandy."

I struggled to pull myself up. "I do not want a brandy," I

cried. "Are you deaf? I just told you there is a body in the lake. Unless I am very mistaken, it is one of the stablehands."

Hands clasped my boot. "What are you doing?"

"Lord, you are a fidget," Damien chided as he undid the laces.

I squirmed back from him but winced as the pain seared through my leg.

"You never learn, Lillith," Damien murmured as he pulled the boot from my fast-swelling foot.

Charles approached, handing me a small snifter of brandy.

"I said I do not want it," I insisted.

"In this case I have to agree with Damien."

"Charles, please, I beg you. Listen to me."

"I will, Lillith, I promise, but first drink the brandy."

I grimaced as I swallowed the amber liquid, which seemed to scorch the lining of my throat. I handed the glass back to Charles, who remained hovering over me. "You are both treating me like a child," I exclaimed. "A man lies dead in the lake and you behave as though nothing has happened."

"Lillith, you are in shock," said Damien firmly.

"What is it you thought you saw, Lillith?" Charles inquired, placing a pillow beneath the small of my back.

"It is not what I *thought* I saw," I argued. "If you will not go down there, then send someone."

"If you have not noticed, it has started to storm," Damien advised. "Besides that, it is pitch dark out there. If as you say there is a man's body in the lake, we can do naught for the chap tonight. I will have it looked into in the morning."

I turned to Charles, but just then Marisse entered the library. "Damien, when did you get back?"

Before he could reply she continued, "What is going on here? What is wrong with Lillith?"

"She took a fall," Charles supplied. "It appears she may have injured her ankle."

Marisse came to stand over me. "You certainly are prone to accidents, my dear."

"Do not let her compassion overwhelm you, Lillith," Damien murmured.

"If you would be so kind as to hand me my boot, I should like to go to my room," I requested.

"And how do you think you are going to do that?" Damien charged.

I swung my legs from the couch and snatched at the boot he had placed on the floor. Beads of perspiration formed on my brow as I struggled to pull the leather over my swollen foot.

"Aunt Jess," Damien called out, "I am glad you are here. Perhaps you can talk some sense into our Miss Chatfield."

"I would thank you, Damien, for allowing that I know what is for my own good," I snapped. "You ought to be far more concerned about that poor soul down in the lake."

I did not have an opportunity to continue, for there was a knock at the door and Sommers announced that the Farklans had arrived. Struggle as I did to replace my boot, it would simply not accommodate my foot.

"Charles, if you might be so kind, I expect I must have someone to lean on, just until I get up the stairs."

Jessica Darby thrust her cane forward, blocking his path. "Don't you do as she asks," she commanded. "The last thing she ought to do is navigate those stairs. There are rooms down here. One of the maids can set one up quickly, and Lillith can remain there until she can walk again."

"Really, all this fuss is unnecessary," I said despairingly.

Damien wheeled his chair back. "You are right. There is a far simpler solution. Lillith can stay in my quarters."

James Farklan had entered the room behind Marisse. "Obviously I have missed something here."

Leaning on the rolled arm of the couch, I pushed myself to a standing position. As I did so, my leg buckled under me. I expect I would have fallen if Charles had not been beside me so quickly.

"I think you had best come with me," Damien said.

Without a word Charles swept me into his arms and followed Damien.

"This is jolly entertaining," James Farklan said, chuckling.

"Please put me down, Charles," I begged as he carried me along the hallway through the doors towards Damien's suite of rooms.

"Lillith, it is only temporary," he argued. "Just until we can fetch a doctor and get you on your feet."

Tears welled in my eyes. "Please, I do not want a doctor. I just want to go to my room."

He slowed his gait. "You sound almost frightened," he murmured.

I bit my lip. Of course I am frightened, I thought, but how do I tell you that? Months ago Charles would have been the last person I trusted, so why did I feel that I might confide in him now? And what was I to confide?

"You have had a nasty scare," he continued. "The shock of such a fall is nothing to dismiss, Lillith. But we'll have you to rights again very soon."

I wished I had not acquiesced and taken the brandy, for my head was spinning. I clutched at the fold of his sleeve. "Charles, do me one favor. Fetch Amanda. Bring her here, please."

"Of course, if that is what you want," he assured me.

We moved through the parlor of Damien's suite. "You can take her in there," he advised. "There is a candlestick by the bed. Fetch it for me and we can light the sconces."

As much as I had fought, I felt relief as Charles eased me onto the soft bed. He returned almost immediately with the lighted candle, using it to illuminate the gilt wall lights. When he finished he turned to leave.

"Where are you going?" I demanded.

"I will be right back, Lillith," he answered.

I lay very still, my eyes roving over the circumference of the room. I was ever amazed by the unexpected detail given to Darby. The paneling was exquisite, the cornice enriched

255

with pairs of carved consoles. The window-reveals were delicately carved and gilded, festooned with curtains of ivory silk brocade, fringed and pelmeted. And yet here again there was a disquieting force to the room. Between the fluted Ionic pilasters framing the doorway was a vigorously carved head, horned and laughing, protruding from the architecture. The entablature of the door was supported by bolection molds of writhing snakes. The overall effect was a strange counterpoint of beauty and beast, of good and evil.

When Charles returned Damien was with him.

"If you can manage to lie still for a few minutes, I'll have a look at that ankle," Damien offered. "I would send for Rendcomb, but I am afraid in this weather he would never make it."

"I do not need you or anyone else to fuss about me," I countered. "What should suit me best is to go back to my room."

"Well, then, you are not going to be very happy, because you are not going anyplace," Damien argued. "You will be undisturbed here. I will see to it that one of the maids fetches your clothing and whatever else you might need, and then in the morning we can see about getting a doctor."

"I really don't think you have a choice, Lillith," Charles counseled.

I lay back against the pillows. "Would you ask Mary to come?"

"Damien, I will stay here with her," Charles offered. "Just until the maid comes."

Damien looked from one to the other of us. "Let it not be said that I would interfere."

I waited until I heard the latch of the outer door before turning to Charles. "I am quite certain of what I saw down in the lake. I am not deluded."

"I did not suggest that you were, Lillith," he replied, coming closer. "It must have given you a terrible turn. You indicated you knew who it was."

"I am certain of it. I just know it is the stablehand. The one they call Heathy."

"The best thing you can do is put it from your mind, Lillith," he suggested.

"No, that I cannot do," I insisted. "I have to know what happened."

He studied me curiously. "The chap obviously had an accident. You do not expect it is other than that?"

"I do not know," I murmured.

"Lillith, you cannot think—"

He broke off as Damien came into the room with Mary in tow. "She cannot think what, Charles?" he queried, his eyes trained on me.

"It is not important," I said quickly. "But now that Mary is here, I should be most grateful if you would leave us. That is, unless you will reconsider and take me to my room."

Damien shrugged. "Perhaps you can talk some sense into her, Mary. If you need anything, Lillith, you need only ask."

I watched the two men leave as Mary laid a robe beside me and placed some toiletries on the nightstand.

"I am so sorry to add to your duties," I said.

"Don't ye be talkin' nonsense, Miss Lillith. Now let me 'ave a look at this leg o' yers." Gently she turned my ankle between her plump little fingers. "Kin ye wiggle yer toes?"

It was uncomfortable, but I managed to do as she asked.

" 'Tis a good sign," she said encouragingly. "Ye won't be dancin' a jig soon, but ye'll be right as rain. Now ye change yer clothes an' settle under the covers. Cook's fixin' a tray fer ye, an' aye'll be back in a wink with it."

As soon as she had left I swung my legs off the bed and, balancing against the bedpost, tentatively attempted to stand again. It was useless. I fell back against the covers, realizing that no amount of determination would allow me to leave this room on my own. Angrily I pulled at my clothing and, divesting myself of it, pulled my nightdress over my head. I sud-

257

denly felt terribly cold and shivered as I clumsily drew up the covers.

Mary bustled in with my tray, Chips at her heels. "Now this is jest the thing," she announced. "Ye take some nourishment an' 'ave a good night's rest, an' tomorrow things'll look a lot brighter."

She propped the pillows high at my back and set the tray before me. "Aye've te get back te the kitchen, but ye jest set yer tray on the stand there when yer finished."

I studied the tray before me. "What is this?" I asked, picking up a small vial.

"Oh, aye near fergot," she fretted. " 'Tis from Lady Jessica. Real insistent she was that ye take it. Says 'twill 'elp ye sleep. An' there's somethin' else."

She left the room and returned with a cane. "This was sent along as well. Jest if ye 'ave te rise in the night."

She called to Chips, who had curled up beside the bed.

"He is all right here with me," I assured her.

"Then aye'll be leavin'."

As she went towards the door I sat up in the bed. "Mary, is there a lock on the door?"

She appeared surprised. "Miss Lillith, there's not a door in this 'ouse that doesn't lock."

"I know," I murmured. "All too well."

She closed the door behind her and I was left in the solitude of the room with the gently snoring Chips as my only companion.

The cook had taken great care with the preparation of the food, but as I picked at the leg of mutton and creamed onions my mind was miles from it. No matter where I looked, the picture of the inert form floating in the lake flashed before me. Charles had been quick to term it an accident. And yet I was still uncertain. Why? I did not even know the man. Indeed, I could not even be sure that it was the stablehand. It was reasonable that it should trouble me, but there was something deeper than shock which plagued me. I had no idea of the depth of the lake, but how was it, I asked myself, that one familiar with the property could come to such an end?

I swallowed a morsel of the succulent meat, telling myself that I must not allow my imagination to run away with me once again. I had done it too often since coming to Darby and it had served me ill.

Mary would chastise me, I was certain, but I had no appetite for the turnips or honeyed tart. Awkwardly I placed the tray aside and settled back. I tried to turn my foot against the weight of the covers and was totally discouraged as pain flashed up my leg.

Why had I gotten myself into this predicament now, when I was but days away from finishing the cataloguing? If I were superstitious I would think it an omen. Everyone obviously faulted my conviction that I should leave Darby, and yet even my best determination these days appeared foiled.

Chips raised his head suddenly at the sound of approaching footsteps. The door opened a crack and it was with relief that I saw Amanda peering in.

"Oh, good, you are still awake," she said as she entered the room. "I thought that draft might have put you in a deep slumber by now."

I glanced at the vial on the tray. "It was kind of your aunt to send it on, but I really had no need."

"Nonsense," she objected. "There is no cause to be stalwart. It will simply allow you to rest."

"Amanda, really, I—"

"Now, I shan't take no for an answer," she commanded, pouring a full measure of the liquid into the small teacup.

I accepted it from her and drank it down, screwing up my face at the bitter taste.

"That is better," she said complacently, drawing up a chair. "Now I shall stay here with you until you drift off."

I shook my head. "You go back to your dinner, Amanda. I've upset enough people for one day."

She frowned. "You must have been the one who was upset, Lillith, thinking that you spied a body in the lake."

"You sound as though you do not believe me."

"Well, you must admit it is a curious story."

"Is that what everyone thinks? That I fabricated this horror?" I demanded.

She reached across and placed her hand atop mine. "Now, do not fret. If it will make you feel any better, I am certain it will be looked into tomorrow, and then we can put your mind at rest."

I wanted to protest, but the draught had commenced to take effect and I felt myself sinking into oblivion.

I found myself walking along a dark hallway which seemed to have no beginning and no end. Someone was calling to me, my name echoed throughout the chamber, but no one was in sight. There were endless doors to each side of the hall. Something told me not to open them, but a strange urge demanded that I see what was beyond. I tried the first door, then the second, and on and on, but they were all locked. Panic overtook me as I started to run, desperate to escape the maze. But there was no escape.

I awoke with a start. The room was dark, but I sensed I was not alone.

"Who is there?" I murmured, pulling the covers up about my neck.

I recognized the whir of the wheels against the carpet.

"What are you doing here?" I demanded as his chair approached the side of the bed.

"I came to inquire how you are," Damien replied, "but you were sleeping so soundly that I decided not to disturb you."

"How long have you been here?"

"An hour, perhaps two."

I struggled to sit up as he lit the candle on the nightstand. "I shall have you know I do not take kindly to men invading my privacy."

He smiled. "I ought to remind you that these are my quarters, Lillith."

"Well, I did not choose to be here."

"That is true," he acknowledged, "but there is no reason why we cannot make the best of a bad bargain. You look so enticing lying there. Not unlike the first time I saw you—also in these quarters, lest you have forgotten."

I flushed deeply. "I must ask you to leave this minute, Damien."

He wheeled closer. "No, this time I am not going to leave, Lillith."

"I warn you, Damien, if you move any closer I shall scream."

"To what end?" he challenged. "No one will hear you at this end of the house."

I struggled to pull the covers aside, wincing at the pain in my ankle. "Have you no regard for me, Damien?" I cried as I swung my legs over the side of the bed.

He swore. "Lillith, do you not see that it is because I have regard for you, as you put it, that I want this sparring to stop. It is not what I want and it is not what you want, but you are too damn stubborn to see it."

"I warned you the last time, Damien," I said through clenched teeth as I pulled myself up to a standing position, "go back to your concubine, or whoever you have been spending these last days with, but leave me alone."

It happened so fast that I had no chance to react. As I had started to take a step forward his arm had flung to my midriff, forcing me back on the bed.

"Stop your histrionics and listen to me," he demanded, his dark eyes flashing. "I left Darby because I had to get away from you. Do you understand?"

"No," I managed to whisper.

"I could not go on any longer sitting there day after day, watching you, wanting you as I do. Had I been able I would have come to you long ago and taken you in wanton abandon. Perhaps it would have purged me of this obsession. I thought if I left here I would see the folly of it. But the irony was that, while you were the last person I wanted to give thought to, I have thought of nothing else."

"Why are you telling me this?"

"Because I am going to ask something of you, and I wanted you to know that I have not come to it easily."

I waited for him to continue. For a moment I thought he had changed his mind, for he turned away from me, staring into space. When he turned back there was such sadness in his face that despite my frame of mind I grew concerned.

"I want you to marry me, Lillith," he said slowly.

My expression must have revealed the shock I was experiencing, for he repeated the proposal again, this time, it seemed, with more conviction.

I drew a deep breath. I would have thought it a joke or trick of some kind, but I had never seen Damien so serious.

"Have you nothing to say?" he finally asked.

"Only to ask who put you up to this?" I challenged.

He shook his head. "Your problem, Lillith, is that you do not listen."

"Then why do you want me as your wife?"

He ran his hand through his dark locks. "Because, God help me, I cannot imagine life without you."

I was trembling, and I knew it was not the chill of the room. I stared at him, my eyes filling with tears. "Do you really mean that?"

His eyes softened. "On my life, whatever it is worth, I do."

I struggled to gather my thoughts, but each one seemed in opposition to the other. "Your offer is very kind, Damien," I replied finally.

Again the earlier sadness seemed to return. "Kind is far from what my request is. If I were truly kind, Lillith, I would have seen you gone from Darby and thanked God that I had done at least one decent thing in my life. But the thought that

I should not see you again, that you would be out there, lost to me save for in memory, was inconceivable. Before you say anything else, I want you to know that I do not expect an answer tonight. I have heard you say that you are not as desirous of me as I am of you, but beware of the vehemence of your denial. Like it or not, Lillith, there is a magnetism, a bond between us that is larger than our very selves. Call it what you will, but I think if you are honest, truly honest with yourself, you will see that we are each other's destiny. If you think that you can leave Darby and never look back, never once regret, then I shall be alone in wondering what might have been. But if there is the slightest doubt, then there is enough to build on."

He turned his chair around and wheeled it towards the door. "You needn't worry about locking it, Lillith. The only intruder you may have in the early morning hours will be Chips, who, though unable to plead my case, I think shares my hope that your answer tomorrow will be yes."

With that he was gone. My head was swimming. The effect of the sleeping draft had not wholly disappeared, which frustrated me, for I desperately needed a clear head. Whatever scenes I had played out in my mind, in my wildest imaginings I could never have predicted that Damien Darby of his own volition would ask me to marry him. My first inclination was to dismiss it as but yet another aberration of his. But I could not. There had been many times when I had mistrusted Damien since I had come to this house, but this was not one of them.

Strangely, what puzzled me most was his demeanor. He had asked me to marry him, and yet that restless storm which ever seemed to brew within him was distinctly absent tonight. He spoke of passion, but I heard something else in his voice. Was it a sense of defeat? Why did he acknowledge that it would be kinder to send me away, yet in the same breath beseech me to stay?

Did he think himself so diminished by his infirmity that by

marrying me he must condemn me to a less than full life? It was not impossible, I supposed. How could I think of him now as a husband when but days ago I was troubling over why a young girl, now dead, had expressed such fear of her own brother? And why, I asked myself, did everything inexplicable at Darby always take me full circle to Anitra?

Lady Lillith Darby. My lips formed the words again and again. It was ridiculous, of course, but then it was not every day that Lillith Chatfield received a proposal of marriage. How distant it all seemed from those days of innocence when Rebecca and I would conjecture about our future spouses.

The candle flame flickered out, leaving me alone again in the dark of Darby Manor.

Save Marisse, there was no one who had not encouraged me to marry Damien. Jessica, even Amanda, suggested that he harbored a fondness for me. Then why had I not seen it? Was there a seed of truth in what Damien had said? Were these swells of animosity our own way of denying an attraction?

Certainly I found him attractive, but then almost any woman would. And there were moments, when I had relaxed my guard, when I had even found him charming. We shared a love of the arts and I, as he did, felt at home in these remote northern climes.

But these were not reasons to marry. Or were they?

I mulled over all he had said. He had made it clear that he wanted me. He had gone so far as to say that he could not imagine life without me. But one word had been distinctly absent from his soliloquy. There had been no mention of love. It was not a word to be used lightly. But it was a word which for me was inextricably tied to marriage.

What if I were to accept Damien's proposal? Would he, once his passions were sated, abandon his commitment to me? Was he asking my hand in matrimony only because he saw no other way of conquering what had thus far eluded him?

If I left Darby I would never be certain. And that finally was the heart of my dilemma. Could I leave here and never look back? I knew the answer, but the reason was far more complex. Until a few months ago I had never even known Darby existed. And yet slowly, almost insidiously, it had become a part of me. I had cherished Bostworick Hall, but my feeling for Darby was different. As fanciful as the notion seemed, it was as though the manor was asking something of me, pleading that I not abandon it.

17

I AWOKE to find Chips's muzzle touching my hand where it lay on the coverlet. "I fear when I cannot romp with you today you will be quick to abandon me," I suggested.

"He is hardly as fickle as that."

I started, looking across the room to see Damien just beyond the half open door. I scrambled to pull the covers about me as he maneuvered his chair into the room.

"What right do you have?" I demanded as he wheeled towards the bed.

Instead of being put off he appeared amused. "Unless you can manage better than you could last evening, I fear you are my captive," he replied.

"I shall be out of your way as soon as I am allowed privacy to dress," I snapped.

His eyes narrowed. "I do not want you out of my way, Lillith. I thought I made that quite clear last night. Speaking of which, I should like an answer."

"You have hardly given me time," I countered.

"To wait would only be to do us both a disservice. I have asked you to marry me. It requires a simple yes or no."

His tone was so changed from last night. Today I felt he was offering me a position rather than asking me to be his wife.

He withdrew a small box from his pocket and laid it on the coverlet beside me. "Perhaps this will help you decide."

I picked it up and released the small gold latch. Inside, nesting against a cushion of velvet, was the most exquisite ring I had ever seen. "It is breathtaking," I managed.

"It was my mother's, and my grandmother's before her," he replied slowly. "Try it on."

I hesitated, feeling it was somehow tantamount to accepting his proposal, but finally I withdrew the square of emerald surrounded by diamonds. It slipped easily onto my finger.

"Somehow I knew it would fit," he said.

I took it off and placed it back in the box.

"Am I to take that as your answer?"

I looked at him. The defiance was gone, replaced with a look of sadness, or resignation, I knew not which.

"I only wish I could be as certain as you seem to be," I answered. "I care too deeply for you, Damien, to enter blithely into a marriage which might cause you any more pain than you have already suffered."

"It is pain which you would release me from," he murmured.

"I am not certain I could be what you want me to be, Damien. What if I were to disappoint you?"

He smiled. "I am not asking you to play a part, Lillith. I am only asking you to be yourself. Save for perhaps that stubborn streak of yours."

"Stubborn!" I gasped. "You are the one who is stubborn, Damien Darby."

Almost simultaneously we burst into laughter.

"It seems we have come this way before," he recollected.

"I suppose we are a pair," I admitted.

"Yes we are, Lillith, and it is high time that you saw it. Marry me. Let me prove it to you."

Our eyes met, and in that instant all my doubts and fears seemed to fade away.

"It appears your father will get what he wanted after all," I said finally.

"Does that mean what I think it does?"

I nodded.

Whereas I had expected his reaction to be jubilant, he appeared strangely sobered.

"I shall post the bans immediately," he said. "But I would ask one thing: that nothing be said to the household—that is, not for a few days. It may seem peculiar to you, but I have my reasons."

"As I have no friends or family hereabouts, I would hope that we might keep the service simple," I requested.

"That would suit me as well," he agreed. "Though I expect it will be met with some opposition. But I will do all I can."

Chips got up suddenly and scampered to the door. Damien turned round to see Mary juggling a breakfast tray.

"Oh, aye be beggin' yer pardon," she spluttered, looking from Damien to me and back again. "Aye knocked at the parlor door, but aye guess ye didn't be hearin'."

"It is all right, Mary," I assured her.

She came forward hesitantly and placed the tray on a table at the far side of the room. As she did Damien reached forward and took the box containing the ring. "I shall just hold on to this for a few days. If you need anything, I shall be in the studio."

"But what about the body in the lake? Surely you are going to have it investigated," I blurted out.

From the far side of the room there was a crash. I turned

to see Mary staring helplessly at the splinters of porcelain on the floor. "A body," she mumbled, her mouth aquiver.

Damien shot an angry look at me. "It is nothing to trouble about, Mary," he said tersely. "Lillith thought she saw something in the lake, but she had had a nasty spill."

I was incredulous at what he was saying. Certainly I had been thoughtless about Mary's presence, but he was making it sound as though I had imagined it all. Mary, who seemed appeased, busied herself with clearing up the fragments of china. I was fuming as I turned to Damien.

"Why did you say that?" I whispered angrily.

"Do you want this place in a frenzy?" he charged. "You had best learn now, Lillith, that discretion is a must in a household like Darby. It will be looked into, I promise you that, but the less you say the better."

Numbly I watched the man I had just agreed to marry wheel himself from the room. I had no chance to wallow in the confusion which raged within me, for Mary had bustled the tray over to the bed and set it down.

"There's porridge an' eggs an' the fresh 'am ye like," she announced, "an' aye'm te stay till yer done. Cook says so. Course, that's only 'cause Mrs. 'Orsley's gone to town. She won't spare me a moment, that one."

I picked up my fork as she hovered over me. "Is she unkind to you, Mary?"

Her face reddened. "Oh, Miss Lillith, please don't be sayin' nothin' te the master. Aye need me spot 'ere. An' the Darbys, they don't take kindly te talk."

I swallowed a morsel of ham. "I am just finding that out," I muttered.

" 'Ow's yer leg?" she inquired.

I tried to move it under the covers. There was a distinct soreness, but the agony I had experienced the night before had disappeared.

"Better, I think," I replied. "Mary, why do you not sit with me. As you seem determined to stay, you would do us both a service if you relaxed a bit."

Tentatively she sank into the chair. "Aye've te tell ye, Miss Lillith, ye shook me underpinnin's when ye said somethin' 'bout a body. But then aye guess the shock an' all got ye confused."

Thoughtfully I spread the thick jam on my toast. "Have you heard anything about Flo?" I asked, straining to keep a lilt to my voice.

She shook her head. "Ye know, 'tis odd ye should ask, 'cause jest last night somethin' real peculiar happened. Me room was stuffy an' aye was restless. Aye was about te go out te the 'all when aye 'eard footsteps. Bein' a cowardly type, aye stayed in me room, but aye peered out. Would ye believe, aye saw Mrs. 'Orsley an' Sommers. Went into Flo's room, they did. An' then they came out. They were carryin' somethin', but aye couldn't see what. Well this mornin', afore aye came te the kitchens, aye decided to see what it was all about."

"And what did you find?" I asked, caught up in the fervency of her story.

She leant forward and whispered conspiratorially, "That's the lot o' it. There was nothin'. Not a uniform, not a comb, nothin'. 'Twas like she never existed."

"Perhaps she contacted them and asked for her things to be forwarded," I suggested.

Mary considered this for a moment, but then she shook her head. "Ye 'ad te know Flo. Spent all 'er wages on fancy duds, she did. She'd never leave 'em behind. Not unless she met up with a dandy, an' there ain't much chance o' that."

I pushed the tray aside. "You really are worried about her," I said.

" 'Tain't like we were chums," she replied, "but it gives me the jitters, this place. Much as aye 'ate te see ye leavin', ye'll be well gone from 'ere."

I turned away from her, fearful that my expression might give hint of my recent decision.

271

"You know, Mary, I think I will try to get up. I want to test this ankle of mine."

She removed my tray as I swung my legs from the warmth of the bed. Gingerly I stood up. The feeling of soreness increased sharply as I took a step. Mary sprinted for the cane and handed it to me. Loath as I was to admit it, I was not going to be able to navigate without it.

"Shoulda sent fer the doctor," Mary stated as I moved towards the water closet, "but they don't take te outsiders at Darby."

I bit my lip. Mary was surprisingly open this morning, and though I was tempted to try to elicit information from her, I was for the first time aware that gossip did not become my new role at Darby.

When I had finished bathing she helped me dress. I was anxious to get to the studio. I could not abandon the cataloguing simply because I had agreed to marry Damien. But my main concern was what the search of the lake would reveal.

I turned to study myself in the mirror and drew a loose tendril of hair high on my head. I did not know what I expected of my reflection, but I was almost disappointed to see myself unchanged. It was not every day I accepted a marriage proposal, and somehow I had expected my countenance to reflect this pending change in my life.

I wondered as I approached the studio whether I had not been overzealous. My ankle throbbed, and I was experiencing waves of dizziness.

Damien was obviously surprised when he answered my knock. "You should not be up and about," he advised.

"I am still in your employ," I reminded him. "Besides, I quite enjoy the cataloguing, and I am nearing the last of it."

He wheeled back, allowing me to pass. "I hope you do not intend to persist with this once we are man and wife."

"And why not?" I asked, amazed. "I was hoping that you might be agreeable to my sending a few of the paintings off to London. I am certain that if they were seen by my friend's father he would be able to elicit interest. Of course, the galleries would want to send emissaries to Darby, but I am convinced it would conclude in a showing."

"Lillith, I am flattered, but I have no such ambitions. Beyond that, I will not have a lot of strangers traipsing about this house. We lead a very private existence here, as we choose to do. I hope you are not entertaining chimerical ideas about changing things at Darby."

"What do you expect me to do with my time?" I demanded.

His expression was stern as he watched me settle before my work table.

"When we marry you will be mistress of Darby. You will not be wanting for things to do. There are tenants to look to, charities which will call upon your time."

I drew the ledgers towards me. "Would those duties not fall to Marisse?" I pursued. "I mean, once she marries your father she will be Lady Darby."

"My dear, we have suffered enough ignominy without the scheming Lady de Wentoff," he replied sarcastically. "Actually, I am most eager to see her reaction when she learns that we are to be married. She will be livid."

"Perhaps I am naive, but why should it have import for her? I expect she finds me unsuitable, but—"

"Lillith," he interrupted, "this has naught to do with your suitability. Marisse de Wentoff is an ambitious woman. Do not let her spin you into her web, for in this case the spider has a fatal sting."

There was such venom in his voice that I was fearful of challenging him.

I was surprised when there came a knock at the door. Visitors to the studio were less than infrequent. I could not see who it was, but the voice, though hushed, was definitely male. I expected to see the man enter, but when the door closed I realized that instead Damien had left with him.

I waited, half expecting him to return, but when he did not I addressed myself to the work at hand. Half an hour later I scanned the few entries I had managed to make, realizing my mind was obviously elsewhere.

When Damien finally returned I was almost grateful. Being alone was giving me too much time to think.

"That was one of the stablehands," he offered. "I had asked him to look into that little matter at the lake."

"Little matter?" I said, astounded. "I scarcely think a man's body is a little matter."

"Lillith, listen to me," he demanded. "Wills found nothing in the lake. No body, nothing."

My eyes flew open. "But that is impossible," I exclaimed. "I know what I saw."

"You know what you think you saw," he countered.

I was trembling as I burst out, "You really do not believe me. You would take the word of some stablehand over that of the woman you have just asked to be your wife. Is this the kind of trust, of belief, on which this marriage is going to be founded? Well, if it is, I want no part of it."

"Lillith, come down from there," Damien pleaded.

"Why?"

"Because I want you here beside me when I say what I have to say."

Warily I took up the cane and moved down to the seat opposite him. He extended his hands, asking me to place mine in his. I was surprised that such large strong hands displayed such a gentle touch.

"Now hear me out. It was dusk when you were out. That lake is covered with surface flora. It would not be difficult to mistake a cluster of fronds for a human form. Wills was instructed to examine every part of the lake. He found nothing untoward. He has no reason to lie to me, and I have no reason to lie to you."

"Don't you?" I asked softly.

He let go of my hands. "What do you mean?"

"I do not know," I sighed. "I am just upset. I could have sworn . . . I am not given to imaginings, truly I am not."

"No one suggested that you were," he answered. "It was an illusion, nature's deception of the eye. I work with it every day in my paintings."

I sank back in the chair, feeling sure he must think me a foolish hysteric. "I am sorry if I have upset the household."

He smiled. "It is not so serious as that. But I should give up the ghost, as it were. There is no need to trouble anyone any further."

I suddenly felt weary to the bone. "Would you mind very much if I retired to my room? I am not much good at cataloguing today."

He studied me intently. "I should have insisted that you stay in bed. Do you want me to fetch Mary to help you?"

I shook my head. "All I need is rest. I ought to be fully recovered by tomorrow."

I knew he expected that I would return to his quarters, but my need for privacy challenged me to tackle the main staircase. I was so absorbed in my progress that I did not see Charles until I had reached the top.

"I was just inquiring about you," he said. "Mary told me you were up and about."

"I fear I am up but not yet about," I admitted.

"It must have been an enormous shock," he went on. "First finding a body in the lake, then your fall. You gave me quite a fright."

"Well, it seems I brought it on myself," I replied.

"I cannot see how," he mused.

"Damien had the lake investigated this morning," I told him. "Apparently what I thought was a body was simply weeds. I feel such a fool, but honestly it seemed so real. I know now I was mistaken, but I cannot stop seeing it in my mind's eye."

Charles put his hand on my arm. "You needn't fret about that now, Lillith. Frankly, you look particularly pale. Direct me, and I shall accompany you to your room."

The earlier dizziness had returned and I welcomed his help.

I cannot remember crossing the length of the room, only thinking, as I lay down, that a bed had never felt so good. When I awoke it was dark and I felt numb with cold. I had not bothered to undress. I did so now, though with such lethargy that I grew concerned. I usually brimmed with energy, but at this moment all I wanted to do was crawl back into bed.

When I next awakened it was to find Mary creeping towards me looking like a dog pointing its quarry.

"Oh, now aye've gone an' done it," she said, troubled. " 'Tis only aye've brought yer tray."

"What time is it?" I asked, sitting up in bed.

"Almost seven, 'tis," she replied, setting the laden tray before me. "Miss Jessica was real specific that ye should eat."

"You know, I actually think I have an appetite," I admitted. "Given that hours ago I thought I was dying, I would say it is a healthy sign."

Mary laid the fire as I started eagerly on the breast of capon.

"Master Damien was fit te be tied when 'e found out ye'd come back up 'ere," she offered as she dusted the soot from her apron.

"This *is* my room," I pointed out.

"Oh, aye think 'e was jest worried 'bout ye climbin' the stairs an' all."

"If you see him, please assure him I am all right," I requested.

Cook, I decided, would have been pleased with me, for there was not a morsel left on the tray when I placed it aside. I was feeling so much improved that I decided to pen a letter to Abraham. That I had not heard from him was worrisome, particularly as he had been in ill health, but I did not trust that Mrs. Horsley was as exacting with the post as she claimed. This letter, I decided, I would entrust to Mary.

I had just gathered a few sheets of writing paper when there came a knock at the door. Thinking it was Mary returning for the tray, I bade her enter. As I looked up to greet her I started, for it was not Mary but Charles.

"I did not mean to frighten you," he assured me, "but I must speak with you."

He appeared so agitated that I allowed him to advance. "I have only a moment. I excused myself from dinner with a rather lame explanation, but I felt it imperative I speak with you tonight."

"What is it?" I pressed him.

"When I saw you earlier something did not ring true," he began. "You strike me as many things, but not as one to fabricate. After luncheon I decided to take a walk on my own, down to the lake."

My heart was beating as he reached into his pocket and withdrew what appeared to be a swatch of fabric.

"I saw no body, but in searching the banks, I found this."

I took the still damp fragment from him. "But this proves nothing."

He nodded in agreement. "Not by itself, I agree. However there was something else. Beyond where the bridge forms, there were marks as though something or someone had been dragged into the dense woodland. I followed the tracks, but they appeared to stop abruptly."

"Are you suggesting I was not mistaken in what I saw?" I demanded anxiously.

"Let us say I do not think it was coincidence."

"But then why . . ."

"Why would Damien or his man have lied about their findings?" he finished.

"I was not going to say that," I said defensively. "Perhaps the stablehand was more cursory in his examination than you, or perhaps one thing had nothing to do with the other."

"I do not think you believe that any more than I do," he protested.

Before I could answer, there came a knock at the door.

"Lillith, it is Amanda. Might I come in?"

Charles shook his head furiously, but I saw no sense in denying her entry. She knew I was there, and if I turned her away she would only become more persistent.

"It is open," I called out.

She saw Charles first.

"I was just leaving," he said.

"Not on my account," she bristled, turning round. "Obviously I have come at an inopportune time."

"Amanda, wait," I said.

"We will continue this tomorrow, Lillith." Charles strode past her without a word and closed the door behind him.

When she turned to face me I actually cowered at the fury I saw there. "It is not what you think," I told her.

She shrugged. "What you do in the confines of your room is none of my business, Lillith."

"I simply do not want you to misinterpret."

She glanced at the bed, which was still turned down. "I do not think interpretation is my problem. Just how many nights have you and your paramour tittered over my interest in him?"

"You cannot possibly think that of me," I exclaimed as I watched her pace before me.

"What do you expect me to think?" she raged. "Oh, never mind, what does it matter anyway."

"Amanda, it *does* matter," I cried. "It matters very much what you think. But I swear to you, you are wrong."

"Then prove it."

"I am going to marry Damien." As soon as I had blurted it out I was sorry. He had exacted only one promise from me, and I had already broken it.

You might have thought from her reaction that I had slapped her senseless, for she could only stare at me.

"You heard me correctly," I said.

She moved forward and sank into the chair opposite me.

"You took my advice," she said finally. "But at dinner, Father made no mention."

I smiled. "Your father does not know. And you were not to learn of it either—at least, not for a few days—save that now I have broken my word to Damien."

"I wish you would not be so oblique, Lillith," she complained. "You have accepted my father's proposal, but you say he does not know. Or perhaps that is why Charles was here? He is making the arrangements?"

"Amanda, I accepted Damien's proposal, not your father's. As for Charles, he knows nothing of this."

She was looking at me, but it was as though she was not seeing me. "I was hoping that you would be pleased," I offered.

"Pleased," she echoed. "Yes. Yes, of course I am pleased. Why would I not be?"

I toyed with the satin tie of my robe. "Amanda, I think I can be honest with you and say that it is as much a surprise to me as it is to you, both Damien's proposal and my acceptance. But I shall try to be a very good wife to him, I promise you that."

She stood up suddenly. "Damien has always been full of surprises, but I think this is by far his best to date. As for myself, the secret is safe with me. I should hate to steal his thunder."

I reached out my hand to her. "Thank you, Amanda. Admittedly I made the decision on my own, but you must know you had great influence on me. And I do hope you will be often at Darby. It struck me only a while ago that by marrying Damien I shall be gaining a family again."

She placed her hand in mine and, leaning down, kissed me swiftly on the cheek. "I quite think this will change my plans altogether. Why, I may even move back to Darby. However, for now I had best get back to dinner and repair what damage I might have done with Charles."

We agreed to see each other in the morning. My earlier determination to write Abraham was gone. The tumult of the evening had left me edgy. I seemed less able to concentrate on my impending marriage than on the discovery Charles had imparted earlier.

Was it coincidence? I wondered. Charles obviously did not think so. But, assuming that he was correct, the implications were chilling. Damien had sworn he was being honest with me, and I had believed him. Even now I could conceive of no reason why he would lie. Unless, of course, he thought it kinder to spare me the awful details. There was one other possibility, but it was too daunting to consider. For it meant that Damien might be lying to protect someone or, worse yet, himself.

If the latter were true, then there might be reason for me to fear the very man I was to marry. I found myself staring at the dressing table. Was it coincidental that Anitra had been frightened? What was it that she had feared? Was it Damien himself? Or had she, as I had, found herself at the center of a mysterious incident?

I rose and hobbled over to the dressing table. My fingers slid across the silky inlay, trembling as they pulled forth the drawer and reached back to clasp the leather-bound volume. I traced, as I had done before, the name emblazoned on the front.

"I *have* to do this," I whispered. "It is the only way."

My hand pressed at the lock, but it did not budge. Of course! It would not have been left unlocked. But where might she have left the key? Even as I searched the corners of the drawers, I knew my search would prove fruitless. The secret of the key's hiding place had gone to the grave with Anitra.

There had to be a way of opening the diary. I could take a scissors or knife to it, but that seemed an almost barbaric action.

Where the key should fit, there was only a minuscule aperture. If I could find an object slim enough to fit into it I might be able to move the tumbler. I withdrew a comb from my hair and broke off the end tooth. Taking the sliver of tortoiseshell firmly between my fingers I pressed it into the opening. As I did there was a whisper of a click, and the lock released.

I turned back the cover of the diary, taking care not to break the binding. The paper was fine, and as the writing was small I pulled the candle closer.

The date of the first entry was February 1845. She would have been but thirteen. I leaned closer, my eyes scanning the page.

> Dear Diary, I shall make a pledge to you. I, Anitra Celestine Darby, shall faithfully share with you all my most private thoughts and actions each day forever more. You will be my most intimate friend. All my secrets will be your secrets. We shall be one you and I.   A.

I smiled to myself at the fervency of dedication with which she had begun this journal. Although the entry told me nothing, it suggested a passionate nature at a young age.

The successive entries were typical of a young girl keeping a diary for the first time. Literally every thought, every action had been meticulously recorded. Finding the entries ingenuous but hardly revealing, I moved to the middle of the diary. The date here was June 1847.

I was immediately struck by a change in the penmanship. The painstakingly neat hand of the early writing had now taken on sweeping flourishes. The change was so great that it might well have been enscribed by another. I read on:

> I cannot go on this way, but where am I to turn? There are days when I fear for my life, and then others when I wonder whether I am not tainted by the madness. The same blood pulses through our veins. Even if I escape, I shall never escape the taint of Darby.

I slammed the diary shut and fumbled it back into the drawer. I felt as though I was going to be ill. What was so horrific that it had made the lovely young girl question her own sanity?

The answer was in that slim volume, I was certain. Then why could I not bring myself to read on? Only this morning I had professed the need for faith and trust between two people who were to pledge their lives, one unto the other. Did I thrust the diary from me out of disgust at my driven need to lift the veil of secrecy from this house? Or was I truly afraid of what I might find?

I picked up the candlestick and with the aid of the cane moved back to the bed. Whatever well-being I had experienced earlier had left me. But whereas my earlier malaise had been physical, my sickness now was of the heart.

I slept fitfully, waking almost hourly. Thus when Mary arrived with my basin I could barely rouse myself.

"Afore aye ferget, Master Damien said ye were te stay in yer room today. Seems real concerned 'bout ye, 'e does."

I splashed the warm water on my face and accepted a towel from her. "Where is Damien?"

" 'E said 'e was off te the studio, but aye don't be thinkin' 'e wants te be disturbed," she related. "Miss Amanda was real specific 'bout wantin' te see 'im, but 'e said no one was te come round."

"Where is the rest of the household?" I inquired, sitting down to examine my ankle.

"Looks a mite better today," she observed. "Now, let me see. Lady de Wentoff's takin' a carriage te town, an' that nice Sir Charles, 'e's with Lord Darby an' 'is sister."

"It seems I am relegated to my room."

She crossed to the draperies and drew them back. " 'Tis a gloomy day. Yer just as well te keep 'ere by the fire."

"I have some letters to write," I admitted. "Which reminds me, would you mind posting them for me?"

"Aye'd be pleased te but 'twouldn't be till Thursday, when

aye go te me mum's. But ye kin give 'em to Mrs. 'Orsley."

"Thursday will be fine," I assured her.

Mary left me, to return shortly with my breakfast tray. I ate sparingly and then settled down to my correspondence. It was several hours and dozens of crumpled sheets later when I finally finished the letters. Upon rereading them I found the tone hollow, unconvincing. But how, I wondered, could I convince those closest to me that I was doing the right thing when I was not convinced myself.

I had not even suggested that they attend the wedding. The trip, I expected, would be too arduous for Abraham. I knew Rebecca would be disappointed and hurt, but I did not think I could risk having her about. It would take her no more than a morning to sense my misgivings. Later, when the deed was done, I would invite her to visit.

Deed, I thought to myself. It sounded more like a crime than a marriage. As I slipped the letters into their envelopes there came a gentle knocking at the door. I drew the cane to me and went to open it, pleased to find Amanda beyond.

"I hope I am not interrupting," she said, "but I was desperate for some adult company."

"Of course not," I said, ushering her in.

"How is your ankle?"

"Much improved."

She clapped her hands together. "I was hoping you would say that, as there is something I want to show you."

"What is it?"

Her eyes danced mischievously about the room. "You will see soon enough. I think you will be pleased. Just follow me."

As we walked in tandem towards the back staircase, I wondered what this mysterious thing was that she was leading me to.

"Be careful," she advised as she started up the narrow wooden steps. When we reached the top she paused to open a door at the attic landing. She had to struggle some moments before she was finally able to free it.

I fought to suppress a sneeze as the dank air filled my nostrils. "I hope this is not where the servants live," I gasped.

"Goodness, no," she replied. " 'Tis an odd attic, in that it is divided. The servants' quarters are back there over the west wing."

I lifted the skirts of my gown as I followed her along the rough pine flooring. A thick layer of dust covering stacks of valuable but long-abandoned furniture told me that we were the first to intrude upon this space in a fair time.

She had reached a spot under the pitch of the roof. Turning round, she seemed perplexed. "I know they are here someplace."

"If I knew what you were looking for I might help," I offered.

Amanda moved down to the far end where sheets covered bulky shapes. She drew them back, revealing several domed trunks. "I knew they were here," she exclaimed as she knelt down before the largest and commenced undoing the heavy straps.

As I reached her she lifted the dome of a trunk and I saw that it contained a cache of rich laces and silks. She rummaged deep among these goods but apparently did not find what she was looking for, for she quickly moved to a smaller trunk. "Phew, it is dusty up here," she exclaimed, raising the lid, together with a small cloud.

I stepped closer, as she gently lifted a gown from the top of the trunk's contents.

"Oh, Amanda, it is exquisite," I murmured as the endless lengths of white satin inset with alençon lace drifted to the floor.

She held it away from her at arm's length, as though there was a taint to its memory. Her voice was faint as she murmured, "It was my mother's wedding gown. I recalled it last night and thought you might want to wear it."

I reached out and fingered the series of rosettes adorning the sweep of the skirt. "It is breathtaking, Amanda, and it's so thoughtful of you to suggest it, but I cannot imagine that your father would approve."

She appeared surprised. "Lillith, my father will be so happy to see Damien married that what you wear will be of little consequence. Besides, it is not doing any good shut away up here, and I am quite certain that with a few cinches it will fit you perfectly. Why do we not go back to your room and try it on right now?"

Before I could argue, she started for the stairs, holding the train high off the floor. Realizing that she had neglected to close the first trunk, I crossed to it. As I drew the heavy lid towards me my index finger caught on a rough place on the dome. I peered closely and saw that it was not the result of some accident.

I stared transfixed at the crudely carved heart. Inside there were two initials: *D* and *A*.

"Are you coming?" Amanda called out.

My heart was pounding as I made my way back to where she waited on the landing. It meant nothing, I told myself. It was a playful whim, likely done by a child naive to the implications. Then why did I have this sickening feeling in the pit of my stomach? Why did every word from that last diary entry resound in my ears, forcing me beyond rationalization. *I wonder whether I too am tainted by this madness. The same blood pulses through our veins,* she had written.

I drew a deep breath of fresh air as we reached the second-floor landing.

Amanda turned around and said quickly, "Are you all right, Lillith? You are so pale."

"I should just like to sit down for a bit," I managed to say.

"I should never have dragged you up there," she apologized as we returned to my room.

As I sank into the sofa before the fire Amanda laid the dress across the bed. "What you need is some tea," she announced. "I shall tell Cook to send our luncheon trays up here."

The last thing I wanted was food and company, but I did not have the heart to contradict her.

I sat watching the flames in the grate, desperately trying to rid myself of the insidious suspicions which had taken seed. Could Anitra's torment have been born of passion and not of fear? Was her terror bred of unnatural feelings for, or perhaps even an association with, her own brother? Or was it an unrequited obsession?

By the time Amanda had returned I had managed to get hold of myself. Carving on a trunk was hardly evidence that unspeakable sins had been committed at Darby. I was over-wrought. The incident yesterday, the timorousness with which I was entering into this marriage, had obviously upset me more than I was willing to admit.

"How is Terrence?" I inquired as she crossed to the bed and lifted the gown.

"He is with Mrs. Horsley," she replied lightly. "You know, I think you ought to try this on. It might need a few altera-tions."

"Amanda, we have not even announced our intentions," I protested. "Damien wanted to wait a few days."

"I wonder why?" she mused.

"He did not tell me," I admitted. "Frankly, I did not object, as it gives me a little time to accustom myself to the idea."

"Just the reason you should try this gown on. There is something about a wedding dress. It seems to dispel any qualms a bride may have."

"What makes you think I have qualms?" I inquired as I began unbuttoning my gown.

She regarded me curiously. "Damien is not just any man. He is very passionate about . . . about life. But surely you have discovered that by now."

I flushed at the directness of her implication.

"I see I am mistaken," she concluded.

"You sound surprised," I commented as I slipped the dress over my head.

"I am, but I should have known better."

She arranged the fullness of the wedding gown. I was amazed as I wriggled into the Edwardian sleeves how well it fit.

"It would take me an hour to do all these buttons," she said, "but I will fasten just enough to get the effect."

When she had finished I turned around. "What do you think?"

"See for yourself," she instructed as I ran my fingers over the smoothness of the satin.

"It is exquisite, Amanda," I murmured.

"You will make an exquisite bride," she answered. "It is a pity . . ."

I met her eyes in the mirror, waiting for her to finish. When instead she turned away, I reached out and touched her elbow.

"It is a pity about what?" I pleaded.

"Oh, nothing," she said lightly. "It was foolish of me to say anything."

Something told me her hesitancy was too important to disregard. "Please tell me what you were about to say."

She bit thoughtfully at the full flesh of her lip.

"I should not burden you with this, Lillith," she said finally, "but ironically, you are the only one who can help."

I placed my hand in hers and led her to the couch.

"I am at a loss to know what it is, Amanda, but if there is some way I can help you, you know you need only ask."

"It is not for me, Lillith, but for Damien that I would ask this of you. You know how pleased I am that you are going to marry. Certainly I championed it from the first. But I always assumed that if it came about it would have been my father's offer you accepted."

I smiled. "He should be very happy to learn that I have saved him a considerable sum of money."

She shook her head. "No, you do not understand. You see, there is no question in my mind that Marisse is determined to marry my father for only one reason, and I assure you it is not love. Why, I do not know, but he is vulnerable to her. If she gets her way and becomes Lady Darby, she will have a fortune at her disposal. For myself it has no import; I am more than amply cared for. But it is for Damien that I am concerned. Darby and all the holdings should by all rights go to him some day."

"I do not see what I could do."

She sighed. "There is one thing. You could accept my father's offer, but with the addition of one request. That Damien be his principal beneficiary."

"But it would be a total deception," I gasped. "Besides, when your father found out he would not only renege, but he would be enraged at being so manipulated."

"Not if you were very clever," she insisted. "At present he knows nothing of your plans. You could go to him this very day and tell him that you have reconsidered."

"He would never believe me, Amanda."

"There I think you are mistaken," she assured me. "My father believes that people are principally motivated by greed. Ironically, he deludes himself about Marisse's appetites. Tell him anything. Tell him that now that you are facing return to London, you see that you can ill afford to be independent of spirit without the means. Tell him that I have tried to dissuade you from leaving. The only thing you must not tell him is that you have already agreed to marry Damien."

I could not believe my ears. Her very vehemence told me she was not jesting. But it was inconceivable that she would be sitting before me asking that I perpetrate this hoax on her own father.

"Before judging me too harshly, Lillith, think of it this way; would you want Darby to fall into the hands of someone like Marisse, who cares naught for it, but only for what it affords her? There are hundreds of people who depend on us—the workers, the tenants. We have a responsibility to these people.

I would be loath to see that entrusted to Marisse."

"I do not know, Amanda. I would have to discuss it with Damien."

"Damien?" she exclaimed. "He is the last person you should tell. Can you imagine the pain it would cause him, to learn one day that his inheritance was due only to your arrangement with Father? He has caused Damien enough anguish, Lillith."

"You really think this is something I should do?"

"If you care for Damien it is what you *must* do," she insisted.

I looked down and, realizing that I had not removed the gown, asked if she might help me change. No sooner had I donned my walking dress than Mary arrived with our luncheon. While she busied herself I whisked the gown off to the closet—the last thing I wanted was to find her curiosity had forced me to break my promise again. And, to my relief, Amanda seemed content to while away the next hour with mere pleasantries.

As the clock struck two she jumped up, saying that she had to reclaim her son from Mrs. Horsley. When I offered to care for Terrence for the afternoon, she advised that my time would be better spent talking to Lord Darby.

It amazed me several hours later to find that having weighed Amanda's request, I saw merit in it. I had no qualms about Marisse, but both Damien and Amanda were obviously distrustful of her. For that matter, Jessica Darby was hardly enamored of her. There was no point in thinking that Lord Darby would of his own volition entrust the estate to Damien. Beyond my conviction that it was rightfully his, I was influenced by the realization that many lives depended on the continuity of Darby. I wished I had days to consider the ramifications of such an action, but time, I knew, was of the essence. Once Damien announced his intentions, all would be lost.

As I made my way downstairs I did so wishing that I possessed even a smidgeon of my mother's acting ability. Deception did not come to me naturally, and I could not allow Lord Darby to suspect for an instant that my motives were not genuine.

I was just crossing the reception hall when Charles came out of the library. "Your leg appears improved," he noted.

"By tomorrow I should even be able to discard this cane," I said.

He looked about, as if to make certain we were alone. "On that matter we were discussing, I have additional information."

"You have found something?" I asked eagerly.

"Not exactly," he replied, keeping his voice low. "I took myself down to the stables earlier today and had a talk with one of the hands. It appears that this stablehand who disappeared may have had reason to do so. But it also may well not have been of his own doing."

"Have you told this to anyone?"

He shook his head. "I do not think it would do any good. Something tells me the less we say the better."

"Maybe it would be best just to forget it," I suggested.

His eyes widened. "I am amazed to hear you say that. Where is the tenacious Miss Chatfield?"

"I could have been mistaken, you know. I just don't want to do anything to upset the household right now."

"Has something happened you are not telling me about?"

I avoided his gaze. "Of course not."

"Then do not allow these people to bring you to mistrust yourself, Lillith."

He should know the whole of it, I thought as I left him and directed my steps towards the library. As I entered I saw Lord Darby seated across the room. For a second I thought he was dozing, but as I tiptoed forward he raised his head.

"If I am disturbing you I could come back later," I offered.

"No, I could use a respite from those damnable finances," he replied.

I approached him tentatively as he picked up a decanter from the table beside him and replenished his glass.

"I take it you have mended from your little escapade," he mused.

"I am much better," I replied quietly.

"Tell me, Miss Chatfield, how is your work with Damien progressing? Why he needs those damn paintings catalogued is beyond me, but then a great deal about my son is beyond me."

"More's the pity," I murmured as I took a seat opposite him. "As I have told you before, your son has great talent. I have worked with his canvases for months now, but I never stop being in awe of them. When I think I have seen the best of them I come upon yet another. There is a sensitivity which captures the rather melancholy beauty of this area. They should not be locked away in the studio. They should be hanging in the great halls where they can be fully appreciated."

Lord Darby shrugged. "I know nothing of art. If you say they are good then I shall have to trust your judgment. It is not my idea of how a son of mine should spend his days."

"And what would you prefer him to do?" I ventured. "Instead of berating him, you should be encouraging him. Perhaps if you did he might gain emotional strength, which might even serve to better his physical condition."

He regarded me intently. "I did not realize you had formed such an attachment to him."

I flushed. "That is not what I said, Lord Darby."

He gulped down some brandy. "I know what you said. But if you have no feelings for him, why would you care what I think of him?"

I willed myself to remain calm. I could feel my throat become dry as the tumult raged within me. But I knew that if I allowed myself to be cowed by him, I should never be able to accomplish what I had set out to do.

"I care about Damien, but not in the way you imply."

"Perhaps. In any event you still have not answered my question. How is your work progressing?"

"Actually, it has almost come to an end," I admitted.

He looked surprised. "I see. And what are your plans now?"

"I have not really made any. I shall return to London and then . . ."

"And then?"

"I have a personal commitment to attend to, and then I shall commence to seek employment."

"This personal commitment; may I ask the nature of it?"

I smoothed the folds of my gown. "I simply want to visit a friend who has been ailing."

"Commendable, I suppose, but scarcely practical," he retorted. "But then if you were practical, you would have accepted my original offer to you."

I straightened in the chair. "I thought we had agreed not to discuss that again."

"And I have kept my part of the bargain. I am not certain that I would have gotten the best of it anyway. Perhaps you did me a favor by rejecting my proposal."

"What do you mean?" I said, bristling.

I waited as he withdrew an ornately carved pipe from his vest and filled it from a small leather pouch. He lit it, and the pungent aroma filled the room.

"I only meant that you seem a very strong-willed young woman."

"And you want Damien's wife to be someone you can control," I charged.

He puffed on the stout teak stem of the pipe. "Now it is you who are putting words in my mouth, Miss Chatfield. What I meant was that a woman who is perhaps more docile—more, shall we say, pliable—would be more suitable for my—for Damien."

"So that he might bully her as you bully him?"

"You do not mince words."

"You do not know your son at all. The last thing he needs is some passive woman who will hover about him, tending to his every whim, whom he can intimidate and reduce to little more than a servant."

"If, as you imply, he would be better served by one such as yourself, then why will you not accept my offer? Why will you not consent to marry Damien?"

I stood up and went to stand by the fireplace, my back to him. I knew that this was the moment to speak, but I dared not let him see my eyes, for I knew they reflected the uncertainty in my heart. I felt as though my body housed two minds, two souls, one which willed to be silent, to flee from the morass of Darby, and the other which could not abandon it.

"What would you say if I were to agree?" I murmured finally.

"My hearing is not what it used to be," he replied.

I turned to face him. "I am sorry. What I said was, what would you say if I were to agree?"

He shook his head. "Either this brandy is having more of an effect than usual or I am misunderstanding you. You can't be saying now that you want to marry Damien."

I placed my hand on the mantel to steady myself. "But that is exactly what I am saying, Lord Darby: that I am willing to accept your offer. That is, of course, if it still stands."

He looked at me incredulously. "You *are* full of surprises, Miss Chatfield. I could not be more dumbfounded and I am rarely at a loss, I assure you."

I waited for him to go on, wary that if I spoke my voice would betray me.

"You will pardon my asking, but has something happened between you and Damien to provoke this change of heart?" he finally asked.

I lowered my eyes. "I assure you, this is my decision. Mine alone."

"Then you are not in the family way?"

I gasped at his suggestion, the flush of my embarrassment prickling my skin. "I should prefer to think you did not intend such an insult, Lord Darby."

He laughed. "This is hardly a time to affect such an aura of propriety, my dear. Frankly, you look very pale. I suggest you come and sit down. This turn of events calls for another brandy, and no matter what you say, I shall pour a drop for you as well."

I did as he bade only because, loath as I was to admit it, my knees quivered beneath me. He handed me a snifter, and clasping it between my palms, I drank. The liquid burned as it slipped down my throat. I cannot go on with this ruse, I told myself. I would tell Amanda that I had failed. But if I abandoned it now I would never have another chance. I owed it to Damien at least to try.

"Now. Why do you not tell me what is behind this change of heart," he demanded.

I stared into the snifter. "It is not a change of heart, Lord Darby. Rather a change of mind."

"And you expect me to believe that just like that"—he snapped his fingers—"you have come round to my way of thinking? I recognize that we have spent little time together since you have been at Darby Manor, but I am aghast you would think me so naive."

I took another sip of brandy, prayerful that the numbing effect would take a quick hold. "I must admit I am surprised at your reaction. For one who was so fervent months ago, you seem now, well, almost suspicious. I would have thought you would be overjoyed. I am acquiescing to what you wanted from the first. Am I to conclude that you now find me unsuitable?"

"What I find, Miss Chatfield, is inconsistency. I accepted your decision, though I admit reluctantly. What I offered you was a name, respectability, not to mention a great deal of money."

"I should remind you, Lord Darby, that I have a name, and

in my own esteem I have respectability."

His lips moved. "So it is the money you admit you lack," he concluded, smirking.

I flinched under his bald examination. "If that is what you wish to think then let it be."

"Decisions have finally always to do with money," he said. "I told you once, but you preferred not to believe me."

"It may surprise you to know, Lord Darby, that I still do not take the stock in it that you do. I will also admit to you that this may be the worst mistake I have ever made in my life. But I face a choice, and if I am honest, I must admit that my alternatives are limited. I am embarrassed to say that. For I was raised within a family who, if anything, believed in and sought after the possibilities in life."

I watched as he drew on his pipe. "And what would you do, Miss Chatfield, were I to withdraw the offer?" he asked.

The stoniness of his regard caused me to shiver. This challenge was the last thing I had expected. I drew a deep breath, realizing that I should have to gamble my fate.

"Then I should ask that you arrange for my departure on the next coach."

He swirled the amber liquid in his glass. "I see you give me no latitude, Miss Chatfield."

I drew a deep breath. "As you have given me none, Lord Darby. You made an offer, I accepted. I suspect there is nothing else to converse about, save whether your original proposition still stands."

"I am not a man who goes back on my word, if that is what you infer," he said deliberately.

I placed the glass on the table before me. " 'Tis all moot, you understand. There is the likelihood Damien will have no part of this."

His eyes widened. "You mean to tell me this is not a conspiracy between you two?"

"I assure you, Damien knows nothing of this," I swore honestly.

"I am amazed."

"Then you are even less attuned to your son than I had thought. Frankly, I cannot predict how he will react. If there is the suggestion of conspiracy, 'twill likely be Damien's belief that you and I plotted this from the first."

"If you want him to believe otherwise then it is incumbent upon you to convince him."

I studied the octagonal vine pattern of the carpet at my feet. "I will speak with Damien."

"When?"

The brandy had taken its effect, and I suddenly felt exhausted. "By tomorrow," I replied resolutely. "But if he balks even slightly at my decision, I warn you I shall not argue it. I care enough for him that I should not want to cause him further misery in this life. If he refuses, I shall be on the next coach to London."

"I would not have thought you a woman to give up so easily," he challenged.

"It is not a matter of giving up, but rather of respecting the wishes of another."

He downed the liquid in his glass. "I do not think I need remind you of the terms of our agreement, Lillith. I am not bargaining for a caretaker for my son but for a wife in every sense of the word. I want heirs to the line. If you wed my son I expect you to bed him as well. Of course, the sooner you produce the offspring I wish, the sooner you will have your fortune. Then you will be free."

'Twas ironic, for freedom was the last thing I thought I should ever enjoy again. But the deed was not done yet. I had to heed Amanda's plea to reach the purpose of this parley, protecting Damien's inheritance of Darby.

"There is one thing," I ventured. "Another concession I would ask you to make."

He eyed me suspiciously.

"I have decided that your remuneration is not enough. If

this is to be my home, I want to be certain it will always be so."

"What are you getting at?" he demanded.

"Just that I want your assurance that Damien will, on the event of your death, be heir to Darby."

I held my breath as he glared at me. "I see I have misjudged you after all. But what makes you think that I would accede to this demand?"

"I would wish it done out of decency, but I shall not delude myself," I replied. "You have been very direct about what you want. I am simply doing the same."

"And if I do not agree?" he challenged.

"I think you know the answer to that, Lord Darby."

I watched him as he poured another brandy. "You are clever, Lillith Chatfield. I will give you that."

"It is not so unusual that I should want to protect my interests and ultimately those of the children born of this marriage. If they are to carry the Darby name, they should stand to benefit by it. And that thread is through Damien."

I knew he was angry, but I prayed he would not vent his rage on me.

"You will have what you want," he said finally. "I will have Sir Charles draw up the papers. The day you marry Damien the compact is sealed."

It was a heartless arrangement, and I could not believe that I had agreed to be a party to it.

"For one who has just beaten a master at his own game, you appear oddly subdued," he remarked as I stood up.

"I scarce feel a victor, Lord Darby," I replied sadly. "Indeed, I wonder who will be the greatest loser in all of this."

He smirked. "Your tune will change when you start reaping the benefits."

I moved towards the door. "Will my future daughter-in-law be joining us at dinner?" he inquired.

"I think not," I answered, recoiling at the sarcasm in his

voice. "It has been a long day. Please give my apologies to Marisse."

I moved to the staircase, using the cane for support as exhaustion overtook me. The faces of the portraits stared out at me as I climbed. When I reached the painting of Damien, I paused. "I hope I have done the right thing," I whispered, peering up at the profile I had come to know so well.

18

BLESSEDLY my only visitor that evening was Mary, who brought my dinner tray. Hiding away in my room was not an answer, but tonight I could suffer none of this household, even myself.

In my mind I argued that I had committed no wrong. I had acted to ensure the Darby legacy. It was what Edmund Darby had wanted all along. But my conscience spoke with a louder voice; I was no better than he, I had succumbed to the callous manipulation which I so detested in the man.

Ever since I had come to Darby I had felt as though there was a part of me which was slipping away from me. All the things I had cherished, the beliefs which I had held close seemed but distant memories. The emotions and actions which had taken their place were new to me. An inner voice told me I ought to mistrust their worthiness.

I knew it was ridiculous to blame Darby Manor itself, but none who lived here seemed spared. It was as though the house robbed one of all that was right and decent. Morality seemed to have no place here.

I awakened the following morning determined to see Damien. He was the only one who could reassure me that, despite all reservations, lives would not be destroyed but enhanced by our marriage. I dressed hurriedly, relieved that my ankle was so improved that I could walk without the cane. When I arrived at the studio, Damien opened the door almost immediately.

"I thought you were Sommers," he said. "He took Chips for an early romp."

"May I come in?" I inquired.

He wheeled his chair back to allow me entry. "Actually, I am pleased you are here. I wanted to speak with you."

I followed him over to the wall of windows. The early sun cast beams through the soaring elms which rose like wooden sculptures on the landscape.

"It seems so peaceful," I murmured.

"Time marches slowly in the North Country," he observed.

I pivoted round to face him. "You wanted to talk to me."

His eyes narrowed as my gaze met his. "Yes I did. Sit down, won't you?" I sank into the chair he indicated.

"I told you I wanted to wait a few days before announcing our intention to wed, but that has changed now," he began. "Jessica informed us last evening that she intends to leave for London on the morrow. I think it only fitting she be informed before her departure."

"Is that really what you want?" I asked. "Perhaps it would be better if . . ."

"If what, Lillith?" he demanded. "If we waited, if we denied what exists between us?"

I turned away from him, fixing my gaze on a branch buoyed by the gusting winds outside. "I wish I knew exactly what *does* exist between us, Damien," I said despairingly.

He wheeled his chair towards me, stopping just short of my knee. I sat very still as he extended his hand and traced the contour of my face with his fingers. A tremor passed through me as I felt his palm on the nape of my neck, drawing my head forward. My breath was stilled as his lips brushed against mine, gently at first, and then with a force which seemed to send blood pulsing through my extremities.

"Tell me you do not feel it, Lillith," he murmured as his hand slipped from my neck down the length of my arm.

"You should not have done that," I said finally.

He lifted my chin up so that I could no longer avert my gaze. "That is not an answer."

Helplessly I felt my eyes cloud with tears.

His hand caressed them from my cheeks, and then he reached into his pocket and withdrew the same box he had shown me the day before. His fingers curled about the yellow gold of the band. "Do not fight it, Lillith," he pleaded as he slipped the glittering jewel on my finger. "There is nothing to fear."

"You seem so certain, Damien," I choked out.

"I am certain that I need you, that Darby needs you," he replied.

I twisted the ring back and forth on my finger.

"We can be married within several weeks," he persisted.

"Why must it be so soon?" I asked.

"Am I to take it that whatever misgivings you managed to develop in the last twenty-four hours have not been put to rest?"

"I made a commitment to you, Damien," I said finally. "I will not go back on it."

He reached out and cupped my chin in his hand. "On my life, I shall do everything to see that you do not regret it." I believed him, but only because I wanted so desperately to believe him. He looked past me. "It is brightening, have you noticed?"

The sun had warmed the ice-laden branches, causing thousands of droplets to rain from their lofty perch.

"The roads should clear by the height of day," he continued. "I thought we might take the carriage out. That is, if you are feeling up to it."

"Oh, I would love it," I exclaimed. "Perhaps you might show me some of the tenant farms."

He smiled. "Since when have you been interested in the tenants?"

"Since Amanda . . ."

"Since Amanda what?" he demanded.

"I know what you asked of me, Damien, and I meant to keep our confidence, truly I did," I rambled, "but something happened and I just blurted it out."

He clenched his teeth, a muscle twitching along his jaw.

"Since you have decided to tell the others anyway, I cannot see the harm."

His hand thrust forward, clasping my wrist. "What did she say? What did she say to you?"

I winced at the force of his grasp. "Damien, you are hurting me," I moaned.

"Tell me what she said to you," he repeated.

"I do not remember," I lied. "She was pleased, she found your mother's wedding gown in the attic and—"

"And what?"

"And n-nothing," I stammered. "I tried on the dress. If that was wrong, I am sorry, but I meant no harm.

He released me as suddenly as he had grabbed me. "I am sorry, Lillith. I had no right."

I shrank from him, staring at my reddened wrist. "Sometimes you frighten me, Damien."

"I have said I am sorry, Lillith. I promise you it shan't happen again."

I stood up, edging past the wheels of his chair.

"Where are you going?"

"I am simply going to try and finish the cataloguing," I replied.

"I thought we had agreed to take a ride," he reminded me. "It would do us both good."

My heart was no longer in it, but I acquiesced, and less than half an hour later I found myself bundled next to Damien, putting Darby behind us, if only for a while. He was silent as the wheels of the carriage clattered against the roads, which had heaved against the harshness of cold and ice. I stared out the window watching the rows of conifers struggle against the weight of ice.

Our route took us through a wellspring of small villages, undistinguished save for their slate-roofed stone houses and small churches. The horses had slowed their pace, and we appeared to be climbing out of the valley.

"This is Bolton land," Damien said suddenly. "It borders Darby on the north."

I eased forward to gain a better view. It appeared a wasteland, save for a solitary four-square edifice rising from a distant plateau.

Sensing my question, he said, "That is Bolton Castle. It has been deserted for almost two centuries now. When Mary, Queen of Scots, surrendered at Carlisle, it was here that she was brought and chambered."

I stared at the grim reminder and shuddered. "How dreadful it must have been for her, sealed off away from everyone. It must have been like a living tomb."

"There are worse things," he murmured quietly. "At least her shame or despair or both were banished from the view of others."

There was empathy in his voice, and I wondered whether Darby had become to Damien what Bolton had been to Mary.

If I had hoped Damien might be more forthcoming in his conversation, I was sadly disappointed. For myself, I drank in each new sight with increasing curiosity. This canvas of old quarries, castle ruins, peaceful valleys, and high fells scored with deep ravines and dashing rivers was soon to become my home. I hoped that if I could see it as Damien did, it might tell me more about this man whom I was to marry, this man who at moments such as this one seemed a stranger to me.

He made not one move to touch me during the entire excursion. I tried to tell myself that he was at least showing me some respect, that after his earlier performance he would not dare force himself on me. But my heart questioned his sudden propriety. Had the touch of our lips when he had been hungry to prove our passion, only disproved it instead? Did he already regret his proposal? When I was no longer an illusion but flesh and blood in his arms, had his pulse not quickened as mine?

Damien had frightened me earlier, but no more than I had frightened myself. I knew not what he had stirred in me, only that it left me wanting more. I wanted to taste again his lips against mine, feel the caress of his hand at my throat. He had awakened something in me. Had he felt it too, or had my inexperience betrayed me?

"You seem very deep in thought," he mused. "Would you care to share it with me?"

I turned straight ahead, the brim of my bonnet shielding my eyes. " 'Tis nothing truly."

"I hope you are not still brooding about the apparition in the lake."

"Even if I were, what good would it do?" I challenged.

"None," he admitted.

"Is that the lot of the Darby women?" I ventured. "Am I, like Anitra, to be relegated to a code of silence?"

The minute I said it I regretted it. I steeled myself for a verbal or physical assault. When neither was forthcoming, I turned to face him. Where I expected to behold anger I saw only sorrow etched on his face.

When he finally spoke his voice was raspy. "Anitra lived as she died, Lillith. I have lived my life in the shadow of it. Each day I bury her again, as I did the first time. Sometimes I used to think there should never be an end to it. That is, until you came to Darby. For the first time I saw a glimmer of hope that I might rise out of the ashes and restore a sanity, a continuity to Darby. If you force me to live with these ghosts, Lillith, you will dash all my hopes of that."

My emotion caused me to swallow hard. "I do not want to hurt you, Damien. Can't you see that?" I beseeched him.

"Then let it go," he commanded. "Let go of those suspicions, those things you do not understand. If you do not believe in me, then believe in us. God help me if I am wrong, but with you I know there is hope. Without you my soul is damned."

I stared at him, struggling to make sense of these last moments. I had blurted out Anitra's name, demanded to know whether I too was to be relegated to a life lived in the shadows. I had expected his wrath, but not his pain. Had I become so obsessed by this child-woman that I had forgotten that Damien was held responsible for her death? Such despair, such unhappiness had been visited on him! Had I been forced to bear such guilt would I have been any different? I knew not. But why did he believe that I possessed some power to save him from his pain? I had but months ago thought I could not rescue myself from the obscurity of my own loss. Why did he think I would deliver him from the abyss of tragedy?

I had not realized until the house loomed before us that we had come full circle to Darby. I alighted from the carriage but did not wait to see Damien's chair brought to him. He was fiercely independent, and attempts to assist him he somehow took as an insult to his virility.

At first I thought I was alone in the reception hall, but as I crossed to the stairs my name echoed throughout the soaring chamber. I turned to see Lord Darby framed in the door to the drawing room.

"Might I have a moment with you?" he inquired.

I was not eager to deal with him, but I knew I could not chance a more public meeting.

As I slipped inside the drawing room, closing the door behind me, he spared the use of subtlety. "Do you have something to tell me?" he asked.

"If you are asking whether I am going to marry your son, the answer is yes," I informed him.

His eyes narrowed. "I expect I ought to congratulate you, but though it seems that the fox has proved craftier than the hunter, I should not be too smug if I were you."

"And what is the meaning of that?"

"My dear, do you expect me to believe that my son has suddenly agreed to marry you, when we both know how distasteful the prospect was to him? No. I think not. What I think is that over these months he has formed an attachment to you—perhaps it is even mutual—and the two of you decided to outwit me at my own game. I cannot fault you entirely, indeed I rather admire your cunning, but stand notice I do not believe this little scheme for a moment. Salina Kent might have succeeded in duping me, but not you, Lillith."

"Do not insult my mother's name," I warned him.

"Well, you might as well admit it," he snapped.

"I admit nothing," I said, hearing the tremor in my own voice. "Damien has nothing to do with this. If you think it a ruse, then so be it. But why should he not have what he deserves? And why would you care, anyway? You have said yourself the one thing you want is to see the legacy of Darby continued." Somehow amidst my own mingling of fear and fury I knew I had stopped him.

"You have me at one disadvantage, Lillith," he acknowledged finally. "Time is on your side. I shall have Sir Charles draw up the papers. You will have them as promised, the day of your marriage."

I had turned to leave when he stopped me. "There is one more thing, Lillith. The less said about all this the better. Though some would doubt it, I do not deceive myself that

Marisse's interest in me is wholly unselfish. My days are numbered, and I am allowed self-deception. She amuses me, and I want her to continue to amuse me, so I should not boast of the arrangement we have made."

I drew a deep breath. "In turn, I would ask the same of you, Lord Darby. Contrary to your insistence, Damien knows nothing of this. You have spared him little else. Perhaps just this once you might see fit to treat him as a son and not as an enemy."

I did not wait for an answer but left him and went to my room. Divesting myself of my cloak and bonnet, I sank onto the edge of the bed, fingering the intricate crewelwork of the coverlet. I felt no joy, none of the exhilaration due the victor. But I could not allow self-loathing at the thought of my manipulations to obliterate my motives. It had been done with the best of intentions. Indeed I would, if he had threatened it, gladly have given up the sums he was to settle on me.

I did not fully understand what my responsibilities would be once I married Damien, but I was determined to see that good would come out of it. The fire years past had claimed more than two lives, and it was time to make a new beginning.

Seating myself at the dressing table, I brushed the snarls from my hair, using only a ribbon to catch the cascade down my back. I was about to leave the room when, remembering the two letters I had asked Mary to post, I crossed to the table by the fire where I had left them. At first I thought I must have been mistaken, for as I riffled through the sheets of paper there was no sign of the envelopes. I would have continued my search save that I had told Damien I would join him for luncheon, and I was late already.

When I reached the studio I was relieved to find that his spirits seemed greatly uplifted since our drive. Even Chips shared his ebullient mood, scurrying between us as we shared portions of guinea hen and corn pudding.

I found myself hoping that that afternoon would mark a change between us. Only once before had Damien encouraged me to talk about myself, but this day he seemed eager for me to reminisce. Whereas before I had found his questions intrusive, today my recollections seemed to have a cathartic effect. I said that he was allowing me to meld my past into the present.

When I retired hours later to change for dinner, the happiness of the past hours paled slightly with the realization that, as much as Damien had managed to elicit from me, I had learned no more about him or Darby. One day he would come to me, but I knew it had to be voluntarily. I had to engender the one thing in him that he seemed to have lost, even in himself: trust.

19

Yo u could have heard a pin drop. Even though I had anticipated it, when the moment finally arrived I was as ill-prepared as the rest.

To my chagrin I had descended that evening to find that James and Maude Farklan had been included in the dinner. Marisse, with whom I had exchanged hardly any words these past few days, was in high spirits, and particularly solicitous, I noticed, towards Lord Darby. Amanda, who had spent most of the day with Sir Charles, was of a kindred mood, and though the repartee was insipid for the most part, I took cheer in the camaraderie.

There was not a meal at Darby unaccompanied by wine, but when Damien called for champagne there was a moment's pause.

Jessica Darby was the one who finally filled the void. "The grape of celebration," she exclaimed as the bubbles rose in her glass. "Or have you decided, Marisse, that we should take on the habits of the French?"

"For once I have naught to do with it," Marisse replied. "Perhaps your brother has finally seen fit to make free with his cellar."

"Is it someone's birthday?" Maude inquired as the remaining glasses were filled.

"What is this about, Edmund?" Marisse demanded anxiously.

Lord Darby faced me squarely, clear challenge in his eyes. "I am as much in the dark about this as you," he said finally.

Damien lifted his glass. "I should like you to congratulate me. Lillith has consented to marry me."

There was utter silence, until Amanda effusively feigned surprise.

Marisse whirled to face me. "Is this true?" she asked incredulously.

I nodded in assent.

She turned to Lord Darby. "Edmund?"

"Apparently we are to have a wedding," he said steadily.

She stood up, almost spilling the effervescing liquid in her glass. "Are you going to tell me you knew nothing of this, Edmund? This is ridiculous. Obviously you and Miss Chatfield here . . . well, we all know—"

"I would not say what you might later regret, Marisse," Damien interrupted.

I stole a look at him, but his attention was focused on Marisse. "Are you not going to congratulate me?"

Jessica Darby raised her glass. "Here, here. I thought I should be six feet under before I saw this day. Lillith, dear, you have given me a new lease on life with this news."

"And you, James," Damien said, "I think this is the first time I have seen you at a loss."

"I admit I am flabbergasted," he replied. "There are more secrets in this house than I dared imagine."

Finally everyone had commented, everyone save Sir Charles, who had not taken his eyes off me since the announcement.

Damien looked from one to the other of us. "I could not blame you if it is envy you are feeling, Charles."

"You have read my mind," Charles replied slowly.

"A wedding at Darby," Jessica said enthusiastically. "When is it to take place?"

"I am not going to give Lillith time to change her mind," Damien replied. "Two to three weeks at most."

"Oh, that cannot be," she argued. "I have just set plans to return to London, and I simply refuse not to be allowed a share in this."

Marisse, who had reseated herself, threw her napkin on the table. "Well, you needn't worry, as there will be no wedding here in the immediate future. You all seem to forget that there is to be a ball at Darby eighteen days hence."

"How can we forget when you remind us daily," Jessica retorted. "But it might now prove fortuitous. Why not make it a wedding celebration. At least then those hoards of guests shan't leave here wondering why they came."

"What would you say to that, Lillith?" Damien inquired.

"I thought we had agreed to a private ceremony."

"By tradition you will have that," Lord Darby informed. "There is a chapel on the westerly land. It is used for all Darby weddings."

When an hour later we had done with dinner, all I could think of was escaping to the privacy of my room. It was obvious that I was to have little say in my own wedding. But if I took exception, it was Marisse who voiced it. The conclusion that the ball should serve to celebrate our union clearly infuriated her. I did not deceive myself that it was her own marriage which she wanted to take precedence. I had tried to argue it, but when I was vociferously overruled I accepted that my own desires were to be subjugated to those of the family.

When we were at last done Lord Darby announced abruptly that he was tired and intended to retire early.

I seized the opportunity to say that I too was weary.

As I rose, Damien looked across at Charles, saying, "You see, old chap, what they say about marriage must be true. No sooner does she agree to be my bride than she tires of me."

"Poppycock," Jessica Darby scoffed. "You men are all alike. 'Tis an emotional time for a woman, and Lillith is right. She needs her rest. You will have a lifetime with my nephew," she said to me. " 'Twill be soon enough."

I excused myself, following Lord Darby from the dining room. I had but closed the door behind me when he stopped and came back to me.

"I do believe that was the most expensive toast I have ever drunk."

His words stabbed at my very being.

"Let me give you a word of caution, Lillith. I have paid a high price for you. Do not even think of being less than a faithful and dutiful wife to Damien, or it will be you who will pay the price."

"Why would you think I would be anything else?" I stammered.

"Because I know my son," he replied.

I stood stock still as he walked slowly towards the library.

As I made my way to my room I fluctuated between fear and rage. How dare he threaten me, and how dare he castigate his own son! I hardly expected him to welcome me into the bosom of the household, but I had hoped we might at least be civil with one another. Yet, in truth, I knew I wanted more than that. With Damien I wanted to open a new era at Darby, but I had to wonder at this moment whether anyone could lay to rest the ghosts of this place.

I undressed and climbed into bed. When I awakened the clock had just chimed midnight. I lay there, praying I could drift back to sleep, but my mind was too full to allow the bliss of slumber.

I had no idea why, but I suddenly found myself thinking of Millie. She had been kind to me when I had needed it most, and for that alone I knew I ought to write her and give her news of my impending marriage. It seemed a ridiculous thing to do at this hour, but it was better than fretting.

I drew my robe about me and went over to the table where I had left the writing tablet, reminding myself to ask Mary about my letters in the morning. As I dipped the pen into the miniature inkwell, I realized the reservoir was dry.

Now that I was up, I was determined to complete the task. Remembering a large inkwell in the library, I decided to venture downstairs.

Thankfully, the house was still as I crossed to the staircase, my candle lighting my way. I opened the library door and carefully closed it behind me.

"I see there was another who could not sleep."

I whirled about to see Sir Charles seated by the fire.

"I ran out of ink," I said quickly. "I shan't disturb you."

"You could never do that, Lillith," he replied quietly.

I crossed quickly to the desk. "Oh, dear," I murmured.

He rose and strode towards me.

"I did not bring my paper with me and I cannot carry that off," I remarked, noting the heavy bronze inkwell.

"There must be some paper in the desk," he said, opening the middle drawer. "Aha, you see," he said, withdrawing several sheets and placing them on the gold-tooled leather top.

"I could not use that," I commented, noting that it bore the Darby crest.

He looked down at me. "A bit premature, but not untoward, if indeed you plan to go through with this."

By "this" I knew he meant my marriage to Damien. I said nothing.

"You cannot truly be serious about this, Lillith."

"And why not?" I challenged.

"Because it is a mistake. I do not know how Edmund convinced you."

"What makes you think that is what happened?"

He looked surprised. "You cannot tell me that you have come to this voluntarily?"

"I am doing this of my own free will," I asserted.

He shook his head. "Nothing will convince me of that. You forget that as Edmund's solicitor I will be privy to certain things. There will, of necessity, be no secrets from me. That is, of course, unless you do not expect to receive an endowment once you marry Damien."

I replaced the stationery in the drawer.

"Your silence says it all," he murmured.

"I do not see what concern it is of yours," I bristled.

He reached out and almost caressingly rearranged a tendril of my hair. "It has become my concern, Lillith," he replied slowly.

I looked up at him. There was a tender determination in his expression. "May I ask why?"

"You should not have to ask that. Can you not see that I have come to care for you? Frankly, I had hoped that you might return with me to London. I might be able to court you properly there. But as things stand, you force my hand."

"Please," I begged, "there is really nothing to say."

He placed his hand on my elbow. "There you are mistaken," he continued. "Lillith, I cannot let you do this. If you think Darby is a haven where you can take refuge, I fear you are wrong. Damien was right when he accused me of envy, but if I thought he was the right man for you I would be silent. I do not know what it is, but there is something very wrong here. There is something unholy about Darby. These people sit about in stony silence or rage. What is there to cause you to remain here?"

"Damien," I replied simply.

He hesitated as my sincerity dawned on him slowly. "You actually care for him."

"Is that so surprising?"

His smile was forced. "I think this is the part where I ought play the good sport. But you will forgive me if I tell you my heart is not in it."

"I do not think we should be here discussing this," I said, drawing my robe closed.

"You know, I will admit to you that at dinner tonight, when I had recovered from the shock of the announcement, I fancied that I would come to you and beg or cajole or even romance you out of this decision. If I have ever suffered in life it has been due to my own reticence. I know we do not know each other well, but I had hopes that once you returned to London I might make amends for my earlier misdeeds."

"That is long behind us now, Charles," I replied.

"At least I can be thankful for that," he murmured. "I should hate to depart without knowing that we are at least friends."

"I did not know you were planning to leave."

"The day after next," he said. "With one exception, I cannot say I will regret returning to London."

"Perhaps one day we will meet again," I offered.

"Oh, you shan't get rid of me that easily, Lillith. I have to return to Darby within the next weeks to settle a small legal problem."

"Then it is possible you will return in time for the wedding?"

"Possible, but not probable," he informed me. "Though I admit I am uncomfortable about leaving you here right now.

315

I am convinced that you were not suffering delusions down at the lake. It is unsettling, at the least."

I had not given thought to it since the last time we talked. "Perhaps I was mistaken. After all, a body does not simply rise and walk away."

"No. But it can be dragged away," he countered.

"Do you know what you are suggesting?"

He frowned. "I know what I saw, Lillith. Though you seem able to rationalize it, I am not so easily persuaded. I would never forgive myself if any harm were to come to you."

"Charles, I am perfectly safe here," I assured him. "There may be some who are not exactly taken with the prospect of my marrying Damien, but there is no threat to me here."

"Just promise me you will be careful," he implored me.

I smiled. "Frankly, the greatest threat to me at Darby is myself. But I hope my series of accidents is at an end. And now, please excuse me; I think I shall retire. My letter can wait."

I started to move away from him, but he reached out and clasped my arm. "Lillith, I want you to know that if you ever need anything, anything at all, you can always rely on me."

As I looked up at him I was struck by the gentleness I beheld in his eyes. If we had met at another time, under different circumstances, I wondered, would I be pledging myself to him rather than Damien?

"Who would have thought we would become friends," I said finally.

He released me. "I wish it were more, but I can at least be grateful for that."

"You know, I think you are overlooking the real prize here at Darby," I suggested. "I think if you were to forget for a moment that you are Lord Darby's solicitor, you might find that you have more in common with Amanda than you think."

He laughed. "I should never have taken you for a matchmaker, Lillith. Unfortunately, I am a man who likes to do his own bidding."

And not a man to be pushed, I thought, as I slowly climbed the stairs. I smiled as the tendril he had arranged fell free again. I was amazed how much Charles communicated with the slightest of gestures. It had been wrong of him to speak of his intentions, but I found myself oddly flattered by it. It was Damien, of course, whom I loved, but I had grown fond of Charles, more than I had realized.

I was just about to enter my room when I heard a sound by the back staircase. As I started towards it a strong draft extinguished my candle. There came the sound of a man's voice. Staying close to the wall, I groped my way forward until I reached the landing.

I was about to call down to see who was there when I heard a man say, "You are a fool, Damien. I am telling you this is a drastic mistake."

I crouched down on the top step and peered through the spindles. The light was dim, but I was certain the man was the same one I had seen slipping out of the house some nights past.

"No good can come from her knowing," I heard Damien argue.

"What if she finds out by accident. Can you think what that might do to her?"

"I will have to take that chance. By the way, since you were fool enough to accept Marisse's invitation, I will thank you to mind your words around Lillith. And be careful leaving. Farklan was here tonight. I am not entirely sure that he has gone, given his obvious shock at my announcement."

As I heard a door close I scrambled to my feet and scurried back along the hall to my room. I was shivering as I climbed into bed and drew the covers close around my neck. Whoever this man was, he was obviously no stranger to Damien, but what was he doing at Darby at this hour, and why was Damien warning him about talking to me? I would find out soon enough, I expected, since Marisse had apparently invited him to the ball.

When I answered the knock at my door the following

morning the last person I expected to find on the other side was Marisse. She looked beyond me, almost as if she expected to find someone there. "May I come in?" she asked.

"Of course," I replied, pushing my hair back from my face.

As she came towards me I was struck by her appearance. She reminded me of sculpted marble, finely chiseled, but frozen. She went to the love seat and indicated that I should join her.

"I think it is time we had a talk, Lillith," she said seriously.

I did not have to wonder at the topic.

"I must say I was at a disadvantage last evening," she continued. "It seems that I greatly misjudged you."

"In what way?"

Her mouth formed a wry smile. "Come now, my dear, let us not play games with each other. We are more of a kind than I had assumed. I cannot fault you for having ambition. What I fault you for is your judgment."

"I do not understand," I replied.

"If you recollect, I have tried to warn you about this place. Several times. Obviously I was not fervent enough in cautioning you. You should have left that first week. I did not think your taking on the position with Damien was wise, but I was convinced that it was purely a business arrangement."

"It was," I said emphatically.

Her eyes widened. "You really expect me to believe that?"

I wanted to say that I did not care what she chose to believe. "It is clear you disapprove of my marriage to Damien, Marisse, but what is your point?"

She drew a breath. "I am certain that the life you have been living here at Darby Manor has been seductive. I can think of few to whom it would not appeal. Save, of course, for its remoteness, which is sadly provincial. But the accoutrements here cannot ever make up for what you will endure."

"If life here is as ominous as you present, Marisse, then why would you choose it for yourself?" I queried.

"Ah, but it is different for me. I am older, more experienced. But most important is that it is Edmund I am marrying, not Damien."

"You do not like Damien, do you?"

"Whether I like him is not the question," she insisted. "But I do know that marrying him would be a terrible tragedy for you."

"Why?" I demanded.

"I cannot tell you that. But I will share with you one thing. It is that Damien can never commit himself to a normal relationship with a woman."

I shrank back against the cushions, horrified by her words.

"I see you are shocked," she continued.

"If that is true, then why were you so eager to warn me of his advances?" I stammered.

"Oh, do not misunderstand, Lillith," she said, smirking. "There is nothing that physically impairs Damien's manhood. It is his sexual appetite, not his performance, to which I refer. You may amuse him for a spell, but you will never really possess him in the carnal sense. And when he can finally deny his obsessions no longer and you lie in an empty bed, it will be too late." She stood up suddenly. "Think about it, Lillith. If you have any sense you will heed my words and be gone on the next coach to London."

"Wait," I cried out. "You cannot come here like this and make such insinuations. What are you really saying?"

"No. I shan't risk that. But if you really want to know, why not ask Damien? Ask him about the fire, ask him about this unholy obsession, ask him about his sister. Ask about Anitra."

The sound of her name seared through me as a knife. "What does Anitra have to do with this?"

She stared hard at me and then, gathering up her skirts, went to the door.

"I said, what does Anitra have to do with this, Marisse?" I repeated.

"Everything," she replied.

The door closed behind her. My heart was pounding so

furiously that I could actually hear its very beat resounding in my ears. The gathering light of day played its beams about the room, and as I stared down at my hands, the light refracted off the ring, displaying the facets of the emerald.

I tried to tell myself that Marisse was only trying to frighten me. She did not want me at Darby. They were wild accusations. But, then why did the words of the diary engulf me like the Swale in spate, why when I looked into the fireplace did I see the charred ruin of the summerhouse, why did the whittled carving on the lid of a long-abandoned trunk seem a fiery brand on my memory?

I was not allowed to dwell on my confusions, for a maid arrived with my morning basin.

"Where is Mary?" I inquired.

"She's gone te 'er mum's," she replied.

I decided that might well explain the missing letters.

"Will ye be wantin' a tray in yer room?" she inquired as she set about making the bed.

"Not this morning. I think I need some fresh air."

By the time I finished dressing I had altered my earlier plans. I simply could not allow Marisse's warnings to fester inside me. She had challenged me to look to Damien for the answers, but that was impossible. Even if I had had the courage to question him about his relationship with Anitra, I knew I would not find the truths I sought that way. It was to Jessica Darby's room that I took myself.

"Come in," I heard her call out in response to my knock.

I opened the door a crack and peered inside. " 'Tis I, Lillith. I did not mean to intrude."

She looked up over her spectacles. "Nonsense. An unexpected pleasure, my dear. I have been avoiding going downstairs, and now you give me the perfect excuse to stay here."

I stepped tentatively into the room.

"You shall have to come closer, my dear. I do not admit it in public, but my sight and hearing are not what they used

to be." She motioned to me to sit on a tapestry-covered Jacobean chair.

"I like this room," she continued. "Marisse calls it a dis-
grace; I prefer to think of it as well worn. A bit like myself,
actually. But now, tell me how is it that I am honored by your
visit? I hope 'twas not Damien's doing. Does he think that
because you two are soon to be wed 'twould be wise to humor
his old maiden aunt?"

I shook my head. "I came on my own."

She tapped the floor lightly with the cane held in her left
hand. "And from the sound of your voice 'tis not merely a
social call."

"I admit I scarce know how to broach this with you," I
conceded. "I know I have no right, but there is something that
I must know."

"If I can tell you, I will," she assured me.

"Has Damien . . . do you know if Damien was ever in love
with someone?"

She appeared thoughtful. "I cannot answer that, Lillith."

"Then there *was* someone," I concluded.

"There may have been. I do not know. But even if there
was, it is obviously in the past. It poses no threat to you today.
And if you are thinking about the little Farklan, I can assure
you Damien is not the least bit interested in her. He may be
foolish about certain matters, but he is not an idiot."

"But what if he cannot forget her, this woman," I persisted.
"What chance would he and I have?"

"Assuming that there was someone, the key is the past
tense. She—whoever she was, if she even existed—will only
be a part of your life together if you permit it. I would wager
that the sooner you put this out of your mind, the sooner you
will be able to build a life anew."

"But what if he cannot, for whatever reason, bury the
past?" I persisted. "What if this relationship so obsessed him

that he can not live in the present. What future would there
be for us?"

She appeared troubled. "Lillith, who has been filling your
head with these notions? Certainly not Damien."

"It does not really matter who it was," I cried. "If there is
even a germ of truth in it, you must see that it would be
impossible for me to marry him."

The line of her shoulders relaxed.

"Lillith, listen to me. I suspect it is Marisse who is behind
this anxiety of yours, but rest assured, you have naught to
fear. I cannot tell you it will be an easy life; heartache has been
a companion to him since the loss of his mother and sister. In
many ways he lost his father as well in that fire. But he cares
for you, deeply. There is a spirit in him which has been absent
for years. I think you have renewed him in a way, instilled
something in him. Hope, perhaps."

"He seems so certain," I mused.

"And you are not?"

"There are moments when I cannot imagine life without
him, and others when I am terrified of life with him," I
admitted.

She tapped her cane on the floor. "Perhaps if you were to
leave here for just a few days it might put things in better
perspective."

"Where would I go?"

"You could come back with me to London. I doubt Damien
would fancy it, but a separation, seeing familiar things again,
might help to allay these doubts you have. I am an old fool for
suggesting it, as I know there is a chance that you might not
decide in my nephew's favor. But I am not an inexperienced
gambler. Which is why I would risk the wager."

I turned her suggestion over and over in my mind. It would
be lovely, I thought, to go back, and certainly it was most
generous of her to urge me to, but in truth such a journey
would not be a return to the familiar but a flight from the
unknown.

I thanked her for her offer. "But my answer is here."

She smiled. "I was hoping you would say that. And if I may offer some unsolicited advice, look to your heart, Lillith. That is where your answer finally lies."

Returning to my room, I changed into walking boots and, pulling my cloak from the armoire, made my way down to the reception hall and out the front door. The air was cold but fresh and crisp as I strode purposefully down through the now-fallow gardens to the path leading to the summerhouse.

Jessica Darby had said that I must put away from me any thoughts of this other woman in Damien's past. Perhaps she was right. But she could not know that the woman of whom I spoke was Anitra. And though I knew she had been laid to rest some years ago, I was not sure that she did not somehow still live within Darby Manor and those who abided here.

As I came round the end of the privet I stopped short, for there ahead of me, staring at this relic of a past inferno, was Amanda. I called out to her and she turned, emitting an audible gasp as she did.

I went swiftly towards her. "I did not mean to startle you," I said quickly.

"For a moment I . . ."

I waited for her to continue. "Is Terrence with you?"

"Terrence? Oh, no, I left him back at the manor. 'Tis not healthy for him to come here."

"I suppose it is dangerous," I agreed, noting that the blackened boards had rotted to reveal what had been a cold cellar below. "The rest of the grounds are so carefully manicured, but this . . . It is like a blight on the landscape. Truthfully, I cannot think why someone has not leveled and removed this debris."

She looked slowly around. "We could not do that, Lillith. This place is a reminder. I actually find it almost peaceful at times. If you listen very carefully you can almost hear the silence. 'Twould be a desecration to destroy it."

"But there can be no tranquillity here for Damien," I countered.

Her mood seemed to change suddenly. "I really do not want to talk about this. What I want to know is whether you spoke to my father. I mean, did you go to him? Did you accept his proposal?"

It sickened me even to think of it. "I have never felt so deceitful, Amanda. He thinks Damien . . . he thinks it a collusion between your brother and myself."

She frowned. "Are you telling me he did not agree to it?"

I shook my head. "He agreed, but I pray I did the right thing by taking your advice. It is all such a sham."

She reached out and clasped my shoulders, shaking me slightly. "Of course it is right."

"How can you say that?" I said in amazement. "He is your own father."

Her hands fell away from me. "My allegiance is to Damien. I would do anything for him."

I fell into step with her as she turned back to the house.

We had just crossed back to the terraces when I recognized Perse crouched below one of the stone lions which flanked the cascade of steps. He was turning to load a juniper bush onto a wooden cart when he looked up. As I waved a greeting to him the prickly shrub slipped from his brawny arms. I watched stupefied as he stumbled backwards and disappeared suddenly behind the lower hedgerow.

"He seemed so frightened," I said.

"You must not take it personally. Perse is afraid of his own shadow," Amanda replied. "He should not be kept about, but as long as . . ."

I waited for her to complete the sentence, but she did not.

She put her arm through mine, almost propelling me towards the house. When we reached the front door Amanda paused to use the brass boot scraper. We had just crossed the threshold when Sommers appeared from the far vestibule.

"Begging your pardon, but Sir Charles was looking for

you," he said. "He asked that you meet him in the library."

Amanda broke into a wreath of smiles. "This day is turning out better than I dared imagine," she said warmly.

Sommers looked confused. "Oh, 'twas not you, Miss Amanda, but Miss Chatfield whom he asked for."

The look Amanda gave me was one of unabashed fury. "One is not enough, I suppose," she hissed.

I was so stunned that it took me several seconds to recover. I nodded to Sommers, and once he had left I turned to Amanda cautiously. "What did you mean?"

As angry as she had been, she was now the model of contrition. "Oh, *do* forgive me, Lillith," she beseeched me. "I cannot think what made me say such a dreadful thing. Disappointment I expect. It was only I hoped that before he left Charles might make some overture, some small statement of intention."

"I did not realize things had progressed so far," I ventured, thinking that she would be devastated if she knew of my encounter with Charles the previous evening.

"Oh, they have not," she assured me. "But I think he is rather shy and intimidated, being Father's solicitor."

"Perhaps if you just let things take their course."

She regarded me seriously. "Do you think so? I suppose you might be right. Perhaps I am just getting caught up in the moment. You and Damien . . . 'Twould be lovely if we could all be married and live here at Darby."

I thought it would only complicate matters should I remind her that Sir Charles resided and worked in London.

She leant forward conspiratorally. "You can be a dear and put in a word on my behalf. Nothing obvious, of course. Something subtle like, 'Do you not think Amanda superb?'"

I would have been surprised save that her peal of laughter told me 'twas all in fun. "Well, he would be a fool if he did not pursue you," I concluded honestly.

She clasped her hands. "My thoughts precisely. Now be gone with you to start your good deeds."

Sir Charles was alone in the library, so absorbed by something atop the desk that he did not hear me enter. Positioning
myself before him, I cleared my throat. "I believe you were
looking for me."

I wished he had been less obviously pleased as our eyes met.
"Thank you for coming." he said.

I looked down at the scatter of papers as he stood up. " 'Tis
not my doing," he replied. "Were it for me to say, I would rip
all this to shreds."

His vehemence was perplexing. "What is it?"

"Your marriage contract," he said flippantly. "Such as it
is."

"Oh."

"Oh? Is that all you have to say?"

"Is there something out of order?" I asked.

"Oh, nothing is out of order, as you put it, if you insist on
going through with this."

"It is called a marriage," I reminded him.

He slammed his fist down on the stack of papers. "Call it
what you want, but do not insult me by referring to it as a
marriage. That would be hypocrisy. The irony is that last
night I actually believed you cared for him."

I reeled at his assault. "What right have you?" I challenged.
"How quickly you forget that from its inception you have
been a party to it."

"That was different, Lillith. Everything has changed since
then," he argued.

I went to the fireplace and sank into the wing chair.
"Oddly, little has changed," I murmured, "except myself."

"What do you mean?" he demanded.

I stared ahead. "I am not certain," I responded finally. "But
please do not try and dissuade me again from this marriage.
I am too tired to fight you, or it."

He strode over to me. "Even more reason, Lillith, for you
not to sign these papers. Come back with me to London.
Think on it and—"

"No," I exclaimed.

"All right," he conceded. "Stay here. But do not sign these papers. I shall return to Darby in two weeks. If, after that time, you still insist, I will not stop you. I am not asking this of you solely for myself, of that I assure you."

His plea was so impassioned that, if but for a moment, it gave me pause. "And what of my commitment?" I ventured finally.

"Damn your commitment. You have made none until you sign these papers."

I knew he was right. As long as I did not put my name to the agreement I was free to do as I pleased. But what he could not know was that I was not free, signature or not.

I had argued that I had given my word, but the truth was, as I suspected Jessica Darby already knew, that I had given my heart. Somewhere amidst the confusion, apprehension, and suspicion of these last months, I had fallen in love with Damien Darby.

I stood up and went to the desk. "I trust you will tell me where my signature is required," I said resolutely.

"There is nothing I can do to convince you?" he entreated.

I turned to look at him. "Please do not make this more difficult for me than it already is. I know what you are trying to do. But you needn't feel now, or ever, any guilt about this. It is my doing. If I am to suffer as a result, then so be it."

He studied me some moments before coming to join me at the desk. Silently he searched through the papers, and selecting one, he drew his finger along an open empty line.

As I took up the pen his hand closed over mine.

"I pray to God that Damien Darby grows to know where his fortune really lies."

327

20

I N the end I almost regretted not accepting Jessica's offer, for I realized how lonely Darby would seem these next weeks. When she and Charles left on the coach for London the following day, Amanda was with them.

It had been a last-minute decision, made possible by my offering to care for Terrence while his mother was away. She had approached me, saying she longed to visit the shops, but I suspected her real motives were centered around Charles. Although I thought she ought be more reticent in her pursuit of him, I couldn't deny her. Besides, I decided it would give me an opportunity to get to know this boy who was soon to become my nephew.

Though I had not warmed to the child, I felt sorry for him. Most of the time he was relegated to his room, and I could not think that the companionship of Mrs. Horsley gave him reason for cheer.

As the weather had turned inclement the afternoon of their departure, I decided to find some indoor amusement for Terrence.

Mrs. Horsley and I had managed to keep our distance since our last encounter, but separation had not quelled her hostility.

"I have come for Terrence," I explained as she wedged her bulk between me and his door.

"I am perfectly capable of seeing to him," she snapped.

"I am certain you are, but I told his mother I would look after him in her absence."

She did not budge. "The child does not care for strangers."

I sensed she was deliberately testing my patience, but I kept my voice even as I replied, "Well, I am not a stranger to him, Mrs. Horsley."

"You will always be a stranger here, Miss Chatfield," she scoffed.

I drew a deep breath. "On the chance you have not heard, Damien Darby and I are to be married."

She gave me a look of total disdain. "There is nothing that escapes me at Darby. But that does not alter the fact that you will never belong here. You can marry Master Damien, you can live within these walls, but you will always be an outsider."

Ignoring her venom, I kept to my purpose. "I will ask you again. Please fetch Terrence for me."

I breathed a sigh of relief as she turned and called to the boy, who came reluctantly to the door. I wished he could have looked happier to see me, but I tried to disregard his sullen expression as I extended my hand to him. "In the event you are looking for us, we will be in the studio," I advised the housekeeper.

"I shouldn't do that if I were you," she called out as I started to lead the child down the hall.

Deciding I should not dignify her comment with a response, I continued along the hall and down the stairs with Terrence in hand.

"Perhaps your Uncle Damien can find you some oils and you can paint for a while," I offered, hoping to cajole him into a brighter mood. "And after that, we might go to the library. Would you like that?"

Dark, penetrating eyes so like his grandfather's lifted to mine. I did not know what I beheld there, save that there was no trace of the impish innocence of youth. Indeed, his expression was more that of a wizened old man.

Realizing he had no intention of answering me, I proceeded towards the studio. Never could I have prepared myself for Damien's reception of us.

"What do you think you are doing?" he demanded as Terrence let go my hand and dashed past him into the studio.

"I intended to work on the cataloguing. And since I have Terrence in tow while Amanda is gone, I did not think you would mind if he dabbled with a few of your paints."

"Well you are wrong," he announced. "You know I allow no one in here other than yourself."

"I know that, Damien," I replied, keeping my voice low, "but he is only a child and I am certain he would not be disruptive. Besides, I think he needs companionship."

"Then you entertain him, Lillith," he flung at me, "but I do not want him here today, tomorrow, or any other time, for that matter."

There was no point in arguing. I could tell by the set of his jaw that he could not be persuaded. Moving past him to search out the child, I heard a whimper emanate from behind a rack of canvases. Peering behind, I saw Chips, who, on recognizing me, bounded forward.

"It is all right, Chips," I murmured as the dog peered warily from behind the fold of my skirt.

As I leant down to pet the spaniel there was a sudden crash at the far end of the studio. Somehow Terrence had managed to topple the easel. I sprang forward, alarmed that he might have been hurt by the massive oak frame, but as I reached him my concern turned to bewilderment, for his face was wreathed in pure glee at the chaos he had created. I started to reprimand him and then stopped myself. Though instinct told me he had done it purposefully, I could not prove it. "Now do you see why I do not want anyone in here?" Damien demanded as I struggled to right the mess. "Just leave it, Lillith."

I took hold of Terrence, left the studio, and made my way to the library. I supposed I could not blame Damien for being angry, but I sensed there was more to it than mere irritation at the intrusion on his domain. He clearly had little regard for the boy. Admittedly, I found Terrence a strange child, though perhaps I unfairly compared him to Elijah. But then Elijah had been loved and nurtured, and though I was certain Amanda had done her best with the child, he had undoubtedly suffered because of her own grief these past years.

I decided then and there to make a special effort with him. There was a certain irony in it. I had come to Darby assuming that governing would be my lot. Little had I thought that my energies would be dedicated to a child who would soon become my nephew.

21

UNFORTUNATELY the strides
I had hoped to make with Terrence
in the ensuing days were never realized. Although I took full
charge of the boy and tried to be as inventive as I could within
the confines of Darby, I was discouraged when he continued
to be unresponsive. It was not, I concluded, a matter of intelligence, for the boy possessed a high level of reading and verbal
skills for his tender years. But he took no joy in anything,
seeming to prefer his own introspection to the company of
others.

I was to see a different side of Darby in those next weeks.
Whereas I had hoped that Damien and I might take advantage
of the quiet and come to know one another better, I saw him

hardly at all. I had first thought 'twas because I had Terrence in hand, but even when dusk robbed the studio of light he sequestered himself away from the rest of the household. I had expected Marisse to use the time to try and dissuade me from marrying Damien, but instead she seemed almost studiously to avoid me. Her entire focus, it appeared, was on the approaching ball. Indeed, the manor was turned inside out in readiness for its first grand occasion in many years.

As I sat each night in my room, stitching nips and tucks into the gown I would wear for my wedding, I felt nothing of the joy of a prospective bride. Had it not been for Mary I might have lost heart completely. She had returned from her mother's, and on learning of my impending marriage she had expressed such happiness that if only for a few moments I was swept into a mood of enthusiasm. And I was relieved to learn that she had taken it upon herself to mail my letters.

I was at least spared unpleasant exchanges with Lord Darby, for, as Mary informed me he had taken ill and was keeping to his quarters. I supposed the indisposition could not be too serious, since Marisse made no move to curtail her plans, but perhaps she did not realize the gravity of his condition.

As the days turned into weeks whatever cheer I had managed to muster disappeared, and I experienced a loneliness the like of which I had not known since the death of Father and Elijah. I was at my lowest ebb when Mary arrived one afternoon with a package.

"What on earth is that?" I puzzled as she handed it to me.

"Come by the post, it did," she replied, regarding me eagerly. " 'Twas sent special—ye kin tell by the markin's."

I asked her to fetch a scissors. "I cannot imagine who has sent this," I murmured as I undid the elaborate wrappings.

"There should be a note inside," Mary offered.

It had all been so carefully packed that I had to smile when I finally withdrew the small box from the mass of tissue. There was an envelope atop it which bore Rebecca's handwriting. Mary moved closer, eagerly peering inside. With care I pried apart the final crating, exclaiming as I withdrew the porcelain figure it held.

"Oh, 'tis grand," Mary murmured as I set the cage of twisted gold wire containing the most diminutive of songbirds on the table before me. "And so unusual."

It was not merely ornamental. Winding the key at the base, I paused to listen as it played a simple minuet.

"Ye should take it down straightaway an' show the master."

I shook my head. "Somehow I doubt that he would be interested."

"Well, 'e wants te see ye, in any event. Said ye were te meet 'im in 'is quarters."

If I had not felt that he had been purposely separating himself from me, I would have thought nothing of this summons. But as things were, I experienced some anxiety.

"Tell Master Damien I shall be along soon," I replied as I replaced the cage in the box.

As soon as she had left I reached for the envelope and spread the pages it contained before me. It read:

Dear, dear Lillith,

Like as not, by the time you receive this you shall be Lady Lillith Darby. I cannot tell you how thrilled I was with your news though I admit it reminds me of my own prospects, which at present appear bleak.

But I prefer to think that I shall have the privilege of learning through your experience. You simply *must* tell me everything.

How thrilling it must be! A lord *and* an artist. It is fitting somehow. You always did, I suppose by birth, have some appreciation of the finer arts. Your Damien must feel fortunate to find one with your understanding of a world I admire but admittedly do not understand.

I was cross with you for not inviting me to the wedding, but as you suggest, perhaps 'twould be more reasonable to come in the spring. Your description of the North Country is indeed eloquent, but I admit to you I find even the tranquillity of Devon tedious. I cannot wait to return to London.

I hope you do not mind, but I simply had to share your good fortune with Mother and Father. Mother, of course, is thrilled. Father was rather odd about it all. He knows of the Darbys but seemed more disturbed than pleased about your prospective marriage. Something about a fire. I naturally argued that our Lillith was far too reasonable to become entangled in anything untoward. I am correct, am I not?

Of course I am. Which is why I shall not trouble myself about you. Of the two of us, you have always been the even, sensible one, and I am assured of your conviction that you are doing the right thing.

I shall write more later. I hope you will not think the bird an oddity. After I had bought it I had a moment where I thought it inappropriate. It does seem rather trapped in that gilded cage, not at all what I envision your marriage shall be like.

In fact I do hope, my dear friend, that you shall soar to heights still unknown to either of us. (Well, at least, to myself.)

Do write often. And pray do not be as oblique as you were in your recent letter. I promise I shall hold all you say dear.

Awaiting your intimate words of what marriage is all about (I shall languish if you do not write soon!), I am,

Lovingly as ever,
Rebecca

Slowly I refolded the writing paper and replaced it in the envelope, clutching it to my breast. How I missed her, but

336

how relieved I was that she would not be attending my wedding. I could deceive certain people, but not Rebecca. In her own naive way she would be certain to ferret the truth out of me.

I took a moment to secure the combs in my hair before going downstairs. I tried not to trouble myself as to why Damien had sent for me, but I was nervous as I rapped at the door to his quarters.

"You wanted to see me," I said as he opened the door.

"There is someone I should like you to meet," he replied.

I followed him into the parlor.

"Reverend Holmsby, this is the woman I have been telling you about," he said to the tall man who crossed to me.

"So this is Lillith," the reverend said effusively as I extended my hand. "You did not tell me what a beauty she is, Damien. Had I known, I should have made a point of paying my respects long before."

I took an instantaneous dislike to this man who leered at me through thick, dark-rimmed spectacles.

"The bans have been announced," Damien informed me. "As Reverend Ghent is indisposed, Reverend Holmsby will perform the ceremony."

"May I inquire what church you belong to my dear?" the man asked.

I looked to Damien. "None I fear, not formally."

"You did not tell me that, Damien," he said in an accusatory tone. "I do not see how I can sanctify this marriage when Miss Chatfield is not of the faith."

"I have not been a communicant, Reverend Holmsby, but I am not without religious training," I argued.

"You needn't defend yourself, Lillith," Damien said. "It is not as though the Darbys have been churchgoing. And as we will make a substantial contribution to your rectory, Reverend, I think you will find your way to being charitable in this matter."

"Of course," the reverend stammered. "I doubt whether the Lord will frown on one small accommodation."

"Then I think we have little else to discuss," Damien concluded. "I will show you out."

The reverend gathered his hat and cloak, saying, "I know the way." He bowed slightly to me. "I will see you Friday next, then."

"I am sorry I had to put you through that," Damien apologized when the man was well gone.

"It is something we never discussed," I replied, going to sit on the couch, "but then there is so much that we do not know about each other."

"Sometimes the less one knows, Lillith, the better."

"Is that why you have been avoiding me these past weeks?"

He studied me. "I think that is in your imagination, Lillith."

"That seems to be your answer for everything," I countered.

"What is it that you want from me?"

"Damien, we are to be married," I said despairingly, "but sometimes I wonder if this is truly what you want. At least when I was cataloguing your work we shared something, but of late we have not even had that."

I sensed by his expression that my words had touched him.

"Be patient with me, Lillith," he beseeched me. "There are things I must deal with which have nothing to do with you."

"If something is troubling you, Damien, perhaps it would be helpful to share it with me," I offered. "I do not want any secrets to come between us."

"What makes you think there are any secrets, Lillith?"

I stared down at the carpet. This was my opportunity to have him lay to rest my suspicions, those things that were the hidden, dark side of Darby. Whether because I lacked the courage to speak or because I feared a truth too painful to accept, I could not answer him.

He wheeled his chair towards me, reaching out to touch my

face. "Perhaps I have avoided you lately. But not for the reasons you might imagine. When I am with you, Lillith, I am reminded how gentle you are, how unblemished by life, and I have to ask myself what right I have to endanger that goodness. I have only brought pain and suffering to those close to me, and on my life, I want to spare you that."

My eyes clouded with tears. "Damien, it was not your fault. That fire was an accident. You are wholly without guilt. And as to suffering, it is you who have borne the pain of this loss. I am not some fragile flower which will wilt if faced with hardship. Can't you see that I do not want you to spare me, but to enfold me into your life? I want us to share wholly, without question, without reserve."

Gently he lifted a lock of my hair. "I cannot do that, Lillith."

I shook my head. "In time, we—"

"Do not ask me for more than I can give."

It came as no surprise to me. In my heart I had always known that even as his wife I would only be married to a part of Damien. The other part would always elude me. And yet, like a spider trapped by its own design, I was caught in the intricate web which was Darby.

He drew away from me. "I suspect by week's end you will relish the solitariness of these past weeks. My aunt is returning tomorrow. Amanda and Charles are accompanying her."

"I have missed them," I said. "And truthfully I am eager to find out if things developed as Amanda had hoped."

"What do you mean?"

"I think Amanda has hopes for Charles," I revealed.

"Is that what she told you, or is this another one of your notions?"

I stood up. "I am sorry I said anything."

"Where are you going?" he demanded.

"I am going to look in on Terrence."

"You prefer the child's company to mine," he charged.

I strode past him. "Terrence does not accuse me of having notions."

"If it is an apology you want, you have it," he called out.

My hand clasped the brass of the door handle. "What I want, Damien, is there to be no reason for apology between us."

This time I did not wait for his reply. I went towards the library, thinking that I would search out a book for the boy. I was only steps away from it when I felt a comb slip from my hair. As I bent to retrieve it, I heard someone utter my name. Seeing that the reception hall was empty I tiptoed towards the closed doors.

"You are a fool, Marisse," the voice charged. "If you had done what I told you she would have been gone from here a long time ago."

"Perhaps," I heard Marisse reply. "But I still hold the trump card."

"And when are you going to play it?"

"Soon."

"You are not really going to let her marry him? Do so and you won't see one penny of his money."

The voice was that of James Farklan, I was certain of it.

"Actually, I think it might serve our purpose better than I expected."

"I think I have heard enough, Marisse."

"Please do not leave," she begged.

I did not wait to hear any more but, gathering my skirts, flew across the hall and up the staircase. So Amanda was right. I had been sickened by my own duplicity with Lord Darby, but at this moment I knew I had done the right thing. How naive I had been! But what was this trump card Marisse held? Did they really think they could keep me from marrying Damien? I was obviously a threat to this scheme of theirs, but what threat were they to me? What lengths would they go to to see me gone from here?

As Mrs. Horsley seemed to have Terrence in hand, I returned to my room. I had been there only a few minutes when Mary arrived.

"The master told me aye'd find ye 'ere. Thought ye might like a spot o' tea."

"You needn't have troubled, Mary," I said as she set the tray down.

"Te be truthful 'tis givin' me a break from polishin'. Ye'd think the queen 'erself was comin', the way Lady de Wentoff is givin' orders."

"There is another cup on the dresser, Mary. Why don't you sit with me a while?"

"Oh, aye couldn't do that," she objected, "not with you marryin' Master Damien an' all."

"Nonsense. Just because Damien and I are to be wed, that should not make you any less my friend." I fetched the cup and poured the steamy brew. "How did you find your mother on your last visit?" I inquired.

"Oh, she's after me again to leave Darby. Aye shouldn'ta told 'er 'bout Flo."

"You still have had no word from her?"

She shook her head. "Somethin' tells me she's come te no good. Me mum says aye'm te keep quiet 'bout it or aye'll be gettin' the boot."

"Not as long as I am here," I assured her.

"Ye've bin so kind te me, Miss Lillith. Ye deserve the very best. Aye hope ye kin find it 'ere."

"I hear some doubt in your voice."

"Oh, 'tis a grand place, but aye don't think there be one 'ere who takes a pot o' pleasure in it."

"It is a house which has borne great tragedy," I offered.

She set down her cup. "Aye've te get back te the kitchens. Will ye be wantin' yer tray in yer room tonight?"

"I had not thought of it, but yes, I suppose I will."

After she left I regretted my determination to keep to my room. Now that I knew my opposition, it would not serve me well to shrink from it. I had no intention of confronting

Marisse, but I was also determined to somehow discover what threat she posed to me at Darby. In the end I busied myself with penning a letter to Aunt Millie and retired early.

When I awakened it was dark and I was shivering from the cold. Realizing that the fitfulness of my sleep had caused the covers to cascade from the bed, I leant down to retrieve them. As I did I started, for I had heard the door latch click.

"Who is there?" I called out with some temerity.

When there was no response I gathered my robe to me and gingerly crept towards the door. Hearing nothing beyond, I closed my fingers about the knob and, drawing it towards me, peered out into the dark beyond. The hallway was empty. I was about to step back into the room, deciding it was likely a draft which had shaken the door, when I stopped. It was vague, but there was scent in the air. Once before its pungency had lingered in my room. There was a sweet, almost cloying quality about it. Jasmine. It was like jasmine.

Anxiously I stepped back into the room, turning the key in the lock. I had not been deluded. Someone had been at this door. But who? The servants were long abed, and I could not imagine why they would be intruding at this hour. I was certain of only one thing. It was a scent worn by a woman.

I climbed back in bed, my ear trained on the door. I tried to tell myself I was being foolish, that I had nothing to fear, but I could not dismiss Charles's warnings.

I was glad he would return on the morrow. If I made mention of this to Damien, he would only dismiss it. I knew I could not live here, starting at the slightest noise, but there were too many things I did not comprehend. If Darby was to be my home I had to lift the veil of suspicion which clouded my understanding of it.

I had bathed and dressed and was attempting to cajole Terrence into finishing his breakfast when I heard a commotion downstairs. Minutes later Amanda burst into the room, her arms full of packages. "Mrs. Horsley said I would find you here," she exclaimed, setting down her parcels.

She strode forward and gave Terrence a kiss. "Have you been a good boy for Lillith?"

"We have had a pleasant time," I offered. "I am afraid the weather has not been on our side, but we have managed."

"Oh, you were good to see to him," she gushed, "and wait till you see what I have brought you."

"You needn't have done that, Amanda," I said, embarrassed, as she searched out one of the larger packages and dropped it into my lap.

"Nonsense," she argued. "Actually, unless you have had second thoughts it is quite practical."

"Second thoughts about what?" I inquired as I undid the elaborate wrappings.

"Oh, hush. Just open it."

I gasped as, folding back the tissues, I lifted out the most beautiful wedding veil I had ever seen.

"I hope you like it, as we had a beastly time getting it completed."

"Like it? I am speechless," I replied as I admired the yards of lace which fell across my lap from a tiara of seed pearls.

"You know, I should love to show you all my other purchases, but might I impose on you just a little longer and ask you to look after Terrence this morning. I feel rather dusty from this traveling."

"Of course," I assured her. "We will take a stroll outside. Would you like that, Terrence?"

I sensed he was less than enthusiastic, but I went to deposit the veil in my room and fetch my cloak. Amanda had readied Terrence by the time I returned.

"We'll have a chat later," she suggested as I took the child in hand.

As I went past the drawing room the doors opened and Jessica Darby stepped into the hall.

"Just the two people I was hoping to see," she exclaimed tapping her cane. "Now come over here and give your aunt a proper greeting."

343

.

I prodded the child forward and watched as the woman enveloped the small rigid figure. She stood up and reached out to me, drawing me to her. "That means you as well, Lillith. We are practically family, you know."

I drew away from her, puzzled. It had only been for a split second, but something had jogged my memory.

"Are you all right?" she inquired. "You seem troubled by something."

"I . . . 'tis only your scent. I thought I recognized it."

She laughed. "And I gather you did not care for it."

"No, it is not that, it just seemed familiar."

I looked around as Charles appeared behind her. "I thought I heard your voice," he said smiling down on me. "How have you been, Lillith?"

"Very well, thank you," I replied. "And you?"

"Other than needing to stretch my legs a bit, I am just fine."

"I was just about to take Terrence out. You are welcome to join us."

"A splendid offer!"

"Now, don't you go getting any ideas, Charles," Jessica admonished. "I have come all the way back here for a wedding, and a wedding I shall attend."

His eyes bore into mine. "I sense you have nothing to worry about Jessica."

As the three of us stepped out into the brisk morning air, Terrence broke from my grasp and ran on ahead.

"Do not venture too far," I called out.

Charles crooked his arm and I slid mine through it. "We do not need any more mishaps on these steps."

We walked in silence, following the child's path. "Is it my imagination or are you particularly pensive?" he inquired.

"I am sorry. I expect it is just nerves about the wedding."

"Then you still plan to go through with it?"

"What makes you think otherwise?"

"Hope," he replied simply. "You know they say it springs eternal."

"You mustn't say that, Charles. You know—"

"What I know," he interrupted, "is that I can only be honest with you, Lillith. I know you say it is what you want. Believe me, I have reminded myself of that daily. But every mile of the way back here I prayed that I would hear you say you had made a mistake."

"I have made a decision, Charles," I replied slowly. "Please try to be happy for me."

He halted. "If that is what you want, then how could I deny you?"

"Tell me," I said, resuming our pace, "did you see Amanda in London?"

"It was hard not to."

"And here you were the reticent one," I chided.

He frowned. "I think you misunderstand. Frankly, the whole thing was worrisome. Naturally I offered to escort her to dinner and the theater one evening. I felt obliged to, if only out of politeness. It was a great mistake on my part."

"I think you should explain," I suggested.

"Would that I could. It was not as though she said or did anything truly untoward. It was more her manner, I suppose, which I found so peculiar."

I waited for him to continue.

"She became terribly forward after that first evening. We had had a pleasant time, I admit that to you. I felt rather friendly towards her, but nothing more. Well, the next morning she was at my office, arriving just as my man opened the doors. It quickly became clear she had no intention of leaving. Fortunately, I had only one client expected that day, because she seemed determined to monopolize my time. Under other circumstances I should have been forced to be quite blunt. But I shall be honest with you; the Darbys, I have come to see, were given preferential treatment by Father. Politeness required that I see her."

"Then certainly you could afford to spare one day."

"But it was not one day, Lillith," he argued. "It was every

345

day. A pattern had been set, and I knew not how to break it."

I kept still. I knew of course that Amanda had been attracted to him from the first, and I knew her to be frank. She was no will-o'-the-wisp, mind or body. Unfortunately, her eagerness had simply overwhelmed him.

"If I were you I should be flattered," I advised.

"You know I might have been, truly I might. But her insistence took such a turn on the third, perhaps 'twas the fourth day, that I cannot even explain.

"We were at dinner. I admit I was tired. I had found myself working until all hours to compensate for my lost time. She must have asked me a question. In truth I cannot recall if I either did not hear her or whether I simply had a mental lapse. With no seeming provocation she threw her napkin to the table. 'You are thinking of *her*, are you not,' she flung at me. I was so shocked I could only stammer that I did not know what she was talking about. 'Lillith,' she continued. 'You are thinking of Lillith.'

"I must have appeared inordinately guilty, for, at that very moment, I admit to you that it was you who preoccupied my thoughts. Without even waiting for my response she commenced a tirade the like of which I hope never to experience again. I really could not even tell you the substance of her ramblings, save to say that one word, one name kept coming through: Anitra. Anitra this, Anitra that."

"But what does Anitra have to do with me?" I cried.

He shrugged. "I wish I knew, Lillith. I am not certain there was any connection. If the situation had been different, I might have tried to reason with her, but she had caused such a stir that all I wanted to do was get away."

"Later, the next day, did you ask her about it?"

"I tried to, but she acted as though it had never happened."

I drew my cloak closer round me and called to Terrence. "We ought get back to the manor."

He looked to where the child stood, defiant to my entreaties. "The boy is as odd as his mother, I fear."

"That is a terrible thing to say," I chastised him. "I would have expected you to be more charitable. You know Amanda lost not only her mother and sister but her husband as well in a very short space of time. On the surface she seems to have borne it well, but it must have been terribly difficult for her. Raising a child alone is not easy. And it is hardly as though she receives much support from her family."

"And that is the family you are about to join," he reminded me.

"Which is even more reason, Charles, that we should not be discussing them this way. If I am to be part of Darby, I cannot go about speculating with you or anyone else about the place that will be my home. I have to learn to accept those things I cannot change."

He paused and turned me to face him. "Has something happened since I have been away? Has someone said something to you?"

"Why do you ask that?"

He frowned. "There is something different about you. Two weeks ago you were convinced that you had been witness to something untoward here. And, if you recall, I took your part. Today you talk about acceptance. I am puzzled."

"Charles, can't you see that if I persist in this I will be opposing the man I am to marry in three days? I admit that there have been things which have troubled me, but they are fragments of a past that has little if anything to do with me. If I am to have a future here, I have to lay these things to rest. Damien has told me there was nothing there, and I have to believe him."

His face softened. "I said to you once that I hope he knows where his fortune really lies, and I meant it. I will not try and dissuade you again, or interfere, or ask you to question this place or these people. But I hope that in trusting Damien you will not lose trust in yourself, Lillith."

"Thank you," I murmured.

"For what?"

"For understanding. For being a friend."

"You know if I can ever do anything for you, Lillith—but then I've said that before."

I hesitated. "You know, actually there is something you can do. I want to give Damien something, a memento of our wedding. Not anything material, but I have had a plan for some time now. I just need help in executing it. His work is so good, Charles, and I know that if they were seen by someone of influence his paintings would be in great demand. If I were to borrow a few canvases, perhaps when you return to London you could show them, perhaps enter them in one of the exhibitions."

I was taken aback when he laughed.

"He really is talented, you know," I bristled.

"You mistake me, Lillith. It is only that you and Damien are more kindred minds than I had earlier assumed."

"What do you mean?"

He winked. "You will see soon enough. But, certainly, I would be happy to try to place them in the right hands."

"Only, Damien must not know," I insisted.

"My lips are sealed."

"I am not certain when I might take them out of the studio, but somehow I will get them to you before you leave."

I called to Terrence again, who this time was more cooperative.

We had just reentered the manor when Mrs. Horsley called down, from the stairs. "There you are. I am to take Terrence to his aunt." I encouraged the boy to follow her.

Charles leant over and whispered, "That woman hardly warms the cockles of one's heart."

"Going back on your promise already?" I chastised him.

His mouth formed a boyish grin. "No. But you must admit she is hardly a model of jocundity."

In spite of myself I laughed. "If you will excuse me I think I will go to the studio."

"And abandon me here?" he teased.

"Oh, I think you will find plenty to busy yourself with," I retorted as I moved away.

I felt more spirited than I had in days as I made my way towards the studio. I would have scoffed if anyone had told me months ago that I would be glad that Charles would be here for my wedding. But then, months ago who would have thought that I would be marrying Damien? I had just reached the studio and was about to knock when beyond the door I heard Amanda say, "You cannot tell me where to live, Damien, any more than you can tell me whom to love. Darby is as much in my blood as it is in yours."

"Amanda, after the wedding, after the ball, I want you to take the boy and go home, do you hear me?"

I was embarrassed at the thought that I was eavesdropping, but I was also horrified, not only by what Damien was saying but by the harshness of his tone.

"You will be sorry for this," Amanda threatened. "You think you can—"

My knock interrupted her sentence. Whatever their argument, nothing was worthy of a rift between the two. Damien opened the door, seeming more than a little surprised to see me.

"I hope I am not intruding. I just thought I might try to finish the cataloguing."

"This might not be the best time, Lillith," he suggested.

I started to turn away, but Amanda came past his chair. "We will continue this another time, Damien."

"Please do not leave on my account, Amanda," I beseeched her.

She smiled. "I shan't. But for now I think perhaps I will see what Charles is about."

"I just left him in the main hall, and Mrs. Horsley was taking Terrence up to your aunt."

She thanked me. "Come see me later, will you?"

I agreed that I would and went past Damien into the studio,

where Chips nearly bowled me over with his greeting.

"How long were you standing there, Lillith?" Damien demanded.

"Long enough to know that you and Amanda were arguing," I confessed. "I couldn't help overhearing. I do not understand why you want her to leave Darby."

"It is none of your business," he snapped.

"That is not true. This is to be my home as well, Damien, and I cannot think why Amanda and Terrence should not be welcome here."

He was visibly agitated. "This is not something I wish to discuss with you. Just trust that it is better for all concerned if she leaves Darby."

"Have you ever considered the fact that she offers me companionship?"

"I had not realized you were so lonely," he observed.

"I expect we have a great deal to learn about each other," I replied quietly. I climbed to where I had left the ledgers and drew them to me.

"I have to leave you for a while," he said. "I will leave Chips here with you, if that is all right."

"Of course," I agreed, trying to conceal my disappointment. I had told myself that I had missed the cataloguing, but it was really Damien I had missed these past weeks. For someone who had been so passionate in his declaration of need for me, I sometimes wondered if Damien truly needed anyone.

It was dark when I made the last entry. Whereas I had once thought I would feel some exhilaration at this moment it now seemed anticlimactic. Completing my work had once meant freedom from Darby, freedom to start a new life. Little had I thought that, instead, it was to mark the beginning of a new life at Darby.

22

THE following three days passed without event. As the manor was being turned upside down in readiness for the ball, the public rooms, save the library, were closed. Amanda was determined to spend as much time as feasible with Charles, and though she tried to inveigle me into joining them on several outings, I refused. I did not want her to think she had any cause for jealousy.

With Damien off working in the studio I had nothing but time on my hands. I filled most of it reading and walking the grounds and visiting with Jessica Darby. We grew close in those hours when she spent recalling her youth at Darby. And though I was to learn no more of the lives of those who dwelt within the manor, she did offer insight into happier times. In turn I reminisced about my own youth at Bostworick Hall, realizing as I did that the memory was less painful to me now. I would never forget my loss, but time had begun its own healing process.

The night before my wedding day I spent alone. Amanda had wanted me to take dinner with her, but I begged to be excused, saying that I had a slight headache. The truth was that I realized it was my last night as Lillith Chatfield, and there was almost a need to savor myself as I had been, not as I would be when I became Lillith Darby.

Though I had gone to bed early I was too restless to sleep. The wind was almost of gale force, and rain buffeted the facade of the manor. I drew my robe about me, deciding to go down to the library. Jessica had told me that somewhere in those shelves was a volume on the history of the Darbys. As I was soon to be one of them, I decided I might as well start learning about their ancestry.

When I opened the door to the library I was startled to find Charles inside.

"What are you doing up at this hour?" he inquired.

"I couldn't sleep," I admitted. "And you?"

"Just meditating."

I crossed to him. "You seem upset. Is anything wrong?"

He picked up an envelope from the table before him and handed it to me.

"What is this?" I asked.

"Officially I was not supposed to give this to you until you are Damien's wife," he said, going to sit on the settee. "But I cannot see what difference a few hours will make. Go on, open it. I think you will find it all in order."

"I am certain it is," I murmured, placing it back on the table.

"So when I see you next you will be a married woman."

I went to sit beside him. "That almost sounds as though you are not going to attend the ceremony."

"You will forgive me if I say I would find it difficult."

"I am sorry you feel that way, Charles. In some ways I suppose I was counting on you."

"You really want me there?"

"I think I could use a friend to stand by me," I admitted. He sighed. "Then a friend you shall have."

"Then you will come, you will be there?" I said delightedly.

"Only if you promise me the first dance at the ball."

"You drive a tough bargain," I teased.

I had not bothered to close the door and had not heard Damien enter.

"It appears I should have been keeping a closer eye on you, Lillith," he charged as he wheeled his chair abreast of where we sat.

"I think you are more than a little out of order, Damien," Charles accused.

"Then would you like to tell me what this tête-à-tête is about?"

"Damien, please, Charles was only—"

"You go on to bed, Lillith," Charles interrupted. "This is between Damien and myself."

I was shaking when I finally reached my room. How dare he suggest what he had! He had assumed the worst. What did he take me for? Was this how we were to start our marriage, under a cloud of suspicion?

When I opened my eyes the next morning I shut them again quickly, as if by doing so I would blot out the day. Even if I imagined it possible, Mary's arrival brought reality quickly to the fore.

"Yer still abed?" She giggled. "Why, aye would thought ye'd bin up fer hours. An' lookin' so calm, ye are. Why, aye'd be in a tizzy, I would."

"Do not let appearances deceive you," I advised.

" 'Ow aye wish aye could be there," she mused as she set fresh towels beside the basin. " 'Twill be ever so grand. Lord

Darby's 'ad the great coach brought out. They bin polishin' it since last night."

"I thought this would be a simple ceremony," I moaned.

She looked bewildered. "Aye suppose it's all in what a body takes as simple. Ye know it's not as if yer goin' te be just any Mrs. So-an'-so. Ye'll be a Darby."

"At one time you did not seem to think that was necessarily a good thing, if I recall."

She regarded me nervously. "Aye did not mean anythin' by it, Miss Lillith," she stammered. "An' besides, that was all before, ye know, before ye came 'ere te Darby."

I pulled my robe about me. "You mean the fire, do you not, Mary?"

"Aye'll be fetchin' yer tray now," she mumbled. "Ye'll need a hearty breakfast. 'Twon't be another meal until yer weddin' dinner before the ball. Yer te be ready by ten."

"Ten?" I gasped. "Why so soon?"

"'Tis a stretch te the chapel, it is. Aye've only bin there once. Way te the west, it is, on the furthest part o' Darby land."

"What a strange place for a chapel," I murmured.

"Oh, 'twas there afore the manor," she replied. "Nigh unto a relic it was, till Lord Darby's father 'ad it rebuilt."

I had finished bathing when Mary returned with my tray.

"Will ye be wantin' 'elp, with yer gown an' all?"

I shook my head. "Amanda shall be here, I am certain."

"Well then, aye'll be leavin' ye. But afore aye do, aye wanted te give ye a little somethin'. 'Tisn't much, ye realize, but aye made it meself."

Carefully I opened the small package she entrusted to my hands. Inside there was a linen handkerchief with the initials *L.D.* embroidered in one corner.

"Oh, it *is* lovely, Mary," I said admiringly, "but you should not have done this."

"Me mum taught me 'ow."

"I shall treasure it always," I assured her. "In fact, I shall carry it with me today."

She was flustered by my embrace and was quick to take her leave. As she did I moved to the dressing table, taking stock of my appearance. My hair shone even in this light, but the veil's tiara demanded that I wear it knotted severely at the nape of my neck. Doing so seemed to accentuate not only the size of my eyes but the almost iridescent quality of my skin. I was not terribly adept with powders and rouge, but when I had finished, I was not dissatisfied with my appearance.

I was about to rouge my lips when I realized I had not touched the food on the breakfast tray. I was anything but hungry, but if Mary was correct, it would be hours before I saw food again. Each mouthful seemed to stick in my throat. I drank the whole of the pot of tea, using an uncommon amount of sugar to bolster my energy, and returned again to the dressing table, where I applied the light rose coloring to my lips.

But I was not easy in my mind. The drawer containing the diary seemed almost to pulsate before me. These last weeks I had put it out of my mind, so why now, why today did I feel it beckoning me? Why did I feel Anitra with me on this, the very day of my wedding?

I opened the drawer and stared down at the volume within. My fingers had just curled about the diary when there was a knock at the door. Nervously I slammed the drawer shut as Amanda peered around the door.

"Could a future sister-in-law be of some help?"

"I fear I am dawdling a bit," I admitted as she closed the door.

"That is why I am here. I thought you might do with a bit of encouragement. Father is anxious to be on time, as the guests will soon be arriving for the ball."

I crossed to the armoire and carefully withdrew the wedding gown.

"Let me help you," she offered.

Ten minutes later she had fastened the last of the seed-pearl closings, which ran the length of the back through the small bustle to the train. I leant down as she lifted the veil and set the tiara on the crown of my head, allowing the yards of lace to cascade over my shoulders.

She took my hand and led me to the mirror. "Now, look at yourself."

I stared at my reflection. There was no question that I looked the part, but that was the problem. My mirrored image was that of a young, expectant bride. But I felt that I was regarding myself from afar, as though the real Lillith was watching this other Lillith in a tableau which had no basis in reality.

"You look very beautiful, Lillith." As Amanda appeared behind me in the mirror I found her expression almost wistful. I wondered if she was thinking back to her own wedding day.

"I cannot believe that in only a few hours I will be married," I admitted. "Somehow I thought when this day came I would feel . . . I don't know. Different, somehow."

"A typical case of nerves," she chided. "It will pass."

"Have you seen Damien?" I inquired.

She shook her head. "You know, I have to fetch Terrence, but I will come back for you if you like."

"There is no need. I have only to fetch my cloak and I will meet you downstairs."

When she had left me Mary arrived. "I snuck out o' the kitchen," she whispered, "aye simply 'ad te see ye. A real vision ye are."

I withdrew her handkerchief, which I had tucked into the sleeve of the gown.

"It's like a part o' me will be there with ye. May God be with ye, too, Miss Lillith."

I asked her to help me with my cloak. "I expect I am as ready as I will ever be," I murmured.

We parted in the hallway. As I started down the main staircase my eyes were drawn to the portraits. One day I supposed I would take my place in this gallery of those living and those long lost to Darby. I wondered if years from now some other young woman would stand before my likeness and ponder the story of Lillith Darby. Or would I, like Anitra, remain faceless, a missing link in the history of Darby?

It was Charles who waited for me when I reached the reception hall. "If there is envy written all over my face you will forgive me that," he murmured.

"Where are the others?" I asked.

"Already in the coach. I admit I hung back purposely."

"Is there anything wrong?" I asked, troubled.

He shook his head. "I just wanted you to know that Damien and I settled our differences last night. At least, on the surface."

"I am so sorry that happened, Charles."

"It was not your fault, Lillith. Damien is very possessive of you. I expect were I in his boots I would be as well."

"It is odd you should say that," I countered. "Sometimes I feel he wants to push me away instead of drawing me to him."

He frowned. "And yet you still want to marry him."

I smiled. "It is my destiny."

He offered his arm. "Then let me not stand in the way of what is preordained."

The air was crisp as we stepped outside the manor. "What is the matter?" Charles inquired as I hesitated on the top step.

"There is only one coach," I fretted. "It is bad luck for the groom to see the bride before the service."

"Superstition, I assure you," he replied as he led me down the steps.

Lord Darby, having spotted us, stepped down from the coach and offered his arm.

"A momentous day," he uttered as he came to assist me.

But before I could climb into the carriage, Marisse, whose visage was in shadow, spoke up. "Edmund, truly, I do not know why we all have to be jammed into this one carriage. I have not sufficient room as it is."

"Marisse is right, Father," Amanda chimed in. "Even with Terrence on my knee I cannot see how we can travel so."

"A fine thing to decide at this hour!" Lord Darby exclaimed. He turned to one of the stablehands nearby. "Pull out the other pair and be quick about it."

"Charles and I shall follow in the other carriage," I said quickly.

Lord Darby appeared relieved. Fortunately, the driver brought it quickly, for I had worn light boots which gave little protection from the icy ground. It was only when we were under way when I realized there was no rug in our carriage.

" 'Twould have been warmer in the head coach," I said as I drew my cloak closer. "I should not have volunteered you as well."

Charles laughed. "Frankly, I am grateful I need not ride up there. Besides, this way you can rid your mind of that earlier fear, even if it is superstition. Damien need not see you until we reach the entrance of the chapel."

As the carriage turned out onto the main road Charles seemed to sense that I was not given at the moment to idle chatter. From the window I watched the landscape unfold. There was always something new to behold in the torsions and rills of the dales. A fragment of rainbow pierced the overlay of clouds, giving the skies a dark, turbulent appearance. There was something restless about the Darby land, even in the still of winter. I would always be fascinated with it, but I wondered if anyone could ever really take root in it.

"You shall tear those gloves to shreds," Charles warned as he turned back to me.

"I wonder if we have much farther to go."

"Unless I am mistaken, the horses have slowed," he replied.

"We took a turn a while back. This road appears far less traveled."

I leant forward and peered through the window. "I think I see a building ahead."

" 'Tis a chapel, there is no doubt. Unusual out in the middle of nowhere like this."

I told him briefly what I had learned of its history. The carriage jostled suddenly and I heard the driver calling to halt the horses.

"Why are we stopping?" I asked.

"I do not know," Charles replied, "but I certainly hope they do not expect you to trudge up that hill to the chapel—if that is indeed our destination."

We waited a few moments. I was surprised to see Lord Darby approach.

"We shall only pause here briefly," he advised.

"Is there some problem?" I inquired.

He shook his head. "Our family is going to have a small service before the ceremony."

With that he turned abruptly and walked away. Curious, I opened the door of the carriage and looked ahead. They had gathered at a simple cemetery and I had no doubt who was laid to rest there. I watched mesmerized as the coachman struggled to wheel Damien forward. His hat hid his face, and something told me it was best I not see his expression. Marisse and Jessica strode forward to take their places beside Lord Darby and the reverend. Only Amanda hung back, which I gathered was for the sake of young Terrence.

I closed the door and sank back against the leather seat.

"It is hardly a festive way to start your wedding day," Charles said sarcastically.

"It makes no difference," I assured him. "It is, after all, a fair distance from the manor. They likely have little opportunity to pay their respects."

359

"You seem ever able to make excuses for them," he said with exasperation.

"They say that to forgive is divine. Perhaps I am aspiring to some higher plane," I teased.

We fell silent, out of hearing of the reverend's eulogy, but respectful. It was, as Lord Darby had promised, a brief service, and in less than fifteen minutes our driver had started the horses again. When we had come to a stop once again Charles said, "Wait for me, Lillith. Once everyone is seated I shall come for you."

I did as he instructed.

When I finally alighted from the carriage I recoiled at the grim structure before me. There was no grace of line or color. Heavy dark stone set up on the barrow gave frame to a building which gave no hint of welcome.

"So this is where I am to be married?" I mused.

Charles put his arm about my waist. "Take heart. However foreboding it is outside, it is really quite pleasant within."

As we reached the heavy nail-studded oak door, we slowed our pace. "It is time to remove your cloak," he advised. "I shall place it on a near pew so you might retrieve it later."

I did as he instructed.

"I was wondering what I would say to you at this moment, but it was actually you who brought something to mind," he said quickly.

"What is that?" I inquired.

"When you referred to your destiny, it reminded me of a stanza from a young poet I quite admire. His name is Whittier. It goes,

The tissue of the Life to be We weave with colors all our own And in the field of Destiny We reap as we have sown."

I shuddered suddenly. He could not have known the impact the verse would have on me. Since coming to Darby I had threaded the eye of a needle that unseen hands seemed to have placed into mine. And I had commenced to weave myself into the pattern of Darby. Damien proclaimed it our destiny.

"What is it?" Charles asked.

I managed a smile. "I was just wondering what the harvest will bring."

His eyes met mine. "I never thought I would hear myself saying this, but I hope it is bountiful for you, Lillith."

I rose up and kissed his cheek.

"And now the veil," he announced.

I lowered my head as he lifted the face veil and let it fall to cover my face. As I watched him take his seat with the others, music from a pipe organ lilted through the peaked rafters. My legs felt like the blowing leaves of a season past as I commenced walking down the narrow aisle leading me to where Damien sat, his eyes directed not at me but straight ahead of him. I wanted to scream to him to turn around. I wanted his eyes to beckon me to him, to reinstill in me that faith which he had declared in our union, but he gave me not even a glimpse.

I drew abreast of Damien and the reverend instructed me to kneel on the long velvet stool which abutted his chair. As I did I turned to face Damien but even now he would not meet my regard. Was he as nervous as I, or was he for some reason avoiding me?

The awkwardness of the scene intensified when the reverend looked out into the nave and inquired who was giving my hand in marriage. It was I who broke the chilly silence. "I alone give myself to this union."

I will never be able to recollect even one word of the prayers. One seemed to melt into the next.

"I do," I suddenly heard Damien mutter.

"And do you, Lillith Bairns Chatfield, take this man, Damien Edmund Darby, under the laws of God and the Church of England to be your lawfully wedded husband?"

The words played over and over as a chorus in my mind.

I was aware suddenly of a hand on my shoulder. I looked up to see the reverend frowning over me.

"I do," I managed to say.

I felt Damien's chair move suddenly. "Place your hand in his," I heard the reverend instruct.

The position Damien had moved to made it impossible for me simply to reach across to him. Shifting my weight, I leant forward, stretching my arm before him. He made no move to take it but slipped a simple band encircled with diamonds onto my finger. As quickly as he had done so he withdrew his hand, almost as though my very flesh was burning to his touch.

"And therefore in the name . . ."

Damien and I were man and wife. I turned to him expectantly, but instead of reaching out to me he spun his chair about. I shrank back at the expression of pure disdain on his face. It startled me so that I almost fell from the kneeling bench. Without a word his hands clasped the wheels of his chair, directing it back down the aisle. When after a few moments I was able to regain my composure, I looked out to where those who had witnessed this union had congregated. Amanda was smiling. Surely then 'twas only myself who had experienced this bizarre antipathy of Damien towards me.

I felt almost as though I was in a trance as I rose and followed the chair along the dusted splay of marble. As we reached the nave Damien turned to me, saying, "You will allow me to be settled before you enter the coach."

Lord Darby was the first to reach me. "You are a Darby now, Lillith, and I expect you to act like one. Go after him and spare us all."

"Spare you?" I muttered. "What do you mean, spare you?"

He said not a word but strode past me to Marisse, who was assisting Jessica.

Had it not been for Charles I would have been left to struggle alone with my cloak. Tucking the fullness of the veil under its hood I was fearful of uttering a word to him lest the tears which were poised to flow should express the turmoil within me.

When at last I settled back against the seat of the carriage I prayed for some word, some gesture, but there was none forthcoming.

As the horses pulled down past the simply marked graves I turned to Damien. "If visiting here today was painful for you I can understand that, but please do not shut me out this way, Damien," I implored him.

"I will do with you what I wish," he jeered.

His words pierced me like a knife. Up to this moment I had been experiencing hurt, but now it was fear which riddled my very being.

"Damien, I am your wife," I stammered, "not some slave to be bartered."

"Ah, but you bartered well in becoming my wife," he muttered.

"What would make you say such a vicious thing?"

I watched as slowly he reached into the pocket of his coat and withdrew an envelope, which he dropped ceremoniously on my lap. "I think this says it all, my dear."

I looked down at the envelope, which I recognized as the one Charles had given me the evening before. In the heat of the confrontation I realized I had left it there on the table.

"How you must have gloated in that instant, when, with a mere 'I do,' you were no longer the impoverished Miss Chatfield but a woman not only of status but of substantial wealth."

My heart was pounding. "Is that what you think?" I murmured weakly.

"Have at least the consideration not to deny it, Lillith," he demanded.

The tears which until now I had kept in check spilled down my cheeks. "You do not understand," I cried, "you—"

"Spare me this performance," he interrupted. "I must say you have acted brilliantly. Your mother cannot have had a

363

finer hour. And here I have been accusing Marisse of avarice. How blind I have been!"

"You have to listen to me," I begged him, "you have to let me explain. I did this for you, Damien."

"You lie, Lillith," he seethed. "You deceived, you manipulated. There was nothing selfless in this scheme of yours."

I struggled to catch my breath. "If you really believe that, then why did you marry me?"

364

"What better way to ensure my inheritance," he replied bitterly.

"And that is the only reason?"

He turned to me. Only once before had I read such anguish in his eyes. I reached out to touch his arm, but he pushed my hand away. "We are almost back at the manor. As you have displayed such talent in theatrics, I would advise that you continue your performance through this day and night. Our guests will be curious, and I should do or say nothing to give them reason to suspect that we are not the blissful newlyweds."

"If you think that I have any intention of showing my face tonight, think again, Damien," I warned. "Unless you will hear me out there is nothing more for me to say to you or anyone else."

"You will be there, Lillith, and you will keep up appearances. I have kept my part of the bargain. This is yours. I suggest you honor it, or be willing to pay the consequences."

"Is that a threat?"

He shrugged. "Take it as what you will."

The carriage pulled to a stop and a footman helped me alight. Warily I waited until Damien's chair had been lifted down and he had been eased into it.

"A hunt shall commence momentarily," he said. "Though I obviously will not be riding, I will be expected to attend the call. But as you look a bit tired I think you should rest a while. It will be a long night, and I want my new bride to be radiant."

I felt a hand at my elbow. "Of course she will be radiant," Jessica Darby assured him. "My dear, I cannot tell you how happy this day has made me. I wanted to tell you back at the chapel, but Edmund was shuffling me about so. I am so pleased you are now officially part of the family. I only hope that nephew of mine understands the full bounty he has received."

Damien flashed her a charming smile, which I knew to be false. "Oh, let me assure you I know better than any my bounty, as you so well put it. And I assure you I shall not let a day pass that I don't remember it."

I climbed the steps to Darby with Jessica on one side and Lord Darby and Marisse on the other, telling myself it was only a few more paces until I would reach the sanctuary of my room. Blessedly, no one was present in the reception hall.

"You will excuse me," I said hurriedly, "but I think 'twould be best if I lay down for a while."

"And miss the hunt?" Marisse queried. "I shan't tell you what to do, but I would have thought you would be relishing your first appearance as a Darby."

It was Jessica who came to my aid. "Never mind, Lillith, 'tis nonsense anyway, this galloping about after a poor creature who wants only the safety of his den. I quite agree with you. A proper nap is in order. Tonight we celebrate."

I climbed the stairs alone. My cloak seemed suddenly a weight about my shoulders, and I shed it, allowing the fullness of the gown to trail behind me. If in that instant I had wanted to forget that I was a bride, the bride of Damien Darby, I could not, for the mirrors lining the hallway, reflecting one to the other, reminded me with each successive step that the deed was done.

When I reached the door to my room, seeing that it was ajar, I slipped silently through. I could only stare mutely at the sight before me.

Mary, startled by my entrance, almost leapt away from the

trunk by which she was crouched. "Miss Lillith," she cried. "I mean, madam, ye scared the life out o' me."

My eyes were fixed on the trunks laden with my own clothes. I asked, "What are you doing?"

She seemed puzzled as she replied. " 'Twas orders, it was. Aye mean, yer te be moved to the master's suite now that yer married. Ye did marry 'im, didn't ye?"

"Who told you to do this?" I said in consternation.

She let the petticoat she had been folding slide from her hands. "Aye didn't mean ye no 'arm, I swear. Mrs. 'Orsley told me aye was te pack yer things an' move 'em."

I looked from the trunks to Mary, who almost seemed to be cowering behind their bulk. "Mary, I am so sorry," I stammered. "Truly, I did not mean to accuse you of anything. I . . . Damien just had not made mention."

Instantly she seemed to relax. "Ye didn't think ye'd be stayin' up 'ere, did ye? Aye mean, yer weddin' night an' all."

I crossed to the bed and sank onto the edge of it. "You know, Mary, I never gave any thought to it," I said, pondering my own admission.

She stared at me incredulously. "Ye can't mean that, madam."

I plucked at the crewel on the coverlet. What were the words he had used? I fought to recollect them. *Performance, appearance.* There were others, but those were the two I remembered best.

"Of course not," I lied. "But for the rest of the day I think I will stay right here."

As Mary resumed packing she prattled on, amazed that I was actually a Darby now and enthusiastic about the ball that evening. I could have cried with relief when she rose finally, saying, "That should do it, save fer yer toiletries."

I looked across at the dressing table. "I will do that," I said quickly.

"Then aye'll be sendin' the footmen up later."

I cared not that my veil was crushed under my weight as

I threw myself onto the bed. My head was spinning, and I fought the waves of nausea which flooded my being. I tried to tell myself it was all a misunderstanding, that once Damien heard me out he would see that I had only done what I had out of love for him. He was angry now, but the anger would dissipate in time. Then why did I have this overwhelming sense of despair, this hopelessness?

The usual stillness of the manor changed as I lay there counting one hour rolling into the next. Carriages could be heard along the drive, and the strains of an orchestra tuning up lilted from the floor below. I stared across at the darkening sky outside the windows realizing that I had to get up. Pulling out the combs which had held the tiara, I let the veil fall to the bed. I did not need the mirror to tell me that my face bore the streaks of my anguish.

The water in the basin was cold but soothing as I splashed it against my face. When I had finished repowdering and rouging and had dressed my hair high on my head, I was amazed at the transformation. From the outside no one would ever guess my inner tumult.

When I heard a knock at the door, I assumed as I crossed to answer it that it was the man who had come for my trunks.

"You see, you *are* ready," Amanda triumphed. "I had no more than entered the drawing room when Damien insisted that I come back up here and fetch you."

"Is everyone else downstairs?" I inquired.

"I think Marisse invited half the county. I wish you had attended the hunt. It was truly spectacular."

I lowered my eyes. "I needed some time alone, Amanda."

"Lillith, did something happen between you and Damien?"

"Yes," I admitted. "But I hope you will understand if we do not discuss it tonight."

She studied me curiously. "All right, but I want you to know that you can come to me any time. Damien is a bond between us now."

I reached out and embraced her. As I pulled away I said,

"You know, I have been so preoccupied with myself that I did not tell you how lovely you look."

She pirouetted before me. The emerald silk swung out from the tight-fitting bodice, creating a rustle which reminded me of leaves shimmering in the wind. "It *is* lovely, is it not? I had it made when I was in London. It was naughty of me to be so extravagant, but if it makes Charles sit up and take notice 'twill be worth every pound."

As we reached the staircase I paused, watching elegantly attired figures descend to the floor below.

"The tall woman with the red ostrich plume in her hair is the wife of Lord Dardington, and the girl stuffed into the ridiculous pink gown is her daughter," Amanda whispered. "The daughter is older than I am, but her mother thinks if she keeps Sarabeth ever the ingénue, it will take years off her own age."

We were halfway down the stairs when she gasped.

"What is it?"

She motioned me to look over the railing. "You see that man who is just crossing from the library, the one with a slight limp?"

I nodded.

"His name is Samuel Fenn. He is a notorious philanderer. I cannot believe that Marisse has invited him here."

"You seem to know everyone," I said.

"There was a time when this house was filled with people," she mused.

As we reached the base of the steps, Marisse, who had been talking to some people on the far side of the hall, swept over to us. "Well, if it isn't the bride keeping company with Damien's dear Amanda."

"Where is my father?" asked Amanda.

"He is in the drawing room," she replied icily. "The guests are waiting with bated breath for official announcement of Damien's rumored marriage."

I moved through the sea of faces, feeling as though every

eye was trained on me. The doors of the drawing room were opened wide, and above the din of the guests I heard Damien call my name. As I went towards him in the center of the room, the cadence of chatter and laughter slowed to a hush.

"If it is not my little bride." His voice was slurred. "This vision you see before you this very day became Lady Lillith Darby. Now for those of you who must wonder how a cripple managed to wed this beauteous maiden, let me tell you how I accomplished it."

My hand trembled as I clasped the back of his chair. My God, he is drunk, I realized, as he downed the glass of champagne in his outflung hand.

Suddenly I heard the sound of a single person clapping. I looked up to see Charles applauding deliberately. His effort was infectious, for soon what began as a smattering grew to a hearty sound of congratulation.

The bevy of well-wishers silenced whatever mockery Damien was attempting. When the crowd had finally ebbed it was Charles who stood before me.

"Thank you," I murmured as he took my hands in his.

"Remember, you promised me that dance," was his only reply.

I nodded as I felt a tap on my shoulder. I turned around.

"You will pardon my intrusion," the man said, "but like everyone else I wanted to pay my respects."

I looked up into the face of a man I did not know but who was no stranger to me.

"I fear I truly did startle you," he apologized, regarding me warily. "I am Victor Brathwaite."

"Not Dr. Brathwaite," I blurted out.

He smiled. "Obviously my reputation precedes me."

My eyes took in the shock of white hair, the full jowls, the distinctive roundness of the shoulders. Without hesitancy I knew that this was the man I had seen not once but twice leaving the rear entrance to Damien's quarters. But he was also the man the very mention of whose name had thrown Damien into a rage.

"I can only be surprised we have not met during your recent visits to the manor," I said.

He turned to accept a glass of champagne, appearing disconcerted as he lifted it from the silver tray. I glanced to where his eye was trained and spied Damien staring at him from afar.

"I was asking about your recent visits to Darby," I said.

"You must be mistaken, madam."

"Lillith," I insisted.

"Dr. Rendcomb, the gentleman with Edmund, is the Darby physician. It has been some years now since I have tended the family."

The man was lying. I was as certain that he was the man forewarning Damien some nights past as I was that Damien, by his steely regard, was willing him to deceive me now. But why, I asked myself? Who was Victor Brathwaite, and what was the truth of his relationship with Damien?

Even if I had dared ask I was not going to be afforded the chance, for I was besieged by yet another round of congratulations. One name after another rolled off my tongue as I became the object of scrutiny of the guests. Dizzied by the attention, I was greatly relieved when dinner was announced.

Damien, who had been on the far side of the room, wheeled his chair towards me as couples drifted out into the reception hall. I braced myself as he drew up beside me.

"I must commend you, Lillith," he muttered through clenched teeth, "you are a great success. There is not a man here who does not envy me this moment. Little do they know at what cost you became my wife today."

Suddenly I felt as though the heat of the room would suffocate me. "Damien, I have done what you commanded. But threats or not, I swear to you that if you do or say anything to assault me further, I will walk out on this whole company.

Cause me any embarrassment and I will return it to you in kind."

I walked in tandem with him as he spun his chair around and wheeled it through the hall to the dining room. That no expense had been spared was obvious. Tall tapers flickered in the elaborate bronze sconces as the myriad flames of the crystal chandelier heightened the glitter of the women's fabulous jewels. Down the length of the table garlands of fresh fruit spilled from ice sculpted in the form of gliding swans.

Place cards had been set out, and the guests maypoled around the table until they found their places. I found myself seated to the right of Lord Darby, the earl of Shropshire opposite me. For the next two hours, interrupted only by the serving of six courses, I endured a round of toasts, each ringing more hollow to me than the next. I could not see Damien from where I sat, but I wondered if he found each blessing of our union as empty and farcical as I.

It had been weeks since I had spent any time with Lord Darby. Though I knew he had not been well, I was shocked to find him much enfeebled. He was never loquacious, but tonight his words seemed controlled more by shortness of breath than by thought.

When at last the meal was completed, the earl, who had been ogling me throughout, said, "I hope you will allow me to escort you to the ballroom, Lady Lillith. It would be more than my pleasure to have the first dance."

"That is very kind of you," I demurred, "but I think I should be with Damien right now."

I rose and walked through the emptying room, stopping but steps away from his chair. He turned to face me. "If you are looking for a dancing partner you have come to the wrong place, Lillith."

"I am looking for my husband," I challenged.

"Your husband? The one who trusted you? The one who thought you might be the only person on this earth who could

3 7 1

help him cleanse his soul? Or the one whose fortune you sold your own soul for?"

His words lashed out at me as the tongue of a viper seeking its victim.

"Hours ago, Damien, I knelt beside you and promised to love, honor, and obey. I have obeyed you tonight, and if you reject the love and honor I offer, then so be it. But my promise had nothing to do with money."

I gathered my skirts and swept past the entourage of servants who had begun to put the room to rights. Music flooded the whole of Darby as I joined the milling guests pressing their way into the ballroom. Feeling a hand at the small of my back, I turned to find James Farklan staring down at me.

"You have been so beset by admirers that I have not been able to get within feet of you. Damien is a fortunate man. But then I think this spells good fortune for you as well."

"What are you trying to say?" I inquired.

"I have the feeling you do not like me, Lillith, but I should not be so quick to dismiss my observances, shall we say. Unless I am very mistaken, you have not only become a Darby today but a very wealthy woman."

"I do not have to listen to this."

"No, you do not," he agreed. "But when you learn that this marriage of yours will be in name only, that you will never be able to hold Damien, you may turn to another. I just wanted you to know I am available."

I was too stunned to reply. Indeed I was still staring after him as Charles walked up to me. "I seem to be repeating myself with you, but are you all right?"

"No," I admitted, my voice breaking.

He clasped my arm and drew it through his. "They have just started a waltz. You promised me one, you know, and we can talk while we dance."

I held fast to him as he led me to the highly polished floor, where men twirled their partners about the rotunda. Stars glistened above the leaded-glass dome enclosing the room as we glided to the strains of the orchestra.

"You can talk to me, you know," he encouraged me.

"I know," I replied, "but this is something I have to get through myself, Charles. It is between Damien and me. For better or worse, Darby is my home now."

He bowed slightly as the music stopped. "Which reminds me that I shall be going home soon."

"Oh."

"You seem surprised," he observed.

" 'Tis only that I have grown rather accustomed to your being about. I never gave thought to your leaving."

" 'Twont be for a day or two, but I thought I should mention it, particularly as you had wanted me to take several of Damien's paintings back with me to London."

"It might not be possible now," I replied, "but I will try to get them to you. That is, if you are still willing?"

"Willing to do what, may I ask?" the earl of Shropshire interrupted suggestively.

The music commenced again. "You cannot monopolize this lovely lady the whole of the night, young man. May I, Lady Lillith?"

He smiled lasciviously as, reluctantly, I allowed him to lead me to the formation of a minuet.

" 'Tis a pity your husband cannot have the pleasure," he jibed. "Frankly, I cannot think what he finds so entertaining about Lady Maude, but then I have never known her as intimately as the Darbys."

He twirled me around so that Damien was in full view. It was true that Maude was at his side, but that meant nothing. She was a regular guest at Darby, and if once there had been more than mere friendship, that was in the past. However he felt about me at this moment, we were still man and wife.

I had not the time to consider it further, for when the dance came to an end it was followed by one upon another, with partners who became more faceless as the night went on. When at last the orchestra took an intermission I excused myself from my last partner and made my way through the milling crowd in search of sanctuary outside the ballroom. I found it in a small office off the reception hall. It had been a good half hour since I had seen Damien. He had made no move towards me, but while I had remained in the ballroom his eyes had held me captive. I had been aware when he moved off, surprised that he allowed me out of sight.

I sank into a Jacobean chair, listening to the swish of gowns as guests crossed to the main hall where refreshments were being served. As the music recommenced I realized I could not sequester myself here forever. I rose and was adjusting the train of my gown, which was looped to the top of the bustle, when I spied the wheels of Damien's chair through the archway.

"It is too dangerous to talk here," I heard him say. "Meet me later."

I dared not move lest he see me, but I was compelled to know to whom this warning was addressed. Peering round the molding of the arch, my heart sank, for in that split second a group of people returning to the ballroom obscured my view.

"Where is that lovely bride of yours?" I heard one man ask.

I waited until the group had passed, then slipped out into the hallway. Damien, just inside the ballroom doorway, did not see me as I edged along the perimeter to where Jessica Darby was seated.

"Lillith dear, come sit with me for a bit," she encouraged, patting the vacant chair next to her. She took my hand in hers. "In my heyday I would have found this quite splendid, but as my limbs weakened so did my enthusiasm."

"I fear I find it a bit overwhelming," I admitted. "It makes me realize how tranquil my life has been."

"And you have not found tranquillity here at Darby?"

"I became a part of Darby today when I married Damien.

But I feel as much a stranger here as I did the first day I arrived," I admitted.

"Give yourself time, my dear," she said encouragingly. "Darby is a house, not a fortress. It is not an enemy which barricades itself against you. It is your home now. And Darby will be what you, Lillith, make of it."

I was about to reply when a man to whom I had been introduced inquired if he might have the dance which had just begun.

"You go along," Jessica told me, "but remember what I said, Lillith."

"I will," I replied as I was led to the dance floor.

I found myself partnered for the entire next set, but my mind was not on the music or the idle chatter of the local gentry. Jessica had said that Darby would be what I made of it. But how could I even begin when Damien so clearly shut me out?

"I expect your husband would like me to return you to him," the elderly gentleman with whom I had shared the last waltz offered. "He has not taken his eyes off you." I accepted his arm as he led me to where Damien sat. "Were I thirty years younger I should have given you a run for your money," the man charged.

Damien stared directly at me. "It is Lillith who gave me a run for my money."

Fortunately the remark appeared to have escaped the man, who thanked me for my company and excused himself.

"Damien, I know the evening is not over, but I have done what you wanted. I am so tired, could you not make excuses for me?" I begged.

"No, I cannot make excuses for you, Lillith," he said coldly, "but I expect we both have suffered this evening long enough. When the next dance begins follow me out. The guests will simply assume that the newlyweds, unable to deny themselves any longer, have slipped away to be alone."

I did as he instructed but not without hearing the titters of a few who noticed our leavetaking.

"Good night, Damien," I murmured, as we reached the base of the staircase.

He whirled his chair about. "Where do you think you are going?"

"To my room," I replied gathering the fullness of the gown.

"You have a short memory. You have new quarters now."

"Unless you have changed your earlier opinion, I think it would be better if I remained in my own room."

"Frankly, I do not care what you think, Lillith. But I do care what others think. Your things have been moved to my quarters. They are your quarters now."

He was concerned about appearances, but he was also perfectly capable of making a scene. Where would arguing get me?

I followed him, and as he opened the door to the parlor Chips bounded past him directly to me.

"There is no accounting for taste," he muttered as he wheeled towards a set of decanters atop a butler's tray.

"You once said he was more perceptive than most people," I reminded him.

He filled a snifter half full with brandy. "Did I? Then this is an exception."

"Damien, listen to me," I cried. "We cannot continue like this. I know you are angry, and I see now that I must have hurt you, but you must believe that it was the furthest thing from my intention."

"Hurt me?" he fumed. "No, you can't hurt me, Lillith. I deluded myself. I thought you were the one person who could pluck me from the dark and show me light again. In that I put you in an unjust position. I looked to you as my savior, and now I find you are but a mortal after all."

I steadied myself on the back of the chair before me. "Damien, why do you always talk about wanting to be saved?

Saved from what? From whom? What is this anguish you
bear? Is it the fire? Is it Anitra?"

"I told you never to mention her name," he lashed out.

"Why? What is so painful that you cannot even hear her
name without cringing? What is this secret buried within
you? Is it yourself from whom you want to be saved, or is it
Anitra? Is it her memory which haunts you? Whatever it is,
you have to free yourself from it. Can't you see that we have
no chance unless you do? Please trust me with whatever it is."

For one brief moment I thought I had reached him.

"Trust you?" he jeered. "I cannot believe you have the
audacity to even suggest such a thing. You may have connived
your way with my father, but do not think you can continue
to play me the fool, Lillith."

"Damien, please hear me out."

"Do not insult me with any more of your falsehoods. And
as for Anitra, leave her out of this. There is no secret, nothing
for you to learn. You have a very vivid imagination which, for
your own well-being, you should keep under control. Unlike
you, I prefer not to recollect, not to hold on to the past, and
that is my choice. My mother is dead. Anitra is dead. You saw
their graves today at the chapel. I have buried them. That is
all I have to say."

I fought to keep my composure as he threw the brandy to
the back of his throat and replenished his glass.

"Your things are in the room there," he said, gesturing. "I
thought you were tired."

Trembling, I looked past him.

"You needn't look so terrified," he mocked. "Have no fear;
you will sleep alone tonight. And the next, and the next."

I felt rooted where I stood.

"Please spare me, Lillith," he said before I could speak. "I
think enough has been said."

I raised my head and looked across at him. "The tragedy,
Damien, is that too little has been said."

Without another word I crossed the length of the parlor

377

and upon entering the bedroom closed the door, clinging to the cold of the metal latch behind me.

So this was to be my future as Damien's wife. I was married to a man who wanted no part of me, mistress of a house which gave me no welcome. Jessica had advised me to trust in the healing powers of time. But if she knew what I had done and the consequences of my deed, would she still hold out hopes for the future?

I dragged myself over to the dressing table mirror and fumbled with the buttons at the back of the gown. I wondered what Damien's mother had felt the day she had worn it. Had she, as I, entered marriage with a mixture of anticipation and trepidation, or had she come to it eagerly, certain of her decision? And in those months and years that followed, had she found peace here at Darby, or had it remained as much a chimera to her as it was to me now?

When at last I had snuffed out the candle and climbed into bed, my tumult had given way to a numbness of mind and body. I closed my eyes and slipped away to the blessed nothingness of sleep.

Something awakened me. I drew myself up in the bed. As I did I saw that there was a sliver of light from beneath the door. I was certain that I heard voices.

Slowly I pulled back the covers and tiptoed towards the sound. Pressing my ear against the door, I heard a man ask in hushed tones, "Are you certain she is asleep?"

The answer was unintelligible.

"What do you think she knows?" he persisted.

"I am not certain," I heard Damien reply. "She suspects something. Even tonight she was beseeching me to talk about Anitra, but I think it is all speculation."

"Damien, you have to tell her. This burden has already destroyed your father, and I have seen it eat away at you year after year. What happens if one day she discovers the truth on her own? Can you imagine the terror of it?"

"I have managed to keep it hidden so far, Victor. And what good would it serve?"

Dr. Brathwaite! It was Dr. Brathwaite to whom he was talking.

"What it might do is allow you to lead a normal life, Damien. It might mean that Darby could be a home to you instead of an asylum."

"I will never tell her," Damien argued. "I won't chance it."

"You are that afraid of losing her?"

There was a pause. "I have already lost her, Victor."

I did not wait to hear any more. I tiptoed back to bed and pulled the heavy covers about my neck. I was certain now that it must have been the doctor to whom Damien was talking earlier.

What was the tapestry of Darby which I had from the first been compelled to weave? If I spun these threads of mystery, would I finally have a complete picture of Darby? And if I did, was it a canvas I would wish to see?

Without naming this secret, Dr. Brathwaite had charged that Damien would continue to lead an unnatural life. Even after the heartbreak of this day, I knew that I cared too deeply to allow that. Somehow I was the link, the bridge from his past to his future. He had said that he wanted me to guide him out of the darkness. But what was the path which would allow me to lead him on to the light?

I had promised myself I would never violate her again. But she was the one person who might tell me what I needed to know. Her words were the silken threads I needed to embroider the truth once and for all.

23

T H E distant roll of carriages along the drive was the sound I awakened to the following morning. Realizing it signaled the departure of guests, I knew the hour was late.

I had but risen and drawn my robe about me when there was a knock at my door. Suspecting it was Damien, I crossed to it tentatively.

"Damien?" I inquired through the barrier.

"No, madam, 'tis Elsie with yer basin."

I opened the door to find a robust serving girl I had seen about the manor.

When I inquired after Mary, she simply shrugged, saying

that Lady de Wentoff had informed her that she would be attending my needs henceforth.

I was civil with the woman; it was not, after all, her doing. But I had formed a bond with Mary and I resented Marisse's interference. My first thought was to let it pass, but I did not take to the new maid, who had a decidedly sullen manner. Marisse, I concluded, was testing her authority, and were I to overlook this, it should likely be but the first of many incidents.

Deciding that the sooner I tackled the issue the better, I dressed quickly. Finding the parlor empty, I presumed that Damien had gone to the studio. As it turned out, Marisse had just stepped back into the reception hall after bidding adieu to the last of the guests.

"The blushing bride," she purred as I approached.

"I do not think we need endure a charade," I rebuked her. "That aside, I should like to clarify one thing. Mary has attended me since I arrived, and she will continue to do so."

She gave me a rather supercilious smile. "It seems our meek little Miss Chatfield has found her voice now that she has become a Darby. I should be careful not to let it go to your head, my dear. For the moment you may enjoy the status, but I hold the power here."

I drew a deep breath. "Marisse, I know that one day you hope to marry Lord Darby and become mistress of this house. But until that day comes, I am at liberty to make my own decisions. And Mary shall be my lady's maid."

"Right now you think you hold the cards, Lillith," she replied caustically. "But, mind me when I say you do not. When I play my hand you will see what a fool you have been—a fool to have married Damien and a fool to think that you can carve a life for yourself here. Edmund regards you as little more than a servant. That should not shock you, for you know full well what he thinks of his own son. Amanda, who you think has befriended you, has already manipulated

you into becoming a nursemaid for that ill-begotten prog-
eny."

"Stop it," I commanded. "Amanda has nothing to do with
this."

She smoothed her perfectly coiffed hair. "Have it your way.
But mark my words. One day you will look back on my
warnings. You may not like me, Lillith, but you will learn
that you should have heeded my advice."

"If you insist on making insinuations, Marisse, then why
not back them up?" I charged. "Or is it that these are hollow
threats made by a woman who sees the fortune she has
worked so hard for slipping from her grasp?"

The slap of her hand came so fast that it was not until
seconds later that I felt the searing pain across my cheekbone.

"You little bitch," she said sneeringly. "You may think you
have won, but when you discover your prize it will sicken
you. It will wrench every shred of decency from you. You
will find by this farce of a marriage that you have condemned
yourself to a living hell. I thought once you should learn it
from my lips. But that would be too kind. And it would not
suit my purposes. No. You find out for yourself, Lillith.
When your husband returns ask him. Ask him about Darby.
Ask him about Anitra. Ask him about his beloved obsession."

"Where is Damien?" I choked out.

Her almost demonic gaze altered suddenly. "The new bride
has no idea that her husband left Darby this morning? Now
that *is* interesting. It suggests a rift, or that perhaps on a night
meant for the greatest intimacy there was none."

"I am not going to listen to this," I said, spinning on my
heel.

Her talonlike nails raked across my arm. "When this child
I am carrying is born your usefulness here will be at end. And
then where will you be, Lillith?"

Seeing my surprise, she continued. "That is right. I will
provide the heir to Darby, not you. And when Edmund learns

of this, what place do you think you will have in this house?"

She released me suddenly as voices drifted from the staircase. Desperate to avoid being seen by the last of the guests, I hurried to the studio. The viciousness of her words cut at me as I banged on the door. When there was no response my heart sank. Had she spoken the truth? Had Damien really left Darby? But for what destination, for how long?

My hand fell to the knob. As I fully expected it to resist me, I was amazed when the door swung open into the room. Tentatively I stepped inside. The sun cast an opaline light through the windows, creating a sort of canopy over the endless images captured on the array of canvases. I picked up one of the paintings nearest me, tracing my fingers across the thickly brushed oils which formed tendrils of clouds in a dark sky. Whatever Damien was, for whatever reason his mind and body were the prisoners and not the masters of his fate, he possessed a gift bestowed on few. He could choose to discard me, but I would not allow him to discard himself.

Charles had said he would help me in getting examples of Damien's work into the right hands, and though my heart was not in it at this moment, I realized it might be the one chance I would have to spirit a few of the canvases out of the studio.

My eyes swept the room, focusing on a painting I thought was representative of Damien's work. Its mood was unleashed and wild. Indeed, it was its very brooding quality which caused me to conclude that my second selection should be of a brighter, more cheerful aura. I recalled one work specifically which I much admired, a sun setting on a field of flowers. I went to the ledgers and leafed through the endless pages for the notation which told the location of the painting within the studio.

It seemed forever before I came upon it—*A June Day in Swaledale.* I went to the far end of the room and methodically began going through the stack of canvases. As luck would have it, the painting was nowhere near the front. Cautiously lifting my skirts, I stepped further to the rear, but in making the move I lost my footing. I thrust my hands forward to break my fall and as I did the large canvas behind came toppling over with a resounding thud. It was several moments before I could extricate myself. When finally I did I pulled the large painting upright. Leaning it against the wall, I hastily fetched a candle in order to examine it more closely. Fortunately there seemed to have been no damage to it. Setting the candle down, I started to move the canvas back into its usual place. I realized then that I was standing before a door—the same door which Damien had forbidden me to look beyond.

My hand shook as I picked up the candle and with my other hand grasped the door handle. It was unlocked, but the door fitted tightly to the frame and a sharp tug was needed to force it open.

As I held the flame directly out in front of me, my first thought was that the space beyond was empty. It appeared windowless, and there was no furniture to be seen. Looking closer, I realized that the walls were covered with canvases. I stepped towards the perimeter of the room until the light of the candle was sufficient to illuminate the paintings.

Nothing could have prepared me for what I beheld. My hand flew to my mouth to stifle my horror at what was before me. In desperation I moved from one painting to the next, praying that I might find some relief from this panorama of malevolence. But there was none, for everywhere I turned she was before me, laughing, mocking, suggestive.

It was Anitra, but not the Anitra who had been captured in the sketches in the portfolio. There was no gentleness, no wistful youth in the face portrayed on these walls. Everywhere the eyes mocked me, the mouth jeered, each pose more frightening than the last.

I thought I was going to be ill. This place, this room was like an unholy shrine, a desecration of the very memory of Anitra. There was no love here. The contorted masklike countenance was the creation of an abnormal mind. Something simple and lovely had been disfigured, transformed into an inhuman being by a diabolical use of symbol and line.

I tried to make myself look again at one particularly large canvas where the artist had superimposed Anitra's face on the head of a gargoyle. Evident even through the grotesqueness, there was a seductiveness about her visage which was shockingly blatant. Even through the mutilation of brush and oil she kept vigil, not as an innocent but as a wanton temptress.

How long I stood in that room I knew not. My first instinct had been to run, but it was as though I was mesmerized by the sights surrounding me. I winced suddenly as hot wax dripped from the ebbing candle onto my hand. I must get out of here, I thought as I made my way unsteadily towards the door. I was shaking so much that I had to support myself against the wall. Waves of nausea accosted me, and I drew a series of deep breaths, struggling to regain my equilibrium. Keeping my eyes trained ahead of me, I reached out and pulled the door shut.

"You cannot afford to faint now, Lillith," I told myself as I made certain that the door was secured. Methodically I replaced the larger canvas first, stacking the rest as I remembered finding them. I turned and looked about the room. Nothing must be displaced, nothing must give hint that anyone had been here.

The ledgers, I thought, glancing towards the desk. I crossed to them, hurriedly closing and aligning them. The painting I had selected of Swaledale was propped against the leg of the chair.

I snatched it up and chose another randomly from the racks by the side wall. Taking one last look about the studio, I moved stealthily back to the reception hall, the paintings clutched under my arm. Seeing that Sommers was just crossing to the library I hung in the shadows until he had disappeared from view.

It occurred to me suddenly that, in my near delirium caused by the shock of these last moments, I had not given

386

thought to what I would do with the paintings until I could place them in Charles's hands. If Damien were to return and discover them in our quarters, I would have no logical explanation, and I could well imagine his fury.

The safest place was Anitra's room. Mary had likely tidied it, and it would be shuttered again as it had been before my arrival at Darby. Taking fresh hold of the canvases, I moved through the reception hall. Encountering no one except a maid polishing the stair rail, I breathed a sigh of relief as I reached the second floor.

I had moved forward only twenty paces when the echo of footsteps behind me stilled my gait. I peered over my shoulder.

"Did you not hear me call to you?" Charles asked as he caught up with me.

"No," I admitted.

He stretched out his arms. "Here let me help you with those."

"Actually these are the paintings I spoke to you about. Since you were leaving I thought—"

"Say no more," he interrupted, lifting them from my grasp.

"You cannot be seen with these," I said, flustered.

He looked round. "Follow me."

I did as he bade but stopped short as he opened the door to his room.

"You trust me, don't you?" he teased as he beckoned me in after him.

I slipped in, watching as he carried the canvases over to a gateleg table and gently laid them atop it.

Tentatively I went to where he bent over the canvases. He was smiling as he lifted his eyes to mine. "Figures I understand, but perhaps you can explain what makes these works exceptional."

I gently traced the brushwork of one of the paintings with my finger. "He is a magician when it comes to light. The shading there, you see it gives the sky an almost plaintive quality."

His hand clasped mine. "What I see is that you are shaking like a leaf, Lillith. Your hand is like ice."

I pulled away from him. "You know how drafty this house is," I answered dismissively.

"Lillith, look at me," he commanded.

"I must go, Charles," I objected. "I should not be here."

He stepped into my path. "Something is wrong, very wrong, and you are going to tell me what it is before you leave this room."

"Charles, please," I stammered. "I am just tired. The ball and . . . the rest of it. Yesterday was a long day."

"I cannot keep you here against your will, Lillith, but I do not believe for one minute that that is all there is to it. Where is Damien?"

I felt singularly helpless as tears welled in my eyes. "I do not know."

"And saying that, you expect me to believe there is nothing wrong?"

I hid my face in my hands, struggling to regain my composure.

He touched my elbow. "You can trust me, Lillith, you know that."

I smeared the dampness from my cheeks with my palms. "There is nothing you can do, Charles. This is something I have to resolve on my own. I know you want to help, but you can't."

"I am leaving Darby this very afternoon, Lillith. I can't protect you when I am gone from here."

"What makes you think I need protection?" I challenged.

"Because something or someone has you terrified. The Lillith who came to my offices those months ago carried a great burden, but it was a burden of sorrow, not fear."

"If indeed there is a burden, as you suggest, it is mine to

carry, Charles." I gathered my skirts and moved towards the door, feeling his eyes trained on me as I did.

I opened the door, but then closed it again. Turning to him, I said, "Thank you, Charles. Truly. For everything."

The hall clock chimed the noon hour as I slipped into Anitra's room. Deliberately I turned the key in the lock. If I had suspected before that my only hope for the answers I sought lay buried in the diary, I was convinced of it now. The effigies on the walls of the hidden room forced their debauchery into my mind. How could hands which had the power to mirror and interpret the wonder of nature also create such perversions of innocence? Or had I been mistaken? Had I ascribed guilt to the wrong quarter? Had the artist's eye seen beyond the wispy blush of youth to perceive a soul less gentle, or had he imposed the torture of his own soul on a chosen victim?

I sat down before the dressing table and drew out the familiar drawer. When I reached inside I felt a moment's panic as my fingers met only wood. Thrusting my hand to the back of the drawer I gasped in relief, feeling the mottled leather binding. I withdrew the diary and, carrying it over to the window seat, opened it at random.

Drawing a deep breath I focused on the flourish of penmanship.

How I have loathed this day. Damien agreed to take me to Whitcliffe Scar, but not because he knows I love it so. How cruel he was. Why does he wish to torment me so? I begged him to understand. I told him that I know that he loves me and, Lord help me, how I love him. Damien says we cannot continue, that there are too many lives involved, too many people who could be hurt. He tells me I am wicked and cruel. He threatened that if I do not stop tantalizing him he shall have to send me away. But I shall never leave. I do not care if it is evil or unnatural, as he claims.

He is the only man I shall ever want and I do not care what I have to do. I shall have him.

A part of me said that I should not go on but I knew that I must. I had to know all of it: why Anitra was so frightened of Damien; whether he had been able to deny this passion between them; why, when he obviously loved her, he could have painted her so hatefully; the real truth about the fire. An entry two weeks later read:

> We met at the summerhouse last night. Ah, what a passionate lover he is. We simply cannot deny each other. No matter what Damien says I know it is right for us. He is correct about one thing, we must be careful. I have always thought Mother such a mindless sort—her only real concern seems to be her flowers, but he finds her much wiser. Indeed he thinks she may suspect. I must be discreet, for Damien would protect her over all.

I turned ahead six or seven pages.

> I cannot believe it. Amanda has announced she is with child. Father is ecstatic. It has plunged me into despair. Damien says now we must be done, that if our liaison were discovered it would kill Mother, and the shock might cause Amanda to miscarry. I do not care. Damien accuses me of having no morals, but why must I take the blame for it all? Theirs is certainly a greater crime. I have commenced thinking I must devise a plan.

The next page resisted me, and I had to pull the tissue back carefully to reveal the following entry:

> My head has been hurting so again. I went up to the attic to cut a length of fabric and decided that I would carve a statement of our love on the dome of one of the trunks.

If someone should discover it a hundred years from now, I wonder what they will think.

I feel as though I should die if I must go on this way.

I cannot let my plan wait much longer. Things have become too complicated. If I do not act quickly all shall be lost. My only salvation is to leave Darby.

A click at the door caused me to snap the volume shut. Watching as the key jiggled in the lock I realized that someone was trying to enter. I sprang up and raced to the dressing table thrusting the diary back into the drawer.

Whoever was trying to gain entry had become decidedly more insistent.

"Open up." I recognized Mrs. Horsley's voice.

I was trapped. I knew I had to open the door. "Just a minute," I called out.

I released the bolt and we came face to face.

"What are you doing in here?" she demanded.

"I thought something had been mislaid when my things were moved," I lied.

She eyed me suspiciously. "You obviously have not found what you were looking for."

"No, I did not. Perhaps you can tell me why *you* are here, Mrs. Horsley."

She straightened her hunched shoulders. "As the housekeeper, the whole of this house is my domain."

"And as Lord Damien's wife it is now mine as well," I advised her. "Which calls to mind that I should like you one day soon to give me a complete tour of Darby."

Her eyes narrowed. "I do not see the necessity of that. You have been here long enough to acquaint yourself with the manor."

"There is an entire wing of this house which I have not seen, not to mention the lower levels that open into the back gardens."

"They have been sealed off for years," she snapped.

"Well, perhaps it is time they were opened again," I countered.

"I take my orders from Lord Darby or Master Damien."

"Then I shall have to ask them to instruct you to do as I wish," I concluded.

She shrugged. "Do what you will. But I shouldn't be too surprised were I you when they disallow it. And now if you will excuse me, I have a house to put to rights."

I took the back stairs in returning to my new quarters. Someone had brought a luncheon tray to the parlor, hours earlier, I gathered by the chill of the tea. My stomach churned against the food smells, but I knew I had to eat. I needed strength if I was to interlace the filaments which would weave the final pattern.

Something told me I must unravel every stitch of this obsession. The picture forming was of depravity and fear. Once it was completed, what else would I behold?

I had told Charles it was something I had to do on my own, but the more I thought, the more confused I found myself becoming. Something nagged at me. There was something missing.

It was a risk but I decided I had to take it.

I left my quarters and walked deliberately to the second floor. I drew a deep breath as I raised my hand and knocked at Jessica Darby's door. When she bade me enter I did so.

She was seated at the far end of the room, a book in her lap. "Lillith dear, what an unexpected surprise!" she greeted me.

"You are certain I am not intruding?"

She waved me to her. "Nonsense. You know how much I enjoy our visits. But you are the last person I expected to see today. I thought that nephew of mine would keep you under wraps for days on end."

"Damien apparently left Darby this morning," I revealed as I took my seat.

"Left?" she exclaimed. "Are you certain?"

I nodded mutely.

She pressed her spectacles high on the bridge of her nose. "This is not a mere social call is it, Lillith?"

"No," I admitted. "I need some answers, and I am hoping you can give them to me."

"About Damien?"

"About Damien, about Darby. About Anitra."

She lowered her gaze. "I see."

"You have told me that the past is best laid to rest, but in this instance I think it stands between me and any hope I may have for a future here."

"Go on," she said encouragingly.

"I have not been completely forthright with you in the past," I continued. "My curiosity about Anitra and the events which led up to the fire was not mere inquisitiveness. By accident I came upon a diary. Anitra's diary. Had a page not slipped from it I would never have violated her most private thoughts, but that and a series of other things—"

"So you read this diary," she concluded.

"Not the whole of it, but enough to know that although Anitra died in that fire, she lives on in Damien's heart. I am competing with a memory, and it is stronger than I am."

Suddenly Jessica pressed her index finger to her lips as if to silence me. My eyes followed hers as they turned towards the door.

"What is it?" I whispered.

"I thought I heard something," she murmured.

"You do not think someone was listening to us?"

She appeared troubled. "I am not certain. But I think it would be best if we did not talk here."

"Then there *is* something you can tell me, Jessica?" I asked eagerly.

She heaved a deep sigh. "You should have been told before, Lillith. I am sorry I was ever a party to this. By keeping my promise . . . well, it has brought no good. I can't protect Edmund anymore."

"What does Lord Darby have to do with this?"

"A great deal," she replied sadly. "Lillith, I want you to meet me outside in exactly one hour."

"All right," I agreed, "but where?"

"At the head of the path to the summerhouse. I know it may seem an odd place, but it has a great deal to do with what I am going to tell you."

"Are you certain you can manage it alone?" I asked her.

She picked up her cane. "I am slow but steady with this stick of mine."

I rose, bending over to kiss her lightly on the cheek. "Thank you."

"I doubt that you will thank me when you hear what I have to say. But I know now it must be told."

I stepped out into the hallway. It appeared to be empty, but I had a peculiar feeling that I was not alone. I had dismissed it as pure anxiety by the time I reached the reception hall.

Chips jumped from his place on the sofa as I entered the parlor and trotted at my heels as I went in search of my cloak. When I sat down to change my slippers for heavier boots, he nuzzled my arm incessantly.

"You want to go along, do you?"

He cocked his ears.

"I expect it would do no harm," I allowed.

He bounded forward and I followed his lead, deciding to go to the path to the summerhouse from the rear hall.

With a half hour free before I was to meet Jessica, I decided to wander over to the terraced gardens, allowing Chips to romp a bit. As I passed through a topiary arch of pruned oak I noticed a figure in the clearing at the far end. The man was waving and when I was clear of the overhang I recognized that it was Perse. I called out to him.

When he whirled about I realized I had startled him.

"I am so sorry, Perse, I thought you were waving to me," I said as I looked towards the manor to see whose attention he had been seeking. Even if anyone had been there, the glint of the sun sinking to the west marred my view.

When I turned back to him he looked so alarmed that I said, "You are not frightened of me, are you?"

He shook his head.

"I am relieved to hear that. The last time we met here in the gardens, the day I was with Miss Amanda, you ran away from me."

He suddenly pressed his palms together in a prayerful attitude and shook his head.

"I don't understand," I admitted. "Are you trying to tell me you did not mean to run off?"

His eyes pleaded with me, but I could not guess his meaning.

"Can you write, Perse?"

He shook his head.

"Perhaps we can do something for one another," I mused. "I would teach you to write, and in return you could teach me about all these gardens. Would you like that?"

A smile warmed his face.

"Good," I answered as Chips, who had meandered off, bounded back to my side. "We will commence one day soon. But for now I have an appointment to keep."

I started on the path towards the summerhouse and had just reached the fork in the hedge when I looked down and realized that a thaw had made the earth muddy underfoot. Knowing it might prove treacherous for Jessica, I decided to return to the head of the path and await her there.

As I turned, looking down at Chips to be certain he would follow, I stopped. There were marks in the ground, indentations which seemed to parallel each other, running the length of the path. They were obviously wheel marks, the spread of which I thought would be about the same as the wheels of Damien's chair.

Chips scampered ahead and I followed quickly, puzzling over the impressions. I supposed it was not unusual for

Damien to venture out alone; he was remarkably adept at maneuvering his chair. But these tracks had to have been made that very day. The ground had been hard until now.

I pulled my cloak tighter around me as the glowing sphere of the sinking sun became obscured by haze. Surely well over an hour had passed since the arranged time of our meeting, I thought. Soon whatever illumination was left would be gone. I paced back and forth, while Chips, who had finally sat back on his haunches, watched me, obviously perplexed by my unease. Had she changed her mind, I wondered? Had she decided not to risk telling me whatever it was? Would the dark secret of Darby never be revealed to me?

I waited as long as I could. The air welled in gusts now, and I fretted perhaps it was not a change of heart which was keeping Jessica away. I would never forgive myself if she had fallen. Rounding the path to the drive, I spied no evidence of her and concluded that my earlier concerns had not been for naught. She too would keep this covenant of silence.

I had just gathered my skirts to climb the stone steps to the house when my very breath was stopped by the sound of a bloodcurdling scream, followed by another, and another.

I flew up the steps to the door and threw myself against it. I saw Jessica immediately there at the bottom of the staircase. Her spectacles lay a foot from the spun gloss of her hair, reflecting light from the shattered glass within their rims.

As I raced to the crumpled mass I saw a figure at the top of the stair.

"Amanda, what happened?" I screamed.

She ran down the stairs, her eyes wide, as I supported Jessica's head under my hands.

"Is she alive?" she asked as I loosened the ties of Jessica's cloak.

"Jessica, can you hear me?" I begged of the inert figure. "She is breathing," I said with relief, "but I do not think she is conscious. We need a doctor."

I looked up to see that a swarm of servants had surrounded us.

"Someone send for Dr. Rendcomb," I commanded.

From the top of the staircase Mrs. Horsley answered, "I shall have the doctor here in a few moments."

"What happened, Amanda?" I asked again as she bent close to Jessica.

"I have no idea. I was walking down the hall, to come and look for you, actually, when I heard a scream, and then a crash. I saw her at the same time you did."

"Where is your father?" I asked. "And Marisse, where is she?"

"I do not keep watch over everyone in this household, Lillith," she retorted.

I smarted at the harshness of her tone but decided she too was upset. "I only meant they need to be told."

Hearing footsteps descending the stairs, I looked up to see Dr. Brathwaite. As he set his black satchel down he said, "Let me have a look at her, Lady Lillith." I rose and watched as he rolled the doll-like figure onto her side. "We need to get her upstairs," he said finally.

Mary, who was now beside me, told him, "The men are eatin' in the kitchen. Aye'll be fetchin' 'em."

True to her word she returned with several able-bodied men and within minutes Jessica had been carried to her room.

"I had best get to Terrence," Amanda said as we followed the entourage.

I nodded. "I am going to wait here until I know something."

It was a half hour before the doctor reappeared.

I jumped up from the hall chair. "How is she?" I inquired, reading the gravity of the situation in his expression.

"It is not good, Lady Lillith," he allowed. "She is awake, her eyes are open, but I am not certain what is registering there."

"You mean she is in shock?" I persisted.

He rubbed his chin. "It may be that, but I fear 'tis more. She is not moving. There is only the slightest tremor in her right hand. And she seems unable to speak."

"Oh no," I gasped.

"I am quite certain she can hear me, but when I asked her to respond she only stared back at me. It might only be temporary. Only time will tell—whether her heart can survive it, and whether she will experience a return of these senses."

"It was fortunate you were here. I thought all the guests had long departed."

"Yes, it was," he replied simply.

"Might I see her, Doctor?"

"If you wish," he agreed. "But only for a few moments."

I stepped into the darkened room and tiptoed over to where a single candle burned an oblique flame of light. The paleness of her hair and face against the white of the sheet made her seem more an apparition than flesh and blood. As my hand covered hers the dusting of lashes fluttered open.

"It is Lillith. Everything will be all right," I reassured her. Her pupils seemed to dilate with a look of such terror that I was immediately daunted. "I am sure the doctor told you you had a terrible fall," I said slowly. "When you did not appear at the summerhouse I became concerned and returned to the manor. I was the first one to find you—well, Amanda and I. She had to go to Terrence, but I am certain she will be in soon to see you. I fear I do not know where Damien is, or Edmund or Marisse for that matter, but I will find them."

Her eyes darted left and right. I held my breath as I watched her lower lip quiver. She was trying to say something.

I placed my palm to her brow. "You must rest now, Jessica. I know you were on your way to me, and I know you are trying to tell me something now. But it can wait. The important thing now is getting you well again. I had best leave you to rest."

Her expression implored me to do or say something, but I knew not what. I stayed only a moment longer and then left to seek out Amanda.

I was totally unprepared for her verbal assault when she opened the door.

"Do you know that Charles left Darby today?"

"I know he was planning to leave," I admitted.

"Then why did you not say anything?"

"Amanda, it did not occur to me," I apologized. "I expect I thought you knew."

"For someone who was going to champion my cause you have scarcely been a friend," she accused.

"Amanda, your aunt is lying near death but rooms away, and you choose to attack me for reasons I do not understand," I said in despair.

"Oh, Lillith, I am sorry," she apologized. "I am just upset."

"We all are," I consoled her. "Jessica looks so fragile, it is heartbreaking."

Her eyes widened. "You have seen her?"

I nodded.

"Did she say anything to you?"

"The doctor is not certain why, but she seems unable to talk."

She appeared thoughtful. "I expect then that I shall be staying at Darby after all."

"I did not realize you had been planning to leave." From the background I heard Terrence call out to her. "You go on, Amanda," I suggested. "I will talk to you later."

As I moved past Jessica's room Lord Darby was just leaving it. The burden seemed to have shrunk him bodily.

"How is she?" I asked him.

He shook his head. "She is sleeping now."

"If you do not mind, I think I will sit with her," I offered.

"You will let me know if there is any change?"

I assured him I would and slipped silently into the room, taking a seat near the bed.

Jessica had not come to be injured through divine intervention, of that I was certain. But it did seem that there was a force beyond the human realm which would keep me from learning the truth I sought. What was this promise which Jessica had kept, that now might be locked away forever?

Though I now knew for certain that the brother and sister had been bound together in an unnatural affection, not as siblings but as lovers, the fear which had threaded through those pages of the diary was still unexplained. Anitra's fear was not of discovery but of Damien himself. There was evidence he had tried to end their relationship. Had the threat of that so terrified her, or did she fear something greater than rejection?

I did not know what had driven Damien to create that macabre shrine in the studio, but I was certain there was a link. If he had loved Anitra how could he so desecrate her memory? Or had he painted what he saw?

Several hours passed before Dr. Brathwaite returned.

"You must be tired," he said. "I am going to stay with her the remainder of the night. Likely she will sleep, as I gave her a fairly potent draft."

"I could do with some rest," I admitted.

The house was still as I crossed the hallway to the staircase. I shut my eyes as I imagined Jessica plummeting from the very spot where I stood. But even if she had misstepped, how could she plunge the full length of the stair? Perhaps she simply had not the strength to clasp the uprights of the balustrade to break her fall.

As I slipped into bed an hour later I did so wishing that instead I were rising from it to discover that the events of the past days had been a dream. I felt like a boat adrift in a sea whose turbulence I was powerless to battle. Would I, like Father and Elijah, be dragged to its depths, silenced forever?

Could I live on this way? By marrying Damien, had I joined his living hell?

Something awakened me. I started to rise, realizing that the covers, which I had pulled tight around my head to block the agony of the day, were no longer about me. As I sat up an arm flung out against me, knocking me back.

I opened my mouth to scream but was aware that I emitted not a sound. The lips that covered mine were full. A tongue forged into my throat, laden with the taste of brandy. I pushed up with all my might, but I seemed impotent against this brutalizing force. In my mind I spat every unutterable curse, but I was rendered speechless by the pressing insistence of my attacker.

In those first few moments his identity did not even enter my mind, so desperate was I in my attempts to repulse him. But the moment he uttered my name I knew.

His hand moved to the lacy bodice of my nightdress and I flung my leg forward to free myself from his, which pinned me as a dead weight.

"Fighting it will only be worse," he whispered as his lips explored my face and neck.

"I beg you, Damien," I choked out as I fought to free my hands, still pinned at my back. My eyes widened as his palm covered my mouth. Breath seemed to ebb from me.

"I want you, Lillith. You have your stud fee. Now you will have your stallion."

My screams, my pleadings were helpless against his force.

"I warned you to leave here," he slurred. "I told you it could come to no good, but you would not listen. In that you remind me of another. She too would not listen, and see where it led her."

It was as though her name were a firebrand on my brain: *Anitra, Anitra.* I wanted to shriek my own name. I wanted to scream it, as though its very sound would shock him senseless.

But at that moment it was as though she and I were one, fighting a force which in some way neither had the will to resist, yet terrified that it should be our total demise.

I was powerless, powerless against one who seemed to possess a superhuman strength.

When the fight left me I do not know, save that my own strength was spent. The last thing I remember before he entered me was the tearing of my gown. The one vilified me physically, the other audibly. I might have cried out were I not so broken. His penetration was deep, swordlike, stretching it seemed to the very base of my navel. At that moment I thought it would end, for it was then that his grip seemed to release. But seconds later he renewed with such a fervency it took my breath away. The brandy on his lips was such an intoxicant that I felt as though I had drunk of it myself. Each thrust seemed to have a greater insistence than the last, his swelling not lessening but growing, seeming to invade my every organ.

If pain and pleasure can be one, I was to learn it that night. I had stopped fighting initially because all my strength was gone, but as I lay inert, the pressure of his weight holding me as in a vise, the searing pain ebbed as quickly as it had come and was replaced with a spasmodic tingling which seemed to flow from my every pore. Involuntarily I felt my body move, rising up to meet his until we were lifting, rocking together, the song of our limbs a perfect unison.

I felt as though I was drifting upwards, soaring as a bird which seeks the highest climes. His thrusting became more rapid now, my own frenzy meeting his. When the moment of release came it was so intense that our shuddering lasted not seconds but minutes.

He rolled away from me without a word, his labored breathing slowly abating to the evenness of sound sleep. I lay motionless, waiting for a touch, a glance, the mere sound of my name. But nothing came.

Tears welled fully in my eyes, trickling, then streaming

402

down my cheeks. If there were but one gesture, one attempt to reach out to me, I knew at that very moment that I would forgive him. Forgive him not only for taking me as he had done here this night, but for everything else. But as the minutes and hours ticked past, with the sound of his breathing the only companion to the charity born of love that I was willing to impart, the act of forgiveness was replaced by a sense of despair.

He had said I would sleep alone, so why had he come to me this night? It made no difference really. Whether it was this night or the next, he had not come to me lovingly, not even needfully. He had broken his pledge, but why not? I was, after all, his wife. He could do with me as he chose, and there was not a law in the land which would condemn him.

What frightened me most was that if he had come to me with passion I would have accepted him, even knowing it was not born of love. I would have taken him to me, hoping that he would find in me the absolution which he sought. Instead, in an inebriated state, he had simply forced himself upon me, caring only to sate his own appetite.

Had it been this way with Anitra as well? Had he taken her against her will and thereby enslaved her in a hell of their own making? If that were true then one could certainly understand her fear, her terror.

He had left me with nothing. He had taken my pride and now my body. He had compromised me fully, even to the point that I had been willing to compromise myself.

24

I AWOKE suddenly. There was no one beside me in the bed. I struggled to sit up, aware as I did of an ache low in my groin. That and a heavy body scent were the only remaining vestiges of the night before.

I could not even remember falling asleep, only the sound of the rain, as incessant as my tears. The draperies were closed and I had no idea of the hour.

My hand moved over the sheet where he had lain. He had not even had the courage to face me this morning. Had I really expected I would wake to find him beside me, repentant for his deed? Surely he would say *something* to me, or would he retreat from me, retreat to the studio and act as if nothing had happened? There was nothing I could say or do. He would know that.

But I simply could not lie here mute night after night, wondering when he would violate me again. I did not think I could endure it—his taking me, using me—not when, Lord forgive me, he was able to rouse such stirrings in me. Let him go to another. For my own sanity I could not allow him to come to me again. Not ever.

I had to make certain he would never intrude on me again, but I would be naive to think that I could stop him by locking my door. No, I needed to do something more, something which might instill the same fear in him as he had in Anitra.

I formed her name with my lips. It was Anitra herself who would keep him from me. There were many things the Darbys could afford, but not the threat of scandal, at least not one of such a shocking nature.

Finding the weapon which I might use against him seemed to give me renewed strength. I pulled myself out of bed. The water in the basin had not been replenished from the night before, but I could not await the maids this morning. I scrubbed myself until my skin was raw, as though the soapy water might magically cleanse me of my inner wounds. Wincing as I rubbed my lower arm I saw that an ugly bruise was forming. Fortunately, my winter garb would cover the visible reminder of emotional scars I should bear for life.

When I had dressed I turned to study myself in the mirror. My appearance amazed me, for whereas I expected to see the ravages of the night reflected there, my color was high and my eyes no less bright than usual.

A breakfast tray had been left in the parlor. Food was the last thing on my mind, but I was going to need all the strength I could muster for the days ahead. Jessica, at least, would need care, and if I was to carry out what I was resolved to, I needed to nourish both body and spirit.

When I had finished I went directly to Jessica's room. I took heart as I reached her door, for I recognized Amanda's voice from within. As she caught sight of me she broke off in mid-sentence.

"How is she?" I asked as I approached the bed.

"Much the same," Amanda replied.

"When I heard you talking I thought perhaps she had regained her voice."

"No, I was just telling Aunt Jessica that I would care for her."

Seeing that the older woman's eyes were open, I turned to her, saying, "I am certain that is a great reassurance to her. But why do I not sit with her for a while?"

Amanda stood up. "Actually you might do that. There is something I need to discuss with Damien. I understand he has returned."

When she had left I took her seat, drawing the chair closer to the bed. Seeing a glass of milk on the nightstand, I picked it up and asked Jessica whether she wished to drink any of it. I took the closing of her eyes to mean she did not. She opened them again, and I was disturbed to read in them the same intense panic which I had seen the night before.

"I know this must be frightening for you," I said gently, "but I am certain you will improve."

It was obvious my reassurances were doing little to assuage her fears. She closed her eyes again, seeming to prefer the retreat of sleep.

As it turned out, it was Lord Darby, not Amanda, who took over the vigil, leaving me free to carry out my second resolution for this day.

I left Jessica and went directly to Anitra's room. Without hesitation I withdrew the diary from the dressing table drawer. It opened almost automatically to where I had bent the binding on my last reading. Hurriedly I turned the pages to an entry dated May 1848.

I cannot go on. It is all such a sham. D tells me he will bring an end to it, that he will find a way to extricate us from this hell we have found ourselves in. I cannot imagine what he plans. But I also cannot go on pretending. The one thing on which we agree is that others know or suspect. At first I thought it a lie, but now I am uncertain.

I turned the page, almost hungrily, abashed by what I found. The subsequent pages had been ripped out. Who had done this? Why?

The next entry was short:

D and I have formed a plan. Mine he said was too drastic. His I find naive, certainly if only that we shall have no money. What can we live on? I have nothing. Surely Father will cut us off. And though I wish not to debase our love by thought of monetary gain, I admit I am afraid. But then fear is not new to me. I have lived with it for years now.

I paused, trying to take stock of what I had read. There seemed a new resolve here. Obviously the two had made a pact of some sort. Were they to have run away together? I wondered. Surely that is what she had meant by suggesting that Lord Darby would cut them off. But why, when Damien had seemed to decry her wishes before, had he succumbed? Or had he been unable to stop himself? Had the torment been so great that he had been willing, as she had, to abandon all else for the sake of their union?

I had to keep reading, but I dared not risk being found there. Besides, I had to take possession of the diary now. Once I had regarded it as a strange companion. Today it was a weapon.

I shut the drawer and, clasping the diary to me, left the room. I was so intent on secreting the volume in my room that I did not see him seated in the parlor of our quarters. Were it not for Chips I might have been more startled than I actually was.

"What are you doing here?" I murmured to the dog as his cold muzzle nudged my hand.

"I think the better question is, where have you been?" came a voice from the shadows.

"Damien," I managed to utter. "I did not expect to find you here."

"Unless you have forgotten, it is where I live," he retorted sardonically.

"I thought you were in the studio."

I could hear the grate of the wheels as they approached. I tucked the hand which clutched the diary behind me.

"I was. But someone had let Chips out. He would not come back on his own."

" 'Twas not I," I said defensively. "I have been with Jessica."

"Why didn't you tell me what happened?" he demanded.

"Tell you," I cried. "I do not recall your giving me a chance to say anything."

I stepped back as he wheeled his chair closer. "You act as though you are afraid of me," he said accusingly.

"Do not come any nearer, I warn you."

If I had not been frightened before, I was now, by the steely resolve I saw in his eyes as they met mine.

"Never threaten me, Lillith. Do you hear? Never."

As he propelled himself towards me I tried to go by him. I would have cleared him fully had Chips not crossed my path. I cried out in pain as Damien flung his arm against my elbow, dislodging the diary from my hand. It hit the floor with a resounding thud.

"What is that?" he demanded, his grip tightening on my arm.

"It is nothing," I said. "Only a book I was reading."

"Well, I should like to see it," he retorted, his grip on me slackening. "It might prove illuminating to see what my wife amuses herself with."

"Stop it," I insisted, squirming to free myself from his grasp.

"What a high regard my little Lillith seems to hold for herself."

With one determined effort I shook myself free. "Regard? You talk about regard?" I said accusingly. "You have left me with none for myself. You obviously have none for me. And you are leaving me with none for you."

"What are you talking about?" he demanded, wheeling to where I stood.

"How can you sit there and even ask me that?" I demanded. "Have you no decency? Have you become so depraved that you have lost *all* reason?"

"Depraved? What are you talking about? Last night? Are you going to tell me that you did not enjoy it?"

"I will not listen to this," I choked out. "But I shall tell you one thing, Damien; that was the first and last time. By God, I swear it."

"I told you not to threaten me, Lillith," his voice boomed. "And do not oblige me to hear your sanctimonious drivel. You made your bed and you will lie in it, when and if I want."

In the midst of this heated exchange I leant down to retrieve the diary. "That is where you are mistaken," I warned. "If you ever approach me again I shall reveal you for what you are."

"There are some who take well to what I am," he countered.

I reached out to support myself on the back of a chair. "But they do not know what I do, Damien."

Our venting our fury on each other had been so rapid that I was momentarily surprised by his silence.

"And what do you think you know, Lillith?" he asked finally.

"I know everything. I know it all. About you, about Anitra—everything."

For one split second I thought I had alarmed him. "You do not know what you are talking about. Deal with me if you want, but do not defile Anitra's memory."

"How can I not speak of her?" I cried. "She is as much a part of you as this house. Can you deny that?"

I knew I had to get out of the room. I could no longer know what I might say or what he might do. I dashed forward blindly, almost whimpering in relief as my hands found the cold brass of the door handle. I escaped into the bedroom, closing the door with a fury that frightened even myself.

Fumbling, I found the lock and turned it. The silence now was as frightening as the skirmish which preceded it. My back was still against the door as there came a pounding upon it.

"Lillith, open this door," I heard Damien call out.

The reverberation beat against the small of my back.

"I said open it, damn you."

I stood pressing all my weight against the door.

"Lillith, for God's sake, open it," he entreated me again. "I have to talk to you."

"Go away," I pleaded, the tears falling freely from my eyes. "I beg you, go away. I cannot take any more, Damien. If there is one shred of decency left in you, please let me be."

I waited for renewed pounding on the door, but there was none. The only sound clear to me was that of my own labored breathing.

The diary was as a burning artifact in my hand. I wanted to move, but seemed unable. I fought to make my breathing easier, but I could not. I realized with sudden horror that there must be another key to the door, that this barrier was temporary at best.

I waited as a creature hunted. Time, I surmised, was in my favor. He could not lie in wait forever.

How long I remained fixed in one spot I know not. It had been some time since I had heard Damien wheel his chair from the door and the door to the hall close behind him. I sensed that I was alone again, but I could not chance that he had tricked me. I had no intention of making myself a prisoner in my room, but the better part of valor told me to wait.

I had stunned him with my revelation. It had been my salvation. But I had not thought through fully how he might react. As long as I was in possession of this diary I had him at a disadvantage. But Damien would not be disarmed for long. He was a man who wanted control, and I knew that I mustn't relax my guard. My triumph, if I had had one, would be short-lived. But how far would he go to ensure my silence?

25

During the week which followed, the squalls of winter howled about Darby like baying wolves. By contrast, the house itself was so still you could almost hear the silence.

I spent most of my waking hours with Jessica, whose condition remained unchanged. Whether out of concern for his aunt or actual fear of some reprisal from me, Damien kept his distance. Indeed I saw little of any of the household, including Amanda, who I surmised was occupied with young Terrence.

Seated there hour after hour, day after day, watching a life in the balance, I had more than enough time to reflect on my own life. One thing was clear: I had to leave Darby. I knew not where I would go, but that seemed almost irrelevant. If

I remained, slowly I would become like Jessica, a shell of my former self. There was something insidious about Darby. The house was like a thief creeping stealthily in and snatching bit by bit, relentless until it had taken all. My will was the one thing it had not robbed me of as yet, and while I still possessed it I had to escape.

Yet a part of me wavered in my resolution. The tapestry was still incomplete. If I left it unfinished, would I be leaving in defeat, not by choice? In returning to the known, would I be ever haunted by the unknown?

Jessica opened her eyes, and I leant forward so that she might see me. As had occurred so many times, her lower lip quivered. I closed my hand over hers.

"I know you are trying to say something," I told her. "I only wish I could fathom what it is."

Suddenly I felt her hand draw up against mine. "Jessica, you moved," I exclaimed, watching the bony fingers as they played across the coverlet.

The movement was slight, but it was enough to encourage me that she might, if I placed a pen in her hand, be able to write whatever it was that was preying on her mind. I crossed to the desk and, withdrawing pen and paper, returned to where she lay.

When I had set the paper under her hand, I leant down and supported her at a slight angle with my arm. At first, as the instrument scratched raggedly across the manila sheet, I thought our effort futile. But as I returned the pen to her fingers she seemed to call up a new determination. The effort was so arduous that I felt it within my own being. I watched spellbound as I saw the pattern she traced on the paper. She had been able to write only one word: *Anitra.*

Gently I laid her head back on the pillow. Her eyes closed and I realized she had succumbed again to sleep.

What was this covenant she had entered into about Anitra? I wondered. What, if fate had not intervened, would I have learned?

I took my dinner tray, as I had on the nights preceding, in Jessica's room. Marisse, I knew, had invited the Farklans for the evening. It ought not to have surprised me that she placed her social engagements above all else, but I need not be party to her insensitivity, I decided.

It was almost eleven when I returned to our quarters. I stiffened at the sight of Damien seated in the parlor. Drawing a deep breath, I gathered my skirts and swept past him, but he called out my name.

"What is it, Damien?" I inquired, my back to him.

"Have you seen any change in Jessica?"

"No," I replied, going towards the bedroom.

"Wait," he called out. "I have something for you."

I turned round. "I do not want anything from you, Damien."

His face contorted. "You insult me and yourself by such falsehoods, my dear. In any event, I believe this is due you."

He thrust an envelope out to me. When I made no move to take it he threw it at me. As it fell to the carpet a stack of pound notes spilled forth.

"Pick it up," he commanded as I stared silently at the money. "I expect it seems a paltry sum to you, now that you are assured a fortune. But I pay my debts."

Tears swelled in my eyes. "You can keep your money, Damien," I choked out.

"A winning performance, Lillith," he snarled, "for such a cunning little vixen. But you would never be so grand with my father. Just how long did you connive with him? From the first? Tell me, Lillith, when did your little scheme take form?"

I was helpless to suppress the sobs which racked me now. "You do not know what you are talking about," I cried. "There was no scheme, no plot. If Amanda had not convinced me that I must do it for your sake, I should never have gone to Edmund and humiliated myself as I did. You should be thanking me instead of spiting me. Now that Marisse is with

4 1 5

child, at least you will have the protection of the estates."

He stared at me incredulously. "What are you saying? Do you expect me to believe any of this?"

"It does not matter anymore, Damien."

"To the contrary," he argued, "it matters a great deal. Who fabricated this nonsense about Marisse?"

"If you do not believe me, then ask her yourself," I challenged as I whirled away from him to seek seclusion in my room.

The ferociousness with which I slammed the door told me that I was angry as well as hurt, angry at Damien, and angry at myself for being totally truthful. He need never have known that Amanda's encouragement had precipitated the agreement with Lord Darby. If he had listened to me the very day of our wedding, he would have known that I had not done it to malign him. I had done it to secure his heritage, and what had I received in return? He had defiled both my body and my spirit.

As I sank before the dressing table and reached back to uncoil the chignon at the nape of my neck, one of the diamonds on my wedding band scraped along my earlobe. I watched the blood trickle to my shoulder, thinking it ironic, for indeed it was this very union which had bled me of all that I had deemed sacred.

I had gone to my bed uneasily since the week before. Though I knew the linens had been changed not once but twice since then, the sheets seemed somehow imbued with the memory of that night. The raw scent of his flesh, the hardness of his muscles trickling with sweat, still lingered with me. I pressed my hands across the flat of my thighs, remembering the depth of his invasion, remembering that despite denial, pain had become pleasure.

In those spasms which had quelled the surging as he took me, had he experienced any joy, or had he only used me to spend himself? I remembered the intoxication of his breath as he had slurred, "I want you, Lillith." But was I really the object of his desire, or was I merely a substitute for the woman who even in death seemed to possess him?

I lay staring at the ceiling as the clock ticked away the night. I counted the chimes as it struck five. As their peals echoed into stillness other sounds brought me alert. They were muffled, but I was certain I heard voices in the parlor. The light of the moon sent a silver beam across the length of the room, and slipping from the bed I tiptoed along its path to the door.

I had seen him numerous times since Jessica's accident and recognized his voice instantly.

"I am telling you she is not capable of it," Dr. Brathwaite argued.

"All I know is that I have a very dead stablehand rotting away in the old forge," Damien replied. "I won't have any more blood on my hands, Victor."

My hand flew to my mouth, silencing my panic.

"You do not even see what all this has done to you, Damien," the older man castigated. "Edmund will never recover from it. I thought when you married Lillith that there was a chance, but you simply have spun the web more intricately. I repeat to you that when, not if, she finds out the truth about Darby, you will lose her."

"It is your job and Mrs. Horsley's to be certain she does not. I know she is suspicious. She has not disguised her doubts. But she is also confused. I need time. There were things I learned tonight which might change everything. If I confirm that there is any validity in what Lillith told me . . ." His voice trailed off.

"Do you understand what you are asking of me?" Victor demanded.

"It may not be necessary, but during this interim, if she should come to you or try to elicit your confidence, I want you to dismiss anything she says as preposterous. Tell her she is under stress, tell her anything but the truth."

"There again I think you are wrong. Why don't I talk to her

and find out what she knows. It would not be difficult, since she is always with Jessica. I can do it this very morning if you want. I shall be careful."

Again the next exchange was muffled. Only the last two words, "tomorrow then," came through.

My heart was beating wildly as I crept back to bed. Anitra had been frightened, and I was certain that it was fear that I saw in Jessica Darby's eyes. Now I too was afraid.

Victor Brathwaite was an unwilling conspirator, but a conspirator nonetheless, in something which had its roots in evil. Whatever this secret was it carried with it a malevolence that I was now certain controlled the lives of everyone at Darby. Damien would see it guarded at any cost. Even murder.

Where would he stop with me? Would he, if I challenged him outright with all that I knew, not only deny it but claim I was unbalanced? Would he connive with the doctor to try and make me and the others believe that my brain was addled? It was insidious but clever.

I felt a very real presence of danger. I had determined that I must leave Darby, but I had never thought I would have to escape from it. I could not do it on my own. I had to have help. But to whom could I turn? Until I could form a plan, I knew I had to keep my wits about me. I could not let anyone suspect what I knew or what I intended.

It was several hours later when I heard Damien leave the parlor. I did not wait for my basin to be brought but dressed hurriedly. Kneeling before the armoire, I lifted the serge skirt from the bottom and withdrew the diary from its folds. If I was going to have to do battle, I needed to be armed with the one weapon I had against Damien and against Darby.

Slipping it into the pocket of my cloak, I prepared to leave my room. I had to get outside. I had to clear the clutter of my thoughts and start afresh. I suspected I had all the elements to complete my picture, but they were in disorder. Somewhere I had dropped some stitches, and now they were the key not only to the tapestry, but perhaps even to my own safety.

But first I would see Jessica. One of the maids had just finished bathing her when I arrived. I waited until she had gathered the towels and basin and left us before taking my place beside Jessica's bed. I withdrew from the nightstand the book in which I had concealed the paper she had written on. Holding the paper up before her, I asked if she remembered it.

Her eyelids closed and opened again.

"If that means yes," I said eagerly, "blink once again." When she did as I asked, it dawned on me that there might be a way for her to communicate with me after all. I replaced the paper in the drawer and turned back to her.

"Aunt Jessica, I know you are trying to tell me something," I said as I leant down to her. "And it may be very important for me to learn what it is."

Her lower lip trembled.

"No," I continued. "I know you cannot talk, and I do not want you to try. But I am going to ask you a few questions, and you can answer me with your eyes. If the answer is yes, blink only once. If it is no, blink twice. Do you think you can do that?"

Her response was yes.

I sat on the edge of her bed, trying to calm my nerves. "There is a secret here at Darby," I commenced. "And it has to do with Anitra?"

Again her answer was yes.

"I know that Anitra was frightened," I went on. "Did she have reason to be?"

She did.

"Was it Damien whom she feared, Jessica?"

Where I expected to see her blink but once, her eyelids flickered twice. Convinced she had misunderstood my question, I repeated it.

When again she closed and opened her eyes a second time, I clasped her shoulders.

"Please, Jessica, you *have* to tell me," I begged her.

A vein which ran like the jagged course of the Swale pulsed down the side of her temple. I released her, suddenly sickened by my importunings. What had I come to, I asked myself. The woman was barely clinging to life and I was shaking her, demanding her to respond.

"Oh God, I am sorry," I whispered as she sank exhausted from my grasp.

Her eyes opened slowly and a single tear trickled down her cheek. I reached down and dabbed the sadness and frustration from her face with a corner of the sheet.

I had not heard the maid slip back in, but when she brought the tray to the bed I arose. "You need to eat and I need to think," I said as I patted Jessica's hand. "I will be back soon. But I promise, no more interrogation."

I sensed that she wanted me to stay. But I was driven by a need to get out of this house. I needed the snap of this northern air to clear the cobwebs and bring clarity to my thoughts and actions.

I had no particular destination but found myself ambling down through the avenue of trees to the point by the lake where the water tumbled in distinct falls beneath the low arches. The wind whistled through the distant willows, with their brown polished winter bark. I stepped closer to the pool, watching the water trickle over the flint-faced plinths, then hanging like iced teardrops from their edges.

To the naked eye it was such a peaceful setting. I shut my eyes as I remembered the body I had seen floating amongst the water lilies and newts. Had he unraveled the mystery of Darby? I wondered. I knew from the conversation I had overheard at the stables he held information which was a threat to someone here, and that someone was a woman. But who? I supposed it could be Flo, the young serving girl who had disappeared, but that made no sense. And so who was left? Jessica, Amanda, and Marisse. I knew now that Marisse could not be trusted, but could she do murder? No. Even if she were capable of it she would never soil her own hands.

420

.

Other hands would surely carry out her orders.

Instead of returning to the drive I took the shorter path round the stables to the terraced gardens. As I reached the crest from which the land dropped to the rear of the house, I paused. I had an eerie feeling I was being watched, or followed, or both.

I quickened my pace as I followed the slope towards the path leading to the summerhouse. As I scurried through the maze of privet I was certain that I was being pursued. I heard my name being called, and though the cold made breathing difficult, panic set me running. I did not see the rock which had been heaved up by the frost, and though I clutched at the hedge I could not break my fall.

I lay there for only a moment before hands clasped my shoulders.

I cried out as a voice bade me, "Lillith, just lie still."

As I turned, the hood of my cloak fell back. "Charles," I gasped at the figure hovering over me. "What are you doing here?"

"I arrived last night. I thought you knew," he replied.

"Thank God it is you," I whispered.

"Can you stand?"

"I think so," I allowed.

Gently he helped me to my feet. "Lillith, you are trembling so. You were racing along as if you were terrified of something. I called to you. I thought you heard me."

I clutched at the sleeve of his coat. "You have to help me, Charles," I pleaded.

He placed his arm about my waist, offering me support. "Just lean on me and I will take you back to the manor."

"No," I cried. "You don't understand. I cannot go back there. Not until you have listened to me." He waited as I continued. "You were right. I never should have married Damien, but not for the reasons you think. When you suggested that things were not right here at Darby, I denied it. Perhaps it was because I did not want to admit it to myself."

"You really *are* frightened," he said, amazed.

"I have reason to believe," I went on, "that Damien, with the help of Dr. Brathwaite, will try to discredit me, that they will claim I am unbalanced."

"In heaven's name, why?" he demanded. "Lillith, Damien and Brathwaite loathe one another."

"No," I argued. "It is all a deception. The two are conspirators in something I do not completely understand. But trust me, I know they are in league."

He rubbed his brow. "I admit I am in the dark."

"I have evidence," I blurted out, "evidence which could ruin Damien, perhaps even destroy the Darbys entirely. There is a secret here, a dark, terrible secret. And I fear the two will do anything to silence me."

"Do you realize what you are saying, Lillith? My God, what is this secret?"

"I cannot tell you that now, Charles, save to say that it centers about Anitra and the fire and who knows what else. The body that was in the lake, the one Damien denied existed—well, it was very real. And the man's demise was no accident."

"How do you know that?" he persisted.

The words tumbled out as I told him what I had overheard the night before.

"I knew I should never have let my suspicions rest," he chastised himself. "I was uneasy when I left Darby. Something kept nagging at me. Call it superstition, but I had the feeling something was very wrong here. Then to return and find Jessica as she is . . . I started to wonder whether I did not have some sixth sense."

"She was coming to tell me something when she fell."

"You *do* think it was an accident?"

The very suggestion that it might have been otherwise sickened me. Had I misread the fear I had seen in her eyes day after day? Was she frightened not of her condition, as I had assumed, but of someone responsible for it?

"You are not sure, are you, Lillith?" Charles surmised.

"I am not sure of anything anymore, Charles. I thought if I could piece the puzzle together I could face this unknown. If I could bring it to light it could no longer haunt or hurt anyone here."

"What are you going to do, Lillith?"

"I have to leave here. At least for a while. I feel as though I am on the verge of the truth, but I am also terrified that I am going to fall into a great precipice. I can't do this alone, Charles. It's strange, these twists of fate. In many ways you brought me to Darby. And now I am asking you to help me leave it."

"If that is really what you want, then of course I will arrange it," he assured me. "But I should warn you that my intercession will not be welcomed. You don't think that Damien is just going to let you go?"

"Then what am I to do?" I asked despairingly.

"You said that the doctor was to see you this morning."

I nodded.

"You also indicated that Brathwaite appears opposed to this scheme, or whatever it is that is going on here."

"Yes."

"Then I am not certain you have anything to fear from him."

"You are not suggesting I meet with him?" I gasped.

"Precisely that. You will have to convince him, of course, that you are naive about this evidence you say you have. And do not allow him to suspect that you have enlisted my help. I need time to think of some way to extricate you from this place."

I managed a smile. "Oddly, time is what Damien told Brathwaite he needed."

"If you think you can walk on that ankle, I suggest we get back to the house."

I accepted his support gratefully. We had just come

423

through the terraced gardens when I paused suddenly.

"What is it?" Charles asked.

I looked up at the manor. "I do not know. Earlier I had the feeling that I was being watched, and I have it now. Likely 'tis just my nerves."

"I did not think they used this end of the house," he mused, following the direction of my glance.

I shrugged. "Maybe they shan't have to go very far to convince me that I am suffering delusions."

"Lillith, you are as sane as I," he said as he guided me towards the drive. "You cannot allow doubt to undermine you now."

I looked up the steps to the manor. "When I lost Father and Elijah, I felt robbed of choice. Here again I have no choice as to what I must do. I will not be dissuaded by my doubts."

We were only steps away from the landing when the doors were flung open.

"It is Damien," I murmured.

"Stay calm," Sir Charles said, tightening his grip on my arm.

"Good morning," he called up to the figure seated above. "I seem ever present in times of emergency, but your wife seems to have taken a nasty fall and turned her ankle. 'Twas lucky that I chanced upon her when I did."

I could feel the bitter regard of Damien's eyes upon me. "Then 'tis fortunate that Dr. Brathwaite stayed over last night. He should look at you straightaway, Lillith." I bit my lip, willing myself not to panic. "He is in the library," I heard him say. "I shall fetch him." He swung his chair about and wheeled away from us.

"I cannot go through with this," I whispered.

"You can and you will," Charles insisted. Then, raising his voice so Damien would hear, he added, "Can you make it on your own, Lillith?"

He pressed my arm.

"Yes, thank you," I managed to reply.

As Damien's chair disappeared from view he said, "Remember, I shall be close at hand. Whatever you do, keep calm. Say little. Try to keep the conversation on your ankle."

He released me and I limped forward, praying with every step that God would give me the strength for whatever lay ahead.

Damien did not reappear. It was Dr. Brathwaite who found me there in the reception hall.

"I understand you have had a bit of an accident."

"It is nothing truly," I assured him.

"Nonsense," he countered. "By your expression alone I can see you are in pain. If you will just give me a moment I shall fetch my bag. Nothing is broken, I am certain, or you would not be able to walk on it. But a wrenching can be just as painful. If we wrap it well and keep you off your feet for a while we should have it put to rights in no time. Why do you not proceed to your quarters, and I will meet you there."

Do not argue, do not divulge anything, Charles had told me. I took a deep breath. "That is very kind of you."

With every step I took I willed myself to be strong. I had come this far. I was not alone anymore.

The diary bulked under my hip as I lay down on the bed and let my cloak slip open. The doctor returned within minutes and silently withdrew the boot from my foot.

"You have taken a nasty turn there," he said finally. "I shall bind it to keep the swelling down. If you keep off it for three or four days, it should be fine."

My heart sank. Three or four days seemed a lifetime when the next minutes and hours held my fate.

I watched him warily as he wound the support about my ankle.

"That should do it. Just heed my warning. You do not want permanent injury to that leg."

I thanked him, but instead of taking his leave, he hung back.

"You seem anxious, Lady Lillith," he offered. "Is something else bothering you?"

425

"Of course not," I lied.

He buckled the strap of his bag. "We have not had much opportunity to talk, you and I. But now that you are a Darby, I hope we can become friends. You are rather stuck with me as your doctor, you know."

"I thought Dr. Rendcomb was the family doctor," I challenged.

"He has treated certain members on occasion," he replied.

"But it was you who saw to Damien. After the fire, I mean."

He nodded.

"Then why is it that you and Damien are at such odds, Dr. Brathwaite?"

The minute I had blurted it out, I was sorry. Charles had warned me to keep silent, but I felt like a river in torrent with no dam strong enough to stop me. I knew I had struck a nerve, as he immediately averted his gaze.

"That sometimes happens in these cases," he replied.

"It is a pity the two of you cannot communicate and settle whatever differences exist," I persisted.

"That is the way it must be."

I gritted my teeth. How far would his lies go, I wondered.

"And Anitra, I gather you were her physician as well?"

He frowned. "What makes you ask about Anitra?"

I chose my words carefully. "Only that she was so young and died so tragically."

"The loss of both her and Lady Darby was a great shock."

"Particularly to Damien."

"It has been a great burden for him."

A shiver passed through me. "A burden, Doctor? That implies he was somehow responsible."

"Did I say that?" he replied quickly. "A poor choice of words."

"Was it? Was it really?" I cried out.

He reached out and took my hand. "Lady Lillith, I think

you should talk to me. You are more unnerved than I thought. I can help you, you know."

I snatched my hand from him. "I do not have to listen any longer. You think you can deceive me, that you can lie to me, but I warn you as I have warned Damien, I know everything. I know about Anitra and Damien, I know the secrets of this house, I know that you and he are conspiring to ensure my silence, but it is too late for that."

I had dashed all of Charles's warnings in one hysterical outburst. I was sobbing uncontrollably now. Nothing seemed to matter any longer. All caution had been thrown to the wind.

Again he reached out to me.

"Do not touch me," I said chokingly.

"Lady Lillith, get a hold of yourself," I heard him command. "I do not know what you think you know, but Damien and I have no malevolent intentions towards you, I swear it."

"Are you going to tell me that you were not here last night, the two of you?" I accused. "And spare me any further deceit, for I know this was not the first time."

He hid his face in his hands.

"What is the truth, Doctor?" I begged. "What is the truth about Damien and Anitra? What *really* happened at the summerhouse? Was it truly an accident, or are all of you hiding something as you are hiding the death of the stablehand?"

He drew a deep breath. "I cannot answer that."

"Why?" I demanded. "Because you share guilt for this secret you all harbor?"

"I cannot because I have given my word," he replied, his voice filled with despair.

I reached down into the pocket of my cloak and withdrew the leather volume. "I have not finished reading this, but I have seen enough," I said sadly.

He looked down at the volume, which I clutched tenaciously. "And what, may I ask, is that?"

"Anitra's diary," I replied.

"I see," he said thoughtfully.

"Your expression speaks a thousand words, Doctor. I obviously do not have to tell you of its contents. You know. You know that Damien felt something other than brotherly affection for Anitra. You know that within these very walls they conducted their clandestine affair. You know that they were lovers."

He gasped, his face contorted in shock. "My God, is that what you think?"

"Now you are going to tell me I am mad, deluded, but you see you cannot. Because it is all here in her own words. Did you know that they were planning to go away together? But something happened, something was frightening her. As passionately as she loved him, she was terrified of him."

The doctor picked up his bag and went to the door. "There is nothing more I can say to you, Lady Lillith. In my wildest imagination I cannot think what has caused you to arrive at such conclusions. I can only tell you I do not find you deranged. Mistaken, horribly so, but not deranged."

"Where are you going?" I demanded.

"I am going to fetch Damien. It is time for this burden to be lifted and the past buried once and for all."

There it was again, the reference to a burden. The burden of what? Of what he had done? I was confused. Was this another attempt to dupe me? I was almost convinced by the doctor's fervent denials, but how could I be, when I held the very proof of Damien's damnation in my hands.

"I do not want to see him," I exclaimed.

He left without another word.

I lay there for a few moments, too distraught, too bewildered to move. The doctor had warned me about putting weight on my ankle, but I could not stay here.

I had to find Charles. I swung my legs off the bed, almost shrieking with pain as my foot hit the floor. The wrapping was such that I had difficulty pulling my boot over it. I withdrew the diary from my cloak and tucked it deep into the pocket of my skirt. Beads of perspiration formed on my brow as I limped from my quarters through to the reception hall.

"God, let Charles be nearby," I murmured to myself.

I dragged myself across the marble floor to the library. The door was ajar, and I saw Charles pacing by the fireplace. I called out to him and he strode swiftly towards me.

"I have been distraught," he murmured, clasping my elbow to give me support. "What happened in there?"

"There is no time to explain," I retorted, "but you should know that I said far more than I should have. Dr. Brathwaite has gone to fetch Damien. I cannot see him. You simply have to keep him from me."

He stepped closer to me, his arm encircling my waist. As he did I was accosted by Damien's voice behind me.

"A touching scene, but I would remind you, Charles, that Lillith is my wife."

As I spun around, his dark eyes flashed at mine.

"I do not know fully what is going on here, Damien," Charles retorted, "but I know that Lillith is terrified of you, terrified of this house. I should tell you straight off that I am taking her out of here, away from you, away from Darby."

Damien's eyes were unflinching, never leaving my own. "Is that what you want?" he demanded of me.

My eyes filled with tears. "Yes," I murmured.

His expression surprised me. It was a mingling of pain and sadness. "I won't stop you," he said finally. "Not if that is truly what you want. But before you go, I want some time with you. Alone."

I turned to look at Charles, who had not relaxed his grip on me. "It is up to you, Lillith."

"I do not want to hear what you have to say to me, Damien," I managed to say.

He gripped the sides of his chair. "I ask you to ask yourself only one thing. Can you leave here without the slightest doubt left in your mind?"

It was the one question he could have posed which could cause me to waver.

As if reading my mind he said, "Then spend this time with me. In a way, you owe us both that."

I drew away from Charles. "You are sure?" he demanded of me.

I nodded.

"Not here," Damien said. "Let us go to the studio."

"Good Lord, can't you see she is in pain?" Charles said angrily.

"Beside the door, there in the Chinese stand, there is a cane," he replied.

Charles searched it out and brought it to me. "Can you manage?" he asked me.

With some trepidation I placed my weight on the cane and took a step. "I am fine," I assured him.

I followed Damien to the studio, thinking as I did how long it seemed to have been from that first day, when I began as his assistant, to this, which would be my last at Darby.

I felt a moment's panic when he shut the door behind me, but he quickly distanced himself, the light of the windows at his back. I sank with relief into a chair, watching him apprehensively as he poured a brandy.

"May I offer you some?"

I shook my head.

He swirled the liquid in the glass. "Since it would appear that you are in the accusatory position, perhaps you should tell me whence these charges come."

"What good would it do, Damien?" I said in despair. "Has not enough pain been caused, and enough lives ruined?"

"In that alone you may be correct," he acknowledged. "But you have made some very harsh allegations, and I want to know how you think you can substantiate them."

"I know about you and Anitra," I mustered the courage to murmur.

"You have said that before," he replied tersely. "But I think you should explain what you think you know about Anitra and myself."

"Must I say it? I am certain Dr. Brathwaite has already told you of my revelations."

He nodded. "I want to hear it from you."

"I know . . . I know that you and Anitra—" I broke off.

"Go on," he pressed. "That Anitra and I . . ."

"That you were lovers."

His eyes were fixed upon me. "I did not hear you."

I clutched the carved head of the cane. "That you were lovers. That you and she were lovers. I know why you once told me that your life, here within these walls at Darby, was—is—a living hell. I also know that Anitra was terrified of you. And I am left to wonder if that fire was really an accident."

I shuddered, frightened by my own vehemence.

He uttered not a word but drank down the rest of the brandy, refilling the glass almost immediately.

"This knowledge you think you possess, Lillith, is there any evidence that what you say is true?"

I reached into my pocket and withdrew the leather volume. As I had done so often before, my fingers traced the name emblazoned on the cover. I held it up for him to see.

"Do you know what this is?"

He studied it for a moment. "I think I do."

"Then you admit to it?" I asked, amazed.

"What I admit to is that I recognize it as a diary which I gave Anitra. 'Twas some occassion, Christmas or a birthday."

"Do you know its contents?" I inquired.

"By its very nature, a diary is a private matter, or so I thought," he berated me.

"Whatever you think, I did not mean to violate that intimacy."

"It is not your violation but your conclusion which troubles me, Lillith."

I fingered the strap of the leather volume. "Damien, this is not conjecture. This is Anitra's own voice."

"Then open it. Read it to me. I am anxious to hear what she will divulge."

I pulled the diary open at random.

" 'Dear diary,' " I read. " 'It is all such a terrible mistake. How, with all that has happened between us, can D do this? I shall not abide it, I swear to you, it is too cruel. You cannot abandon me now.' "

"Go on," he said slowly.

The next page I came to was all too familiar to me.

" 'I cannot go on. It is all such a sham. D tells me he will bring an end to it, that he will find a way to extricate us from this hell we have found ourselves in. I cannot imagine what he plans.' "

"Stop there," Damien demanded.

"I can understand that you would not want to hear any more of this," I allowed.

"You understand nothing, Lillith," he countered bitterly. "I see what you have done. And I expect from your vantage point there was a logic to it all. But you have allowed yourself to be grossly misled."

"Do you mean to tell me you are going to deny this?" I cried.

"Of course I am, because your assumptions are completely erroneous."

"Tell me how," I demanded.

"Answer me this, Lillith. Is there anywhere, anywhere in the entirety of that diary that her lover's name is mentioned?"

"What are you talking about?" I lamented. "It is here throughout. D this, D that."

He slammed his glass to the table before him. "D this, D that," he mimicked. "But where is there mention of *Damien?*"

For a moment I was taken aback. I opened the diary and frantically began leafing through it.

"You will not find it," he advised. "Not with the inference you drew."

432

My eyes near fled through the pages.

"But it is all here," I argued desperately.

"Lillith, put it down. Stop this foolishness and listen to me."

I sat almost as if frozen to the chair.

"The D that Anitra refers to, Lillith, is not Damien. It is Donat, Donat to whom she refers."

I searched my memory for recollection of the name. There was none.

Seeing my bewilderment, he continued. "You would know him better as Robert. His full name was Robert Donat Craigmoore. It was only Anitra who called him Donat. His French ancestry she found romantic. But then Anitra had many romantic notions."

I started to interrupt him but he demanded that I let him finish.

"She was my sister," he continued. "And whatever you think, I cared deeply for her. She was a late child. An enchanting child. I wish to God I knew when I sensed the change. My father adored her. She was more of an encumbrance to my mother, but Mother was willing to forgive her as well. In retrospect, she was different, volatile from the first. But the manifestations of her complexity did not become obvious until later. There were so many signs. And then so many words and actions. But if you are close to someone you tend to overlook their vices."

I wanted to argue, but had I not indeed done that with my own father?

He ran his hand through the waves of his hair. "Believe me. I charge myself perhaps more than any other."

"Are you telling me that D, this Donat you refer to, was the one Anitra was enamored of?" I asked, astounded.

He nodded.

"But Robert Craigmoore was the name of Amanda's husband."

"Tragically, one and the same."

"If this is some ruse, some tale you have concocted to take blame from yourself, Damien, then you are even more depraved then I thought," I charged.

"What I am about to tell you is known—at least I pray 'tis true—to only two people, Victor Brathwaite and myself. Had you not come here and found that diary, it likely would have died with us. Whether you choose, after hearing what I have to say, to remain or to leave Darby, I only beseech you to have the sensibility to keep this confidence."

I acquiesced mutely.

"Robert Donat Craigmoore came from a wealthy family hereabouts. His grandfather, like mine, unfortunately culled a fortune from those damned mines which mar these northern counties. Though several years my junior, Craigmoore and I were acquainted, never close, but as our parents exchanged social amenities he was certainly no stranger to me.

"He was a devilishly handsome chap, and it was on a day when he and his family were visiting when I realized Amanda was taking note of him. Indeed, I was stunned to see this direct, purposeful sister of mine play the coquette. At first Robert seemed not to pay much attention to her. Frankly, when his interest seemed to change so abruptly I questioned whether there had not been undue pressure placed on him by his father, who was an opportunist of the first order.

"In any event, he courted her and they married. Perhaps because Amanda missed the ties of her family, the two returned here frequently. I thought little of it, but in retrospect, as the visits lengthened almost into permanent residence, I should have suspected something.

"How long it had been going on when I discovered them there at the summerhouse and which of them initiated it, I do not know. Likely the diary you have there would tell us that.

"My initial reaction was a fury the like of which I had never known. If Anitra had not been there I wonder if I should not have killed him right there that day. But whereas I assumed that he was a despicable cad who had taken advantage of a young innocent, Anitra made it very clear that theirs was a mutual passion. She was of such a tender age that I dismissed her cries.

"I was in a quandary about what to do. I threatened them both, making them swear they would put an end to this liaison. My first reaction had been to expose him, banish him from Darby and the family. But Amanda was so blind to him, so in love with him, that I knew she would be destroyed by the knowledge.

"For a while I believed that it was over, but at the time I had not appreciated the turns of Anitra's mind, the pure selfishness of her nature, the maliciousness of her intent. Her behavior became obsessive, wanton."

"But surely your family saw," I interrupted. "Particularly Edmund, who was so close to her."

"I know it is difficult to imagine, but you would have had to know Anitra. She was calculating, and adept at keeping all suspicion at bay. With Edmund she continued to be the delicate, endearing child he worshiped. Anitra and my mother had never been close; perhaps Mother was more aware of her true nature than I ever knew. Around others save the servants she was the epitome of decorum and charm. But that simple, thoughtful guise masked a dark side."

"You talk as if she were two people," I charged.

His eyebrows raised. "An astute observation. For indeed, within that one body there raged two souls. I won't trouble you recounting the endless pleadings and threats I visited on them once I was certain they had never even interrupted their affair. I decided then that my silence was not serving anyone, particularly Amanda."

"And you told her?" I asked, amazed.

He shook his head. "I never had the opportunity. For simultaneous with my decision, Amanda announced she was with child. You can see that the shock might well have been too great. Oddly, at that time something seemed to change. I

4 3 5

.

do not think that Robert cared a pence for Amanda, but I have reason to believe that at that juncture he actually tried to end his relationship with Anitra. Her reaction was tempestuous, bizarre. Her swings of temperament were more frequent now. She would go from crying, seeming contrition, to explosions of laughter. But it was not laughter born of humor, it was a hideous cacophony.

"I had known something was wrong but I was now convinced that she was ill. That is when I enlisted the aid of Dr. Brathwaite. I knew that she would not permit him to see her, and since there were no outward physical signs I could not alert my parents to the necessity. He agreed, however, to frequent the manor more often under the guise of assisting me with a study of anatomy which I might use in my paintings.

"It did not take long for him to confirm my worst fears. This was not simply the case of a high-strung, overly sensitive young girl."

"But what of treatment, some medication? Certainly there was something," I said.

"We tried," he said despairingly. "But where we thought that by doctoring her food or drink we might at least calm her, there was no change. In retrospect, I think she may have grown suspicious, perhaps even avoided those herbal teas. Brathwaite believes she had progressed too far into that shadowy world ever to be reclaimed."

I sank back in the chair, too drained to speak. My mind was roiling with my efforts to bring some reason to all that Damien had laid before me.

He replenished his glass once again. "None of this is easy, Lillith, but as you may suspect, the worst is yet to come.

"Whereas I thought that Terrence's impending birth had had some influence on Robert, the change in him was short-lived. Later I learned that he succumbed again, but this time for different reasons. Anitra, sensing she was losing her grasp, threatened to blackmail Robert. If he did not resume his affair with her she would go to Amanda and tell her everything. Anitra became obsessed with the idea that the two of them would go away together. I think it was at this juncture when Robert saw there was more to the folly than he had ever anticipated. Whereas he had been harsh with her in trying to put it all asunder, now I think he was actually becoming frightened of her, and so he cajoled her into believing that he was in sympathy with her.

"Although I have gone over the events of those last days thousands of times, some of it is still a blur to me. Amanda had returned to the manor, leaving Robert behind. That afternoon there was a dreadful quarrel between my mother and Anitra. What was said, I shall never know, and perhaps that is best. What I suspect is that Mother confronted Anitra, that she by this time also knew of the liaison and, like me, had come to fear for Anitra's mind.

"I was busy in the studio the next morning trying to clear up some things before Brathwaite and I were to leave for London. He knew of a specialist there, and as a last resort we had decided two days thence to take Anitra to see him.

"I had seen Amanda at breakfast in the morning room. She had told me that she was going to take a walk down to the summerhouse, as the doctor had advised a daily constitutional. I remember seeing Anitra at the top of the stairs as I crossed to the reception hall. If she spied me she did not acknowledge it.

"It must have been about ten when I decided to go down to the stables to saddle my mare. Before I reached them I was aware of an acrid burning smell. I began to walk faster, thinking that it might be coming from the stables themselves, when I turned to see smoke billowing from the east. I broke into a run. Before I even saw the flames leaping like spires to some celestial realm I knew it was the summerhouse. All I could think of was Amanda. The heat of the fire was so intense even from afar that I knew I had no time to enlist aid. Save for the left wing, the place was an inferno. I burst through the door,

437

screaming for Amanda, the smoke so dense that it seemed to singe the very pupils of my eyes. I had gone no more than ten paces when I stumbled against something soft. As I knelt down I realized with horror that it was my mother, or the remains of what had been my mother. A burning beam had fallen across her. Her face was charred almost beyond recognition. I had to put my hand to my mouth as waves of nausea o'ertook me."

He paused for a moment. "You wanted to hear it all, Lillith," he murmured. "I knew she was dead," he continued, "and, though it sickened me to leave her there, my prayer was that I might find Amanda unharmed. I pressed on towards the wing still relatively untouched by the flames, hoping she had managed to crawl there to seek escape. But I never reached it, for suddenly I spied a form pinned under fiery debris. I pulled off my shirt and tore at the fallen rafters. When they came free I was shocked to discover it was not Amanda, but Anitra. She murmured something as I lifted her up, clutching her to me as I fought to escape the flames. For a moment I thought we were going to get clear, but in one split second the fire, which had only lapped at this area, tore through, collapsing the ceiling. My body covered Anitra's. Her breath, though shallow, gave me hope. I tried to rise but found I could not. By some force beyond my own I was able to drag, push, roll us out of the conflagration."

He cringed. "I will never forget her eyes. They were wide open. There was a look of wild, maniacal panic about them. Blood trickled from the corner of her mouth, and she choked as she tried to say something. I cradled her head against my arm, begging her not to talk, but it was as though she was possessed, driven to tell me something. I pressed closer to her in time to hear her say, 'I did not mean to, I swear, I did not mean to, Amanda, she . . .' and with that she was gone. I remember looking back towards the house and screaming. In Anitra's last moments she had somehow tried to undo all she had done.

"I must have passed out, for when I awakened I was at the

manor, in bed. My arms were bandaged up to my shoulders. I remember thinking I had to get up. I tried to move my legs, but strain as I did they would not budge. I sank back down in bed as Dr. Brathwaite came in.

"I remember asking where my father was, and he told me that he was in the library. Amanda was with him. I do not know whether my gasp was from shock or relief or both. I demanded to know if she was all right. Brathwaite told me she seemed to be taking it very hard, particularly the news of Mother. He had sedated her, but he was concerned. When I inquired how she had escaped, he did not know what I was talking about. It was only moments later when I learned that Amanda had not been in the summerhouse after all."

"But where was she?" I asked, bewildered.

"It seems, thankfully, that she had felt fatigued and returned to the manor. I was in no condition to attend the funeral. Though the doctor assured me that my arms would heal, he gave me little hope about my legs."

"It must have been dreadful for you," I stammered.

"Truthfully, I thought little of it those first days and weeks. I felt the loss of Mother and Anitra far more than my inability to walk. Besides, there were other concerns I had to face. The authorities were called in. It is routine in this kind of thing. Father was too distraught to face them. Robert came for Amanda, who had seemed to be moving trancelike through the house since the fire. I decided, even with everything which had happened, that it was better for her to be away from the manor for a while."

I waited, my nerves on edge, as he paused to down his brandy.

"The fire was not an accident, Lillith. It was set. Deliberately. But not, as you think, by my hand."

"Then who?" I gasped.

"Obviously it was Anitra," he moaned. "All I can fathom is that she must have thought Amanda was still ensconced there at the summerhouse."

"And your mother?"

"I have tried to tell myself that that was a mistake. If they had not had that quarrel, I would be certain of it."

"Damien, do you know what you are saying?" I asked, astounded.

He hung his head. "I know, at times it seems incredible even to me, Lillith. But you had to know, to see what she had become. There was no reason left in that mind. I prefer to think it was not even Anitra at the last. She had always been rivalrous of Amanda. When they were younger, Amanda always gave way to her. It must have been painful for her, particularly when my father showed such favoritism towards Anitra. But to give up her husband to her younger sister? No, I think not. I believe that in her madness Anitra would have done anything to be with Robert, or Donat, as she called him."

"Even murder?"

"What else am I to think? The fire was set deliberately. Her last words still ring in my ears . . . 'I did not mean to,' she said. Perhaps at that one instant before death she was repentant."

Something was troubling me. "But, Damien, if that were true, why would Anitra, if she had set the fire, have fallen victim to it? It makes no sense."

"I thought the same thing at first," he agreed. "But it is the only answer. Perhaps somehow, inexplicably, she became trapped. What I prefer to conclude is that she may have realized, too late of course, that it was not Amanda she had set her wrath on but her own mother and gone in after her. The authorities were willing to concede the latter theory."

My head was pounding. "Damien, if all this is true, why does Edmund blame you?"

"That is simple," he sighed. "I concocted it so he would."

"You did what?" I asked, perplexed.

"The shock to Edmund had been almost unbearable. Can you imagine what it would have done to him if he had learned the truth, learned that his adored Anitra had set the fire which had killed his wife, taking her own life as well? Reputation aside, it would have ruined him. And all the sordid details, the history of it all, would eventually have come out, destroying Amanda too. So I bribed the authorities to keep it quiet, saying that some oils and varnish had been left carelessly. As I am the only one in the family who painted, the guilt was mine."

"And have you bribed the authorities about the stablehand as well?" I asked accusingly.

His expression told me I had caught him off guard.

"You see, I overheard you and Dr. Brathwaite, Damien. Do you have an explanation for that as well?"

He shook his head.

"Then why did you lie to me?" I demanded.

"Lillith, I am not certain what happened there, but the one thing you do not understand is what it means to be a Darby. We cannot afford even a hint of scandal here. You know my father is not well."

"A man has likely been murdered, and all you can think of is scandal," I said, astounded. "I am your wife. Surely you could have told me the truth. But instead you conspire to make me think I am suffering hallucinations."

"We have no proof that the man was murdered, Lillith," Damien countered.

"Well, I happen to believe that he was blackmailing someone at the manor," I revealed.

He frowned. "What makes you say that?"

I related what I had overheard down by the stables.

"Why did you not tell me, Lillith?"

I was incensed by the very suggestion. "Do you really believe you have given me reason to share anything with you, Damien?"

Our eyes met, and the pain which I had read there oft before flooded his. My name took form on his lips, and I knew that he was reaching out to me.

"I can't, Damien," I said slowly. "I must have time to think. Too much has happened."

"You are leaving Darby then?"

"I do not know, Damien," I replied quietly. "I just know I need to be alone. I need to find myself again." As I rose to leave I turned to face the room, the room I had once seen as a chamber of horrors.

"I have seen the paintings in there," I confessed.

"I see."

"I suppose now I understand, or can try to understand why—"

"No. Truthfully I do not even understand it myself," he interrupted. "If I could remove them without creating comment, I would have done so long ago. I started them while she was alive. In a strange way the paintings reflect an earlier awareness of her illness than I would dare admit to myself. After the fire I could not go back to them. You probably noticed that several remain unfinished. I have no excuse for them, save that they reflect the frustration and fear I felt those months before her death. She was obsessed. But in some strange way, I had allowed her to obsess me as well."

26

I LEFT the studio and limped across the reception hall to the library, where I knew Charles would be waiting. I was surprised and slightly disappointed to find Amanda with him. I sensed from her regard that I had interrupted at an inopportune time.

I was too tired, however, for amenities. "Amanda, might I ask a favor of you?" I said. "Would you be so kind as to leave Charles and me alone. Just for a few moments. It is very important I speak to him privately."

She looked over at Charles, who had not taken his eyes off me. I knew she was far from pleased, but she agreed, and I went over to where Charles sat. As she closed the door he put his finger to his lips and crossed past me to the door, where he stood listening for several moments.

"She is gone," he told me.

"I hardly think she would listen," I rebuked him.

He shrugged. "You may be right. For myself I am not so sure. There is something about Amanda Darby I do not trust. But that aside, I must tell you this last hour I have been like a cat on a ledge. Are you all right?"

I tried to force a smile as I smoothed my hair away from my brow.

"Do you want to tell me what happened?"

I shook my head. "I have not even sorted it out for myself."

"Do you still want to leave Darby, Lillith?" he persisted. "If you do I will see to it right now."

I shook my head.

"Does that mean you are staying?" he asked, amazed.

"Charles, right now everything is a blur," I replied feebly.

"Lillith, hours ago you were begging me to take you from Darby," he reminded. "You thought—and you had convinced me—that you were in very real danger here. What of this evidence you claimed you had?"

"I was not lying to you, Charles, I swear it. But there were things I did not know."

"Knowing them now, can you remain here, Lillith?"

I raised my eyes to find a gentle clarity in his. "I will tell you what I told Damien. I must have time, Charles. You have been a good friend, and I owe you an answer. But at this moment I do not know the answer myself."

"I am going to look in on Jessica," he said. "If you need me, you'll find me there."

We parted at the staircase. All I could think of was retreating to the sanctuary of my bedroom.

When I reached it, Chips, who had nestled into the coverlet, looked sheepishly up at me. As I sank down beside him he moved over and licked my hand.

"You are a faithful fellow," I said, ruffling his silken coat.

He nudged into the crook of my arm, and I welcomed the close warmth of his body against mine.

Where to begin? I wondered. I had sought the truth and I believed that Damien had spoken it. I had watched him, seen the pain etched in the planes of his face, heard the aching despair in his voice. If only this one time, I believed he had been honest with me.

But how could I have been so mistaken? And if I had gone to him with my misgivings, would it have made a difference?

I could not even fathom the burden he had borne these last years. It was not my place to judge whether what he had done was correct, but none could argue that it was selfless. He had been left crippled, diminished not only by his physical disability but by Edmund's rejection of him.

My mind replayed over and over what Damien had told me: Anitra's relationship with Donat, her slow loss of reason, the fire. Acceptance did not come easily. I trusted he had spoken the truth, but there remained a gnawing sense that something was missing. Intentionally or not, there were words left unspoken.

Perhaps what troubled me most was that we had come to each other falsely: he believing it was greed which had brought me to this union, and I suspecting that Anitra, if but in memory, would always be his mistress. It was a marriage conceived in misconception, a marriage now in tatters, and I knew not whether it was possible to pick up the pieces.

I stayed in my room the rest of the day. Mary brought a tray in the evening and, sensing something amiss, kept her conversation to a minimum. When at last I disrobed and curled up in bed I welcomed my exhaustion. All these months I had been obsessed with finding answers. I had them now. But somehow the tapestry was still unfinished.

I reached across the coverlet, my hand closing about the diary. There was more here to be read, more that I needed to understand. I had to be freed from the past before I could decide if there was a future for me at Darby.

I closed my eyes, welcoming the drift of sleep. When I awoke the room was pitch dark. I listened for a moment, thinking I heard some commotion in a distant part of the manor. Chips, who had not left my side, apparently heard it as well, for he sat up, his ears cocked expectantly.

I had no idea what time it was. Chips whimpered suddenly, leapt off the bed, and began scratching at the bedroom door. I waited, thinking it was perhaps Damien retiring for the night. I sat up in bed as there came a shallow knock on the door.

"Lillith? Are you awake?"

"Who is it?" I called back.

"Victor Brathwaite. May I come in for a moment? I must talk to you."

I remembered with everything that had happened I had not bothered to lock the door.

"Come in," I said, reaching down to the foot of my bed for my robe.

"I am sorry to intrude on you at this hour, my dear, but something has happened I think you should know about."

His tone was so dour that I knew it was serious. "What is it? Is it Jessica?"

"No, no it is Lord Darby. He has suffered a heart attack."

I gasped. "Is he . . . ?"

He stepped forward. "He is alive but frankly I do not expect him to last the night. Damien is upstairs with him now."

"Upstairs?" I gasped as I fumbled with the sash of my robe. "How did he get upstairs?"

He seemed puzzled. "The way he always does. The ramp to the west wing."

"I do not know of any ramp," I said, bewildered. "I thought that wing was sealed."

"Did you and Damien not talk earlier? About Anitra, I mean?"

"Yes we did," I replied, "but—it is not important now. Could you hand me the cane?"

"I do not think you should get up, Lillith," he advised. "That ankle of yours needs rest."

"My place is with Damien," I replied with certainty.

"You may be of more help to Amanda," he replied. "I have sedated her, but I have not seen her in such a state since her mother died. She is in the library now."

I left Chips behind in the parlor. The doctor saw me to the library, saying, "I had best go back up. There is little I can do, but this has to be particularly hard on Damien."

"I understand that now," I replied quietly.

I entered the library and found Amanda seated at the far end of the room, staring straight ahead. I crossed over to her and, placing my hand on her shoulder, suggested we move over by the fire.

She shrugged my hand away, saying, "Do not touch me."

I could not have been more startled if she had slapped me.

My instinct was to reach out to her again, but something told me she would not be receptive. I could not be harsh with her. It had not been that long since I had lost my own father, and I recalled that in those first hours and days I was more comfortable being alone in my grief.

I sat listening to the clock, whose ticking was like a prophesy of death. Perhaps an hour had passed when Damien entered the library.

I looked up at him expectantly. Our eyes met for but a moment before he turned to Amanda. "I think you should go up now."

She stood up and strode past me, pausing before Damien.

"No matter what you say, no matter how hard you try, in the end you know there is no escape." Without another word she left the room.

"I know Amanda is upset, but what did she mean by that?" I asked him.

"Nothing," Damien replied.

His response had a hollow ring, but I did not challenge it.

"Is Edmund conscious?" I asked.

He wheeled his chair over to where the decanters were placed. "He goes in and out. I am not certain he knows much of what is happening."

"Perhaps that is for the best," I replied. "But it is so sad that, well, that the two of you might not reconcile before it is too late."

He filled his glass. "It is already too late, Lillith. Perhaps in some other realm he will learn the truth and forgive. I cut a bargain with myself those years ago, and though at times I have wrestled with it, I would do the same thing again today. As I see it, I really had no choice."

I smoothed the folds of my robe. "Where is Marisse?" I ventured.

The muscles in his jaw tightened. "You tell me," he replied caustically.

"What are you saying?" I puzzled.

"So you are naive in that as well," he chided.

"Damien, please do not use that tone with me," I pleaded. "It has been a long arduous day for all of us, and it is not over yet."

"You are right," he apologized. "You didn't deserve that. To answer your question, Marisse is not in the house."

"But it is one o'clock in the morning," I said, amazed.

"That is true. Usually she is back by this hour."

"I think you had best tell me what this is about," I murmured.

He swallowed his brandy. "Marisse de Wentoff is James Farklan's whore."

He raised his head and looked at me. "You do not seem surprised."

"I think now I am beyond shock, Damien. I cannot say that I knew that they were intimate, but I did know they consorted together."

"Surely Marisse never admitted that. Or are you somehow implicated in this scheme of theirs?"

His words raked over me like the sharpened tines of a fork.

"If you had heard Marisse threaten me, you would never accuse me of such a thing," I cried.

"She threatened you?" he demanded.

"Does it really matter now, Damien?" I said in despair. "There is one very real problem here, however. Marisse is carrying a child—a child that she will at least claim is Edmund's."

"I suspect it is a ruse," he replied. "But if Marisse is *enceinte* it is by a Farklan, not a Darby, of that you can be certain."

I started as I distinctly heard the lock turn in the front door.

"Stay where you are," Damien instructed, wheeling himself to the door of the library.

I waited, hearing the heels of her boots click along the marble floor.

"A bit late for a stroll, do you not think, Marisse?" Damien called out to her. I could not make out her reply. "You had best come into the library," he continued, wheeling back within the room.

"The nerve of you, to think you can order me about," she accused, sweeping into the room. She stopped in her tracks when she saw me.

"Lillith, what are you doing here?" Then, whirling to Damien, "What is this about? What are you two up to?" she demanded.

"Edmund has had a heart attack," Damien said bluntly.

She paled considerably, her hand flying to her throat. "Where is he?" she murmured.

"Upstairs."

"Oh, my poor Edmund," she exclaimed. "I must go to him."

Damien wheeled his chair directly into her path. "Spare me your histrionics, Marisse. You are not going anywhere except out that door you just entered."

It was clear he had unnerved her. "How dare you talk to me that way. You will be very sorry when I tell Edmund of this."

449

"My father is beyond hearing any more of your nonsense, Marisse."

She looked truly frightened. "He is dead?"

Damien shook his head. "But it is only a matter of hours, perhaps even minutes, according to Brathwaite."

She sank into a chair.

"I shouldn't get too comfortable if I were you," he continued, "you have a lot of packing to do."

"Do not threaten me, Damien," she warned. "You may be surprised to learn that I am carrying your father's child. We will see what the courts have to say about this."

"On what basis?" he challenged. "You are not married to my father, and besides, we both know that it is Farklan's bastard you are carrying. I wouldn't put much stock in his claiming it, though. He may enjoy sharing these little trysts, but I doubt very much he will share his name with you."

She looked so pathetic sitting there that I could not help but feel some sympathy for her.

"Perhaps this is not the time," I said to Damien.

She shot me a hateful look. "I do not need *you* to intercede, you little—"

"Shut up, Marisse," Damien demanded.

"Look at her there," she continued. "Miss prim, miss purity. Smug, aren't you? You think now you stand to inherit all of this. Well, we shall see about that. You may think I will be the only one out in the cold, but mark my words, you'll follow soon after. You don't suppose that Damien, once Edmund is gone, will bother with the likes of you."

Her threat was like a knife in my stomach.

"That's enough," Damien exclaimed. "Get out of here. Now."

"You expect me to leave at this hour?" she replied, her voice quavering.

Damien lowered his head. "Just be sure you are not around in the morning."

As she passed by him she spat out. "This is not the end,

Damien, I swear it. You cannot dismiss me like this, because you know that your secret is not safe with me."

I watched as Damien put his head in his hands.

"Damien, what does she mean? What secret?" I pleaded.

He had not the opportunity to respond, for Dr. Brathwaite appeared at the door. I think Damien and I both knew the news before he said a word.

"Amanda was with him at the last," he offered. "Though I have given her some additional sedation, she did not seem herself. She is in bed now. Perhaps a night's sleep will help. Speaking of which, you both ought get some rest. Particularly you, Lillith."

"I am all right," I assured him.

"There is nothing more you can do here tonight," Damien told me.

"What of you?" I ventured.

"There are plans to be made, and I could not sleep if I tried." He looked alarmed suddenly. "My God, in all of this I never even gave one thought to Aunt Jess."

"I looked in on her," Dr. Brathwaite assured him. "She is sleeping. I expect at some point she will have to be told, but we will come to that."

I bade them good night and returned to my room. I could not help but smile as I heard the gentle snoring of Chips, who had remained curled up on the bed. At least there was peace for one member of the household here at Darby, I thought. The reality of the loss had still not caught up with me. Edmund Darby had seemed so invincible to me those many months ago, and now he was gone. I had not liked the man. Indeed, I had found him despicable. It would be deceit to feign a sense of loss. But my heart went out to Damien. His father had damned him unjustly, and now there was no chance for reparation. Death had cheated him once again.

27

As if in acknowledgment of Edmund's passing, the following day seemed drenched in gloom. There was a colorless quality to the landscape as though all life had been drained from it.

I felt relief as I dressed that the injury to my ankle had been slight. The ensuing hours would, I knew, be difficult and I would need to deploy all my energy.

Damien had not returned to our quarters during the night. I could not know whether he wanted me near him, but I with certainty knew that I must be there for him if he needed me. Was it a sense of obligation? I did not know. Only that I would not abandon him. Not now. Not yet.

I was crossing to the morning room when, hearing voices

from the library, I redirected my steps. As I entered I found Damien engrossed in conversation with Charles.

"Am I interrupting?" I inquired.

The night had taken an obvious toll on Damien. Dark shadows emphasized the deep set of his eyes. "No, I think we are finished," he replied. "Now if you will excuse me, I need to make some arrangements with Victor."

As he wheeled his chair from the room Charles pointed to the tray by the fire. "There ought to be some tea left, Lillith. You look as though you could use some."

I admitted that I could.

"I knew Lord Darby was not well," he offered, "but somehow he seemed beyond mortality."

"I thought the same thing last night," I murmured.

As I drank the tea Charles lapsed into silence. I had not noticed it at first, but now as I watched him I thought he seemed troubled.

"You seem very far away, Charles."

"Perplexed is more apt," he replied. "I suppose I am breaking a confidence, but perhaps you can explain this to me. Damien has instructed me to draft an agreement with Marisse."

"What kind of agreement?" I pursued.

"It is very simple really. As long as she never mentions Darby, she is to receive a monthly stipend for the duration of her life."

My expression must have revealed my shock, for he added, "Precisely my reaction."

"But just last night, Damien, if he could have, would have thrown her bodily out of the manor," I said.

"What do you mean?"

Slowly I recounted the events of the night before.

When I had finished, he said, "None of this makes any sense. Unless, of course, Damien is uncertain that it is James Farklan's child she is carrying, and not Edmund's."

"There is another possibility," I offered. "Perhaps Marisse knows something that is a threat to Darby."

"I know I have no right to ask you this, but could it have anything to do with what Damien told you yesterday?"

"It could," I admitted. "But now, with Edmund gone, I wonder if it really matters, save perhaps to protect Amanda."

"That is another subject I do not understand. I know you champion her, Lillith, but there is something very peculiar about that girl. You know, I used to think she and Damien were close, but if you could have heard the quarrel they had this morning, I think you would have concluded, as I did, that there is more there than meets the eye."

"Amanda and Damien were fighting?" I asked, amazed. "About what?"

He shrugged. "I am not certain."

I stood up. "I had best see her. She is taking this very hard, I am afraid."

"And you, Lillith? How are you?"

I knew he was not referring to my ankle. "I do not know, Charles," I confessed. "Perhaps I am alone in this, but I believed those vows I took, for better or worse. Damien is my husband. And, deny it or not, I think he needs me now. What the morrow will bring is still to be seen."

I found Amanda in her room, staring sightlessly out the window. She did not budge as I approached her.

"Is there anything I can do for you, Amanda?" I asked gently.

She turned her head a little towards me. "You can leave Darby," she muttered dully.

For a moment I was certain I had misheard her.

"You want me to leave Darby? Why? Have I said or done something to offend you? You know 'tis the last thing I would wish."

"There is nothing for you here," she said simply. "If you stay, Damien will make me go. And I cannot have that."

"I do not understand, Amanda. What does my being here have to do with you?"

She turned away, staring into nothingness again.

"Amanda, talk to me, please," I begged. "I know the pain you must be feeling right now. But you needn't be alone. Talk to me, or cry, or do *something*, but do not shut me out this way."

My pleadings were to no avail. Completely deflated, I left her alone in her misery. I tried to dismiss what she had said, but I was hurt by it, and also bewildered. I had felt almost a sisterly bond with Amanda. Certainly she had encouraged my marriage to Damien. So why now did she want to see me gone from Darby?

I decided while I was upstairs to look in on Jessica. Mary was just removing a tray from her nightstand.

As she carried it towards me she muttered, "Oh, madam, 'tis a bleak day 'ere at Darby."

I pressed my fingers against my lips to silence her. "She has not been told, Mary," I whispered.

" 'Tis kinder that way, aye expect."

"I thought this was your day off," I recollected.

"Mrs. 'Orsley says we're low on staff," she explained.

"Nonsense," I argued. "There will be nothing to be done about the manor the next few days. Go visit your mother. I will deal with Mrs. Horsley."

"Yer sure?"

"Absolutely," I assured her. "You go on now."

She left and I went to the bed. Leaning forward, I stroked Jessica's brow, noting that the once burnished halo of white waves framing her face had lost all its luster. This house had seen so much tragedy! It was almost as though there was a malison on Darby.

I smiled as her eyes fluttered open.

"I saw from the tray that you did not eat very much," I said. "You have to keep up your strength, you know."

There was a different look to her eyes today. It was not fear that I read but a certain despair, a hopelessness.

I drew up a chair. "Jessica, I think I may know what you were going to tell me about Anitra. Damien and I talked yesterday. When I read her diary, I drew some conclusions which I know now were mistaken. I should have left it buried with her, but I simply could not."

I followed her eyes as they darted towards the door. I knew she wanted to tell me something, but I was going to keep my promise to myself that I would not tax her strength again as I had the other day. "I am going to let you rest now," I said. "But I will be back later."

I decided to take a walk outside. Likely with all that had happened no one had given thought to Chips, and he was the last thing Damien needed to trouble about today. I had just stepped into the reception hall when I saw Marisse directly ahead of me. Her eyes were catlike as she stepped towards me.

"Come to bid me adieu, have you?" she purred.

I decided not to dignify her comment with a response, and gathering my skirts, I started to move past her. She was too quick for me and blocked my path.

"I doubt that your precious Damien has told you, but despite his outburst of last night, he is not throwing me out of this house. He is *paying* me to leave it, Lillith. And rather handsomely, I might add. Why he would think that I would want to remain in this—this asylum anyway, I have no idea. But you may want to ask him why, when he is so certain that it is James's child that I carry, he has made me such a generous stipend."

"We have nothing left to say to each other, Marisse," I replied.

She shrugged. "Have it your way, Lillith. But one day when this place comes crumbling down around you, you will think of me."

I stepped around her, going towards our quarters. Why was

Damien paying Marisse, I wondered. To protect Darby, but from what? If I asked him, then I chanced betraying Charles. It was suspicion which had led me astray in the first place. Was I going to fall prey to it again?

As I suspected, Chips had been overlooked. He seemed very grateful when I let him out the door through the back hall.

Meandering along the earth's crusted surface, it struck me that I had not even realized that the Yuletide was but weeks away. Darby would, of course, be in mourning, but I hoped that I might convince Damien, if only for Terrence's sake, to honor the occasion.

Would I even be at Darby then? I wondered. Even were I willing to stay, would Damien want me? By the time the complexion of the landscape had changed and spring had brought the heather to bloom, might not the manor itself be brought to new life? If only Damien and I could be as one?

Something told me not to make my decision just yet. The wounds ran deep. But time had healed wounds before.

28

I T rained steadily for the next week. Though none, save perhaps Amanda, truly grieved for Edmund, his loss was carried about like an empty valise.

Damien was with Charles when he was not secluded in his studio. Though I hoped he would reach out to me after the shock of the first days had abated, he seemed to prefer to lose himself in whatever remedy his painting offered him.

I was deeply concerned about Amanda, who seemed to have slipped into a dreamy realm where none could reach her. On Dr. Brathwaite's urging I kept my distance, allowing her to make peace with her anguish.

Save for my strolls with Chips I rarely left Jessica. Although she had not been told about Edmund, there was an increasing despondency about her. Sometimes in those hours where she drifted in and out of a comatose state I wondered whether we would not soon be laying her to rest as well.

The funeral had been a simple one, with Reverend Ghent presiding over a short ceremony in the Darby chapel. Never had I thought weeks back that I should be returning to it so soon again—particularly not to bid good-bye to its owner. Amanda, as she had done the day of the wedding, again hung back from the grave sites. It was almost as though by not viewing the simply inscripted slabs which etched into the earth she avoided the fact that these lives had been given and taken.

It was five days after the service when I decided once and for all to conclude what still seemed unfinished—the reading of Anitra's diary.

I do not know what I expected to find there. Damien had told me everything, I believed. But some compulsion would not let it rest. I sank into the chair by the fire and drew the volume to me.

Recognizing pages I had already read, I turned to a later page, dated July 1848. If I recalled properly, that would have been the very month of Anitra's death. "Amanda and D have arrived," it began:

He is acting strangely. Perhaps it is my imagination, for if the plan succeeds we shall be gone from here by week's end. I do not think I can bear it until then. Seeing her plod about, her enlargement a constant insult. It sickens me how he dotes on her. He tells me he must for appearance' sake, but at times I should like to tear at her very belly and snatch that proof of his unfaithfulness from her.

I felt a shiver go down my spine. Damien had been agonizingly descriptive of the depths to which she had plummeted, but it was one thing hearing it from his lips and quite another seeing it penned by her own hand.

Quickly I turned the page.

D tells me I am wrong, but I think not. I see the way she looks at me. She has never liked me. She was always jealous. Of course, I give her credit—she *was* always clever. Pretending to be generous and care for me. But I have never been fooled.

Riveted, again I turned a page ahead.

Why will he not believe me? He says he loves me, but if that were true would he not heed my warnings? It is all so unjust. Amanda says nothing, but she stalks me as a leopard does its prey, watching, waiting. There are those who would say it is I who am evil. Perhaps I am. No, that is wrong. D loves me. I cannot help what we feel. It is a destiny that is stronger, larger than us both. But through that veil of propriety and calm I know there lurks a venom, a hatred which frightens, even humbles one such as myself.

There were only two other entries.

The first read simply "D has left as we planned. In two days we shall be done with Amanda, done with Darby forever."

The last was obviously scrawled so quickly that it was almost illegible. I strained to read these, her final words:

I was right. She came to me last night. She knows everything. I wanted to argue but my head is hurting so again. Why did I wait? I should have left yesterday with D. She meant to frighten me. But the point of my blade is sharper. Because, God forgive me, I know the truth.

It was almost an hour before I closed the diary for what I knew would be the last time. I rose and blew out the candle and, moving to the bed, lay down upon it. Over and over, the words reverberated in my mind. Amanda knew! By the time I fell asleep I had a dread fear that I had happened upon the piece of the puzzle which till now had been missing.

I awoke the next morning bathed in a pool of perspiration, the sheets beneath me sodden reminders of my nightmare-filled sleep. In my dreams the paintings, the grotesque shrine to Anitra, came alive, the gargoyled androgenes reaching out to me and finally giving chase. I remember running, my lungs constricted with pain, fear driving me forward like a frightened doe. The direction I took seemed vague but suddenly I found myself standing amidst the charred remains of the summerhouse. I stopped, thinking I had escaped my predator, when suddenly a clawlike hand curled about my arm. I swung about, gasping, for the face distorted by reptilian markings was not that of Anitra but of Amanda.

Shaking, I managed to pull myself from the bed. I had to busy myself, to push these thoughts from my mind. The events of these past months and weeks had taken their toll. I had been so wrong before in my conclusions. Would I never learn from my mistakes? Could I not let well enough alone?

My ankle, thankfully, was almost recovered and I bathed and dressed quickly. It was a gray day, the sky hanging low and heavy over the hills. Not a scene which invited one out of doors, but I was determined that, no matter what the weather, I would enlist Damien's aid in obtaining a Yule tree.

I was surprised to find him seated in the parlor of our quarters. Chips, who was at his side, scampered to me as I entered.

"Abandoned me last night, did you?" I said as I knelt down to him.

"That was my doing," Damien said. "I thought it likely you needed a sound sleep."

"How are you, Damien?" I asked tentatively.

"I expect I have not given myself time to think," he admitted. "Charles and I have finished our dealings. Thanks to you this is all mine now. The irony is, I do not give a damn about it."

"Not even Darby Manor?"

He smiled wryly. "This place has been a perverse mixture of pleasure and pain. There seems no middle ground here."

"I doubt that you would ever be happy in a middle ground, as you refer to it."

He regarded me quizzically. "For once, you may be right, Lillith."

I winced at his "for once," but I expected in his eyes that was all I could be credited with.

When I made no move to leave the room he turned back to me. "Is there something else?"

"Actually there is," I admitted. "I know it's painful for you, but there is one aspect of what you told me about Anitra, the fire, which still perplexes me."

"What is that?" he inquired.

"You said when you reached the summerhouse it was an inferno."

He nodded.

"And when you entered, if I remember correctly, you said you had only gone a few paces when you stumbled upon your mother."

He closed his eyes. "That is right."

"And then you went towards the back of the summerhouse, desperate to find Amanda. But it was Anitra instead that you came upon."

"Yes," he replied.

I paused. "Was there a back entrance to the summerhouse?"

He looked confused. "No. There had been once but my father had had it sealed off. There had been trouble with vagrants entering there. But I do not see what you are getting at."

"Do you not think it odd that Anitra was at the rear? If indeed as you suspect she realized somehow that it was your mother and not Amanda who was trapped inside, why would she have needed go to the back of the building. She, like you, could only have entered through the front. She, like you, would have had to come upon the body."

I knew that I had jogged his memory and that he found my conclusion perplexing.

"Then you think that the authorities were mistaken? That the fire was an accident after all?" he asked.

I bit my lip.

"Well, is that what you are suggesting?" he persisted.

"I do not know," I replied, avoiding his gaze.

"Even if you are right, what difference would it make now?"

"I think it is terribly important," I argued, "if only for your peace of mind."

He sighed. "Peace only comes, Lillith, to those who are not at war with each other or with themselves."

From the very first I had known that there was a battle raging within Damien. But I still did not understand what it was that he fought. I left him as he seemed to prefer to be left—alone.

I fetched my cloak and, finding that Damien had left himself, decided he must have gone to the studio.

It was warmer than it had been for some weeks, the recent rains having cleared the landscape of all traces of snow. I drank in the air, which had an uncommon freshness.

I ambled down the path through the gardens, noting that hay had been placed over the beds to shelter the plants until spring. Only a week ago I had held out hope that with that season there would be a rebirth for Damien and myself. But not now. Charles had said that he thought Damien had been most generous. But it was not his benevolence I wanted, it was his love. And that was the one thing my heart told me he could not give.

I did not want my last memories to be of the summerhouse. When I looked back on Darby I wanted to picture the wildflowers on the fells and sheep dotting the dales. But I needed to see the ruin just one final time.

The charred carcass seemed to beckon me as I stepped down to where the columns, which had escaped remarkably unscathed, rose in remembrance of the entry. My eyes searched through the rotted structure, seeking to reconstruct the edifice as it once had been. It was clear that there had been a front hall. But unlike the one in the manor, this one had been far from grand; it had been small and narrow. To reach the central part of the house one would have had to pass through a doorway at the rear of the hall. To get to the back of the house, off of which was an extended wing, it appeared that one would have had to proceed through not one but two other rooms, each of considerable size. I stared at it all, imagining again and again the original configuration of the house.

It cannot be, I told myself, as realization came on me as the dawn of day. But something had been missing and I knew now what it was. The authorities had been right. This had been no accident. The fire had been deliberately set, but *not* by Anitra's hand. She had victimized others, but finally it was she who had fallen victim.

I did not need to ask myself who had done it. I knew. 'Twould never have been Edmund. And Robert—Donat— had left Darby the day before. Damien had despaired about Anitra, but he had no reason for this. The words of the diary replayed over and over in my mind. Why had I not seen it before? Repeatedly I had read two words: *She knows.* But "she" was not Lady Caroline Darby.

There was a sound behind me, like the snapping of a twig. I whirled about only to find Amanda some ten paces behind me.

I stood stock still.

"You look frightened," she said, her eyes boring into mine.

" 'Twas only that you startled me," I replied slowly. "I cannot imagine why I did not see you approach."

"I did not take the main path," she replied. "There is another one down there. You likely have not noticed it. It has been left to overgrow since the fire."

I looked about. "Is Terrence with you?"

"Terrence? No, he is in the house."

"What brings you down here, Amanda?" I asked.

"I saw you from the window. And I wondered why, when you have been warned about this place, you keep coming back to it."

She moved suddenly, taking several steps towards me. I stepped back, my hand reaching one of the columns as I did. Her gaze was so intense that though I wanted to look away I stood transfixed by her regard.

"You know, don't you, Lillith?" she said finally.

"Know? Know what?" I heard myself reply.

"Pretense is not going to get us anyplace. I see it in your face."

I sighed, feeling so broken, so despairing, that I clung to the column for support. "Yes, I know, Amanda. God help me, I know."

"When did you find out?"

"I found Anitra's diary. I mistook a great deal at first. It was only recently Damien told me about the fire. But I kept having this feeling that there was more."

"Why did you not leave Darby?" she cried.

"Amanda, I thought we were friends," I pleaded. "You encouraged me to marry Damien."

"Of course I did," she snarled. "It was the one way I could be certain he would inherit Darby, that I would never have to leave here. And now that he has it, there is no place for you here, Lillith. No place at Darby. And no place in Damien's life."

"Why?" I asked, anguished. "Why did you do it, Amanda?"

"I had known for a very long time about their liaison. At first I did not believe it, but there was evidence, small notes, absences, more than enough proof."

466

"And you kept it locked up inside you?"

"I did not care, until I found out I was carrying a child. Suddenly it was very important that Robert appear the solicitous, loving father-to-be. Actually, for a time he was. But then a few incidents caused me to suspect that I was losing him. I knew I had only one recourse. I had to confront Anitra."

"And what did she do?"

"She laughed. Can you imagine, she actually laughed."

I waited for her to continue.

"I do not remember much about the next few days. Robert left the manor. Every time I would see Anitra, she would look at me in that supercilious way of hers. Then there was that morning. I left the manor to go to the summerhouse. When I got there I found that Anitra had gone there before me. She did not see me, but I could see her through the windows."

"And your mother, did you know she was there?"

Her face twisted in pain. "I did not know, I swear it, I did not know. She was oft up early, but usually to putter in the garden. There was no reason to believe that she too had come here."

"And then what happened?"

Her eyes clouded over. "That is the part I do not remember very well."

I swallowed hard. "But you *did* set the fire."

She nodded. "I waited until I was certain it had taken hold. It was a very hot day and rain had been scarce that year. It ignited much more quickly than I would ever have dreamed. I took the lower path, returning to the house by the rear of the manor. I had been in my room only minutes when I heard the shouts. I remember looking out the window, seeing the flames and thinking how high they soared."

"And what did you feel?"

"Nothing really, except an overwhelming sense of relief. Can you understand that?"

I sank down onto the step of the portico, too exhausted, too sick to reply.

"You know, for a while, Lillith, I was actually going to let you stay here. If you had only helped me with Charles, things might have been different. But you weren't satisfied with just Damien. You had to take Charles as well."

I rose wearily. "Amanda, it is not Charles that I want, it is Damien, Damien who I love." I stepped forward, extending my hand to her. "Take my hand, Amanda," I pleaded. "Come with me back to the manor. We will find a solution together."

I took heart as slowly, tenuously she extended her arm, her hand clasping mine. But as our fingers entwined she jerked me with such ferocity that I fell to the ground. Her boot came up over my head and I rolled to the side, narrowly escaping the heel, which came down with a vengeance. I struggled to get up, my hands scratching against the blackened boards beneath me. She had circled in front of me now, and though I could not make it out I could see that she had picked something up and held it high above her head. I moaned as a nail tore against the inside of my arm.

Suddenly I heard my name being called.

"Damien," I murmured, my lips pressed into the dirt beneath me.

I lifted myself in time to see Amanda's eyes raise, the board she had claimed as a weapon suspended in midair. Fear had replaced the frenzied anger there but seconds before.

Damien's voice was like an echo as it rolled down the hill.

It was over so suddenly that I lay there in disbelief. With the exception of my arm, which was bleeding profusely, my body was whole. Whether reality had touched Amanda suddenly or whether the shock of seeing Damien there had halted her intent, I knew not. But, dropping the splintered wood, she had taken flight.

I dragged myself to my feet, looking up the path. I realized with horror that Damien's chair was poised on a precipice which, if he moved but inches, would catapult him down the hillside.

"Lillith," he called.

"Do not move, Damien," I choked out. "The chair . . ."

I gathered my skirts, moving as fast as my feet could carry me up the incline. "Lean back," I instructed. "I have to get you up on the main path."

"You cannot do that alone," he argued. "Go for help."

"Just do as I say," I demanded, knowing I could not risk leaving him there.

How I was able to summon the strength I know not, but finally, my arms feeling near ripped from their sockets, I pulled the full weight up to the flat safety of the path.

As I did, Damien clasped my arm, drawing me around to face him.

"My God, you *are* hurt!" he exclaimed.

He reached into his pocket and, withdrawing a handkerchief, commanded, "Kneel down, and lay your arm there against the rest."

I did as he instructed, clenching my teeth as he fashioned a tourniquet out of the linen cloth. When he had finished I raised my eyes to meet his. "We have to find her, Damien, to bring her back."

"She won't go far," he replied. "Charles was taking a few of the stablehands down the other way."

"Charles?" I whispered. "How did he . . . I mean—"

He placed his finger to my lips. "When you left this morning I couldn't get what you had asked me out of my mind. With all the hours I had spent reconstructing what had happened, the most obvious thing had escaped me. When Anitra had whispered 'I did not mean to,' I took it as a final repentance for her crime."

"But she added one word," I reminded him.

" 'Amanda'," he acknowledged. "But, you see, I thought she was trying to tell me that Amanda was inside. When in fact she was telling me that she knew or suspected it was Amanda who had set the fire."

"I am so sorry, Damien," I murmured.

His eyes roved over the skeletal structure below. "All these

469
.

years. Why did she never tell me? Oh God, what have I put her through?"

I reached out and touched his arm. "Let's go back, Damien."

I do not know how we made it back to the manor. Not a word was exchanged between us until we had reached our quarters.

"I want you to stay here, Lillith," Damien instructed. "I will send for Victor."

"And then what?" I asked.

"Just stay here," he repeated.

"Someone has to see to Terrence," I advised.

"I will tend to that," he replied.

When he left I went to the bedroom, intending to clean the wound on my arm. Instead, my head hung over the basin and the bile of my own fear and shock spewed forth like the lava of an erupting volcano.

When would this reign of terror cease, I wondered. It was as though Darby served sentence on all who lived here. It was a harbor of sinister words and deeds from which none seemed able to sail free.

I had no idea how much time had passed before Victor Brathwaite arrived. "I am sorry I did not get to you sooner, Lillith," he apologized as he opened his bag. "I had to see Amanda."

"They found her then?" I asked as he withdrew an ointment which he spread liberally across the wound on my arm.

He nodded.

"How is she?"

"From what I have heard, I am surprised at your concern," he said as he covered the liniment with a length of gauze.

"At least for now I am still a Darby, Dr. Brathwaite. This house and all its members are my concern."

"I believe you mean that, Lillith. Which is why I begged Damien to be honest with you. If he had been from the first, much of this might have been prevented."

"What is going to happen now?" I asked as he released my arm.

He frowned. "That is up to Damien. Frankly, I think Amanda for her own safety and the safety of others should be put away. But Damien has locked up secrets here before, and I expect he will again."

"You think she should be institutionalized?" I gasped.

"To turn Amanda over to the law would in my opinion be a crime greater than the one she has committed."

"And there is Terrence," I offered.

"Yes, there is the boy to consider," he agreed. "But I should tell you what I have told Damien. Even if she is committed, I cannot wholly predict how Amanda will be."

"What do you mean?"

"The mind," he continued, "as we are coming to learn, is a complex thing. Far more complex I suspect than the body, certainly in its ability to recover."

My heart sank. "Are you saying Amanda will never recover from this?"

He closed his bag. "She may remain as she is now, she may descend more fully into a world unknown to us, one which she uses to shield herself from the real world, or she may return to the girl she once was. I simply do not know."

"I see."

"I have to get back to her, Lillith," he concluded, "and while I am here I want to see Jessica. My best advice to you is to try and get some rest."

Rest was the last thing I could think of. Awkwardly I changed my gown, selecting one with a looser sleeve. When moments later I entered the library, it was Charles who I found there.

Wordlessly he rose and crossed to me with outstretched arms. I entered them without embarrassment. I needed solace, and in his silence he understood that.

When at last I pulled away he led me to the settee by the

fire. As I watched the flames lap at the blackened stone I cringed.

"You know, when I was a little girl I used to sit by the fire with my father," I said finally. "And I used to think how peaceful it was."

"You have to put it behind you, Lillith," he counseled.

"What you mean is, I have to put Darby behind me."

"That is between you and Damien."

"Have you seen him?"

He nodded. "I assume he is still with Amanda."

"I cannot believe how mistaken I was, Charles," I conceded. "She duped me completely. From the first I thought we had a special camaraderie, but it was all deceit. She used me, she tricked me. She must have known that when Damien found out about my agreement with Edmund he would misinterpret it as greed. And, as is now obvious, that he would want me gone from here."

"But why, Lillith?" Charles asked. "Have you asked yourself that?"

"I can only conjecture," I replied. "Amanda always stood in the shadow of Anitra. I suspect she thought she never really had her father's love, and perhaps she transferred her need to Damien. Then, when she thought she had lost her husband, Damien became the one constant in her life. Perhaps some convolution of her mind caused her to believe that I would rob her of that. In a bizarre way I stood for Anitra, who had always come between Amanda and the love she so desperately sought."

Charles stood up and went to stand by the mantel. "I have to ask you something, Lillith. Do you think Amanda had anything to do with the man in the lake?"

My eyes flew to meet his. "Oh, Charles, you do not really think . . ."

"It has to be asked," he said.

I had concluded that somehow a woman was involved. But not Amanda. It could not be. Unless of course somehow that stablehand had discovered the secret of Darby. Had he known that it was Amanda who set that fire? Had he blackmailed her, and had she in the panic of discovery silenced him?

"From your expression I read that you do not think it impossible."

"No," I whispered. "But Charles, you must promise me not to say anything to anyone. Dr. Brathwaite indicated Amanda would never survive if the authorities were called in. What good would it do anyway? If only for the boy, I beseech you to be silent."

Thankfully, Charles agreed with me.

"You know, in the melee since my return," he said, "I have not had an opportunity to tell you that I managed through a client to place Damien's paintings with a man who is an agent to the Royals."

"And is there any word?" I asked eagerly.

He smiled. "These things take time."

"I know. But it seems even more important now. I do not want this time spent here to have been wholly in vain. Out of the ashes there must rise some good. Tragedy has been a constant flame in Darby too long. It must not be allowed to become its legacy."

29

I L E F T Charles, and as I crossed the
reception hall I noticed that the post
had been left on one of the consoles. I shuffled halfheartedly
through the envelopes. It had been some time since I had
looked for word from Abraham. Thus it was with some disbelief when I came upon the letter penned to my attention.
Eagerly I took it back to my room and breaking the seal
withdrew the sheets of familiar script.

My dearest Lillith,
    Forgive my delay in responding to your news. I suf-
fered a slight relapse, but this too has passed. I cannot
believe that my sweet child is a married woman now.

Would only that your mother and father could have shared this day with you. Theirs was such a special relationship. It was not without strife, but they had the one thing that allowed them to find happiness: love. And that is what I pray you have found.

My tears clouded the rest of the page. I loved Damien but it was not enough. If he did not reciprocate, what chance might we have? If some night he came to me again, I could not let him take my body unless he also accepted my heart. He would possess the whole of me, and what would I be left with?

There was a chill in the air, and I crossed to the closet to search out a shawl. As I did I spied the trunks and valises buried at the back. There was no reason to delay the inevitable, I decided as I withdrew them.

It was nightfall when I laid the last gown into the portmanteau. I was about to undress when there was a knock at the door.

I opened it to find Damien beyond. He looked past me to the open trunks.

"I have obviously interrupted you," he murmured.

"No. I think it is all finished," I said.

"I see. How is your arm?"

I reached to the swathe of gauze. "It will heal."

He lifted his eyes to mine. "How did we manage to wound each other so, Lillith?"

I sighed. "I do not know. But we are not the only ones who have suffered. How is Amanda?"

"You really care, after all she has done to you?" he asked with amazement.

"I feel no bitterness, if that is what you mean," I replied. "Have you thought about what you are going to do with her?"

"I will see that she is cared for. And the boy, of course."

"I am glad. She needs you, Damien."

The tragedy of these past days were clearly etched in his

eyes. "No. I am the last person she needs, Lillith."

"How can you say that?" I argued.

"Because in many ways I am responsible for all of this. But I do not want to talk about Amanda any longer. Charles is leaving tomorrow. I gather from your bags that you will be joining him. I know I may not have the right, but there is one more thing I should ask of you. Would you come with me just this last time to the studio?"

I felt a moment's trepidation. Not from fear of Damien. Fear of myself perhaps. It was a place which evoked too many memories for me, a place I had tried all of this night to part myself from.

Sensing my apprehension, he added, "It shan't be but a moment."

We moved in tandem, I lighting the way to the entrance of the studio. The door was closed and I allowed him to open it. I paused once inside the door.

"It is there," he said, "over by the windows."

So often had I been there, I could have walked to the end of the room blindfolded. But I moved forward cautiously, as if I were a novice within these walls. I came through the stacks of paintings to where his easel stood, noting as I did that there was something set upon it, hooded by an enormous drape.

"I have accused you of being stubborn," he said, "but never have I doubted your curiosity. Go ahead and look."

I stepped forward, holding the candle high, and reached out to clasp the heavy black cloth in my fingers. Slowly, I pulled the shroudlike drape from the easel.

At first I thought I was mistaken. I stood transfixed, my own likeness reflected back to me.

"How? Where?" I gasped.

"I wanted it to be a wedding gift," he replied, wheeling his chair towards me. "You had made mention of it. I did not know until Charles secured it for me and brought it here that

I had known the artist. He is dead now. But he was a great master under whom I was privileged, if only briefly, to study."

I drew closer to the painting, the painting of my mother which Sir Henry Willferth had purchased from me for a pittance.

"It was not until I took receipt of it," he continued, "that I realized how alike you were. Indeed, if I were to put the portrait I completed of you beside this one some might assume the subject to be one and the same."

I reached out, tracing the dappled oils which constituted the best memory of my mother.

"It is yours, of course. Yours to take."

I shook my head, overcome by gratitude and grief.

"Though I know I also offered you the one I painted of you," he continued, "I should rather like to keep that."

I welcomed the darkness of the room as a single tear crossed my cheek.

"I meant you no harm, Lillith. We are all victims here, you know. Victims of our own suspicions and passions and torment. I cannot forgive myself, for I refused to spare you that. I have seen what Darby can do to people. But you were like the zephyr which sweeps through the dales in May, cleansing the hillsides of the debris of winter. You brought a freshness, an innocence here. I actually believed that you could dispel the taint of this heritage, that out of the web of Edmund's resolve some good could come. I saw you as a chance, a chance that Darby might survive after all."

"And now? How do you see me now, Damien?"

"I see you as I always will, Lillith. As the woman I love."

I steadied myself against the frame of the easel. I had waited so long to hear him say it. But why now? Was it only to sweeten the sorrow of our parting?

"Why, Damien?" I cried out. "Why, if you love me, do you want to see me gone from Darby?"

"It is *because* I love you, Lillith, that I do."

Wiping the moisture from my cheeks, I turned back to the painting of my mother. For years after her death, when I had misstepped or misspoken in my quest to discover who I was, I had come to this picture. So many times she had seemed to reach out to me from the canvas to offer counsel or solace. It was her guidance I wanted now.

"Do you remember, Damien, one night during dinner, our reciting some lines of Shakespeare?"

"Very well," he replied.

"You gave me the answer before," I reminded him. "I want you to give it to me again."

I traced the slow upturn of my mother's lips on the canvas with my finger.

" 'I'll set a bourn how far to be beloved,' " I murmured.

I turned and looked across at him.

" 'Then must thou needs find out new heaven, new earth,' " he completed.

I walked slowly towards him and knelt down by his chair. "I want to find my new heaven, my new earth here with you, Damien. At Darby."

He reached out and stroked the waves of my hair from my brow. "Would that it were possible, Lillith."

"We can make it possible," I argued. "At least we can try. Damien, once Darby was merely a destination. Today I know it is my destiny."

"Fate can sometimes deal a cruel hand, Lillith," he warned.

"Or a gentle one," I murmured, slipping my hand into his.

30

DAYS turned into weeks and weeks into months.

Charles had left Darby alone the following day. When I had gone to tell him of my decision, I think somehow he already knew. I suspected he felt that I was making a grave mistake, but he made no attempt to dissuade me. I knew our good-byes were only temporary, but it was still with some sadness when I watched the coach disappear down the drive.

I cannot say that as time passed the kingdom of Darby had become wholly peaceable. Indeed, but two days after I had pledged myself to Damien and Darby Manor, my resolve was tested.

It had to do with Amanda. I knew that Damien could never

face putting her away. And I was not certain that that would be in hers or Terrence's best interests. I had not discussed it with him. I had just assumed they would remain with us at Darby. I admit I did not reach the conclusion without some trepidation. Whether Amanda would actually have brought bodily harm to me if Damien had not stopped her, none of us would ever know. There would, I supposed, always be some menace to me if time did not heal her troubled mind. But for now the woman who stared aimlessly, wordlessly out the window posed no threat. It was as though some metamorphosis had taken place and her spirit was utterly broken.

That was why, when I learned that Damien had arranged to have her removed to the stone house below the manor, I was dumbfounded. It made no sense. But the more I argued it, the less explanation he would give. He said he and Victor had decided it was for my own protection, but if anyone needed protection from her, it was Amanda herself.

He was so adamant about her exile, exacting a promise from me that I would never venture down there, that some of my old fears about Darby seemed to come flooding back. But it was suspicion which had been our downfall before, and I could not allow it to destroy us again.

As my resolve was tested it was also rewarded. We drew closer and closer, Damien and I. With the thaw of spring we ventured out almost daily through the reeded fields up to the rocky combs about the Creg. From there one can see the Swale at the very point where the two streams merge to become one great river. That union reminded me of our own. We were as separate streams, gathering and carrying as we rushed headlong, our waters surging finally to flow together as one.

And yet, as intimate as we had become, a part of the stream which was Damien was held back by some unseen dam. I would lie awake some nights, drenched by the heat of our shared passion, and wonder what it was about him which still eluded me.

Our excursions seemed to have given him renewed inspiration, and I took heart as he absorbed himself fully in his painting. Though I would have been happy to simply sit and watch him, he guarded his privacy jealously during that time, which left me at something of a loss.

I spent hours upstairs reading to Jessica, whose tenacity for life ever astounded me. We told her finally of Edmund's passing. It was simply too cruel to have her think he avoided her. As for Amanda, I simply told Jessica she had decided to go home with Terrence.

Oddly, I had anticipated that the news would make her more distraught, but she actually seemed more peaceful after I had imparted it. Dr. Brathwaite advised that she would never regain her speech or the use of her limbs, but I had not given up hope. I had come to know her determination. If it were humanly possible, I knew she would talk again.

It was in February when I kept the promise of my offer to Perse. He was like a bashful child as I took him in hand and slowly began teaching him his letters. I spent only a few hours with him each week, but I was encouraged by his progress. That is, until one afternoon when I had decided to teach him to write his name. I had penned his, then Damien's, then my own, following it for no particular reason with *Anitra*. As his hand traced the outline of her name tears filled his eyes. I might have thought nothing of it, except that in the sessions which followed he copied her name over and over again. Somehow I knew that he too had been touched by her life— and perhaps by her death as well.

It had not been an easy task for me to lay her memory to rest. I was no longer obsessed by her, but I supposed there would always be a lingering curiosity about this girl who had unwittingly changed the face of Darby. Purposely I kept away from the summerhouse. Its remains were only a reminder of how many lives had come to ruin here. And I knew if I ventured that far that I would be tempted to take the path less traveled to the stone house.

If Damien visited her there I did not know. Several times

I had interrupted him and Victor Brathwaite. I suspected as they fell suddenly mute that they had been conferring about Amanda, but her name was unutterable between Damien and myself.

As March brought the peeking bulbs to the increasing verdure of the land, I began to notice a change in Damien. His normal introspection took on more the form of withdrawal. There was a faraway look in his eyes and a melancholy in the tenor of his voice. I tried to dismiss it, telling myself that he was not a man without complexity, but as the mood persisted and I felt him slipping from me I became concerned.

It only intensified when he came to me one afternoon after my visit with Jessica and informed me that he was going to leave Darby for a few days. When no explanation was forthcoming, I inquired where he was going. His response was simply that there was something he needed to attend to.

He had given me no reason for mistrust these past months, but try as I did to dispel my fears, I could not. A small part of me wondered whether there was any truth in Marisse's prediction that Damien would never wholly be mine. He made love to me that night with such hunger, such ravishment. It was as though he wanted to prove something. But I did not know whether it was to me or to himself.

I decided after Damien had left the next morning that it was time for me to put my own imprint on Darby. It was a house, but I wanted to make it a home. I had written to Rebecca and Abraham inviting them to Darby in May, and if I was going to attend to matters too long neglected, I could not delay.

The post had arrived, and searching through it, expectant of some word from them, I came upon a small envelope addressed to me. Seeing that it bore the Grout seal I opened it, eagerly anxious for news from Charles. "Dear Lillith," I read:

Only recently I have come upon some of my father's old files. The ones relating to Darby contained some rather disturbing information. I have wrestled with myself over whether I should impart this to you and have decided I must. I am leaving on the morrow for Darby. Please make no mention of this to Damien. I pray you are well.

As ever, Charles

If Charles had meant to frighten me he had succeeded. Whatever his discovery, I knew it was not insignificant. But what could it be, and why was I supposed to keep it a secret from Damien?

When an hour later I found myself pacing blindly about the library I knew I had to get hold of myself. Whatever Charles had uncovered it was part of the past, I told myself.

I searched out a pen and paper, deciding to occupy myself with listing the needed improvements at Darby Manor. The public rooms, I concluded, needed only fresh paint and some change of upholstery. It was the second floor which demanded a more thorough renovation. As I walked the length of the hallway I resolved that the first change would be the removal of at least some of the mirrors. From my early days at Darby I had puzzled at their placement. I did not know whether Damien would permit it, but I would ask him if we might soften the illusion by hanging some of his paintings. I lost count of the number of rooms I meandered through over the next hours when at last I stood before Anitra's. I had not come to it since that day in December when I returned the diary to its rightful place.

I opened the door, closing it softly behind me. At first I thought it was my imagination, but as I stepped forward the scent stayed with me. I inhaled the sweet perfume again. It was jasmine. I shivered. Its lingering pungency recalled those days at Darby I had worked so hard to lay to rest.

I was leaving the room when my eyes went to the dressing table. I crossed to it and, placing my tablet on the satinwood inlay, I gingerly picked up the small sprig of heather which rested there. I twirled it around in my fingers. The seed pods clung to the tapered shoot, and I concluded it was fresh. But what was it doing here?

Don't do this, Lillith, I told myself as I placed the heather aside and withdrew the drawer containing the diary. But my will was not strong enough. The book almost seemed to burn in my hand as I withdrew it and placed it in my lap.

I leafed through the pages, wondering why I had succumbed once again to this preoccupation. As several pages seemed to stick together I turned forward. As I did I stared disbelieving at the date. I blinked, thinking I must have misread it. But there was no mistake. This entry had been penned this very month.

Who had done this, I despaired. Who would desecrate the diary this way? Was this some sort of prank? But who other than myself even knew of its existence? Damien and Jessica. And Amanda, I realized with dread. Had she somehow returned unseen to the house? Had the distortion of her mind led her to do this? Had she known about this diary all along?

I was trembling as my eyes drank in the distinct flourish of the pen.

When will it all end? This madness that is Darby. I never told Damien the truth. Why I protected her I do not know. Perhaps out of some guilt which I bore. And now even Father is gone. At least, perhaps he has found peace. Victor has told me that Lillith does not know. We have all been amazingly clever at locking our secrets away. I believe in my heart she is the one person he has ever truly loved. But it is not enough. Not as long as she survives. Would that I could warn her! She might escape what none of the others of us can.

The gardens will be in bloom soon again. I look out on them from this sepulcherlike prison to which I am condemned and see dear Perse. If only I could be as his roses and come to flower again!

My pulse was like the beat of an anvil as I thrust the volume back into the drawer. Anitra is dead, I protested to myself. I did not know what it meant or who had written this but I was going to find out.

I ran to my room for my cloak and left the manor. The sky was arched with the suggestion of a rainbow as I scurried down the steps towards the terraced gardens. When I reached the point where the stone lions stood guarding the parterre below, I looked up. The gardens were in full view only from the west wing. But that was the shuttered wing of the house. Mrs. Horsley had been very specific about that.

The only way was to see for myself. Now. Today. But how, if it was locked, was I going to gain access? If only Mary were not on holiday! I could trust her. Suddenly I remembered that in the galley between the two kitchens I had seen a panel which held a set of keys. They might, I thought, be duplicates of the ones that Mrs. Horsley carried about.

I took the back entrance to the kitchens. The cook, who was hauling a kettle from the fire, was surprised to see me.

"Where is Mrs. Horsley?" I inquired, trying to keep my tone bright.

"She's gone te town, Lady Darby," she replied. "Sommers too. We got a tad low on provisions."

"I see," I replied.

"Kin aye be doin' somethin' fer ye?"

I shook my head.

Thankfully the galley was empty. I pulled the oak door of the panel open. There seemed to be hundreds of keys of all shapes and sizes. But as I peered closer I was relieved to see that each set bore a label. Finally I found the ones marked WEST WING. I slipped them from the nail and placed them in my pocket.

I did not bother divesting myself of my cloak. I had no idea how long Mrs. Horsley would be absent. Why I was intimidated by her I was not certain. I had every right to look in the west wing.

There were four keys, and the third fitted the lock. I had not even thought to bring a candle. The door led through to a hall. It was dark, but as my eyes adjusted to the light I started down the passage. Realizing there was a door on the left, I placed my hand on the knob. It was unlocked. Warily I stepped into the room beyond. Save for an accumulation of dust it was bare.

There were two other doors beyond. The second room was as empty as the first. As I passed through it, I stopped short. The heady scent of jasmine wafted to my nostrils once again. It grew stronger as I tiptoed towards the remaining door.

My fingers trembled as they closed about the cold brass. There was only a faint click as the latch gave way and the door opened into the room. I crossed the threshold, my eyes searching the shadowed space beyond. It was like an illusion. No detail had been spared, down to the exact weave of the crewel coverlet. It was an exact replica of the room where I had spent so many hours puzzling about the girl who had dwelt there before me.

She was sitting on the window seat, staring out through the sliver between the partially closed draperies.

"You are early today," the childlike voice spoke.

My head was spinning as the figure turned slowly around. She was shrouded, not by shadow but by a veil which covered her head.

Neither of us moved. Neither of us spoke. I thought, if I cross over this bridge of silence to her, I can never come back again.

It was she who broke the silence. "I have often wondered if this day would come. I expect it was inevitable."

My heart screamed denial, but I knew that I had come face to face with my obsession. My lips formed her name.

"Yes," she replied simply.

"But how? Why?" I moaned.

Slowly her gloved hands clasped the opaque veil and lifted it back from her face. Nothing could have prepared me for what I beheld. It was as though the paintings, the grotesqueries secreted off from the studio had suddenly come alive. It was a mask of distortion, the flesh like the charred wood at the summerhouse.

My hand flew to my mouth as I grappled with the horror of it all.

"My heart beats, Lillith," she said slowly. "Blood flows through my veins, but for all intents and purposes, Anitra died in that fire. They could not bear to look at me, and I could not bear to look at myself."

"You mean they all . . . they all know?" I gasped.

She nodded. "Save for Mrs. Horsley and dear Perse, Father dismissed all the servants. You have to try to understand what it did to him. The only way he could cope with what I had become was to deny my very existence."

"But Damien—what about Damien?" I cried.

She reached up and hid her face again behind the thickness of the veil. "There is so much you do not know. It is too late for us, Lillith, but you can still escape. You can still leave."

"Leave? Why should I leave?" I demanded.

She sighed. "Darby is like a disease. Slowly, insidiously, it eats away at you until there is nothing left. We are all infected by it. Even poor Jessica, who managed to escape the weakness of the Darby seed, has finally fallen victim to it."

I stepped towards her. "What do you mean?"

"Just go, Lillith. Go now, while Damien is away from the manor. Go to Perse. He will help you."

I looked past her veil through my own veil of tears.

"You *have* to tell me why. I know that Amanda set the fire. Why did you not tell Damien, why did you let him carry the blame?"

Her head fell. "Because I did not think he could live with the knowledge of what Amanda had done."

"So you allowed him all these years to think it was you?" I gasped.

"I had to, Lillith. He had bribed Donat into marrying

Amanda. I think he really tried. I think he thought if she were gone from Darby there might be a chance for him to live a normal, decent life. But they are drawn to each other like moths to a flame. They are powerless in the heat of their attraction. The seed of Darby was planted again. If I betrayed Amanda I would also have betrayed the child she was carrying. Damien's child."

I screamed, my pain like a rapier thrust into unsuspecting flesh. "You are lying," I accused her. "I do not pretend to know why, but I know you are lying."

She lifted her veil again. Tears streamed over the mottled, disfigured cheeks. "You see me, Lillith. What reason do I have left to lie to you?"

"No," I shrieked in denial. "I am going to find Damien and I am going to bring him here. And I am going to make you repeat every word to him. Every word of these lies."

"Go to the stone house," she challenged. "You will find him there with Amanda."

"I do not know why you are doing this to me, Anitra, but I am going to find out."

I turned and stumbled from the room. I ran pell-mell through the wing out to the second-floor hallway. As I raced down the helix of the stair, the eyes of Darby seemed to follow me. My boots flew across the marble of the reception hall and down the front steps. My body was near collapse, but frenzy drove me on. I told myself I would find her there alone with Terrence, and when Damien returned I would see my nightmare brought to an end. All the lies, all the secrets which haunted Darby would be laid to rest forever.

My cloak caught against an untrimmed privet bough. The ripping was nothing by contrast to the tearing of my heart. I turned onto the path to the stone house. Gloaming hovered over the landscape as I stepped into the clearing. As I crept towards the building, all courage seemed to abandon me. A light shone through a single window at the far end. I crossed to it, thinking as I did that I heard a woman sobbing.

The panes of glass were thick. They could shield a great deal, but they could not protect me from the tableau within.

I watched as Amanda fell to his feet, her arms clutching his legs.

"You cannot do this, Damien," she cried out. "No matter what you say, you will always come back. We are one, you and I."

I had seen the pain etched in his face so many times. But it was only at this very second that I understood it.

"Don't you see how everyone has suffered the consequences of our actions?" he pleaded.

"I did it to protect you," she sobbed.

"My God, listen to what you are saying, Amanda," he wailed. "Our hands are bloodied by this 'protection,' as you call it. I always suspected Robert's death was no accident. But then Heathy, and that poor little maid. I can't go on this way."

She reached up and clasped his arms. "What are you going to do?"

I watched as his hand reached out and stroked her hair.

"This is the last time, Amanda," I heard him say. "If Darby is to survive, my life must be with Lillith."

"But you love me," she wailed.

"God help our souls, I do," I heard him confide. "But it is not like the love I share with Lillith. There is purity there, Amanda. And in that there is hope that this perverted madness we are born of and have continued to perpetuate can be snuffed out forever."

"You can extinguish a flame, Damien," she challenged. "A fire is another matter. You have learned that before, and you will learn it again."

I groped along the stone of the house. There was nothing more to hear, nothing more to see. As I stumbled through the clearing to the path I wished the earth would open suddenly and swallow me. No prior loss had plunged me into the abyss I found myself in at this moment.

I looked up to the heavens and saw a sprinkling of stars to the south. They were like an omen of what I knew I must do. I clawed my way through the tawny gloom of night, running, stumbling, flogged on by the whip of the wind at my back.

The house loomed before me as I dragged myself up the steps and burst into the reception hall. I threw back the hood of my cloak and stared ahead in disbelief.

"Charles," I gasped, "what are you doing here?"

"Now that is no greeting," he chastised me gaily. "Did you not receive my letter?"

I nodded.

He strode over to me and tilted my face up to his. "Lillith, what is it?"

"I have to leave here," I choked out.

"Come into the library and let me get you a brandy," he offered.

"No," I cried. "You do not understand. I have to leave Darby now. I cannot stay here, not another minute."

"Why, Lillith? What has happened here? What has happened to you?"

I clutched his sleeve. "Charles, I am begging you. If you won't help me, I shall find another way."

He looked behind him to the valises at the base of the stair. "As you can see I have just arrived, but the coach is long gone by now. In the morning perhaps."

"The morning is too late," I said in despair.

"Where is Damien?" he demanded.

"He is not here. That is why I have to leave now, Charles. Please do not ask me any questions. Just trust me."

"Wait for me here," he instructed. "I will go down to the stables and see if I can find one of the men to harness the horses."

Anitra's words came back to me: *Go to Perse,* she had said.

"No. There is someone else who can help us. Come with me."

Silently he kept pace with me in my flight down to the stables. "Stay here," I begged.

I rounded the end stalls to the rooms at the rear, where I had come as an instructress these past weeks. "Please be here," I whispered as I rapped at the door.

He opened it almost immediately. I realized as I clutched at the billow of his shirt that I was frightening him.

"I am sorry," I cried, "but I need your help. I have seen Anitra, Perse. I have to leave Darby and I do not want anyone to know. Can you harness the horses? Now? Can you do that for me?"

He nodded. I waited as he pulled a heavy wool vest on and then I followed him back down to the tack room. As he spied Charles he backed into the shadow of the wall.

"No, it is all right," I assured him. "You know Sir Charles. He is helping me."

Warily he set about his task.

The waiting seemed endless. I paced about as Charles stood calmly by.

When at last the carriage was ready, I panicked. I knew nothing about driving horses, and I suspected Charles was as inept as I in these matters.

"We will need a driver, Perse," I said. "Just until we can get to Richmond." He left us, returning moments later with a stocky lad I had seen once or twice about the manor.

"Lady Darby and I must get to Richmond tonight," Charles advised the youth. "Do you think you can get us there? You will be well compensated."

The boy, obviously cheered at the prospect of earning some money, hoisted himself up into the driver's seat.

I turned to Perse. "I won't forget this," I said. "You'll see to Anitra. I know now that she means a great deal to you."

Charles helped me into the carriage. "We will stop at the manor. You can get whatever things you need."

"No," I argued. "I do not want to stop for anything."

Charles pulled the lap robe around me as the carriage rolled across the cobblestones out to the drive. I stared straight ahead as the wheels clattered past the manor.

"You are sure this is what you want to do, Lillith?" Charles asked.

My head slumped against the back of the seat. "It is what I have to do."

He reached over and simply laid a hand on my arm. "We have to talk, you know. Seeing you as you are now, I cannot even imagine what has been going on at Darby these past months."

He was right, but how could I tell him what I had discovered this day?

"You received my letter, Lillith," he persisted, "so you know that I came upon something most troublesome. Somehow I have the feeling that this is all related. In my father's old files I found a will: Edmund's will. I was surprised, because he had made no mention of its existence when he called me to Darby. In it he made a specific bequest to his daughter, Anitra, and to Mrs. Horsley, who was to care for her in the event of his or Damien's demise. The will was dated two years after the fire, Lillith."

I shut my eyes, trying to blot out the vision of her face as it swam before me.

"Anitra is alive, isn't she?" he demanded.

I drew a deep breath. "She exists. But, in her own words, Anitra died in that fire."

The words came slowly at first and then tumbled from my lips. When I was done he put his arm around me and drew me to him. "Let it go, Lillith. If you let these feelings fester inside you they'll destroy you."

I buried my face against the wool melton of his coat but there were no tears. I felt like a tree hollow at its core with nothing but decay inside me.

"We'll get you away from all this, Lillith," Charles promised. "Someday Darby will seem like a bad dream."

But it was not a dream, I thought. And run as I might, something told me that I should never escape it. The tapestry was complete, and I had to force myself to look at it. I had to face the depiction squarely before the weave would fade.

I pulled away from Charles. "I want to turn back," I said resolutely.

"You cannot be serious?" he said, bewildered.

"I have to, Charles. You may not understand this, but unless I go back I sense I will never be able to go on."

"Lillith, I took you at your word before, but this time I cannot allow it," he argued.

I reached up and pulled the cord to signal the driver. He began to slow the horses.

"I have to do this, Charles," I concluded as the driver climbed down and inquired the nature of the problem.

A wall of silence stood between us as the horses covered the miles back to Darby. I had no idea what I would do to bring this all to an end, but with each roll of the wheels I grew more certain that I must try.

The compartment of the carriage had grown close, and I opened the glass side panel. But instead of freshening the air it seemed to admit an acrid scent which stung my eyes and nostrils.

It was Charles who saw it first. "My God," he cried.

I leant forward as the pace of the horse suddenly quickened. Hooves pounded along the undulations of the drive, fighting through billows of smoke. The sky was alight with spires of flames which, as they reached their acme, seemed to explode and shower back down to earth.

The sound of the fire was like thunder as it raged through the manor, drowning the frightened whinny of the horses. They must have reared suddenly, for there was a loud crack and the carriage jolted to a standstill.

I flung the door open, paying no heed to Charles's cries as I ran towards the inferno. There were screams from every-

495

where as if Darby were never more alive than in its dying. Chips was at the base of the front steps. His bark had a plaintive, almost human sound. I watched transfixed as I suddenly saw a figure emerge under the portico. Only when he was steps away from me did I realize that the blanket around the man swathed another body.

Perse laid her at my feet and I knelt down beside her, cradling her head in my hands. "Anitra, it is Lillith," I said. "Can you hear me?"

Her eyes, which seemed to float in the hollowed sockets of her skull, stared up at me.

"Earth to earth and ashes to ashes," she whispered.

"What happened, Anitra?" I choked.

She coughed and I covered the saliva which trickled from nonexistent lips with the sleeve of my gown.

"Damien came back," she whispered. "I had gone to the studio, deciding I would wait, however long it took. I started to tell him what I had done and suddenly Amanda was there. He said, 'I have to find Lillith.' He started to wheel his chair towards the door, but she blocked his way. He reached out to push her aside and her candle fell, the flame catching the hem of her gown.

"It was all so quick. She broke from him and raved about the room, acting as human kindling. By the time he was able to reach her it was too late. He flung himself atop her and . . ."

Her voice trailed off suddenly. Her chest heaved once and all that was left of her was a lingering scent of jasmine. I laid her head in Perse's lap, and he clutched her to him, rocking her with a silent lullaby.

I started towards the house, repeating his name. It was a whisper at first, but as my body gained momentum so did my voice.

"Damien," I screamed. I listened to what seemed to be an echo, but then I realized that it was my own voice shrieking his name again and again.

I felt hands pull me back and I was aware of voices around me, but I did not want them to penetrate this inner sanctum into which I had withdrawn. I had to watch the tapestry burn all alone.

497

■

POSTSCRIPT

A<small>LMOST</small> a year has passed since I left Darby. Only a row of head-stones in the graveyard by the chapel stand as a memorial of what was. I had walked that last day past the names engraved in granite—JESSICA, TERRENCE, AMANDA, ANITRA—coming to rest finally before the plot which was Damien's.

I would never know whether he had thrown himself upon Amanda to save her or to join her in death as he had in life. I knew only that there had been no peace for him on earth, and I prayed that he might have found it at last.

Charles had seen to my safe return to London. There was nothing left to take away from Darby except Chips. We had both lost masters: he, one he could serve, and I, the master of my fate.

Charles had been insistent that I stay with him, at least until I could get my bearings, but I had refused. If I was going to find my way back I knew it would have to be on my own.

I found a house to let not far from Bostworick Hall. It was small but comfortable. Although I was not impoverished, the bulk of my inheritance was Darby, which, left to lie fallow, produced little or no income. I had a responsibility to see Abraham and Rebecca, but as the seasons flowed one into the other again, I was still not ready.

It was spring when Charles, who had reluctantly honored my need for privacy, called on me unexpectedly. He had two things to tell me. First, that there had been an offer for Damien's paintings. In truth, I had completely forgotten about them. My initial reaction was not to sell them. But I had been able to give him little else. It seemed important that this be his posterity.

The second was that Charles had had an offer for Darby. I think he was surprised when I wavered. It was not that the offer was not generous. The sum he quoted would, I realized, make me a woman of inordinate wealth. It was the finality of it which I could not seem to reconcile myself to.

I begged him to give me a little time to consider it. The very next day I arranged for a coach to take me back to Darby. Somehow I knew it was only there that I would find my answer.

As the carriage retraced the journey which first brought me north, I thought that everything seemed changed. But it was not the landscape which had altered. It was not what I viewed, but how I viewed it that was no longer the same.

Chips sat up suddenly, his nose twitching as we approached the manor. I reached out and stroked his head. "I know," I whispered. "It is hard to forget." The orange of the flames had been like a burning sun scorching the very skin of the building. The charred remains were like a flower withered by heat, its former beauty unrecognizable.

I told the obviously confused driver to wait for me. Chips scampered ahead and as I saw him start towards the front steps I bade him stay. He looked up at the manor. His whimper triggered tears which I had thought I could no longer shed.

The lawns and gardens had suffered from lack of care. The bulbs and early perennials bloomed forgotten in the dense overgrowth. A fine mist fell, blurring the scene so that it resembled a fading picture. I paused at the crest of the hill overlooking the summerhouse. Always before it had seemed to beckon me like a siren from some strange shore. This day it did not. Perhaps because it was no longer a stranger to me.

I lifted my skirts as I meandered on through the waves of heather up to the loftiest point of the Creg. Chips bounded ahead of me, the pods of purple blossom clinging to the feathers of his coat.

I knew the winds on high. We had come here often. I had always thought their rawness an assault of sorts, but today they seemed a buffer 'twixt the narrow path between past and future.

The sound of scratching from a thicket beyond reached my ears. I moved towards it to find a newly fledged pipit trapped in a webbing of twigs. I watched as it stabbed with its beak at the greening bark and fluttered to free itself from the trap of nature's tapestry. I knew it was time to let it go. As I drew the twigs aside the bird hopped forth from its prison. Suddenly it stretched its wings and burst into flight.

It would not forget it had been touched by me. Nor would I forget that I had been touched by Damien. But it was free now. And so was I.